SF Books L

DOOM STAR SERIES
Star Soldier
Bio Weapon
Battle Pod
Cyborg Assault
Planet Wrecker
Star Fortress
Cyborgs! (Novella published in *Planetary Assault*)

EXTINCTION WARS SERIES
Assault Troopers
Planet Strike
Star Viking

OTHER SF NOVELS
The Lost Starship
Alien Honor
Alien Shores
Accelerated
Strotium-90
I, Weapon

Visit www.Vaughnheppner.com for more information.

Star Viking

(Extinction Wars 3)

By Vaughn Heppner

Copyright © 2014 by the author.

ISBN-13: 978-1502544292
ISBN-10: 1502544296
BISAC: Fiction / Science Fiction / Military

-1-

The alien didn't look like a bomb.

He stood seven feet tall and resembled an upright tiger, with muscles bulging against his green one-piece. A breather covered his snout, but I could tell he snarled as he raced at me. The Lokhar—that's what the tiger-alien was called—possessed hands like a man. From the fingertips, titanium-tipped claws gleamed wetly. No doubt, the Lokhar meant to shred me from head to toe, leaving my blood splattered against the bulkheads.

Me? I'm Creed, Commander Creed. I'd never liked my first name so I didn't use it anymore. Neither did anyone else.

I'd been inspecting the latest automated factory. This was the last of many imported from the Lokhar Empire. The complex rested a few kilometers outside of Laramie, Wyoming, or what was left of it, anyway. The Earth had died six long years ago, first nuked and then sprayed with a deadly bio-terminator.

The automated factories were huge affairs, bigger than several old football stadiums combined. The Lokhar Empire industrialists who had shipped this one to Earth had used seven freighters to bring it to the solar system. Tramp-haulers had labored two entire months taking the sections from the parked freighters and setting them down in Wyoming. I'd kept track. It had taken four hundred and seventy-three shuttle flights from orbit. A special force-screen sealed the factory from the poisons presently floating through our planet's atmosphere.

Incidentally, the industrialists' reps had left a month ago. The automated systems had run smoothly for two weeks. The giant plant was supposed to be empty. The tiger must have waited a month alone in here to make his attempt.

I was part of the effort to rehabilitate the planet and save the final one percent of humanity. They lived in giant space freighters orbiting our dead world. Ever since we'd learned that aliens inhabited the Orion Arm with us, human survival had been one long uphill battle after another. These automated factories were helping to cleanse the poisons from Earth.

The tiger roared. It was a deeply throaty sound, reverberating off the walls. His running bounds dramatically increased. It seemed as if he had springs in his legs. No doubt, he had bionic enhancements. Yet, Lokhars supposedly abhorred such modifications to their bodies. They didn't even allow fillings in their teeth. Nevertheless, four more jumps would bring those claws to my throat.

I held a .44 Magnum, the same gun that had killed Princess Nee four years ago, the Purple Tamika Emperor's daughter-wife. She'd ordered the death of every human aboard the Dreadnought *Indomitable*. My slugs had stopped the order and ensured the continuation of the mission to the portal planet.

That's a long story, though. Maybe I'll tell it to you someday.

As the Lokhar charged me, I pulled the trigger three times. *Boom, boom, boom.* The shots were deafening within the confines of the corridor. The first slug whipped the head back even as half of it disintegrated in a spray of skull and blood. The second acted like a linebacker, stopping the Lokhar's forward momentum. The third began to put him down.

That's when the tiger ignited. His bones, skin, fur, blood and one-piece vanished in the titanic blast. The concussion and fireball billowed outward.

I said a moment ago that Lokhars were supposed to hate body modifications. The same didn't hold true for me. Now, it wasn't that I loved what the Jelk Corporation had done to me many years ago. It had helped me survive many alien battlefields, though. Just as good, the modifications had allowed me to turn the tables on someone called Shah Claath.

2

That gave us enslaved assault troopers a battlejumper—a spaceship—and began the road to human freedom. That's another long story we can save for a different time.

I'd become gorilla-strong through steroid-68 injections and had become cheetah-fast by having neuron-fibers surgically implanted in my muscles. The Jelk Corporation had supplied all that at the beginning of my term of service. I also wore a bio-suit, symbiotic second skin. My sweat powered the living tissues, allowing them to act as hardened armor on the outside and enhance my already considerable strength. The second skin didn't cover my face, and I could take the suit on and off at will. I wore a helmet with combat boots on my feet.

The tiger exploded, vanishing from existence. The blast lifted me off the decking and hurled me two hundred meters rearward against a bulkhead. The back of my helmet cracked, causing my consciousness to flutter. The cannonball strike also caused my body to deflect to the left. I bounced against another bulkhead, slammed against the decking and found myself lying in a side corridor. It's possible that saved me from dying in the accompanying fireball.

As I lay there, I sweated intensely, which helped to energize my symbiotic skin. At the same time, I wheezed for air. My chest hurt, especially my ribs. My head spun and splotches made my vision blotchy.

At the moment, I couldn't remember if anyone had been standing behind me. Several Earth Council representatives had been on the inspection tour with me.

A distant roar sounded. It iced my spine. Were more Lokhars inside the automated factory?

I contemplated rising to go and find out. Instead of acting on the thought, I expanded my lungs once again to pull down more air. The pain sent waves of nausea against my mind, threatening unconsciousness.

What should I do?

Another roar echoed in the distance. At least one more tiger lurked in the automated factory with me.

You gotta get up, Creed, I told myself. *Lying here is going to get you killed.*

My mind ordered my muscles to respond. They were still taking a vacation, complaining about how much they ached.

I heard claws scraping against metal. It was a distinctive, frightening sound.

In my mind's eye, I saw the Lokhar striding down the twisted corridors. He would be hunched forward in a feral manner. No doubt, his finger-claws would flick in and out of their skin-sheaths.

If the tiger found me lying here, would he lean over and carefully slice my throat? Would he stomp on my face with his heel? Maybe he'd just explode, taking both of us into oblivion together.

The thought brought something extra to the table, a feeling I couldn't quite call anger. I hurt too much to be mad.

Several years had passed since I'd returned from the expedition to the portal planet in hyperspace. At that time, assault troopers had allied with Orange Tamika Lokhars against the Kargs. It had been a bloodbath for all concerned. The humans making the ultimate sacrifice, and those of us who'd survived, had purchased with our efforts badly needed supplies: these automated factories, space vessels to defend the solar system and anti-toxins to cleanse the bio-terminator.

Much had changed since the expedition. Much had remained the same.

It had been several years since I fought in combat. My bio-suit might have forgotten what to do.

No. I felt it then, the old familiar surge of the symbiotic skin secreting berserker-gang into my brain. I remembered how to clamp down on the process. Too much anger made a trooper foolish.

The chemical rage in me drove away some of the throbbing pain. The foggy tendrils of unconsciousness retreated. Lying on the decking, I stirred.

A stab of agony almost snapped me out of the attempt. More bio-suit secretions added to my determination. I had to do this. I couldn't let...

Who was behind the attack?

Don't worry about that now. Kill the other tiger before he kills you.

4

I wanted to follow the advice, but my right leg didn't want to work. The hurt—

The symbiotic suit hardened around my broken leg. It would help me walk. At the same time, more battle chemicals seeped through my regular skin into my blood stream.

I managed to drag myself up to a seated position. With my chin clicking a lever, I attempted to turn on my helmet radio. It didn't even buzz with static. The thing was dead.

Okay. Fine. I was on my own. I'd been in these kinds of situations plenty of times. I could still do this. My gun, where was my gun?

I glanced around. Then I saw my .44 lying on the decking about twenty meters away.

A single try to lurch to my feet caused me to sprawl forward onto my chest. Waves of renewed agony made me groan.

I must be worse off than I realized. No matter. I had my wits, right?

First licking my lips, I began a long, slow crawl toward the Magnum. My legs simply refused to respond. Luckily, my arms worked well enough. I dragged myself along the deck plates. At the same time, the scrape of claws told me the Lokhar neared my position.

My lips twisted with anger. I'd paid for these automated factories with human blood. Too many good men and women had died helping the tigers. For them to turn around now and try to screw us...

"No way," I whispered.

As I reached the bigger corridor, I glanced down it. Ripped bulkheads, torn decking, electric smoke and blue zapping lights showed me the devastation. What had the Lokhar been packing inside his body? Had it been a mini-nuke?

A throbbing pain beat in mind. It seemed to have synchronized with my heart rate.

That didn't matter anymore. Reaching the .44 became my universe. I dragged myself along. Another roar caused me to look up.

I saw the Lokhar. He had to be three hundred meters down the corridor. How had I heard his claws scrape from that distance? Had I imagined the sounds? By concentrating, I saw he wore a green jumpsuit and seemed muscled just like the first one.

This one reached up to his breather and tore it away. He roared with defiance.

In case you're wondering, the tiger didn't need the mask in order to breathe. Lokhars use the same air-mix humans do. The breather was likely a precaution against any bio-terminator in the air that might have seeped through the force-screen or lingered from construction. That he took it off told me he didn't plan to live much longer.

In any case, the Lokhar's roar caused the hairs to stand up on the back of my neck. It must have been a primeval thing, a reaction learned long ago by humans during prehistoric times.

The tiger began to run with his arms pumping smoothly. Then, he began to bound, using super-Lokhar strength. I had no doubts left. These Lokhars possessed bionic enhancements.

Putting my head down, I crawled.

I heard his thuds, the impacts of his feet striking the decking. They grew in volume. I heard his harsh breathing. Metal groaned in complaint at his weight and velocity.

I reached the gun, fully expecting it to have become a pile of twisted junk. No, sir, this was a piece of Earth's finest gunsmith art. I grabbed it, sat up and gripped the Magnum with both hands.

The tiger could move, all right. He was less than eighty meters from me.

I snapped off a shot so the .44 bucked in my hands. The kick hurt my right shoulder, but I held on.

The slug hammered against his left shoulder, blowing off bits of cloth, bone and spraying blood. The Lokhar also lost his smooth symmetry, twisting. The motion caused him to land wrong on his left foot. It slid out from under him. He collapsed hard onto his chest.

That made me grin.

The tiger looked up. Across the distance, I aimed the .44 at his face. He squeezed his eyes closed, scrunching his face.

What was that about?

6

The Lokhar exploded, vanishing in the same kind of titanic blast as the first one.

Had he panicked, blowing himself too soon? I'd say yes. Because he lay down, the strongest concussion and fireball blew up and down instead of side-to-side as the first one had done.

Even so, the blast sent me tumbling backward. As I rolled, I tucked into a fetal ball. I also gripped the .44 tight against my chest.

It was a good thing I did.

As I lay gasping on the deck plates, with my ears ringing, I heard a third roar.

How many of these tiger-bombers are there? What was the point of the attacks? It seemed as if they wanted to assassinate me more than destroy the automated factory. Had the Lokhar industrialists known about the hidden killers? If so, what implication did that have for the last humans in orbit around Earth?

After the destruction of ninety-nine percent of humanity, we'd fought back from extinction. With all our hearts, we tried to walk along the road of recovery. Mankind's unified hope was to take our place beside the many aliens, forcing them to recognize us as equals.

"Commander Creed!" the tiger shouted.

As I lay on the decking, I raised my head. Far down the hall strode another tiger in a green one-piece. Attempting to lift the .44, I discovered my arm now refused to obey my will.

Sweat stung my eyeballs as I strained. My hand worked, but the arm just wasn't going to do its task. Okay. I had to think of something else.

Once more, I raised my head. The tiger marched toward me like final doom. He didn't seem to be in any hurry. Would he have to blow himself up or could he kill me with his hands?

Maybe I shouldn't give him a choice.

I moved my head to the left, searching but finding nothing I could use to defend myself. Turning my head to the right, however, I saw a possibility.

Slowly, I wriggled my body to the right and up several meters.

"Flee, Commander Creed," the Lokhar shouted, "if you are able." Then he chuckled in the throaty tiger manner.

I hated him. I refused to give him the pleasure of dying at his hand—or his blast.

Once I'd situated myself, I waited, gripping the Magnum. My visor had a crack in the HUD, but it was still whole.

When the Lokhar was twenty meters from me, I raised my head one last time. "Who are you?" I asked.

He smiled, exposing his tiger fangs. Both his arms reached out. He let his claws extend. They were titanium-tipped just as the others had been.

"I am Shi-Feng, Commander Creed," the tiger boasted. "I am the purity of the Lokhar. My triad had the duty to expunge you from life. No longer will your existence sully our universe. Soon, you humans will pass into the twilight. No one will mourn your race. You are a foul, barbaric species."

"I have a saying for you, Lokhar," I told him, using my helmet's speakers.

"Speak your death words, and then I will speak mine," he said.

"Don't count your chickens before they hatch," I said.

He furrowed his tiger brow. "What does that mean?"

My .44 rested on the floor. I couldn't lift its weight. Aiming the barrel at his left foot, I squeezed the trigger. A single *boom* was my reward.

Several things happened at once. The Magnum flew out of my hand, jerking my arm. That hurt. Even so, I rolled to the right into a torn hole in the decking. As my body began to drop—the distance to the bottom looked to be fifty meters down—the slug blew away his foot. The Lokhar shouted with pain. The shot blew his leg backward, bringing his body down onto the decking. The tiger exploded—I was hoping prematurely.

Spinning as I dropped, I managed to stare upward at the gaping rent in the decking. The blast blew over it, doing little harm to me.

I grinned. Then I readied myself to hit the ground. I knew the impact would hurt, maybe break more bones. But my bio-

8

suit was built to absorb punishing damage. My muscles and hardened bones could also take much more hurt than average.

What had the tiger said? His *triad* had the duty to kill me. Triad meant three. The Shi-Feng wanted to exterminate humanity. Okay. That meant—

I struck the bottom. It was the last thing I remembered before the impact dashed me into unconsciousness.

-2-

I broke bones, tore muscles, ripped ligaments and tendons and ruptured a kidney. In a phrase, I was a physical wreck.

Fortunately, we still had special drugs and a Jelk Corporation healing tank. Unfortunately, they weren't on Earth.

After my people found me, scraped me off the floor and set me in a special cradle, they lifted from Earth and rushed to Mars Base. There, they soaked me in the healing liquid. Afterward, I was on bed rest for a week.

I suppose an explanation would be in order. The "they" in this instance was the *Forerunner Guardians*, my people.

Maybe I should back up a moment and give you a quick and dirty guide as to how humanity had gotten into this mess in the first place.

A little over six years ago, everyone on Earth was blissfully ignorant about the true state of affairs in our region of the Orion Arm. That's the name of our spiral arm of the Milky Way Galaxy, where Earth resides. Before the Day, we humans went to work, watched TV, debated politics, religion, fashion, cheered our teams, loved our wives—or husbands—and quarreled over everything.

Just before the Day, a Rhode Island-sized alien spaceship zipped past Neptune, Jupiter and Mars to park in Earth orbit. The U.S. sent up a shuttle to greet it. My dad piloted the craft. But when Mad Jack Creed tried to communicate with the alien vessel, it beamed him into oblivion. Afterward, the alien ship launched nuclear-tipped missiles. Moscow, Berlin, Paris, Washington, Los Angeles, Mexico City, Honolulu, Beijing and other great cities vanished in thermonuclear fireballs. A second wave of alien missiles crisscrossed the planet, spraying a deadly bio-terminator everywhere. That was the Day.

On Day plus one, a space lander came to Antarctica near our science outpost—

Look, I won't bore you with too many details. This is supposed to be a quick and dirty guide, remember.

In our region of the Orion Arm, two alien power blocs waged a death struggle against each other. They had been for centuries. The stronger group was the Jelk Corporation, run by small, red Rumpelstiltskin extraterrestrials. They were few in number and were originally from a different space-time continuum. It took me a long time to wrap my head around that idea. Anyway, as energy beings, the Jelk had taken on material forms, given themselves bodies. Supposedly, Jelk lived for profits. They used other aliens to do their dirty work, mostly the lizard-like Saurians.

The other side, the Jade League, run by the Lokhars, learned that the Jelk Corporation planned to recruit hundreds of millions of Earthers as soldiers. Most Lokhars had funny ideas about religion and honor. They figured it would be doing humanity a favor to kill us off nobly rather than let us become Jelk slaves.

I'd never accepted such doubletalk, but that's getting ahead of the story.

The Rhode Island-sized warship had been a Lokhar *Dreadnought*-class vessel, a hyperspace craft. The lander in Antarctica belonged to the Jelk Corporation. A Jelk fleet had chased off the dreadnought.

I'd known no such fine distinctions at the time. With my rifle, I'd gone out to do war against the crew in the alien lander.

For the sake of brevity, I'll fast-forward the situation. We assault troopers got our start with the Jelk, with Shah Claath in particular. After the Earth smoldered in radioactive ruin, he captured us as if he was a big game hunter. Then, he injected

11

his chosen ones with steroids, surgically put in the neuron strings and forced us to fight as corporation slave-soldiers. In doing so, we bought the survival of the rest of humanity, who lived in Shah Claath's worst freighters, which he landed on the poisoned Earth.

At Sigma Draconis, during the middle of a savage space battle against the Lokhars, I turned the tables on Shah Claath. I hijacked his battlejumper. Unfortunately, I failed to kill the bastard, although I destroyed his body, watching him escape as an energy being.

With the battlejumper in my possession, I returned to Earth. There, my people fixed the landed freighters. Each lifted off the poisoned planet. I had plans to do whatever I needed to strengthen humanity's odds for survival.

Before I got very far with that, the second power bloc—the Jade League—made its next move with us.

As I said earlier, the Purple Tamika Emperor led the Lokhar militarists and the league. As a race, they were religious fanatics. They viewed their greatest duty as guarding the Forerunner artifacts scattered throughout the Orion Arm.

What's a Forerunner artifact, you ask? Any machine or device constructed by the First Ones. They're long gone, by the way. The other extraterrestrials remember them as legends, almost as gods.

One of the ancient Forerunner relics had resided in the Altair star system. It had been huge, a gleaming silver donut-shaped object with the circumference of a medium-sized asteroid. In its center had been an artificial black hole. As Jelk-owned assault troopers, we'd tried to capture it. A maze of tightly-packed meteors had orbited the artifact, guarded by the Lokhar Fifth Legion. Before we could reach the thing, it vanished from sight.

Turned out the Forerunner artifact had gone to a portal planet in hyperspace. That had opened a gate into a dreadful space-time continuum. For many millennia, Abaddon and his Kargs, trillions of them in a billion spaceships, had been trying to get out of the dying universe and into ours. This was their big chance. They were xenophobic against everyone, desiring to annihilate all non-Karg life.

Well, after we assault troopers deserted Jelk service, Orange Tamika Lokhars showed up in the solar system. They wanted to make a deal for our help.

The various colored Tamikas were political factions among the tigers. Just so you know.

Now, I bet I can figure out what you're thinking. The Lokhars slaughtered all by one percent of humanity. Why help the tigers at all, right?

At the time, I figured to grab whatever could help humanity out of our hole. I couldn't afford to be choosy. By loading up assault troopers in the Lokhar dreadnoughts—hyperspace vessels—we gained warships of our own as payment, along with automated factories and anti-toxins to clean up the Earth.

My outlook was simple. Survive first. Get revenge second. Besides, if the Kargs reached our universe, neither Lokhars, Jelk nor humans were going to live much longer anyway.

As a Lokhar-allied assault trooper, I finally reached the artifact in the portal planet in hyperspace. There, I convinced the relic to teleport into the solar system's Asteroid Belt. It appeared near Ceres, the biggest asteroid in the belt. With the artifact's disappearance from the portal planet, the passage from the Karg space-time continuum into ours collapsed, stranding the terrible enemy. That saved our universe from the invaders, although my woman, Jennifer, remained behind as a captive.

In hyperspace, I learned that Forerunner objects were alive after a fashion. It was one more reason why the various alien races worshiped at them as shrines to the Creator. The Jelk didn't worship, though. They needed the artifacts in order to split into halves like an amoeba, increasing their population.

The ancient artifacts were incredibly important to Orion Arm politics and war. Earth now possessed one out in the Asteroid Belt.

After our return from hyperspace, the last assault troopers became Forerunner Guardians. We even received three warships from the Lokhars as a gift. They also vacated Mars Base, which the tigers had built for themselves.

I'd become a guardian to an alien shrine parked in the solar system. With the artifact, I was able to bargain from a position of greater strength.

We desperately needed that. The reason was simple. Every alien I'd met thought of humans as beasts. If the extraterrestrials were really kind, they just figured we were hopelessly savage barbarians.

On that basis—our savagery—our bid to enter the Jade League had been denied. They said we weren't ready to join the civilized races. Thus, we were on our own in a galaxy at war, a pimple outpost with barely the strength to halt space pirates from looting our system.

Now, to top it all off, a triad of Shi-Feng Lokhars—whatever they were—had tried to murder me. They'd hidden out in a Wyoming automated factory for at least a month. Had the industrialists known about them? Had the tramp-haulers?

I sat in a chair in my room on Mars pondering the situation.

The Lokhars under Admiral Saris—a Purple Tamika tiger—had built Mars Base beside Mons Olympia. That's the tallest volcano in the solar system. Seems the tigers had liked tramping on the mountain in their atmospheric-suits. Even after years of vacancy, one could still find their footprints on Mons Olympia. A Lokhar flag used to whip about on the pinnacle. My best friend Rollo had torn it down. He'd put the flag in our communal urinal, pissing it out of existence particle by particle.

Rollo didn't like the tigers much. The steroid-68 had given him massive muscles. It seemed to have made him angrier too. Naturally enough, we called it roid rage.

Mars Base was a dome as envisioned by NASA. It shouldn't have been that bad. Lokhars were quite a bit bigger and taller than the average human, so the quarters should have been spacious for us Earthers.

The Japanese used to live in tiny quarters compared to Americans. The Lokhars seemed to embrace this tradition, as well. While most of the quarters felt like closets, mine afforded me a little elbow room and even sported a viewing port. Outside, red sands swirled across the ground as if Mars was a giant Mojave Desert. A star fighter lifted from a pad, hot exhaust sending it screaming up to space.

My bones still mended, bonding the breaks. Most of the tendons worked again and the ligaments had regained their elasticity.

I wore jeans and a T-shirt gratis of an underground warehouse in vanished Denver. My normal six-three frame had bulked up six years ago. Ten regular tough guys wouldn't have stood a chance against me. It wasn't only the greater strength, but the speed, timing and training.

My chamber boasted a military cot, a desk, computer screen, shelf of books and some weight-lifting equipment, along with a well-stocked bar, complete with tall stools. I also had a pool table. Dmitri, Rollo and I played all the time.

We were the starship captains. Each of us commanded a former Lokhar cruiser. Dmitri presently patrolled the belt. Rollo orbited Mars beside my waiting starship. The crew was on vacation.

A beep now alerted me. I looked up from my chair. A pretty receptionist appeared on the computer screen.

"Doctor Sant is ready to see you, sir," she said.

"Send him in," I said.

"Yes, sir," she said, before disappearing.

Doctor Sant was an Orange Tamika Lokhar. Each tiger belonged to a different color, which indicated his faction. Purple Tamika presently held the throne and most major military commands. Doctor Sant had been one of the few Lokhars to survive the portal planet with us, along with several hundred Orange Tamika warriors. I'd first come to know him as their Alien Contact Officer. Since our return, Doctor Sant had taken up residence on Ceres. He studied the Forerunner object and devoured Lokhar holy texts. As I said, they're religious crusaders.

During his last three years in the solar system, Doctor Sant had begun a metamorphosis from a science officer into a religious disciple. His survival on the portal planet had a profound effect on his thinking.

I should point out that during his stay on Ceres, Doctor Sant had enlightened me about several facets of Orion Arm

15

politics. I was hoping he could explain the Shi-Feng Lokhars to me.

That's why I'd summoned him from Ceres. I hadn't been sure he'd come.

A chime sounded by the door.

Pushing up to my feet, I said, "Enter."

The door slid open to reveal a seven-foot bipedal tiger who stooped at the shoulders. He was thinner than the average Lokhar. He had white in his facial fur, and the eyes were a faded yellow. In the old days, he wore a silver and black uniform with orange chevrons. Today, he wore an orange garment like an ancient Roman toga. The hand gripping the front fold showed a gaudy, plastic-looking ring a little girl might have bought in a bubblegum dispenser. A bright orange rose showed in what looked like its plastic bubble.

"Commander Creed," Doctor Sant said in the alien language. "It pleases me you are well."

"I'm glad you agreed to come to Mars," I said, speaking the tiger tongue. I'd learned it aboard the *Indomitable* a little over three and half years ago.

I approached Doctor Sant, smelling a hint of cinnamon. Reaching out, I slid my hand against a furry palm, the tiger form of handshake. Sant was one of the few willing to greet me Lokhar-style.

Moving to the bar, we spoke pleasantries about his trip and life in the tunnels of Ceres. I mixed him a Bloody Mary. He loved the drink. I poured myself a dash of whiskey, barely wetting the ice cubes.

Since I was still feeling woozy from my injuries, I perched on a barstool.

"You seem shaken," Sant said.

"I'm not sleeping as well as I used to," I told him. "But don't worry. It will pass."

We sipped our drinks and swapped a few more kind words. Finally, Sant relocated to my most comfortable chair. Adjusting his robes, he sat his long frame down, stretching out his furry feet. As a religious seeker, he'd given up the habit of wearing shoes.

16

Carefully setting the Bloody Mary on the armrest, Sant told me, "I know something troubling has occurred. It's why I interrupted my studies to make the trip here. Did the Emperor send you a message, perhaps?"

The way Sant asked that alerted me. "Why would he?" I asked.

Sant squinted. I'd been with Lokhars long enough to recognize his sudden discomfort. He thought he shouldn't have said that. Picking up his Bloody Mary—it was his second one—he slurped slowly, as if he was trying to give himself time to think.

"Is there something brewing against Earth in the Imperial Court?" I asked.

He gestured at me with his drink. "My information is sketchy at best. It's far too soon to be certain. Let us wait out events, as I'm sure there's nothing to worry about."

"Okay," I said, figuring we had time to come back to that. "I'm more interested in something else."

"Oh," he said.

"Yes. What can you tell me about the Shi-Feng?"

Sant's reaction startled me. The Bloody Mary tumbled from his fingers, splashing the red liquid onto his robe, staining it. He appeared not to notice. The glass bounced onto the floor, rolling loudly. My gaze followed it until it bumped against the computer stand. When I looked up, Sant sat frozen, staring at me with his yellow orbs.

His lower jaw slid from side to side. Finally, words came haltingly. "You...you should not speak that name."

"Care to tell me why?" I asked.

His head twitched, breaking the spell. Blinking several times, he seemed to consider what I'd said. Finally, he stared at me even more intently than before.

"I do not understand this," he said. "How could *you* have learned of *them*?"

"Never mind that," I said. "Who are they?"

Sant shoved up to his feet. Taking several long strides, he stood before the viewing panel, staring out at the sands of Mars.

On the bar, I rotated my shot glass on its napkin, waiting. Why was this such a touchy topic? I was more curious than ever.

Doctor Sant turned, regarding me. "They...do not exist. They are a legend."

"Go on."

"You cannot know about them." Understanding lit his yellow pupils. He nodded. "Did the Forerunner Object speak to you again? Did it tell you about...*them*?"

"No."

He sagged back as if I'd punched him against the chest. He sounded winded as he said, "No other race has ever learned of the ones you named. You must swear to me, Commander. Never whisper a word of this to anyone."

"I'm afraid it's far too late for that," I said.

Sant groaned. On shaky legs, he returned to the soft chair, practically collapsing into it.

"They're a legend, you say?" I asked him.

"A myth," he said, "a wisp from the old times. It is inconceivable that you learned the name."

I had the feeling he was lying to me. It was time to up the stakes. "Doctor, I know more than that. Some of the Shi-Feng—"

"No!" Sant said, leaning forward. "Do not speak that name. It is an ill omen to do so."

"Why?" I asked.

"I cannot say."

"They work in triads," I said.

He sank against the backrest, staring at me in a stricken manner.

"Instead of killing with claw or gun," I said, "Shi-Feng explode."

Sant's eyes went wide with disbelief. Then a glimmer of horror entered them. He began to breathe more rapidly. The horror deepened, and he whispered, "No. This cannot be. They...came to Earth?"

"Yes," I said.

His panting stopped abruptly until his eyelids fluttered. He worked his jaws but no sounds issued. It seemed to take an

18

effort of will on his part. He finally whispered, "When did this happen?"

"A little over a week ago on Earth," I said. "They were waiting for me in the latest automated factory in Wyoming."

"They waited for *you?*" he asked. "No. That's impossible. You would be dead, then."

"I killed the Shi-Feng, Doctor."

With a cry, Sant lurched to his feet. He wouldn't look at me. He strode for the door. It seemed he might just leave without telling me what I wanted to know.

"Lock," I said.

Inner *clicks* meant the door locked from the inside. Frantically, Sant pressed the exit button, but the door wouldn't open.

"I must leave," Sant said, although he didn't turn to say it.

"We're going to talk first," I said.

"I cannot speak to any *they* have signaled for death."

"You're talking to me now," I told him.

Sant pressed the button again. When it wouldn't open, he began to hammer on the metal.

I waited.

The doctor's actions became more frantic. He pummeled the door. Then, he stepped back and slammed a shoulder against it.

If we'd been on Earth in a regular house, he would have smashed through. The Lokhars had built the dome tougher than that, though. Three times, Sant hurled himself at the door. Afterward, he panted before it. Maybe he realized there was no smashing through. Finally, he whirled around. Madness swirled in his eyes.

"You leave me no choice," Sant said in a harsh voice. Reaching into his robe, he withdrew a white handle. His thumb clicked a button. A force blade the length of a knife shimmered into existence. It was pure energy, able to cut just about anything. "Instead of sullying myself, Commander, talking to you about the indescribable, I must kill you. Prepare to meet the Great Maker."

19

-3-

I hadn't expected this. It was past time to calm him down.

"Hey!" I shouted. "Do you remember that the Forerunner artifact told me its name? You do know that none of the artifacts has ever told that to a Lokhar before."

Doctor Sant roared. It was loud in the small confines of my chamber. With flapping robes and long limbs, he rushed me, thrusting the force blade like a rapier.

Now, it's true succeeding bomb-blasts a week ago had beaten my body and broken my bones. The healing tank at Mars Base had also speeded my recuperation. I wasn't one hundred percent, but I was still an assault trooper.

Even in my condition, I was too quick for him to kill me easily.

With long flourishes and grunting slashes, Sant came after me. The force blade sliced through the bar top. It chopped a lamp on my nightstand and slashed my blanket to ribbons. I'd grabbed the blanket off the bed and hurled it at Sant like a net.

I would have tried to talk sense into him, but he did wield a force blade. They were nasty weapons, perfect for close quarters combat. All he had to do was touch the energy blade against me, and it would cut skin, bones, muscles and interior organs. That thing was no toy.

Who would tire first? Normally, it would be Doctor Sant. Today—

After three passes around the room, I began to pant. His eyes still glowed with righteous fury. He gripped the front of his robes with his free hand and stood still for a moment.

I could see the wheels turning in his mind. I'd been able to dodge his rushes. Maybe he needed a new approach.

A hard grin stretched his lips. Slowly, using his greater reach, he began to back me toward a corner.

First gulping air, I said, "The Forerunner artifact told me its name. That it did so is a sign of my uniqueness. Surely, you realize that, Doctor. I am above your petty rituals and legends. So, these Shi-Feng hunted me in Wyoming. So what? They failed, exploding uselessly. I'm marking *them* for death now, not the other way around. You don't want to keep attacking me or you'll face my wrath."

Sant halted. He tilted his head to the side, appearing quizzical. "I hold the force blade, not you."

"I'm an assault trooper, though."

"No! You are a guardian of the object."

"That's one of my duties, sure," I said. "But first and foremost, I'm an assault trooper. That means I can defeat you."

"Is that why you keep retreating before me?"

"No. It's because I don't want to hurt you, Doctor. You're my friend."

Lowering the force blade to his side, he stood hunched over. From glaring at me, his eyes darted away again. He backed up until he could view the panel. Although he faced me, he side-glanced at the sands of Mars outside.

"I have ridden the artifact," Sant said, almost as if reciting a litany. "I survived the deaths of millions against the ancient enemy. I have been chosen for a holy task. I cannot throw away my life. I have a duty to Orange Tamika."

"This is much better," I said. "Turn off the force blade, and set it down. Let's talk."

He frowned. "Didn't you hear what I just said?"

"Sure I did."

"I am chosen. I cannot throw away my life."

"That means you'd better put down your weapon before I decide I've had enough of this."

21

Sant shook his head. "No. It means you are dead. They have marked you to die. By telling me, by naming *them*, you have brought me into the circle. I cannot stand with you against them. Thus, I must end it here before Orange Tamika loses my uniqueness. If I don't kill you, *they* will learn I heard of their attack in Wyoming. Then, they will come and kill me too."

"You're making a bad decision, Doctor."

With his free hand, he re-gripped the front of his robe. Hunching forward, he began to stalk me again. He held the force blade in front, waving it as if he knew a knife-fighting technique. Maybe he did.

"This is your last chance, Sant."

"Good-bye, Commander Creed." He bounded in a tiger rush, thrusting the deadly knife.

I'd seen his thighs tense, however. His body language had screamed his intentions. The lanky tiger roared at me as he came. Maybe he thought he could frighten me.

No. That was it. I'd had enough already. My mind snapped into overdrive. His movements seemed to slow down. The long arm kept coming as he leaned and stretched his seven-foot frame. He staked all on the thrust. If I'd been a regular human, no doubt the doctor would have skewered me. Instead, I dodged, but I'd forgotten about my bed's exact placement. The side of my leg struck the edge and I toppled. Both us of seemed to move slowly now.

Sant still thrust as I fell onto the bed. He straightened. I rolled across the mattress. My legs shot up and I stood on the other side. Sant swiveled his hips, thrusting again. My feet tangled in the blanket lying on the floor. I almost tripped because of it, but I stilled my momentum long enough to keep standing. That took too long, though, giving Sant the needed time. When my attention riveted back to him, the force blade already thrust at my midsection. Sant's length allowed him to reach widthwise across the bed to reach me.

Even to my speeded senses, my hands blurred. The edge of the force blade touched my forearm. Blood spurted. A loud *crack* told of broken wrist bones: his. Tiger fingers became numb and released the handle. Given the safety design of the force blade, the energy portion of the knife disappeared.

22

Time flowed back into normal channels for me then. Because of my move and throw, Sant sailed over me, flailing his long Lokhar limbs. He crashed against a wall and slid down in a jumbled heap, tangled in his robes.

I clamped a hand onto my bleeding forearm. The force blade had barely touched the skin, but it was enough to spill blood. A fraction more pressure and that end of my forearm would by lying on the bed in a welter of gore. Instead, the white handle lay on the bed.

As Sant worked to untangle himself, I reached down and picked up the force blade. A *hum* warned of the reappearance of the energy blade. I cut the blanket and wrapped part around my forearm. Blood soaked it, but I stanched some of the bleeding.

Turning with his force blade in my hand, I faced Sant. He sat against the wall, cradling his broken wrist.

I walked to the bar, set down the knife and picked up my glass. Ice cubes rattled in it. I drank the liquid. It was barely enough to wet my mouth. Even so, that made my cheeks warm.

"The Shi-Feng is a holy order," Sant said from where he sat. "They cleanse away evil. None has ever seen one. In their purity, they commit deeds no Lokhar would dare. They accept modifications to their body. They commit ritual suicide and they use their blood to wipe away wickedness."

"I'm wicked?" I asked.

"You have learned the name of a Forerunner artifact. You are the chief guardian to an object that belongs to the Lokhars."

"If you're referring to its stay in the Altair star system—"

"I am," Sant said.

"Yeah, well, I didn't move the Altair Object. It relocated on its own, remember?"

"That is not how the Shi-Feng would view it. To them, you are a beast, Commander. It is inconceivable for a creature to do the things you have. No. You must relinquish the Forerunner artifact. You must formally return it to the Lokhars."

"Now you can say their name?" I asked.

"It doesn't matter," he said. With his back against the wall, Sant slid up to his feet. "You're about to die."

I raised an eyebrow. "Why? Are the Shi-Feng about to break into my room?"

"It is not wise to mock what you don't understand."

"That's why I asked you to come to Mars. Explain the situation to me."

"You are marked for death, Commander. That you have resisted your fate endangers the rest of us. I cannot allow that to happen."

I picked up the force blade. "Do you see who has this?"

"I will make your passing quick, Commander. And perhaps it is well for you to understand." He winced painfully, glancing at his broken wrist."

"Let me summon you aid," I said.

"No! I will leave on my own. First, you must know this much. When one mentions the Shi-Feng, it means their actions must be honorable. Without realizing it, you brought the old codes into play."

"What are you talking about?" I asked.

Doctor Sant reached into his robe and pulled out a wicked little needler. He pointed it at me.

"This is a spring-driven weapon," the doctor said. "It holds poisoned slivers. It was fashioned without any ferrous metals. Thus, it passed your detectors."

"If you had that all along, why use a knife to try to stab me?" I asked.

"Didn't you hear my words? You invoked the Shi-Feng. I had to slay you with a knife, washing away your insult with blood."

"What insult?"

"That you, a beast, should name the holy ones," he said.

"Holy ones blow themselves up to kill others?"

"Good-bye, Commander Creed."

"Shi-Feng!" I shouted.

Sant frowned. "Why do you shout those as your death words?"

"I'm invoking them. You have to fight me honorably now."

"I attempted that. Now, you will use dishonor to question me. I cannot allow myself to be captured and give away Lokhar secrets. Instead, I will kill you any way I can."

24

I stared into his eyes. He seemed to mean what he said.

"Listen, Sant," I said. "You don't realize—"

He pulled the trigger seven times, sending seven poisoned slivers into my stomach.

I stared at him. Then, I collapsed onto my knees.

He tucked the needler within his robes. Then he shoved his broken wrist there as well.

I sucked air into my constricted throat. "You shot me," I wheezed.

"I killed you, Commander Creed."

"No," I said.

"Are you daft? Look at you."

"Don't you realize I still have medical monitors in me?"

Sant frowned. Maybe he didn't understand.

Intense dizziness struck me. The chamber seemed to spin. Then the door slid open and several assault troopers rushed in.

Sant managed to redraw the needler in time to shoot the first one. The rest reached him and bore him onto the floor.

That's when I fell unconscious for the second time in a little over a week. I couldn't believe it.

-4-

Sant's poisoned slivers came closer to killing me than the damage I'd taken in Wyoming. I learned this in retrospect after several days with a one hundred and five degree temperature.

I regained consciousness in Mars Base medical hooked to a Jelk machine we'd salvaged from the battlejumper. This time, it took more than the healing tank to save me.

Lying there drowsily, I realized I'd gotten too cocky. I should have been ready for something like that, kept a weapon in my chamber. Sant had surprised me with his force blade and then the needler.

Where others go unarmed, there it is wise to go armed.

It was an old proverb, one well worth remembering. Sant's attack also hammered home the truth of a surprise attack. The Shi-Feng had used tactical surprise as well. Since prehistoric times, it had been a force multiplier, and it would continue to be so in the future. Next time, it needed to be on my side.

I ached all over. My eyelids felt gritty every time I blinked. I thought about getting up anyway. Instead, I drifted back to sleep.

The next day I couldn't keep anything down. The fever returned, this time only reaching one hundred and thee.

I drank liquids and spewed them back up onto my hospital gown. A nurse put a green solution into the tube sticking in my arm.

I slept more. By now, it seemed as if I'd done it forever. The fever broke and then came back at one hundred and six. I had a terrible dream of Abaddon and his Kargs. The reality of it startled me.

I drifted in the void in a spacesuit. Far away in the distance, I saw a stellar snowflake. Stars shined behind it. That didn't make much sense, even in my dream. Then I realized that was no snowflake. It was a giant Karg vessel. We'd faced far too many just like these in hyperspace.

I moved toward the snowflakes, and I realized more were coming. Dread filled me at the thought. The giant Karg ships weren't in hyperspace but regular space. I began counting them, soon reaching fifteen.

Then I saw Jelk battlejumpers, one hundred of them, at least. They moved in a cone formation, with the endpoint farthest away from the Kargs. The open part of the cone faced the giant snowflakes. In front of the cone-formation at a precise distance was a gauzy substance like a titanic lens. It was most odd.

All at once, the Jelk battlejumpers in the cone fired their lasers at the gauzy substance. The rays filled the lens with bubbling light. Suddenly, a gigantic coherent ray beamed from the other side of the lens. It was then I saw smaller Jelk vessels at the edges of the lens. Did the ships do something to focus the massive beam? I suspected yes. In any case, the giant ray reached out and struck a Karg snowflake-vessel.

The beam disintegrated the alien structure, melting what turned out to be individual Karg moth-ships attached to the gargantuan mother ship.

The Jelk lens ray snapped off. The cone-formation battlejumpers had stopped beaming their lasers into their side of the lens. Were they recharging their coil banks?

More Karg snowflakes moved up. Clinging to them were moth-like ships with glowing nuclear eyes. Those vessels detached from the mother ships. Each craft spewed exhaust as they accelerated toward the Jelk lens.

The massed cone-shaped formation fired into the lens again. As before, a coherent beam lanced out the other side. It struck a moth-ship. The giant ray encompassed the entire Karg vessel, and it annihilated everything so the craft disappeared like a giant blowing out a match. The gargantuan ray moved like a swath, destroying one Karg moth-ship after another.

Did I witness a real space battle between the Kargs and the Jelk, fought in the Corporation's core worlds? In my dream, I believed that to be the case. Yet that would imply the Kargs— or some of them at least—had escaped from their space-time continuum.

The cone formation with its lens wrecked savage destruction against the Karg vessels. Finally, however, some moth-ships drew close enough to the lens to attack. The eyes on the nearest Karg vessels glowed brilliantly. They seemed to bubble as if made of red-hot lava. Then, a red ray beamed. It touched the gauzy lens. More Karg beams hit it. In a consuming flash, like tissue in a bonfire, the lens vanished, as did the smaller ships at the lens' edges.

The cone formation advanced, and the surviving Karg moth-ships gathered in a square. Beams flashed back and forth between the two fleets. Ships exploded, often harming its nearest neighbor. I doubt I'd ever witnessed a deadlier battle.

Finally, the last Jelk vessel disappeared under a barrage of red rays. The Kargs had won, but at a dreadful cost. Hulks and pieces of starships floated everywhere.

As I watched from a distance, my fevered nightmare became personal.

During our invasion of the portal planet, Abaddon had addressed me via screen. He'd shown me how he tortured my sweet Jennifer. For years now, I'd agonized over her fate. Maybe that's what powered the horrible dream.

In the nightmare, the feeling of dread grew worse than ever. I watched as Karg moth-ships cruised through the wreckage of battle. More giant snowflakes appeared, with huge exhausts showing they accelerated, traveling who knew where.

I sped toward one of the snowflakes. Believe me, I didn't want to go there. Yet, nothing I did could stop my advance.

No! I refused. I was Commander Creed. I'd defeated the Kargs before. I wasn't their slave rushing to them at their bidding.

With an intense effort of will, I halted my dream plunge toward that vessel.

Then, it seemed that I didn't float in space anymore. Instead, I stood on a bridge. I didn't recognize the type of ship. It must have been a newer style. Before me, a baroque screen sizzled. A fuzzy image appeared on it. I couldn't see the exact features of the thing, but I saw two fiery eyes like the pit of Hell burning at me.

As I stood on the bridge, the weight of those eyes wilted my resolve. The burning orbs had something to do with Jennifer. Bracing myself, I roared defiance at the eyes. I shook a fist at them.

"Commander Creed," said the deadliest voice I'd ever heard. The words rumbled against my chest, vibrating with debilitating power.

"Abaddon?" I whispered.

The sizzling worsened on the elaborate screen. The image grew fuzzier, but the eyes became like twin fires. I felt the gaze, which locked my jaws.

"I see you, foolish mortal," Abaddon told me. "You are far away, and you are desperate."

"This is a dream," I managed to whisper.

"How truly dense you are," Abaddon said. "You think yourself so wise concerning science and reality. Yet you understand little of power and supernatural force."

"You're saying this is real, not a dream?"

"How can you comprehend? Yes, you dream, but I am indeed speaking to your unconscious mind in the manner of my kind."

"You're a demon," I said. "Is that what you're saying?"

"Come closer to me, mortal. Look at me with your soul and lose all hope."

I almost listened to him. "No!" I shouted, averting my gaze from the burning eyes. "You're not my master. You're an invader in a place you don't belong."

"Wrong. I have come home. Now, I shall devour the living along with the dead."

"The Jelk Corporation will defeat you."

"They fight but lose every battle."

"Taking down more of your moth-ships all the time," I said.

"These are the core worlds. I expand my operations, gaining factories every week. My strength grows as I induce Saurians and creatures you know nothing about into my kingdom. If you can survive long enough, mortal, I will devour your paltry Earth. I will take you, though, and force you to serve me for uncounted centuries. You know nothing of despair, although your woman does. She is my slave, mortal. She is my killer, doing my bidding. Oh, how she hates you, Commander. Perhaps I should send her at you like an arrow to rip out your heart."

"You're a lying fiend from Hell," I said. "I'm going to kill you, Abaddon."

"Brave words from a creature locked in sleep. I doubt you shall survive your sickness. Good-bye, little creature. Know that everything you've worked to achieve, I will destroy. There is no hope for your space-time continuum. I have arrived and humanity's end rushes toward completion."

My heart felt sick. What had he done to Jennifer? How had Abaddon escaped hyperspace? Just how many Kargs had he brought through with him?

"*Creed*," a distant voice shouted. "Wake up, Creed. You're having a nightmare."

I blinked, confused. Abaddon's burning eyes disappeared. I no longer stood on the strange bridge. Neither did I drift in space. It felt as if I zoomed upward toward the light.

"Can you hear me, Creed?"

I felt so utterly weary. Even so, I wanted to wake up.

I did, to find a redheaded nurse whose name I didn't know standing over me. She told me I'd been raving, shouting incoherently. Was everything okay?

I blinked at her, confused. The dream had felt so real. Yet how could Abaddon have spoken to me from hundreds perhaps a thousand light years away? That made no sense. What I'd seen couldn't be reality.

As always, my subconscious must have taken many truths and twisted them into the nightmare. Yet, I have to admit, part of me believed I had glimpsed something more. Could I tell anyone about this, though?

I decided to wait.

Whatever else had happened, the fever had finally broken. The nurse let me suck on a straw as she held a can of vile glop. This time I kept the liquids down. That was a beginning.

I vowed never to let anyone shoot poisons into me again. Why had I gotten fancy with Sant? I should have killed the tiger and been done with it before he could use the needler.

Debating with myself what I should have done with the Lokhar—letting the Abaddon dream dissipate back into my subconscious where it belonged—I fell into a deep sleep. I stayed that way for twenty-three hours. Something had exhausted me beyond normal. It had to be the fever, right? A dream couldn't have done it. Only a fool would believe such a thing.

In any case, I woke up twenty-three hours later, scaring the nurse with my red eyes. She called a doctor. He examined them, shining a penlight into the pupils. After he clicked off the light, he patted me on the shoulder and said I was recovering. I shouldn't worry about the redness. It would go away soon.

Finally, two days later—minus twenty pounds and feeling permanently lightheaded—I allowed the nurse to help me stand. I shuffled to a chair, collapsing into it and panting.

"Why are you up?"

Lifting my chin off my chest, I found Ella Timoshenko in the room with me.

A little over six years ago, Ella had been a Russian scientist. I'd first met her in Antarctica the day after the Earth died. Now, she was a former assault trooper turned guardian. Despite the steroid-68, Ella was still thin with a pretty face. Actually, she had sunken cheeks just like a porn star I'd seen in my misspent youth. Her dark hair dangled to her cheeks, giving her an elfin quality. There was nothing pixy about her razor-like mind, though. She enjoyed things you could count and weigh—using the scientific approach wherever possible.

"Hello to you, too," I said.

Ella grabbed a stool, setting it near me, studying my face. "We thought you might die this time, Creed."

"I feel like I've been dead," I said. I wondered if I should tell her about my dream. Then I realized our scientist would be the last person to believe it could have been real.

31

Ella smiled, nodded and turned away. "Maybe I shouldn't tell you this. You're still getting better."

"Are you kidding? I'm sick of being sick. What's the problem? Give me something to think about."

Ella regarded me, biting her lower lip. Finally, she said, "The Lokhars on Ceres keep pestering us about Doctor Sant."

"Oh?"

"They want him back."

That didn't seem right. The Lokhars on Ceres were Orange Tamika warriors. They'd been with us on the portal planet. Out of ten million tigers making the attack, they were the handful who had survived. What's more, they lived because of us. They owed the assault troopers everything. I had the impression they had dedicated themselves to the Forerunner artifact and to helping mankind survive as a species.

"I don't understand," I said. "They want Sant even after he tried to kill me?"

Ella smiled tightly, looking as if she had a secret. "They have no idea what occurred in your chamber."

"You'd better explain that."

The woman's lips thinned as she stared into my eyes. "You have to understand something first. The doctors didn't think you'd make it through this time. You'd just been in the healing tank. A second immersion this soon…"

"Go on," I said.

"We thought you were dying, Commander. You can understand our grief and rage."

"Sure. What did you do to Sant?"

Ella bit her lower lip again. "Rollo and Dmitri agreed with me. They said I should proceed with the experiment. Only N7 demurred."

"What about Diana and Murad Bey?" I asked.

They were the principle Earth Council leaders. The council governed the people in the space freighters, the bulk of humanity, in other words. As Forerunner Guardians, we are outside the Earth Council's jurisdiction. It was something I'd hammered home to the others many times. Even so, I tried to coordinate with Diana. There weren't enough of us left to allow squabbles.

Ella shook her head. "We didn't tell Diana or anyone else on the Earth Council. Rollo and Dmitri agreed with me that we keep the experiment among ourselves."

"Enough," I said, panting. I couldn't believe how weak I'd become. "Just tell me what you did."

"You know my area of expertise, Commander."

I nodded slowly. During the assault on the portal planet, we'd gained a tiny Forerunner artifact the size of a person's fist. In fact, we stole it from the Orange Tamika Lokhars on the Dreadnought *Indomitable*. That's another of those long stories. In any case, the artifact called EP had beamed a pink ray at Ella. It had fiddled with her mind somehow.

Later, EP had helped me move the larger Forerunner relic presently near Ceres. The small object had remained in the larger one. We hadn't seen EP for years now.

What had the pink ray done to Ella's mind? We all wondered that, she more than any of us. That became her devoted area of expertise.

She commandeered every piece of alien equipment that had to do with the mind and thought control. Using the various devices—the primary tool a Jelk machine from our hijacked battlejumper—our Russian scientist had begun experimenting. After two years, Ella had declared herself free of any alien entanglements in her thoughts.

I hadn't been so sure, and I'd made the mistake of saying so.

After that, Ella went into overdrive. Unbelievably, she found several hidden commands in her mind. Using her alien machines, she deprogrammed herself.

Now, I should tell you that I'm skipping tons of technical jargon. I'm not a scientist, though. I'm a fighter. During her experiments, Ella reached dead-ends. She also had two seizures and raved like a lunatic for a month. At that point, I'd had enough. I locked her in a cell for further study.

Three of her assistants broke Ella out of confinement and took her back to the worst machine, the Jelk device. There, they pushed the limit of their knowledge, using Ella's notes to try one last test. It proved to be the breakthrough.

The next day, Ella had greeted me as her loveable self. She went into exquisite detail what had happened. Her fingers kept tapping her reader, showing me brain charts. As if I'd known what any of that meant.

Believe me, I'd still had my doubts about her.

Ella Timoshenko hadn't. She continued working with the machines in the basement of Mars Base. After that, though, the thrust of her experiments changed. She no longer worried about possessing a traitorous mind. Now she wondered how to read, break and recondition alien minds. Ella's ordeals had given her a thirst to mess with the aliens who had messed with her.

Orange Tamika Lokhars happened to be in the solar system, but those tigers were our closest allies. Purple Tamika Lokhars regularly came to Earth to deliver automated factories. A few of those tigers had disappeared here and there. They found themselves in Ella's chambers with the brain machines.

Before you judge us too harshly, listen to our reasoning. The Lokhars had come to Earth, slaughtering ninety-nine percent of humanity. The last one percent barely hung on. We'd tried to join the Jade League and gain greater protection. The Purple Tamika Emperor had vetoed our entry. Okay. We were on our own, right? As the weakest group around, we relied on our wits and complete ruthlessness. If that meant kidnapping an alien or two to work on…we did it.

That doesn't mean I was proud of the deeds. I simply recognized the crisis and acted accordingly.

Ella experimented on Purple Tamika tigers. Several had died. Two become raging lunatics, and one remained a comatose vegetable. I knew her area of expertise, all right. It was one of our darkest secrets.

As I sat in my chair in the medical chamber on Mars Base, I said, "You're not telling me you put Doctor Sant under one of your machines."

"I am, Commander," Ella said.

"Why?"

"At first," Ella said, "we wanted to know what happened in your quarters. It was obvious you'd used the force blade against him, but where had you gotten the weapon?"

"The knife belonged to Doctor Sant," I said.

"I know that now," Ella said, her lips stretched in one of the evilest smiles I'd ever seen.

Seeing the smile tired me out. I sagged against my chair.

"Are you all right, Commander?" Ella asked.

"Give me a minute." My eyes closed of their own accord. I don't remember falling asleep or anyone picking me up.

When my eyes opened again, I was back in my quarters. My blanket—a new one—was pulled up to my chin. I let my eyes rove around. The room looked as good as new. The viewing panel showed the same red sands in their mindless swirling patterns.

"Hello, Commander."

I turned my head in the other direction, spying the nurse, the pretty redhead. She smiled, stood and checked on me. After fussing for a while, she retreated, leaving the chamber.

When the door opened a second time, Ella walked in with a tray of eggs, ham, toast and orange juice.

My stomach growled as I sat up. I felt ravenous. My hand shook as I picked up the fork. A second later, I forgot about that as I tasted the scrambled eggs. They were delicious.

Ella sat on a barstool, waiting. After I wiped my lips with a napkin, she put the empty tray on the bar.

I burped, feeling full, rested and alert. Maybe I could finally start regaining my strength and putting back on the weight I'd lost.

"Do you remember our last conversation?" Ella asked me.

It took me a moment of recollection. "Yeah, you were about to tell me the worst. What happened to Doctor Sant? Why didn't you tell the Lokhars on Ceres about his murderous rampage?"

"I had another breakthrough with the machines," Ella said, with the excitement shining in her eyes.

"Meaning what?" I asked.

"Doctor Sant told me everything that happened in here."

It took me several seconds to catch on. "You're kidding? He gave you a recap?"

"He gave me much more than that, Creed. I know about the Shi-Feng. I know why Sant reacted as he did. I also learned some Orange Tamika secrets."

"You tore those from his mind?" I asked.

"I did," she said.

Doctor Sant had been a good friend once, maybe the only true one we had among the tigers. Why had he gone crazy? I imagine after his ordeal with the mind machine that he raved madly or lay catatonic on a bed, staring up at the ceiling.

"Is Sant still alive?" I asked.

"Oh, yes, Commander," Ella said. "He's quite alive."

I whipped off the bed cover, stared a second and yanked the blanket back over my nakedness.

"Where are my clothes?" I asked.

"Forget about them," Ella said. "Don't you want to hear what I've discovered?"

I realized I did. "Who are the Shi-Feng?" I asked.

"A death cult of assassins," Ella said. "According to Doctor Sant, their origins belong to the pre-Lokhar Space Age. They're also pre-Creator, as in the present tiger religion. Once, the followers of Shi-Feng worshiped anthropometric Lokhar-like gods and goddesses, much like the Greek pantheon. When the tigers become Creator worshipers, the death cult changed with the times."

"Why do they blow up?" I asked.

"As I said, they're a death cult. They believe in purity and right thinking. The Shi-Feng are convinced that only Lokhars were made in the image of the Creator. Their fascination with the Forerunner artifacts is intense. Put the two together, and it is clear why they had to kill you."

I thought about that. "Why did they wait so long to make their first strike then?" I asked.

"As to that," Ella said, "I don't know. It is a good question."

"When you tell me all this about the Shi-Feng, what you really mean is that these are Doctor Sant's views about them, right?"

"That is correct," Ella said.

"I'm not faulting you," I said. "I'm merely saying we don't know everything about the Shi-Feng, just Sant's coloring of them."

"Yes. It's good to remember that."

36

"So why did Doctor Sant attack me?"

"I believe he told you during your confrontation," Ella said. "Among the Lokhars, the Shi-Feng are held in religious awe. They have an amazing mystique. Legend holds they never fail."

"So...?"

"Doctor Sant believes the Shi-Feng wield supernatural powers. You told him about their attack against you. Once he realized you spoke the truth, he believed that he had to kill you immediately. If he didn't, the Shi-Feng would come after him. On all accounts, he couldn't allow that."

"You mean he had to stay alive at all costs?" I said.

"I doubt you realize why," Ella said.

"Of course I do, for self-preservation."

"You're both right and wrong," she said.

"That doesn't make sense," I said, crossly.

"Then bear with me as I explain. Doctor Sant believes he must stay alive at all costs. You're wrong in thinking it's purely because he loves life. In his mind, he must live in order to preach his new message to the others of Orange Tamika."

"What message?" I asked.

Ella slid off her stool and went behind the bar. There, she mixed herself a dry martini, setting the glass on the counter. "Would you like a bottle of water?" she asked.

"Give me a beer," I said.

"You're not supposed to have any alcohol yet," she said, sipping from her martini. "Ah. That's good." She sipped once more, taking the olive and popping it into her mouth. As she chewed, she regarded me.

"You've told me about Sant's metamorphosis from scientist to religious seeker more than once," Ella said. "I know you've told me about him in order to tease me with the idea that maybe I could get religion too."

Ella finished off the martini. She looked pretty doing it. Then she set the glass on the bar. "I never want to become like Doctor Sant. Once, he viewed reality through a common sense lens. Now, he's a mystic. That he survived the transfer from the portal planet to the solar system has taken on religious significance for him. He can't accept that it simply happened. He has to believe it happened for a reason.

"Naturally, what we're seeing is the guilt of his survival. He wants to subscribe greater significance to the event than it warrants. Why would he live instead of the others? He can't accept the luck of the draw."

"Okay," I said.

"In his search for reasons," Ella said, "he pores over ancient Lokhar holy books. He studies the artifact. He ponders his existence."

"Sant told you all this while he was under your machine?" I asked.

Ella nodded.

"And?" I asked.

"He yearns to preach a crusade against Purple Tamika. He believes the Emperor acted without honor in sending Princess Nee to *Indomitable*."

The Emperor's daughter-wife that I shot," I said.

"Sant sees that moment as an act of the Creator. If you hadn't shot the Purple Tamika princess, she would have turned the dreadnoughts back into normal space. We never would have closed the portal planet. The Kargs would be destroying all life in our universe now. In Sant's mind, that was the first strike against Purple Tamika. Since Orange Tamika closed the gate between the space-time continuums, they should hold the throne."

"Doesn't seem so farfetched to me," I said.

"I agree," Ella said. "The only part that's odd is his need to put a religious coloring to his desire."

I pursed my lips, nodding after a time. I could see her point.

"And that is why Doctor Sant had to kill you. He has a holy message to bring to Orange Tamika, or so he believes. If the Shi-Feng slew him, that righteous cause would die with him."

"Okay. I'm following you so far," I said. "But how does Sant figure Orange Tamika has a chance of taking over from Purple Tamika? The Orange lost too much strength in the destruction of the three dreadnoughts."

38

"That's the strange part," Ella said. "I wanted to keep Sant under the machine and learn more. The protestations of his warriors on Ceres meant I didn't have the time."

"What are you talking about now?" I asked.

"I wanted your opinion about what to do next. It's why I spoke to you a few days ago. When you passed out again, I had to make the decision on my own."

"Back up a bit," I said. "What's the strange part first?"

"It concerns the Jelk Corporation," she said. "We know there's been less combat between the corporation and the Jade League these past six years. Sant's heard rumors as to a possible reason why."

"This I want to hear."

"Several major Saurian fleets appear to have left the frontier," Ella said.

The frontier was between the Jelk Corporation and the Jade League. For centuries, the two sides had warred. The majority of the attacks came from the Jelk against the Jade League. Saurians crewed most corporation war-fleets.

"Does Sant know where the corporation fleets went?" I asked, recalling my dream. The Jelk had battled in the core worlds, wherever those where.

"He does not," Ella said. "And that troubles him. It appears to trouble many in the Jade League. Unrest between allies has risen."

"Jade League allies?" I asked.

Ella nodded.

"Okay. I understand that part. What's this decision you had to make?"

"I let Doctor Sant go," Ella said.

"You did *what*?"

"He's back on Ceres among his warriors."

"That's crazy, Ella. The tiger shot me. He tried to kill me. Now, the Orange warriors will take up arms against us. We can't afford that."

"You must relax, Commander." She scowled. "Frankly, your words are insulting. Do you think I'm an idiot?"

"Of course not," I said.

39

"Surely you understand that I used the machine on him," Ella said. "I erased his memories of my questioning. I erased his memory of shooting you. Naturally, I also blotted out mention of the Shi-Feng."

"The machine can do that?"

"On Lokhars," Ella said, "not on humans, though."

"Sure," I said. "That's okay, then, I guess. Do you really trust the machine that much? He could end up remembering. I'm not sure it was worth the risk."

"Don't we want him to spread unrest among the tigers?"

"That's a good question," I said.

"There is something else," she said. "I added something more to Doctor Sant. He is more disposed toward us now. He'll go out of his way to help us any way he can."

I sat in my bed, envisioning Doctor Sant pumping those seven shots into me with the needler.

"I hope you're right about the Jelk machine," I said. "They're a tricky race, Ella. Who knows what you really did to Sant's mind."

"I've been experimenting with the machine for years," she said. "You shouldn't worry so much. I know what I'm doing."

Talk about your famous last words.

"From what you've learned, do you think the Shi-Feng will attack me again?"

"I do."

"Great," I said. "Well, we're going to have to think of ways of catching them before they do it. This time, I don't want to give them the element of surprise. This time, we're going to get it over them."

-5-

The days merged into weeks. The lingering aftereffects of Doctor Sant's poisons refused to let me go.

I stayed in Mars Base for over two months, slowly recuperating. In that time, I only gained five pounds.

In the third month, we received another automated factory. If the industrialist-captain of the freighter flotilla was surprised to see me, she didn't show it.

This factory went to Australia, near Melbourne. It took five hundred and seven shuttle flights to bring everything down. After the freighters left, a team of guardians under Rollo searched the premises for a week. They found nothing.

Five months after Sant shot me, I returned to duty aboard the *Aristotle*. The old Lokhar cruiser ran smoothly. I took it out to the Asteroid Belt, paying a visit to Doctor Sant on Ceres.

We spoke face-to-face in the Lokhar reception center. He wore his orange toga. I kept to a regulation uniform. Sand shifted across the floor. Hot wind blew through the vents. Sunlamps blazed down on us. This was a vaulted room with a high ceiling.

Doctor Sant looked thinner than I remembered. His shoulders stooped more. I gazed into his eyes. Something haunted them. When I stepped close, I no longer smelled the familiar cinnamon odor. I couldn't figure out why.

"How do you feel, Doctor, really?" I asked.

He raised a long arm and flicked his fingers. "I dream more than usual." He glanced down at me. "You're in many of them."

"Oh?"

"I am ashamed, Commander. In my dreams, I shoot you with my needler. I cannot decipher the meaning. I believe your life may be in danger. Not from my hands," he added hastily.

I debated saying the name "Shi-Feng" to see his reaction. I had a good idea what that reaction would be. Instead, I said, "Thanks for the warning."

"You must not dismiss it so easily," Sant said. "I recognize your ways, Commander. You are too trusting of others." He stooped lower as his voice dropped an octave. "Events stir on the border. Jade League members recall old feuds. There is a time of troubles approaching."

As I stood there with him, I didn't detect any duplicity in Sant. I found myself marveling at Ella's skill with the Jelk mind machine.

"Are you well?" Sant asked later, as I made ready to leave.

"Yes, fine," I said. "Why do you ask?"

"You seem tense. I hope it isn't anything I've said or done."

"Don't worry, Doctor. I've had…things on my mind lately."

"Yes," he said. "Don't we all?"

An hour later I headed for my ship, little knowing that nothing was going to be the same again.

***

Three days later, I sipped black coffee on the bridge of the *Aristotle*. The crew sat on tall seats so they could reach their control panels. The ship had been built to tiger-scale, but it was ours now.

I sat in the center with the other consoles facing inward toward me. That way, the personnel could see exactly what I did or said at all times. It was the Lokhar method, not ours, but we had to live with it. Before me on the bulkhead was the main viewing screen.

From the outside, our cruiser looked like a wedged-shaped slice of pie. The bridge was inside the back third area, buried under many decks and protected by the outer armor. The vessel was fast, boasting a heavy electromagnetic shield in front and a weaker one in back—tigers didn't believe in running away. For main armaments, we had medium-strength laser cannons. This was a shoot and scoot vessel, not a big toe-to-toe fighter like the battlejumper we'd once stolen from Shah Claath.

On the view screen in space gleamed the giant, donut-shaped Forerunner artifact that we guardians supposedly protected.

I took another sip, savoring my coffee.

"Commander," Ella said from her station. "The beacon near Neptune is reporting."

"Yes," I said.

Ella studied her board before her head snapped back up. "I'm detecting starships, over twenty of them, so far. More are coming through the jump gate every minute."

I put the cup into its holder, sitting up. "Put it on the main screen," I said. I had to work to keep the bite out of my voice. Twenty starships—I didn't like the sound of that. The next automated factory wasn't due for another three months.

Ella complied, and I found myself looking at shark-shaped vessels of varying dimensions. The gate shimmered yellow. Blue Neptune hung up at the corner about fifty thousand kilometers from the gate. The yellow intensified as another Great White-shaped vessel slid through. According to the scale symbol on the edge of the screen, some of the ships were bigger than several city blocks. The big ones looked to be larger than Manhattan Island.

"Those must be Starkiens," I said.

"I agree," Ella replied.

We'd had our share of run-ins with the Starkiens. In size, shape and disposition, they were baboon-like aliens. They were private contractors without any planetary abode to call home. They roved the star lanes, practicing piracy wherever they could get away with it. As a rule, the other races sneered at the Starkiens, driving them away as squatters. We didn't have the hardware to sneer.

43

I wondered what they doing in the solar system.

"I count thirty vessels now," Ella said.

The shark-shaped vessels kept pouring through the yellow jump gate. That was the main way the aliens moved between star systems. Long ago, the First Ones had laid down jump lanes. How they did this, no one knew. The stellar maze was like a giant connect-the-dots puzzle with various lanes linking different star systems. Some believed the Forerunners had used the artifacts to make the routes.

"Make it forty-five ships now," Ella said.

"Have they tried to hail us yet?" I asked.

Ella shook her head.

Neptune was light-hours away from us, making two-way talking difficult. We'd get a message hours after a Starkien had sent it. Then, we'd send ours after a similar delay. That made distance arguments difficult. Still, as a matter of courtesy, the Starkien in charge over there could have informed us of his presence. That he didn't hail us implied hostile intentions.

"I'm counting sixty Starkien warships," Ella said.

This was starting to look bad. "Is there any sign of Jelk or Saurians among them?" I asked.

"Negative, Commander," Ella said.

I drained the rest of my coffee, tossing the cup to an ensign. After a time, I drummed my fingers on the armrest of my chair.

"Eighty vessels," Ella said. "They're all Starkien so far, sir."

"Yeah," I said. "It's time to talk to Diana."

Ella frowned. "Earth Council warships aren't going to make any difference against these many Starkiens, sir."

"More is better," I said. "Put me through to Diana."

"Yes, Commander," Ella said, tapping her board.

The Lokhars had some nifty tech. One of their coolest was T-missiles. The "T" stood for *teleport*. The concept was simple enough. The missile popped out of existence and reappeared hundreds of millions of kilometers closer to the target. It did this in the proverbial blink of an eye. We'd used a T-missile in the Sigma Draconis system to attack Shah Claath's battlejumper. Six and a half years ago, Lokhars had tried to use a similar trick against us in the solar system. I'd been ready for it, though, and had exploded nuclear warheads in the reappearing zone, killing the elite Lokhar legionaries that had ejected from the T-missiles against us.

The Lokhars had also perfected a communications system that implemented the teleporting principle. It allowed fast two-way communication without the hours of time lag that speed-of-light talk would have taken between the Starkiens and me.

"Diana is ready to speak with you, Commander," Ella said.

"Put her on the main screen."

A moment later, Diana appeared.

In the past, I'd referred to her as the Amazon Queen. She was a tall woman with wide hips, large breasts and handsome features. She had thick dark hair and usually oozed cunning and sexual power. She ran the Earth Council together with Murad Bey.

For six and a half years, Diana had remained in control. During that time, she had solidified her position among the freighter-living humans. More than once, she'd tried to persuade me to put the Forerunner Guardians under her jurisdiction using a variety of power plays. The lady simply didn't know how to quit trying to amass more authority.

This would be a good moment to remind you that the last one percent of humanity was the troublemaking kind: the hard-cases, the gamblers, the lucky and tough-as-nails survivors. That made the Earth Council members the cream de la crème of dangerous.

"Commander Creed," Diana said on the screen. "This is a pleasant surprise. It's been too long." She unbound her luxurious hair, running a brush through the strands. It looked as if she took the call from her bedroom aboard her cruiser, a small room with silks and lace hanging everywhere.

"You're in Earth orbit?" I asked.

"Of course," she said.

"A Starkien armada is coming through the Neptune jump gate," I told her.

Diana set down her brush, giving me a thoughtful study. "How many warships have you detected so far?"

I glanced at Ella.

"One hundred and thirty," Ella told me.

I repeated the number to Diana. The Earth Council leader whistled.

"It's time for a show of strength," I told her.

"Meaning you want the Earth Fleet to join you at Ceres?" Diana asked.

"I do," I said.

Diana glanced elsewhere as if thinking. Idly, she resumed brushing her hair with long strokes. "No," she said finally, setting down the brush for the second time. "One hundred and thirty is too many alien ships for us to defeat."

"They're going to have more than that," I said. "So I want you to bring your warships and every freighter we have. We're going to show them our solidarity."

Diana didn't feign her surprise this time—it was real. "Are you crazy? You want to put the last humans in harm's way?"

"No," I said evenly. "I want to keep the Starkiens from destroying us."

Her brow furrowed. "You think they're here as slavers?" Diana asked.

"Possibly…"

"Commander," Ella said, interrupting our conversation. "I think you're wrong about that. There's only one reason why the Starkiens could have come to the solar system."

"Just a minute," I told Diana. Clicking a switch on my armrest, I muted the Amazon Queen. Then I turned to Ella, raising an eyebrow.

"They're here for the Forerunner object," she said. "From what we know, the other artifacts are heavily guarded. Surely, the Starkiens think we're too weak to hold onto ours. We've always known this day would come, just not that it would be Starkiens."

"Why have they chosen *this time* to make their attempt?" I asked.

"Remember what we learned about the Saurian fleets?" Ella asked.

"A *few* Saurian fleets pulled back, you said."

Ella Timoshenko glanced at her board. I saw her lips moving. Soon, she said, "I count two hundred and ten Starkien vessels. The last two are off the scale for Starkien ships. I

46

suspect those are base ships, Commander. They must hold the young and serve as storage craft and repair yards for the other vessels."

That made sense. The Starkiens fleets were nomadic. As usual, Ella had cut to the heart of the matter.

"They're beginning acceleration," Ella said, as she stared at her board. "Since this information is over several hours old, they've been moving for some time already. By their heading, they appear to be aimed at our artifact."

I muttered under my breath. This was just what we needed. First Shi-Feng, now Starkiens.

With a *click*, I reopened channels with Diana. "The Starkiens have over two hundred vessels and are headed for the Forerunner object. I need your warships here pronto."

"We can't defeat that many enemy ships," Diana protested.

"I'm not asking you to do that," I told her.

"What then?" she asked.

"If it comes to battle, you're going to cover my ship as I attack the artifact."

Diana shared at me in horror. "You plan to destroy it?"

"If I have to," I said.

"How does that help us, Creed?" the Amazon Queen asked. "If the Starkiens have come for the artifact, once you've destroyed it, they'll kill all of us in retaliation."

"Is that how you play poker?" I asked.

Diana stared into my eyes. "I hope you know what you're doing, Creed."

I grinned to mask the fact that I didn't. The one thing I'd learned in life was to show a brave front. I needed Diana. So, she had to believe I had a workable plan.

Yeah, a workable plan. Over two hundred Starkien vessels against our paltry ten starships and accompanying star fighters—I was going to have to pull the biggest bluff of my life. If I failed, the human race would likely perish within the next few days.

-6-

Thirty-six hours later, my three starships drifted between the Forerunner artifact and the asteroid of Ceres.

The cruisers and missile-ships of the Earth Fleet had already begun deceleration from their race here from Earth orbit. Diana had hedged her bet. The freighters holding the last one percent of humanity hid behind Terra. The three hundred fighter-bombers had also remained there.

That gave me exactly ten starships to face down two hundred and fifteen alien vessels along with one thousand seventeen Starkien fighter craft.

"We can't win this battle," Diana told me via screen.

"I know Starkiens," I said.

I'd had personal dealings with them on more than one occasion. They thought of humans as beasts. They were also excitable and sought easy advantages, a good piratical combination. In a sense, they were the scavengers of the space lanes. Did they think of our artifact as easy pickings? I considered that likely. That meant they planned to swoop down and take it.

I had my reasons for stopping that at any cost. A few million humans among the vast hordes of interstellar space—we needed every advantage we could cobble together.

As I've said, originally, the Jelk Corporation planned to use us as slave-soldiers. Starkiens could just as likely attempt to make us zoo-slaves for others. Maybe a few extraterrestrials would even enjoy feasting on us as delicacies.

So far, we had one clear ability compared to the rest of the aliens. We assault troopers could outfight any other alien as infantry. The Jelk, the Lokhars and the Kargs had all learned the hard way what that meant. With a Forerunner object in our solar system, we now had claim to religious importance. If we lost the artifact, we would lose the protection the aura of having a relic granted us.

That meant our survival and freedom demanded we keep the object.

I left the bridge for some shuteye. Stretched out on my bed, I fell into a fitful slumber. A dream coalesced soon enough. I was in the Forerunner artifact again with N7—a former mining-android. Abaddon spoke to me via screen, showing me Jennifer hanging by her wrists, her toes an inch above the floor. He offered me a position in his evil hierarchy, telling me he'd give me Jennifer to boot.

In my dream, I shouted, asking for Jennifer's forgiveness. She understood I had to do this, right.

"Creed!" she screamed. "Save me. I'm your woman. You can't sacrifice me. You're my man. You're supposed to protect me."

"Jennifer," I whispered. "You have to understand."

"No!" she howled, as Kargs applied torture devices to her flesh. "Creed, help me!"

My eyes flew open. I lay on my bed in the *Aristotle*. Sweat soaked my blanket and sheets.

I got up, drank water, ate a sandwich and donned my uniform. What else could I have done back there on the portal planet in hyperspace six and a half years ago? If I'd agreed to Abaddon's deal, our universe would have faced a billion enemy starships and a trillion death-dealing Kargs. I'd done the right thing. Yet, if that was true, why did I feel like such a heel?

The intercom in my room buzzed.

Wearily, I went to it. "Yeah?" I asked.

"The Starkiens are almost here," Ella said. "Their chief wants to speak to you."

"I'm on my way," I said.

***

Back on the bridge, I found myself staring at the Starkien commander, Baba Gobo. As N7 had once told me, Baba would be his name and Gobo was his rank. It meant *lord of ships*.

A regular Starkien was the size of a baboon and looked as furry and as ugly. Baba had two long canines at the end of his wrinkled muzzle, each of them a dirty yellow color. He must have weighed ninety pounds, sporting a big pouch with an obscene belly button, easily the heaviest Starkien I'd ever seen. He had a mane like a lion, although his was stark white. I knew it meant he was old, older than Naga Gobo, a Starkien I'd killed in the solar system many years ago. I wondered if this Gobo had known Naga.

Just as Naga had, Baba Gobo sat on a dais with raised controls around him. I knew the place stank because Starkiens did. When I'd met them in person before on a beamship, the chamber had smelled like a filthy zoo cage. Baba Gobo lacked clothes. Instead, he wore a harness around his body. His was devoid of weapons or tools, having scarlet streamers instead.

The Starkien on the main screen opened his baboon snout. "I would speak to him known as Creed-beast," Baba said.

I doubted he knew English. We used translator devices to communicate.

Ella touched a switch, splitting the screen into two parts. One half showed the braking armada. Long tails of fusion thrust showed they applied energy. The shark-shaped vessels had crossed our star system in a hurry and now slowed down for a meeting. They also spewed out masses of star fighters who swarmed the bigger ships like fleas. The Starkiens came in a crescent formation just as the Spanish Armada had come against the English in 1588.

I had ten old Lokhar cruisers and missile-ships to face the Starkiens. Most of my vessels were bigger than theirs were. Their largest, however, dwarfed mine. Ella informed me that in tonnage the enemy beat us eighteen to one.

I wasn't going to win a Jutland battle or a Midway victory today. Bluff was my only hope...unless I could think of something better fast.

50

Pushing myself off my chair, I strode toward the screen. I'd chosen blue naval uniforms for the guardians. It gave us a sharper image and a link to extinct Earth fleets. Glowering at the Starkien, I said, "Are you the Baba-creature?"

The Starkien stiffened. "How dare you insult me? Do you have any understanding of my exalted rank?"

"Lord of all Smells?" I asked.

"Is that an insult?"

"Will you look at this," I said. "You're too stupid to understand that I am indeed demeaning you before your face. You *are* the Lord of Starkiens after all."

He opened his snout, revealing his dental work. I could only imagine the fogging he'd give anyone near enough to smell his breath. For a moment, I expected him to howl with simian rage.

Instead, Baba Gobo regained his self-control, closing his snout without uttering a hoot. I reexamined his white mane. With age came wisdom. Perhaps the saying was as true for Starkiens as it was for humans.

"You do not appreciate me naming you as a beast, do you?" he said.

"I am a man," I said.

The Starkien nodded. There appeared a depth to his dark eyes then. I fixated on that, and a chill worked down my back. Baba Gobo was intelligent. Worse, he had cunning. Combined with self-control that was a dangerous mixture.

"Why do your ships block my passage to the Sol Object?" he asked.

Once, the artifact had been known as the Altair Object. At the time, the Lokhar Fifth Legion had guarded it, along with a greater number of starships than I possessed.

"We are the object's guardians," I said.

"Ah," he said, before making barking sounds. I recognized it as Starkien laughter.

"I choose who can and cannot approach the relic," I told him.

"What gives a beast the right?" he asked.

I stared at him.

He made a complex gesture with his left hand. "Let me rephrase my question. What gives *you* the right? Surely, not your puny number of warships."

"The artifact once rested in a portal planet," I said. "The planet was in fact a Forerunner machine which the object powered. That opened the way to the Karg Universe. Abaddon would have crossed to our space-time continuum and hunted down all non-Karg life, eliminating it. I stopped that by talking to the relic. Among other things, the object told me its name."

Baba Gobo's eyes shined wetly, greedily. He leaned toward me. "I have heard this story. It cannot be true, though. One such as you cannot possibly *know* the name well enough to repeat it."

I smiled. "Is this the extent of your guile, how you attempt to trick me into revealing the ancient name to you?"

Hooting sounds came out of the background behind Baba Gobo. The Starkien commander whirled around. He beat his chest and screeched.

"He's excitable after all," Rollo said to my left.

I turned around. Rollo was my best friend. Of all the guardians, he most resembled a gorilla with his thick neck, massive shoulders and muscles. The man had the bluest eyes I'd ever seen. I wondered why he was here instead of commanding his starship, the *Thomas Aquinas*. Before I could ask him, Baba Gobo cleared his throat to my back.

I faced the view-screen.

"I have grown weary of your vanity," the Starkien told me. "It is time for us to reach an understanding. Several years ago, you slew my great-nephew, Naga Gobo. He dealt with the Jelk, which was an evil deed. I deplore his memory because of that. Yet, he was kin to me, and he ruled a Starkien flotilla. You must pay the blood-debt of his death."

"Pray tell me," I said. "What does that debt happen to be?"

"I'm sure you already know," Baba Gobo told me. "I demand the Sol Object."

"No," I said. "I don't think so."

"Do not play the fool, human. I have overwhelming numbers at my command. If you resist, I will not only destroy your ten warships, but I will hunt down your freighters as well.

Oh, yes, I am quite aware of them hiding behind your poisoned Earth. I will capture or destroy each craft, eliminating your kind forever. *That* will atone for your vile deed of slaying Naga Gobo and his people."

"I saved our universe from destruction," I said. "You owe me your life. That should atone for your great-nephew's death."

"Words," Baba Gobo said. "They do not impress me."

"Everyone's an ingrate," I said. "Do you realize I lost one hundred thousand troopers saving your ugly hide?"

The Starkien made another gesture. I took it as a shrug.

"You leave me no choice, I'm afraid," I said. "I am the Forerunner Guardian. You cannot have the object, nor can I allow you to annihilate the last humans."

He smirked. "There is nothing you can do to stop me."

"You're wrong," I said. "There is the Samson Protocol."

He paused a half-beat before saying, "I have no idea what that's supposed to be."

"Samson was an ancient Earth hero," I said. "At the time, he was the strongest warrior in the world. His story is told in our holy text."

"I was not aware you beasts had a holy book."

"Oh, yes," I said. "We most certainly do. In the book of *Judges,* we are told that the Philistines plagued Samson's people. He killed many of their soldiers and mighty men. Yet, he had a weakness. Samson loved beautiful women."

"This is a common failing among champions," Baba Gobo said.

Maybe that was another universal principle.

"In the end," I said, "a woman named Delilah wanted to know the secret to Samson's supernatural strength. She nagged him mercilessly, asking him day and night for the answer. He played along, giving her nonsense answers. Each time, Delilah would perform the needed deed to steal his strength. Then, when he slept, she would say, 'Samson, the Philistines are upon you!' He'd wake up and kill them. At last, though, Delilah wept bitterly, telling him he didn't love her. If he did love her, he'd tell her his secret."

"What did your Samson do?" Baba Gobo asked.

"Like the fool he'd become, he told her the secret. Samson had never cut his hair. It was his symbol as a Nazarene, one who had been set aside to the Creator. As he slept, Delilah saved his head. Then she cried out, 'Samson, the Philistines are upon you!'

"He woke up and attempted to defeat them as he always had, but the spirit of the Creator had left him. Samson had become as weak as other men. The Philistines bound him and burned out his eyes. Then they set him to work as a slave, grinding grain."

Baba Gobo bristled. "Is this what you think you'll do to me: burn out my eyes?"

"Not at all," I said.

"Then I do not understand your Samson Protocol."

"That's because you don't know the end of the story."

"Oh," the Starkien said. "By all means, finish it."

I'll say this for the baboons. They like a good story as much as anyone else. Maybe they weren't all bad.

"One day many years after Samson's blinding," I said, "the Philistines worshiped their gods in the city's primary temple. The leaders said, 'Let us bring out Samson to mock him.' They did. The blind warrior asked the boy leading him to set him between the two central pillars holding up the temple. There, Samson prayed, 'Lord, let me die with my enemies. Give me the strength to push down these pillars.' Afterward, Samson strained. As the Philistines watched, the spirit of the Creator came upon him and he brought down the two pillars, and that brought down the temple full of Philistines. The holy text says he killed more that day than he had during his life."

Baba Gobo squinted at me. "What is your point?"

"The Samson Protocol means I will bring down the temple on both of us, killing all of us as I destroy the Forerunner artifact."

"No," the Starkien whispered. "That is blasphemous sacrilege. You would be branded an outlaw, and your people hounded to the ends of the universe."

I laughed. "Do you hear yourself? You threaten to destroy my people, extinction for mankind. That doesn't matter to a race already slain. Do you plan to kill us twice?"

"You do not possess the means to destroy the artifact," Baba Gobo said.

"I assure you, I do."

"You've fitted nuclear warheads onto the relic?" he asked.

"Among other things," I lied.

"You *are* an animal," Baba Gobo said. "It is vile to destroy an artifact of the First Ones. It is unclean to set explosives on the shrine. I abhor you, beast. Listen to me well. Many think lowly of the Starkiens. But today I will sacrifice my flotilla to rid the universe of monsters like you and your ilk. Prepare to die, Creed-beast."

"The explosions will destroy you, too," I said, surprised at his reaction.

"I have no interest in your—" The Starkien paused, and he glanced to his left, my right.

"Commander," Ella said. "I'm receiving a communication from Ceres. Doctor Sant would like to address the two of you."

Baba Gobo regarded me. "I have received a call from Doctor Sant, a Lokhar of Orange Tamika. Did he not return from hyperspace via the artifact?"

"He did," I said.

"Let us hear what the noble Lokhar wishes to say," the Starkien told me.

Why did Doctor Sant call now? Could he have been listening to our two-way conversation? Did the Lokhar have military-grade spy devices on Ceres? What did that say for Ella's assurance that Sant would favor us?

The split screen changed. The image of the Starkien fleet disappeared. In its place Doctor Sant appeared in his orange robe.

Like the Starkien and me, Doctor Sant used a universal translating device to communicate with the two of us.

"I thank both of you gentlemen for taking my call," Sant said.

Baba Gobo stiffened. "I hope you are not equating the *beast* with me. Do you not realize he has just threatened to destroy the Forerunner object?"

"Yes, I know," Doctor Sant said. "It is why I wish to address you both."

"You are a Lokhar," Baba Gobo said. "Of all the races, I know you serve the artifacts with the greatest zeal. Surely, you realize that we must expunge mankind from the star lanes."

Doctor Sant said nothing, although he turned his yellow eyes onto the Starkien. There was something unsettling about Sant, something I'd never noticed before. It was a new majesty, perhaps, an extra weight or gravity to his bearing. Was that due to the Jelk machine?

"You weren't with us in hyperspace, Baba Gobo," Doctor Sant said. "I joined the humans as they battled down the portal planet to the artifact in the center of the great Forerunner machine. I saw Commander Creed in his element. What is more, I saw him walk the curve toward the ancient residence in the inner torus of the object. He disappeared into an olden building. There, he did communicate with the relic, learning the construct's name. He bargained with the tool of the First Ones. In a moment of time, the object now in the solar system's Asteroid Belt left the portal planet and came here. The object has blessed the humans with its presence. It judges them, Baba Gobo. The Lokhars await the artifact's word on the nature of man. Are the humans beasts as you subscribe, or should mankind join the civilized races as guardians of life?"

"He threatened to destroy the ancient shrine," Baba Gobo said.

"He is the object's appointed guardian," Doctor Sant said. "He uses what weapons he has. Yes, Commander Creed is crude and bloodthirsty, yet he saved our universe from destruction."

"We Starkiens will make better guardians," Baba Gobo said.

Slowly, Doctor Sant shook his head. "This cannot be. The object has chosen its residence. Here it must stay until it choses otherwise."

The Starkien's eyes gleamed wetly. "I acknowledge your rank, Doctor Sant. You are a chosen one of the relic. I bow before you. Yet, you should know, acolyte, that you have just sealed humanity's fate. I will annihilate them and take up residence in this star system."

"Then you must slay me as well," Doctor Sant said. "The Lokhars will, of course, learn of this. Then, you will have to pay the price for spilling my blood."

The Starkien stared at Doctor Sant seeming deflated. "Is this your final word?"

"It is," Doctor Sant said.

"You would do this for these beasts?" the Starkien asked.

"I would do it because the artifact has told Commander Creed its name."

"This is true?" Baba Gobo asked.

"It is true," said Doctor Sant.

The Starkien sniffed several times. He avoided looking at me. "We will leave the solar system, Doctor. As one who journeyed with a Forerunner construct, you have my envy and highest regard. Your words have weight, acolyte. I cannot carry them on my shoulders. Thus, I retreat before your glory."

Doctor Sant bowed his head, and then his image disappeared from the screen.

Finally, Baba Gobo glanced at me. There was venom in his eyes. "This isn't the end of it, beast. When the Lokhar—" The Starkien snarled. Then his image vanished.

That left me alone with my thoughts. Doctor Sant had ridden *on* the artifact when it teleported away from the portal planet. I had gone *inside* the object and actually spoken with it. Yet, I was the beast and Doctor Sant the holy acolyte.

In that moment, with a burning in my chest, I vowed to make the aliens of all stripes recognize that humans were equal to any other race in our galaxy.

-7-

The Starkien flotilla left the same way it had come, through the Neptune jump gate.

Seven months later, Doctor Sant informed me that he and his fellow Orange Tamika Lokhars were going home. After what had happened with Baba Gobo, that sounded ominous. Other extraterrestrials feared the Lokhars but had nothing but contempt for us humans. With the last Lokhars gone, what would stop bloodthirsty aliens from ransacking the solar system?

An Orange Tamika starship docked near Ceres. A day later, Doctor Sant and I walked along an underground corridor jackhammered from the asteroid's rock.

I wore my navy uniform, complete with a military cap and sidearm, my .44 Magnum.

I'd finally gained back all my lost weight and felt strong again. The last of Sant's needler venom had disappeared from my system. At no time had he shown any inclination to recall his assassination attempt against me, nor did he ever speak about the Shi-Feng.

Doctor Sant wore his former silver and black garment with orange chevrons. With his greater height, the tiger towered over me.

"I'm not sure I understand why you're leaving," I said. "I thought you wished to continue studying the artifact."

As we walked down the rock corridors, with the stark lights shining down from the ceiling, Doctor Sant glanced at me

58

sidelong. Since going under Ella's mind machine, he had become less talkative and more contemplative.

His strides lengthened and his furry brow wrinkled in thought. I even noticed that his whiskers twitched. Finally, in a grave voice, he said, "Rumors have percolated from deep within the Jelk Corporation."

"What kind of rumors?" I asked.

"They have invasion troubles," he said.

"From where?" I asked, thinking about my nightmare of Abaddon. "And how did you learn of this?"

"Yes, that is the question, from where, I mean. The captain of *Royal Sovereign*—the Orange Tamika warship docked outside—has told me these rumors. They are food for serious contemplation. The captain told me some believe Center Galaxy aliens have invaded down our spiral arm into Jelk territory. Others think that a secret cabal among them is attempting a Jelk coup. A small number of religious adepts believe Abaddon has escaped from hyperspace with a Karg taskforce."

I felt cold inside. "Abaddon is in our universe? You're sure of this?"

Doctor Sant shook his head. "I make no such claim of surety. I relate to you rumors, nothing more. This we do know. Something has shaken the Jelk Corporation. What's more, various Saurian fleets have departed their jump-off points. By this, I mean those fleets no longer poise like spears to jab into Jade League star systems."

"That's good news, isn't it?" I asked.

Sant stared down at me.

"I'm not talking about Abaddon and some Kargs making it into our universe," I said. "That would be terrible—unless they brought Jennifer with them. Then I could try to free her."

"No!" Sant said, horrified. "You must never attempt such a thing."

I snorted. "Are you kidding me? She was my woman. If I have a shot at freeing her, you'd better believe I'll take it."

"That would be ill-considered indeed. The omens all point to one conclusion. If you ever meet Abaddon face-to-face, nothing will ever be the same for any of us."

59

It was my turn to stare. I hated this oblique stuff. Besides, could Sant really be serious about this? What would that make my dream? Would it be a coincidence, or could the demon-lord speak across a thousand light years?

The Lokhars had an oracle, their greatest Forerunner artifact. It liked making ambiguous statements. I think the policy had rubbed off onto Doctor Sant.

"Do you think the Jelk problem is with Abaddon?" I asked.

"I have no way of knowing," Sant said. "I believe it highly unlikely, though. The Center Galaxy invasion sounds more plausible to me."

I nodded. "Sure, Doc—I mean, Doctor." Like all Lokhars I've ever met, Sant was a bear concerning protocol. They disliked informality. "The Jelk are having trouble with someone or something. It has caused them to pull back Saurian-crewed taskforces from the frontier. Now why's that a problem again?"

"I did not say it was."

"Come on, Doctor. You're acting worried over this. Sure, you're trying to hide it, but I know you, remember?"

His whiskers twitched. "You are observant and rash, a unique combination. I wonder if that is the source of your remarkable strength."

"No, it's a bowl full of Wheaties every morning," I said.

"I do not understand," Sant said with a frown.

"It doesn't matter. What's troubling you? Is there something I can do to help?"

Doctor Sant halted and fingered his gaudy ring. His stare became intent as he studied the rose in the bubble. With a swift move, he took off the ring, holding it up to a ceiling light. "Do you know what this ring signifies?"

I wanted to say a lack of artistic taste. Instead, I just shook my head.

"It is an ancient heirloom, my family symbol. My father gave it to me. His father gave it to him. My great-grandfather accepted it as a token from the Orange Tamika Regent-Emperor."

"Wait a minute. I thought all Lokhar emperors belonged to Purple Tamika."

"*No*," Sant hissed. "The Purple are upstarts. Over two hundred years ago, they purloined the throne from Orange Tamika. It almost brought open revolt among the Lokhars."

"What stopped it?" I asked.

"The Saurian fleets poised to strike deep into Jade League territory," Sant said.

I blinked several times. Sure. That made sense. Historically, what kept allies together? A larger threat. During World War II, the Soviets and Americans joined hands against Hitler. Once the Furhur died and Nazi Germany lay in ruins, the Russians and Americans soon began the Cold War. They didn't have a larger threat binding them together anymore. In this case, the once threatening Saurian fleets were like Nazi Germany.

"Do all Jade League members like each other?" I asked.

"No," Sant said, "many loathe the very scent of other races."

"What about the different Tamikas?" I asked.

"You are shrewd, Commander. The Purple Tamika Emperor has moved openly against Orange Tamika. Our dreadnoughts and their elite crews died in hyperspace. Because of that, we have become weak. Some believe the Emperor will attempt to eliminate Orange Tamika altogether, securing the throne for generations to come."

"And he's making these moves now because the Saurian fleets no longer wait to attack?" I asked.

"You ask that as if the Emperor is foolish. The Saurian fleets have not only retreated but also traveled deep into Jelk Corporation territory. In some fashion, the Jelk are divided or under assault. There has not been such an occurrence for time immemorial."

"Maybe it's a Jelk trick," I said. "They're cunning enough to do something like that. I mean pull everything back and leak rumors that a terrible invasion has brought this about. Then, once the Jade League breaks into conflict, the Saurian fleets will return with a vengeance, cleaning up."

"I agree that is a possibility," Sant said. "It's what makes this a difficult decision."

"You mean your leaving the solar system?" I asked.

61

Instead of answering me, Doctor Sant raised the gaudy ring a little higher. "This is my most precious possession. I have worn it with pride. Now, Commander Creed, I give it to you." Sant extended his long arm, shoving the ring in my face.

I reacted hastily without really thinking about what I was doing. "Oh, well, thanks," I said, taking the ring. "Yeah, this is something," I said, hefting it. The ring was heavier than it looked. "I'll treasure this all my life."

Sant closed his eyes, nodding with seeming appreciation, as if this was a holy ceremony. Maybe it was. When he opened his orbs, he watched me expectantly.

"Uh, oh," I said, beginning to understand. No doubt, I was supposed to give him something equally precious in return. This was a swap. I happened to be wearing my .44. I began unbuckling my gun-belt.

"No," Sant said. "I could not accept a weapon of war, especially one that killed the Emperor's daughter-wife."

"Oh," I said. "Well, I'm not sure what I could give you then."

Doctor Sant smiled serenely. "There is a boon I would ask of you."

"Sure," I said.

"You know the name of the Forerunner artifact."

"I sure do," I said.

Doctor Sant waited expectantly.

Maybe I should have just told him. I didn't want to, though. The tiger had shot me with poison slivers. Screw him. He was supposed to aid us, not us him.

"I do not ask for such a thing for myself alone," Sant said. "It is for Orange Tamika that I ask, the brother-in-arms who died for you and your assault troopers, allowing them to reach the center of the portal planet."

"How does knowing the artifact's name help Orange Tamika?" I asked.

Doctor Sant's serene look became strained. I don't think he liked my question.

"I am not here to bargain," Sant said.

Of course you are, old son. For all I knew, the ring was bric-a-brac, a worthless piece of junk. Sant might be pulling a fast one, and I didn't like it.

"Several months ago, I saved you from the Starkiens," he told me.

"Yes, you did," I said. "And you have my most profound gratitude for doing it. I'm the one the artifact spoke and listened to, yet the baboons weren't impressed with me. You just rode on the relic, and they seemed to think you were some holy man because of it. Why did they have the difference of reactions between the two of us?" I asked.

Doctor Sant stiffened, and his fingers twitched. Had I hit a nerve? Maybe I should just make up a name and give it to him. I rejected the idea.

"You need to let me know exactly what's going on here before I give you the artifact's name," I said.

The tiger seemed to consider that. "You are a wily—" I think Sant almost called me a beast, barely stopping himself. "You are a wily dealer," he said. "Because of my journey with an artifact, I am an acolyte now. The Starkien recognized the change in me. I have begun a holy trek, a soul journey. As the speaker for the Sol Object, my words have gravity."

"Wait a minute. Why are *you* the speaker? If anyone should be the speaker, it's me," I said, jabbing a thumb against my chest.

"No!" Sant said, horrified.

I raised my eyebrows.

"Forgive me, Commander Creed. Even after these past years, you are new to the Jade League. You have an exalted post as guardian of the object, but you are not an accredited acolyte. I am Lokhar. I have ridden the relic. I have studied it and now will return to the empire to speak my words to whoever will listen."

This was rich. After all humanity had done for the Lokhars, we were still little more than beasts in Doctor Sant's eyes.

"In other words," I said, "you're going to create trouble for the Purple Tamika Emperor. But you're going to do it with religious coloring, hiding behind your new status."

63

"Please, Commander Creed, I ask that you speak with decorum and forgo your crudities."

I kept thinking about Sant pulling the trigger seven times and the Shi-Feng blowing themselves up to kill me.

"That's right," I said, hotly. "I'm only a barbarian guardian, one of the only people an artifact has ever talked to. Oh, by the way, how many artifacts have told a Lokhar their name?"

"Only the highest priests would know such a thing," Sant said, stiffening.

"You know what I think?" I asked. "If an artifact talked to me, that means I outrank everyone in the acolyte department."

Sant's eyes darted away from mine. I wondered if I'd hit another nerve. Frankly, I hardly cared.

"Look, Doctor," I said. "You and I have been through a lot together. I saved your bacon on the portal planet. The assault troopers saved the universe. Yet, what do we find: insults by everyone who thinks we're nothing but beasts or barbarians. Well, I'm sick of it. No, I'm not giving you the object's name. You can take your ring back if you want."

I thrust it at him.

Sant's eyes widened and his whiskers stood straight out. With a lightning move, he snatched his gaudy ring, stuffing it in a pocket.

"You have insulted me," he said.

"Yeah, right," I said. I almost told him how he'd shot me seven times. Instead, I said, "You've insulted me throughout this entire conversation. You don't see me sulking about it." I told myself to calm down. The tiger was an ally. He'd helped us just seven months ago with the Starkiens. "Look, Sant, you gave me your ring to try to bribe me. I'm betting knowing the name of the artifact would be just about the biggest thing to hit the Lokhar Empire. And you want me to just give it to you. I don't think so."

Doctor Sant hissed with outrage, and needle-thin claws popped out of his fingertips.

I stepped back, thinking: *Here we go again.* I drew my .44.

"You have committed a grave error, Captain Creed."

"Well how about that, Doc," I said, my gun-hand rock steady.

64

He drew himself to his full height, and it seemed he might curse me. Then, suddenly, the claws slid back into their sheaths. His shoulders sloped like normal and he nodded. Was that a result of Ella's protocols at work in his mind?

"I was an Alien Contact Officer before I became an acolyte," he said. "You humans are different from us, Commander Creed. I feel sorry for you, not because you will not give me the name. You are correct. I sought to trick the name from you. It was unworthy of me and unworthy of you. I am sorry, Commander."

"So am I, Doctor Sant. Whatever happens, I wish you luck." I put away the .44.

"May the Great Maker guide your way," Sant said. "You are going to need all your courage and guile to keep your artifact. A time of troubles is upon us. If the Jelk Corporation splinters or falls into civil war, I doubt the Jade League or the Lokhar Empire will survive it. That will mean every race for itself. You Earthlings are too few to last in such a state."

"Yeah, well, we'll see about that," I said.

Doctor Sant held up a hand in a salute. Then he turned away, heading for a hatch that would take him to the Orange Tamika warship. I wondered if I'd ever see him again.

I heard a hatch clang shut. I knew I had to talk with Diana. If things were starting to fall apart out there, we needed a plan. We couldn't just hang on anymore. We had to begin building a fully defensible solar system.

65

-8-

After Doctor Sant and his Orange Tamika Lokhars left, we had the solar system all to our lonesome. For the first time since the aliens had shown themselves, we were the only beings here.

Despite his galling nature, Baba Gobo had taught me a valuable lesson. Actually, he just affirmed what I'd already known and then forgotten. To every alien we'd met, men were beasts at worst and barbarians at best.

The Lokhar Emperor had refused to admit us to the Jade League. He'd thought about letting the Forerunner Guardians join, a backdoor for humans, so to speak. Even that had been shot down in the end.

It left us in a precarious spot. Baba Gobo had probably backed down to Doctor Sant for another reason, one worth considering. The might of the Lokhar Empire had stood behind Sant. What stood behind us? Not a damn thing.

I sipped wine at a candlelight dinner with Diana. Doctor Sant had left two months ago. Since then, three voyagers in three different alien vessels had entered the solar system. Each had claimed pilgrim status, wishing to view the Sol Object. Each had left a bad taste in my mouth. They'd felt like conmen casing a joint, studying the security systems for a future heist. In seven years, we'd had six pilgrims. Now, we'd had these three in quick succession.

As we ate, I told Diana about my worries.

We were in a special dining area of Mars Base. A ceiling window showed the stars. Side screens showed the lonely rock formations of Mars at night. To cap it, the Amazon Queen had worn sheer silks to the meal. Even after all these years, she had to play her predator's games. I could see her breasts under the fabrics, her rouged nipples. She'd caught me staring several times, and it made her smile. A shark couldn't have grinned with more malice as a morsel swam toward its jaws.

Most of me said to go ahead and roll in the sack with her. It would be well worth it. A smaller voice warned me she was a honey trap meant to bury me deep. I had no doubt Diana knew sex techniques that would leave me gasping. She also had a monstrous ambition to run everything.

Was this how she'd taken care of Loki?

There had been three members on the Earth Council before I'd left for hyperspace years ago. No matter how hard I tried to find out, no one could tell me what had happened to the ex-Swedish billionaire. He had simply disappeared one day.

I realized that Diana had no qualms about using whatever tool she needed to achieve her ends. Understanding that, I tore my gaze from the peaches under her silks and found her licking her lips.

"We don't have to be adversaries, Creed," she purred.

In lieu of answering her, I sipped wine. The candlelight in the center of the table flickered, causing shadows to shift along the walls. I don't know why, but it reminded me of everything the coming of the aliens to Earth had permanently stolen from us. There would never be movies in San Francisco with a hot date or pizza and beer on a Friday night after sweaty games of basketball with my friends. That Earth had died. Despite all our automated factories attempting terraforming, we possessed a poisoned planet with bitter survivors hanging on by our fingernails.

"We have to do something new," I said.

"That sounds erotic," she told me.

I clunked my wine goblet onto the table and leaned back in my chair. "Do you remember Demetrius?"

"Of course," she said. "He was a good man."

"He was a rugged son of a bitch," I said, "an ex-SAS trooper who died on the portal planet. He gave his life so we could keep on living." He had been Diana's bodyguard in the early days when the freighters had been grounded on Earth. The man had joined me on the expedition to save the universe. He'd given his life so the rest of us could live. I thought about Demetrius, how I had to turn his sacrifice into something lasting.

"Okay," Diana said, frowning.

"You're not tracking my thoughts," I said. "This—" I waved my hand to indicate the room and everything it entailed— "is our responsibility. You and me, Diana, we're running the show. Mankind lives or dies on our decisions and actions. We don't have time for games."

"If we don't live, are we really alive?" she asked. "There's no point to existing if we don't enjoy ourselves sometimes. Take a break tonight, Creed. You've earned it."

I snorted. "If I genuinely believed you cared a whit about me as a person, I might find your seductive ways alluring. As it is, I realize you're just trying to manipulate me so you can gain more power."

Something hardened in her eyes, reminding me of a boa constrictor squeezing its prey. That disappeared a moment later, and she smiled. The sexual wattage pouring out of her almost made me reconsider the offer. As I debated with myself, the tip of her tongue slowly dragged across her lower lip.

I admit it, my groin stirred. The lady was sexy. I had to do something, or I was going to rip off her clothes and do her on the table. So, I laughed, stood and swept the wine goblet off the tablecloth, letting the glass shatter against the video of Mars at night.

Diana flinched in surprise.

"Wait here," I said. In three swift strides, I opened the door and moved into the hall, shouting for N7.

The android opened a different door, giving me an inquiring glance. He looked like a choirboy with soft blond hair. He wasn't that, but one of the most dangerous beings on our side. He wore a naval uniform and cap. He'd been with me in the artifact's inner sanctum, meaning that N7 also knew the object's name. No one thought to ask him, though. Lokhars in particular had an aversion to treating androids as people. Did androids lack souls? I suppose so because the Jelk built them to order. Even so, N7 had become one of my brothers in arms.

I told him my needs. N7 retreated and returned shortly with a heavy coat.

"Thanks," I said. With the coat, I returned to my dinner date with Diana. "Here," I said, tossing the long garment across the table. "Put this on."

The coat draped carelessly across Diana as she lounged in her chair, messing her hair. She studied me, finally lifting the coat and running her fingers through her hair.

"You're making a mistake," she said.

"Yeah, how?" I asked.

"You should treat me with greater respect."

"If you want respect, give respect."

"What do you think I did by wearing this gown for you?"

"The gown is your teeth, Diana. You're trying to sink your claws into me. I'm interested, but not enough to give you an edge."

"The great Commander Creed is afraid of me?" she asked in a mocking tone. "Is that what you're saying?"

"Call it what it you want."

"This is ridiculous," she said. "But if this is what you're *ordering* me to do—" She slid the gown off her left shoulder. I imagine she planned to strip in front of me.

My gaze locked onto that shoulder. Maybe I *was* being ridiculous. I don't know. Ever since I'd had the nightmare of Abaddon, I'd begun missing Jennifer all over again. I had an ache, and Diana tempted me. Sex and love were powerful facets of human behavior. People toyed with them at their peril. If I slept with Diana—

No! That's not going to happen. But in order to stop that from occurring, I had to change the dynamics. A man can resist sexual allurement for a time. If he remains where the enticement is, though, eventually he'll give in. I had to retreat from the enticement, or it would overwhelm me. Some things are simply too hard to resist over time.

I know. That sounds weeny. A tough guy was supposed to be able to bed any beauty without a thought. To screw like a dog supposedly proved a man's virility. I happened to disagree with the principle. I'd always believed in choosing one woman and committing to her alone.

Jennifer was my woman. Why otherwise did I have nightmares about my abandoning her? Even after the intervening years, the guilt tore at me was why. I refused to dally with Diana while Jennifer—

As Diana removed her silk gown, I turned my back on her.

"Really, Creed?" the Amazon Queen asked.

"I'm going to leave," I told her.

After a short pause, Diana said. "It's safe, Mr. Boy Scout. You can turn around now."

I did. She sat in her chair with the coat buttoned all the way to her throat. The silk gown lay on the floor beside her. After all my interior moral posturing, I still managed to wonder if she was naked under the coat. I couldn't believe it. I found myself wanting to rip off the coat and lay her down on the table.

"Just a second," I said. I stepped into the hall again and shouted for N7. He showed up. "You're coming with me to take notes," I said.

The android frowned. "I have no need of taking notes, Commander. I can remember everything said. My brain core has a computer's total recall."

"Fine," I said. "Sit and listen then. Come with me."

Diana looked annoyed when I returned with N7. I thought she might protest. Finally, she shrugged, tossing her luxurious hair.

As N7 sat in a corner, I talked for a time about our military situation, finally adding, "Our nearest neighbors have bigger fleets than we do and industrial bases. They also have planetary populations. If the two power blocs splinter, it's going to become a grab what you can type of galaxy. How can we compete in that kind of environment?"

"We have our Forerunner object," Diana said. "The solar system has become holy ground."

"Yeah, maybe," I said. "But we just saw the Starkiens trying to grab our artifact. Sure, we can stop a pirate in his spaceship from hijacking the relic. Our ten starships are too many for a lone operator. What can we do against a planet-based foe with a military fleet?"

"The obvious answer is that we have to find our own allies," Diana said. "We have to become enmeshed with others so we're too big to attack."

"I agree," I said. "But who's going to ally with animals?"

"They can't really mean that about us," she said.

N7 cleared his throat.

I laughed sourly. "He's going to tell you they mean it, all right."

N7 nodded. "The Commander is correct."

"Are you saying we won't be able to find allies?" Diana asked me.

"Not as we are now," I said. "Either, we have to change how the aliens think about humans, or we have to seriously strengthen our star system's defenses."

"We need to trade, then," Diana said.

"Will others trade with beasts?" I asked.

"If it's to their benefit I think they would," Diana said.

"Okay. What will we trade?"

"We've been buying these automated factories with fissionable materials and works of art," Diana said. "Why not use those items on the open market?"

"Well, first," I said, "the Lokhars have traded with us because they owed us for the one hundred thousand assault troopers lost in hyperspace. We haven't paid tit-for-tat. If we're going to really trade with others, we'll need mining equipment."

N7 squirmed on his chair.

"Do you want to add something?" I asked him.

"Indeed," N7 said. "At the moment, we possess no mining equipment."

"On Earth we do," I said.

"We have the one operating mine," he said. "As you know, most of the metallic objects on Earth have badly rusted."

"Well…how about extracting ores from our asteroids?" I asked.

"We lack the needed equipment to do that," N7 said.

71

"We lack pretty much everything," Diana said. "And it seems like we have no way of getting a starter kit, as it were. The automated factories we received from the Lokhars barely produce enough to keep the freighters running. Most of their hardware works on restoring the atmosphere. As it is, we're scraping by."

Nodding, I said, "It's as I thought. Humanity is in a hole. We bought our few starships with the lives of one hundred thousand assault troopers. The Lokhars were supposed to be grateful. Now, they're onto the next thing, conveniently having forgotten about our sacrifices."

"Commander," N7 said. "I have a thought."

"Go ahead," I said.

"Doctor Sant told us the Saurian fleets have retreated," N7 said. "Their hasty reassignment likely means certain Jelk Corporation worlds are unprotected."

"What are you suggesting?"

"Perhaps you could send a ship or two to a mining world," N7 said. "You might be able to land and take what you need, along with mining androids to work the machines."

Diana laughed throatily. "That's very clever, N7. You want to us to free your kind, is that it?"

"It has crossed my mind," the android admitted.

"Vikings," I said. "You want us to go a-Viking."

Both N7 and Diana turned to me.

With the flat of my right hand, I slapped the table. It made Diana start and caused cutlery to jangle against the plates.

"We'll be Star Vikings," I said, liking the idea more and more. "We don't have anything to trade, at least not yet or in any real quantity. All the aliens think of us as animals anyway. Therefore, we use the one thing we were able to buy, our ten starships."

"There's a problem with your plan," Diana said. "If those ships are raiding the space lanes, what will protect the freighters back here?"

"Hmm," I said, pondering the idea. "We can't be obvious about this. Ten ships might be too many. Whatever we do, though, we're going to have to move fast. We need tech. We need tools, and we need more starships. If the Saurian fleets

72

really have retreated, now's the time to strike and grab some of the things we need. Yes, I like your idea, N7."

"I don't," Diana said. "Whose starships do we use? Not mine, I'll tell you. We only have so much ordnance. I mean missiles, mines and laser coils. If you become a pirate—"

"Viking," I said.

"Names don't matter," Diana said.

"I think they do."

She shook her head as if I was simple. "Jelk Corporation planets will have missile defenses, I'd bet, and planetary beams. You won't be able to just swoop down and make yourself rich."

"It's time to take risks," I said. "You're right about that." With an elbow on the table, I made a fist and rested my chin on it. "Okay. You don't want to risk your precious ships. I'll use one of mine, then. It's time to make a trial run. I'll need a freighter, though, to carry our loot."

"We can't afford to waste any of our freighters," Diana said. "We have too few as it is."

"Wrong," I said, "we can't afford *not* to use them. But I'll tell you what. Loan me a freighter and I'll give you a percentage of our take."

The Amazon Queen studied me, and I could see the calculations in her eyes. Finally, she asked, "How much of a percentage?"

We spent the next two hours haggling. Star Vikings, I liked the name. It was better than Forerunner Guardians. It was an Earth name rather than one the aliens had coined for us. Now we had to decide which star system to strike.

-9-

Several days later, I took the *Aristotle*, a former Lokhar cruiser, and the *Maynard Keynes*, a scow of a Jelk freighter. Diana had given me her worst vessel, not that I could blame her. Unfortunately, the engines broke down after the sixth jump.

Going through a jump gate took its toll on the passengers. Flu-like symptoms struck just about everyone, even our android. It also produced wear and tear to the equipment.

Thus, for three days, all my engineers and N7 struggled on the freighter's propulsion systems, trying to get it mobile again. Luckily, this was an empty system. There was no one to give us grief. It had a brown dwarf for a star and burnt-out husks for planets. None of the worlds contained atmospheres. Most were ice-balls with particles of nickel-iron and rock.

On the third day, Ella Timoshenko found a drifting body on her scanner. It turned out to be a Lokhar soldier in wrecked powered armor.

"How long do you think he's been adrift?" Ella asked.

I shrugged. I didn't know and didn't care. The raid weighed me down with responsibilities and worries. This wasn't anything like joining Prince Venturi before on *Indomitable*. There hadn't been any choices last time. The Kargs would break into our universe, and that would be the end of life as we knew it. Here, I could make good choices and bad ones. The wrong decisions would mean the end of the human race. Talk about piling on pressure. I felt the weight of past and future generations squeezing me down.

Finally, the *Maynard Keynes* could move again. The endless work had left our engineers exhausted, though. I let them rest and kept the two starships where they were. Soon enough, everyone would have to work at peak efficiency.

I lay on my cot, staring at the ceiling. If you guessed that I was having second thoughts, you'd be right. I didn't mind raiding the Jelk Corporation. That wasn't the problem. I wondered about scale, though. This would solve our dilemma in a pinprick fashion. We needed strategic answers.

Alliance with the Jade League, full-bore military and economic assistance, would have made a world of a difference to what we planned. That's what I'd originally thought I had been buying with the agreement to put one hundred thousand assault troopers into harm's way. It turned out I'd been a fool. Despite the few automated factories they'd brought, the Lokhars had snookered us, and I didn't like it.

With my fingers laced behind my head, I told myself I had to rid all thoughts of squeamishness from my heart. This was like a lioness with a den full of cubs. She went out and killed a baby gazelle or slew the mother and let the baby starve to death. I wasn't in some airy-fairy tale where the universe played paddy cake with the Marquis of Queensbury Rules to guide us. This was the law of tooth and claw, survival of the fittest, baby.

What did that mean? It meant I had to play this as ruthless as I could. I hadn't come to another race and laced their world with nukes. The tigers and, in a way, the Jelk had come and done it to us. Now, we scrambled for any advantage we could eke out. If I failed, humanity sank out of sight, never to lift its head again.

So be it. I would do whatever—

A knock at my hatch startled me. I swung my feet off the cot, stood and pressed a button. The hatch opened and N7 stood there with rolled-up star charts in his arms.

"Do you remember you wanted to look at these?" he asked.

"Sure," I said, having completely forgotten. "Let's take a gander."

For the next several hours, N7 and I pored over his charts. He knew a lot about this region of Jelk space and our target the Demar star system.

It had an "O" Spectral Class Star, a bluish-white furnace that burned at 30,000 Kelvin on the surface. The system lacked any terrestrial planets. In fact, it only had one Jupiter-sized gas giant. The moons of that Jovian world were heavy with mined ores. The Demar system also boasted Inner, Middle and Outer Asteroid Belts. Those, too, were rich in thorium and deuterium, a veritable mother lode of mineral wealth. The system contained a single huge habitat known as the Demar Starcity. It wasn't a pleasure palace or breeding ground for Saurians. Instead, it had a giant processing center with sideline industries that produced finished goods.

N7 stood beside the table, with a star chart magnetized in place. Using a forefinger, he stabbed the starcity. "This is my origin point," he said. "This is where I was built."

I rubbed my jaw thoughtfully.

"Perhaps as important for you, here in the habitat are many military articles."

"Yeah?" I asked.

"I suspect you will find automated missile systems and beam cannons," N7 said. "There will, of course, be mining equipment. Or, if you prefer, you can take gas giant scoopers to mine Jupiter and Saturn for deuterium."

"Seems too good to be true," I said.

"Agreed," N7 said. "This was the base system for the Tenth Saurian taskforce. The fleet wasn't on the frontier between the Jade League and Jelk Corporation territory. This was a secondary force meant to reinforce wherever needed."

"And you think those warships are gone?" I asked.

N7 straightened. "I do not presume to know, Commander. I work only off the information you received from Doctor Sant."

"Great," I said. "Really, we're in the dark about just about everything."

"Yes."

I gazed at the star chart and the Demar system in particular.

"If the Jelk Corporation was in trouble," I said, "I mean against invaders. It seems as if the secondary or reinforcing fleet would be the first one to go."

"That is logical," N7 said.

"The question is, will the Jade League members already have invaded these regions?"

"That is another reason to try here," N7 said. "Logically, the Jade League members would wish to scour star systems close to their base worlds. This is farther away."

"Do you think Doctor Sant told us the truth?"

"I have no way of verifying his words," N7 said.

"Yeah," I said, rubbing my jaw again. I had a bad feeling about this, and I couldn't fool myself. If we failed here, things would likely get even darker in a hurry.

* * *

I'm sure you've heard of deep-sea fish that live in a world of eternal gloom. Well, I mean the fish that *used* to live in the subterranean reaches of the Earth's oceans. I'm sure the bio-terminator had settled down there by now, too.

My point is pressure. Those fish had learned to live with an intense pressure per square inch that would have crushed a human. No submarine had ever gone to such a depth, although a few bathyscaphes had. The fish could take intense pressure because their own bodies pushed outward. The funny thing occurred when that pressure stopped. If a fisherman hooked such a fish and reeled as fast as he could, the deep-sea creature would die. It couldn't live with the lesser pressure.

What did any of that have to do with our raid? The Jelk Corporation had put intense pressure against the Jade League for uncounted years. These last few years, and now even more so, the pressure had lifted. It was gone. Like those deep-sea fish, it appeared that most of the Jade League members didn't know what to do with the lesser threat. It had seemingly unhinged their thinking. It had also apparently opened old wounds among the members.

What we found as we cruised the jump lanes in Jelk Corporation territory was a decided lack of Jade League

77

vessels. Several times, Saurian scout ships hailed us. N7 responded, using old codes.

The Saurian scout commanders always demanded to know why an old freighter accompanied an obvious Lokhar military craft.

N7 told them he was bringing the Lokhar cruiser to Sector Eight Headquarters for study. Each time, the Saurian commander grew utterly still on the viewing screen. Then he would hiss. After the hissing, the commanders told N7 to carry on.

Sector Eight was code for *secret mission.* As had been the case many times in the past, N7 was the source of priceless information.

I had a meeting with my main team: Ella, N7, Rollo and Dmitri. I'd taken them with me, figuring I needed my best people to pull this off.

Dmitri was a Zaporizhian Cossack from the Ukraine. They used to be a hard-riding, freedom-loving people from the steppes or plains of Russia and the Ukraine. They were supposed to be good fighters. Most people knew them as those acrobatic dancers who squatted low, folded their arms on their chests and vigorously kicked out their legs.

Dmitri was as a solid, muscular man, shorter than my six-three. He had taken to wearing his hair in a straight-up brush-cut.

N7 had magnetized the chosen star chart on a wall. We stood beside it, me with a pointer in my hand.

"We're several jumps away from the Demar star system," I said. "Now is the time to decide where in the system we should target. Any thoughts?" I asked.

"I say we get in, hit and get out as fast as we can," Dmitri said. "That means we should strike a weak spot. So, what's the easiest place to hit there?"

We all glanced at N7.

"I would imagine the Outer Asteroid Belt," the android said. "It's closest to the jump gate."

"Everything is relative," Ella said. "We have to know the lay of the system better. What's the most heavily defended location?"

N7 pointed at the starcity.

"That also happens to be the plum prize," I said. "This is our first raid, and as far as we know, the first time the Demar system will have been hit since the Saurian taskforce left. Are they worried? Who knows? But once they've been hit, the word is going to go out. The second raid will be harder. This might be the time to strike big."

"I don't know why they wouldn't be ready for an assault now," Ella said.

"Because this is a secondary area," I said. "As far as we know, no Jade League members have struck the Jelk Corporation frontier. The Jelk have been on the offensive for a long time, remember? They're not going to think of defense right away. At least, that would be my guess."

"Still," Ella said. "With the protecting fleet gone, those left at home have to be nervous."

"That is my own view," N7 said.

"Yeah," I said. "Well, maybe we should try to put them at ease. Besides, I think the closer we can get to our target, the better for us. We don't want to trade shots with the starcity's laser batteries or defensive missiles."

"What do you suggest?" Ella asked.

I stared at the star chart. What had the old-time Vikings done? They used daring and cunning. I remember reading about one chieftain who pretended to die. The raiders had been pagans, striking Christian Europe. The chieftain had his warriors tell the city fathers of one walled town that he'd become a Christian at death, and wished for a Christian burial. The head priest had realized what a religious coup that would be. He'd forced the townspeople to consent, and he even began to write a letter to the Pope about it. Several days later, big Viking warriors carried the supposedly dead chieftain to the town's church. They had laid their spears and great axes under the faker. During the ceremony, the chieftain opened his eyes, rose with a gusty laugh and pitched the weapons to his men. They went berserk and slew the city fathers and their guards. Then, the Norse warriors rushed through the lanes to the main city gate, opening it to admit their hidden men outside. That night, they sacked the town.

It had been a Trojan horse kind of plan. With a grin, I told the others the story. I finished by saying, "That's what we need to do at the starcity."

"Why there?" Ella asked. "The starcity will be the most heavily guarded place."

"Exactly," I said. "If we can storm it, we'll have breached their main defenses. That means we'll be safe enough for a time to pick our plunder. There's another thing to consider. The starcity should have the kind of goods we need. Besides, the habitat sounds like the best place to use assault trooper tactics."

"How to you propose we trick the defenders?" Ella asked.

I glanced at N7. "You know the Saurians much better than we do. You're going to have to think of something."

We waited, and our golden-haired android blinked at the star chart. "I have an idea," he said at last.

"Let's hear it," I said.

N7 began to speak.

***

Two days later, we passed through the final jump gate to the target, entering the Demar star system.

The *Maynard Keynes* led the way. The much larger freighter used a barely-working tractor beam to pull the shutdown *Aristotle*. If our ploy failed, it would take twenty solid minutes to activate the former Lokhar cruiser to full capacity. We were attempting our own version of a Trojan horse attack. Our very weakness demanded we do it this way.

Inside the freighter were two thousand assault troopers. Two thousand combat soldiers ready to try to turn the tide of history that swept against humanity.

On the bridge, I stood near N7, who acted as the freighter captain.

The intense Demar sun shined its fierce light. The starcity orbited it at a Mars-like distance.

"We're being hailed," Ella said, who worked the communications system.

N7 nodded for her to open channels. A moment later on the main screen, a bedecked Saurian peered at our android.

Saurians were two-legged, walking lizards, looking like giant versions of the gecko from the old-time insurance commercials. The creature moved springier than a human would. Usually, a Saurian stood four or four and half feet tall. They called themselves the Family and made better workers than they did fighters. I think the Jelk liked them because Saurians were easy keepers and bred like flies.

"You are not authorized to enter the Demar system," the Saurian hissed. He wore a uniform with fancy braid hanging down from the sleeves.

"I claim salvage rights to the ship I'm towing," N7 said. "Under article nine of the Jelk scavenger code, I must be paid thirty percent of the vessel's worth."

The Saurian eyed N7, finally saying, "You're an android."

"That has no bearing on article nine," N7 told him.

"No," the Saurian hissed. "It appears your logic circuits are in full working order."

"Yes," N7 said in a mechanical fashion.

As I watched the exchange, I could practically see the greed working in the Saurian's mind. He no doubt thought to cheat the foolish android of its treasure.

Ella tapped her board, splitting the main screen. It continued to show the Saurian and now the starcity in the distance. The habitat was a great cylinder, many kilometers in length and width. By rotating, it created pseudo-gravity for its occupants. Three small pinpricks moved away from the platform.

I pointed at them.

Ella tapped her panel one more time.

The three dots leaped in magnification. They were corvettes, star system patrol craft. The *Aristotle* could have beaten them in a straight fight, but we would have taken damage doing it. If the starcity had heavy beams, the enemy might even have destroyed our cruiser. No. We had to do it like this.

"You will bring your cargo to the number seven docking bay," the Saurian said at last.

"I understand," N7 said. "I expect you to have my thirty percent finder's fee ready once I dock."

"You will receive a reward, android," the Saurian said. "Never fear on that score. But if we see you deviate in the slightest, the corvettes will annihilate your freighter and take the Lokhar cruiser for our own."

"I claim independent locator status," N7 said. "That is guaranteed by the Jelk scavenging regulations."

"We serve the Jelk Corporation," the Saurian said. "You do not need to keep quoting your articles."

"This is my lucky find," N7 said. "I will buy many upgrades with my new wealth."

"You are a wise android," the Saurian said. "I will instruct the judicator to ready your fee."

A moment later, the Saurian blinked off the screen.

"He means to bilk you of your fee," Ella told N7.

"Saurians are quite transparent," N7 said. "It is another reason the Jelk prefer them over most others. The Family has never staged a successful rebellion against the Jelk anywhere."

"This would seem like the time to try it," I said.

"No," N7 said. "Not if the main Saurian fleets are deep in the interior systems. As long as they are there, the fleets are hostages for the frontier regions' good behavior—at least concerning Jelk protocols." N7 studied me. "I understand you dislike the other races' view of humanity. It is even worse toward us, the androids. At least they treat humans as something living. To the others, we are simply machines."

I didn't know what to tell N7, so I said nothing.

For the next few hours, we moved toward the starcity. At the same time, the three corvettes drew closer to us.

"They're scanning our vessels," Ella said.

"Let them," I told her.

Rollo's board beeped. "They have radar lock-on," he informed us.

"They've figured out our ploy," Dmitri said. "We're dead men."

I have to admit that I didn't like how my heart rate increased. Radar lock-on had that effect. "What do you think, N7? Is Dmitri right?"

"It is possible," the android said.

"Their laser cannons are hot," Rollo said, looking up from his board. "What should we do, Commander?"

"Complain," I said. "Ella, hail the starcity. N7, I want you to seriously complain about this."

"What good will that do us if we're dead?" Dmitri asked.

"Maybe they're just testing our reactions," I said.

Dmitri stood there blinking in disbelief.

Soon, N7 complained to the same Saurian he'd talked with earlier.

"You are a spy," the Saurian said.

"That is incorrect," N7 said. "I am an honest trader."

"I will send inspectors onto your vessels," the Saurian said.

"Of course," N7 said. "I welcome them. Let them come. I have nothing to hide."

The Saurian eyed him, finally signaling someone off-screen. "You are a legitimate scavenger, android. Proceed to the docking bay."

"First, I want to know why you targeted my freighter," N7 asked.

"As I said, it is our procedure."

"No," N7 said. "I have changed my mind about bringing the Lokhar cruiser to you. I will take it elsewhere."

"It's far too late for that, android," the Saurian said. "The corvettes will escort you to the docking bay. If you deviate from your course, they will disable your freighter and take the prize ship for the Family."

"That is against article nine," N7 complained.

"You have much to learn, android. Now, do as I say if you value a continued existence."

"I will comply," N7 said. "But I plan to lodge a protest against these actions to the governing authority."

The Saurian hissed before blinking off once more.

***

Nineteen hours later, the *Maynard Keynes* braked hard. The strain told on the ancient engines. Not only did the heavy thrust slow our mass, but that of the *Aristotle* as well.

The starcity loomed before us, a gleaming cylinder spinning in the stellar void. The three corvettes paced us, the farthest a mere five hundred kilometers away. They were sleek vessels with stubby wings. At times, corvettes flew within planetary atmospheres. Their laser cannons were no longer hot, primed for firing, but they could become lethal in minutes.

"It is time to match velocities with the starcity," N7 said.

"Yeah," I said. "Ella, you're remaining here to run communications. Rollo, Dmitri, let's get ready."

We exited the bridge, hurrying to our soldiers in the main bay.

I still used the Mongol system for the assault troopers instead of the legionary start we'd had with the Jelk Corporation. The greatest conqueror in Earth history had been Genghis Khan. His Mongols had swept over an incredible area, riding across degrees of longitude and latitude instead of just hundreds of miles.

I'd decided to steal from the great khan's bag of tricks. One thing he'd done was forge an iron law called the Yassa. We assault troopers had our own Yassa. One of its keys was never to leave one of our own behind on the field of battle. Another was to make the smallest combat group a band of brothers. That was an *arban*, ten brothers and sisters in arms. They lived and fought together, and looked out for each other. Ten arbans formed a company called a *zagun* of one hundred troopers. Ten zaguns formed a *mingan* of one thousand. Dmitri led one mingan and Rollo the other. I had overall command.

We went to our staging areas. Like the other assault troopers, I went to the heat unit holding my bio-suit. The green light was on as it should be. I opened the lid and pulled out a hefty black blob that was warm to my skin. I pushed it onto the decking where it quivered in anticipation. Taking off my shoes and clothes, I stepped naked onto the blob. Around me, others did the same thing. The substance oozed onto my legs, coating my flesh. It was a warm, comfortable sensation.

As I've said before, this was second skin, symbiotic alien armor, genetically engineered for human use. Alive after a fashion, it could heal itself at times. The outer surface would harden, and it allowed the wearer to operate in a vacuum, in outer space. The skin also amplified human strength. It was

84

also capable of secreting a battle drug into our bodies when necessary.

The familiar symbiotic skin rushed up my thighs, over my belly button and didn't stop until it reached my chin. I put on my helmet and grabbed a gun, checking the battery pack. It had a bar symbol on it, with the green all the way to the + sign on top. The laser rifle had a full charge. We had taken to calling it a Bahnkouv assault rifle. Dmitri had told us about an experimental Russian laser, the design headed by a Dr. Bahnkouv. I liked the name because it was human.

This was the largest bay, holding two thousand assault troopers.

The headphones in my helmet crackled into life. "Commander," Ella said.

"I'm here," I said into my microphone.

"There's a problem," she said. "The Saurian just ordered us to remain several hundred kilometers from the main starcity docking bay door."

"And?" I asked.

"The corvettes are closing in," she said. "Worse, their laser cannons have just gone hot. The Saurian told me he's sending over an inspection team after all. Something must have given us away."

"I knew it," Dmitri cried. "They're never going to let us enter the starcity. We're doomed."

My spine tightened. I didn't like the feeling.

"What are we going to do?" Dmitri asked me.

Yeah. That was the question.

-10-

My plan rested on nifty little one-Lokhar flyers. We'd faced them in the Altair star system what seemed like a lifetime ago. The one-man sleds were fast, sported a laser cannon in front and were meant for one Lokhar legionnaire laying down to pilot it.

Enough of my people had practiced with them on Deimos, one of the tiny moons of Mars, and off Ceres in our Asteroid Belt.

There were three corvettes out there, a giant cylinder and likely hordes of Saurians waiting on it. Each of those creatures could pick up a wrench at the very least. Too many of them would have energy weapons. We had two thousand Star Vikings—assault troopers with pure hearts of gold—and not to put too fine a point on it, we had me.

The way I saw it, we had no choice in this. We had to go balls-out.

I studied a schematic in my HUD. The last corvette was too far away from us—staying five hundred kilometers out. The other two were several minutes distant from our big Jelk freighter. No one was aboard the *Aristotle*. For this little game, it didn't count. I was hoping no one messed with it, either. We'd need the cruiser to get home.

"Okay," I said, over a wide-speaker. "Here's how we're going to do it. Dmitri, half your mingan will head for the nearer corvette. We'll call that enemy 'A.' Rollo, half your mingan will go for corvette 'B.'"

"What about corvette 'C?'" Rollo asked.

"Don't worry about it for now," I said. "Rollo, I'm going to lead your B team against the corvette. I want you to lead the rest of your troopers to the starcity. Dmitri, you're going to hit the A corvette. Your second team will follow Rollo."

"That's too complex, Creed," Rollo said. "Send me with my entire mingan at the starcity."

"Right," I said. "I don't know what I was thinking. Command and control will be critical. Dmitri, your mingan will hit the corvettes. I'll command one strike, you will lead the other."

"Roger," Dmitri said.

After we settled that, I told them the rest of the idea, detailing their goals.

In fifteen minutes, as assault troopers dashed to their one-man flyers, we were ready to begin. I told Ella. She informed me N7 had brought us to a relative halt. We had the same circular velocity as the spinning starcity. That would be important.

"Here goes," I said. "Good luck to everyone. Ella, open the main bay door."

We lay or stood on the giant deck. Before us, massive bay doors began to open. One quarter of the two thousand Star Vikings would be part of the flyer teams. Three troopers apiece would use a Lokhar sled. It was a tight fight, being the most people we could pack onto one. The rest of the mingans would use thruster packs. They would be slower, but they would eventually get to their destinations.

I was counting on the fact that each of us would make small targets. As strange as it seems, the starcity probably lacked the weapons to repel Vikings. They had lasers, missiles and heavy guns to destroy ships, missiles and possibly big enemy shells.

Stars shined outside the bay doors. The O Class Star blazed with blue-white light. Then I saw the starcity, a gleaming cylinder with docking bays here at the one end.

"Do you see corvette B?" I asked the driver of my one-man flyer.

"I do," the woman radioed.

"Head straight for it," I told her.

She turned the throttle. Thrust ignited from the back, and the narrow sled zoomed off the decking, heading for the dark object less than twenty kilometers away.

What did the Saurians see? Maybe it was like bees boiling out of a hive. Maybe they didn't notice yet.

They did the obvious, reacting against us by lighting up their lasers. Hot beams smashed against the huge Jelk freighter. If they had lit off a few small nukes instead, it would have finished us off.

I didn't think they would do that for several reasons. For one thing, they were too close to the starcity. Nukes this near would damage it. For another, that would take initiative on the lizards' part. I'd fought Saurians before. The day after the Earth died, they'd landed in Antarctica to capture people. I'd turned the tables on them by attacking with ferocity from the get-go. That was my plan here today.

I gripped the flyer as Bess, my pilot, pointed us at corvette B. The small combat vessel had two main laser cannons. We had a smaller shooter, but I didn't give the command to fire yet. I had a different idea.

A glance back showed me hundreds of glowing dots. Those were thruster-packs pushing their troopers at the starcity. Every flyer we possessed aimed at a corvette. If the Saurian pilots woke up in time, they would take off, putting greater distance between the corvettes and us.

What I was counting on was plain, old-fashioned surprise. I had the initiative this time. Besides, we acted like pirates. That's what Vikings had been in the end. We stormed their ships like buccaneers with swords between our teeth.

The enemy lasers began melting the freighter's outer hull. Now, Saurian missiles zoomed at the Jelk hauler. They meant to take us down fast. What the corvettes didn't do was leave. If they would wait just a few more minutes, we'd have them.

My stomach tightened. Then I felt the edges of anger draining the fear away. I knew what was happening. The bio-suit squirted combat drugs into my bloodstream. It wanted me to go berserk. Jelk technicians had made the symbiotic skins for humans. We'd modified them, but those modifications didn't always remain during battle.

88

"Now," I radioed. "Beam at grid coordinates ten-ten-eight."

Our sled shifted, no doubt so Bess could aim at the targeted specifics. All around me, small laser beams fired at the enemy corvette. The Saurian vessel had grown in size. Each flyer-laser now struck at exactly the same hull spot on the corvette. We needed a breach, and we needed it now.

Luckily for us, corvettes didn't have heavy hulls or much armored plating. They were meant as patrol vehicles, needing speed more than anything else.

An explosion behind me threw intense white light outward. I glanced back. The *Maynard Keynes* expanded as light and debris blew outward. Had a Saurian laser hit the main fusion engine? This could be bad.

It would be terrible news for the people orbiting Earth. Six hundred thousand humans had called the *Maynard Keynes* home for the past few years. Now, they would have to stay on the remaining freighters in Earth orbit, increasing crowding. This freighter was never going anywhere again.

With a shake of my head, I ignored that aspect. I found myself snarling, with my teeth clenched. The corvette loomed before us. I could see Saurians peering out of the main viewing port.

Our many small lasers struck the hull at the same spot, turning it cheery-red.

"Deploy!" I shouted.

Bess' head twitched. It let me know I'd spoken too loudly.

I pushed off the flyer. So did Bess and the other assault trooper. All around me, others did likewise on their sleds. I didn't know what happened elsewhere. Here, though, the plan worked.

Flyer after flyer rammed against the corvette's heated hull. Most of the combat sleds crumpled into junk. The last few blasted a hole into the corvette.

I gripped the controls of my thruster-pack. Jamming my thumb on a button, I zoomed for the opening.

All I needed was a few more seconds to reach the breach. I still couldn't believe the Saurian commander hadn't flown elsewhere.

I guess surprise had the same effect on aliens that it had on people. Given time, they could decide on the right course of action. Having to think fast in the middle of a battle was something else entirely.

Roaring at the top of my lungs, I flashed through the opening. Then, I braced myself. Without my steroid-68 enhanced muscles, I never would have tried this. Without the bio-suit to absorb much of the impact, I wouldn't have dreamed of smashing my way aboard another vessel. Too many troopers would break bones. Of that, I had no doubt. The bio-suits could harden there, though, and help them to walk during the fight. It would also pump drugs into the trooper to make him savage enough not to worry about the pain.

I struck a bulkhead, and for several seconds at least, I went unconscious. My eyes flew open. I lay in a heap with others sprawled around me. A few raced out a hatch to attack the Saurian crew. I shouted and gnashed my teeth. My head throbbed as I sat up, and I didn't know if I had any broken bones.

Climbing to my feet, I found that my eyes didn't work quite right. Well, maybe they would get better as I went along. I staggered through the hatch, groaning, tasting blood in my mouth.

I had a Bahnkouv in my hands. Three minutes later, I killed my first Saurian, beaming the suited creature in the chest, burning a hole there. That seemed to wipe away my pains, and I shouted with glee.

What can I say? This was a fight to the death. I stormed corvette B with the others. Like a blood-maddened weasel, I slaughtered lizards as if they were chickens in a hen house. They didn't have a chance against us in this kind of savagery. Thus, twenty minutes after our breach through the hull, we gained control of the patrol vessel.

***

As I said earlier, this was a ruthless situation. Mercy didn't have any part in the process. Would a lioness show a fawn mercy on the Serengeti Plains of Africa? I would like to say I did this the nice way. I'd be a black-hearted liar, though.

Dmitri and I conquered our corvettes. We both did it fast, leaving the interior bulkheads splattered with Saurian blood. I'll give the lizards this. They never tried to surrender. It didn't matter, though. We were at the top of our game and they were amateurs in face-to-face encounters.

The last corvette rushed us as it spewed missiles and pumped its lasers. It would have been better off making a run for it. The last patrol vessel disabled Dmitri's corvette, shredding the outer hull with lasers. That killed five assault troopers, half the number lost in the engagement. We had already deployed our corvette's guns, obliterating the approaching missiles. If the enemy warheads had been nuclear, it would have been a different story. Corvettes didn't carry that kind of firepower, though.

As the enemy zoomed closer, the Saurian captain switched targets, blasting my captured boat. He must have had a marksman over there. The lasers took out our guns. We had no more counterbattery fire. His missiles would have free rein against us, and that would likely kill too many assault troopers here.

What the last Saurian captain must not have counted on was the seemingly immobilized *Aristotle*. Shortly after the first assault, troopers exited the freighter, N7 and Ella, along with a handful of others, had relocated to the Lokhar cruiser. They started the cold engines, working fast to get it mobile. Now, the cruiser's main laser cannons fired red-hot beams. They were battle-grade weapons, not dinky patrol rays. Under the devastating assault, the last corvette shuddered, belching colored lights. Then it exploded, raining hull, bulkheads, engine parts, water and bloody flesh in a growing radius.

By that time, the belated Saurians in the starcity's tactical center began to act. They launched three missiles. One of them struck my corvette, disintegrating half the vessel. Another smashed against Dmitri's hulk without igniting. The last missile died to the cruiser's counterbattery fire. After that, Rollo put a stop to the tactical center's efforts. His thruster-pack assault troopers gained control of the launch sites, disabling the tubes.

From the cruiser, N7 radioed the giant cylinder. The Saurians refused to answer. I guess they wanted us to knock before they talked. That's fine, because we could oblige them.

With its tractor beam, the *Aristotle* grabbed the least wrecked corvette. The cruiser accelerated, dragging the corvette with it. At the last moment, N7 roared past the great cylinder, turning off the tractor beam. The hulk of the corvette smashed against the starcity's hull, breaking through. Air spewed from the gaping hole, a hurricane force that must have meant plenty of Saurian dead inside.

The next time N7 radioed, a bedecked and glum-looking Saurian answered.

"You must surrender to me," N7 said.

Rollo had already broken into the main starcity. Dmitri and I—together with our teams—jetted to join the action. We'd lost another thirty troopers when the missiles hit, but most of us had already evacuated the corvettes.

"I can ram the starcity again," N7 informed the Saurian.

"This is an outrage," the lizard said. "You are a berserk android. We will decommission you and destroy your entire series."

"Very well," N7 said. "With your words, you have sealed your fate."

"No, wait,' the Saurian said. "I...must consider the rest of the Family. On further thought, we will surrender on terms."

I shut off my HUD display. Terms would be fine. The thing was to get in and get out with as little loss of human life as possible.

***

We hit the jackpot with the Demar Starcity. The difference between gross defeat and splendid victory could be a very close-run thing. This time, we had come out on the right side. Instead of hundreds of dead troopers and capture for the rest of us, we had the pick of a major production center. Just as important, we grabbed several small haulers in port.

The haulers were newer and sleeker than the old freighter we'd lost. For the next fifteen hours, our troopers loaded the haulers with missile defense systems: improved Iron Domes as the Israelis used to use before the coming of the aliens. We found planetary laser cannons, air-cycles, newer laser coils, advanced targeting computers, floating gas giant scoopers and the latest combat rifles and packs.

Choosing what we should loot caused arguments among us. N7 suggested we take unpackaged androids along. Dmitri was against it, and Ella hemmed and hawed. In the end, I took several hundred. They might prove useful in the asteroids, because I ordered mining equipment loaded up, too.

I not only wanted fish, but fishing poles. How many times could I pull the stunt we'd managed here today?

Just before departure, I decided to quiz the senior Saurian. Rollo and N7 had been busy watching our captured lizards. They brought me an old boy.

Like Earth crocodiles, Saurians continued to grow as long as they lived. That made it difficult for the aged among them to hide.

I stood in a control room with a view of the rest of the Demar system. With big missiles, we'd shot down two other system corvettes that had raced from the Middle Asteroid Belt to get here. I'd been right in taking the starcity first.

After that, the rest of the system waited to see what would happen next.

Rollo shoved the old Saurian. The creature stood at five and a half feet. His jaws were bigger than normal, and he had huge eyes. It gave him a wondering look, as if he was continually surprised. Instead of a uniform, he wore long flowing robes that dragged against the decking.

"Are you a priest?" I asked.

"I am the Wisdom of the Family," the old Saurian told me.

"What does that mean?"

He blinked his big eyes as if wondering about answering. Finally, he said, "I decide on the code of behavior for the Demas system."

"You're the one who officially surrendered to me?" I asked.

This time he closed his big eyes. I don't think he liked the question. When he opened them again, he must have decided he had to warn me.

93

"The Jelk will remember you," the old Saurian said.

"Of that, I have no doubt. Do you know who I am?"

"A destroyer," the Wisdom said, "a creature vomited from the cosmos to plague the Family and their Masters."

"There you go," I said. "You have it all figured out. Oh, wait a minute. I'm going to leave you your lives. I'm not half the destroyer you and your ilk were to us."

He held his forked tongue as he watched me with his wondering eyes.

"Where did the Tenth Saurian taskforce go?" I asked.

The Wisdom waved a clawed hand as it to indicate into the distance.

"How about you be a little more specific," I said.

"The Masters summoned the warships."

"Sure, but where?"

"Away from the frontier," the Wisdom said.

"Now we're getting somewhere. How far away did they go?"

"This is wrong," he told me. "You cannot expect me to reveal the workings of the Masters. I am loyal to the corporation."

I unslung the Bahnkouv from my shoulder. "You're making a category error, old son. I don't give a fig about your loyalty. What I'm going to do is ask you again." I put the tip of the laser rifle under his jaws. "If you fail to answer, I'm going to sizzle your head clean off your sorry shoulders. Then I'm going to bring the next highest ranked Saurian in here. He or she will first examine your corpse. Then I'll see if they want to tell me what I'm asking."

"You lack decorum," the Wisdom said.

"Yeah, what are you going to do, huh? It's a birth defect I've carried with me my whole life. You have three seconds to start explaining. Then—*pfft*, your turn at life is over."

He took two of those seconds to think about it. At the third, he said, "The Tenth left to join the Jelk Grand Fleet. They speed for the inner core."

"Why build a Grand Fleet there?" I asked.

"To repeal the invaders," the Wisdom said, watching me with his wondering eyes.

So, Doctor Sant had spoken the truth. The rumors were true. I wondered again if my dream about Abaddon meant anything. But how could it?

"What is the nature of these invaders?" I asked.

"I do not know."

"Who does know?" I asked.

"The Jelk," he said.

I studied the robe-wearing Saurian, finally deciding he told the truth. Well, well, well. The Jelk had truly stripped the frontier of warships after all, building the Mother of All Fleets in the core worlds. Who were the invaders?

I shrugged, and said, "Take him away."

"Wait," the Saurian said. "Did you speak the truth earlier? Will you leave us our lives?"

"If you follow my orders, pops, yeah. You'll live."

He folded his clawed hands and those wide eyes become half-lidded. He looked like a Saurian Buddha then. The lizard even managed a half-bow.

"I go," he said, "and you will go. May our paths never cross again."

"Sounds good to me," I said.

We left the starcity three hours later. To ensure their good behavior, and from those in the rest of the system, we left seven floating missiles as active drones. I radioed the Wisdom and told him the missiles would attack whatever moved. It would be best to let whoever entered the system next deal with the waiting drones.

Afterward, with the *Aristotle* leading the pack, we entered the jump gate, heading home. Given what happened later, I should have made different plans.

-11-

When we returned to the solar system, I felt like Sir Francis Drake. I knew a little about the famous sailor who had gone against the Spanish Armada.

Drake had plagued the Spanish Main in the Caribbean Sea, raiding settlements as he sought the gold of the Incas. During his trip around the world, he passed through the Strait of Magellan, a horrendous passage between South America and Antarctica. That put him on the western shore of South America. His ship, the *Golden Hind*, had been the biggest and baddest cannon-armed vessel allowing him to raid the Spanish settlements at will. At first, they had no idea an Englishman had made it onto that side of the world. By the time they understood, he was gone.

Drake packed his galleon with loot and set out across the Pacific Ocean. The return to England proved to be a harrowing voyage. Most of the crew died of scurvy, a vitamin C deficiency. When he sailed into Plymouth, he met cheering crowds. His investors were rich from his plunder, and Queen Elizabeth had taken her share, too.

It was like that only better when we returned with our haulers, mining equipment and armaments.

The next few days proved sharp with haggling. Diana demanded more as her share. I gave her less, keeping two of the haulers for the Star Vikings. One of those vessels I proceeded to sink into the poisoned Caspian Sea. The other kept watch near Ceres, as we unloaded the last missile launchers and beam cannons onto the asteroid.

Maybe I should have turned around fast and gone on another Star Viking raid. One thing after another kept popping up, though, needing my attention.

Three months and four days after returning from our raid, Admiral Saris reappeared in the solar system. That changed the equation in a way I hadn't foreseen. It happened like this:

Dmitri roved the jump gates. Sometimes, he used the Pluto gate. Other times, he went through the Neptune route. I wanted more advance notice of approaching aliens. This seemed like the best way to get it. Sure, it used up fuel and put a strain on the starship, but we had spare parts now and extra fuel coming from our scoop floating in Jupiter.

The Jupiter scoop was nothing more than sturdy balloons floating in the higher atmosphere. There, the processor dangling under the inflatables collected rare deuterium swirling here and there in the clouds. When the time came, a booster launched a filled cell, which arrived at a container tube fifty thousand kilometers from the gas giant.

It felt as if we were getting somewhere. Given enough time, who knows what we might have achieved. The aliens never wanted to give us that time, though. The Lokhars were the worst culprits in that regard. This time it was no different. At least it wasn't another triad of Shi-Feng. I wondered if they still thought about me. I certainly thought about them and their so-called holy order.

I remember exercising in the *Aristotle's* gym with Rollo. We did bench presses. My best friend had become a monster. Before the coming of the aliens, he'd been lanky, and I'd always been the stronger one between us. Now...not so much.

As I spotted, Rollo breathed heavily as he lay on the bench. He reached up with his paws, the palms covered with chalk dust. He tested his grip several times, finally settling into the right spot. Then he braced himself while taking a deep breath. With a grunt, he shoved up as I helped him lift the bar off the rack.

As he lay there on the bench, the crazy man balanced one thousand pounds on the bar. This would be a new max for him.

With an intake of air, he lowered the bar so it touched his muscled pectorals. Then, Rollo strained, his face turning red. He actually raised the weight. I watched spellbound. My best had been seven hundred and fifty pounds, and I'd considered myself Hercules because of it.

To my amazement, Rollo shoved the one thousand pound barbell up to the rack, slamming the metal into the slots. Then his arms collapsed and he lay there on the bench, breathing hard and grinning like an idiot.

The intercom buzzed.

"What now?" I asked. Stepping to the intercom, pressing the button, I said, "Creed here."

"Commander," Ella said. "You'd better get to the bridge." I heard the fear in her voice.

"Is something wrong?" I asked.

"Dmitri just came through the Pluto gate," Ella said. "He said the entire Lokhar Fleet is heading our way."

"What?" I asked. "You're kidding, right? How many ships does he mean?"

"Dmitri said he stopped counting at three hundred. That was a little over half in his estimation."

A cold feeling erupted in my chest. "Is he counting space fighters?"

"Cruiser class or bigger, Commander," Ella said. "We have a situation on our hands."

"Yeah," I said. "I'll be there in a minute." I clicked off the intercom.

"Trouble?" asked Rollo. He sat up, mopping his sweaty face with a towel.

"Looks like its hitting the fan," I said, "and the Lokhars want to stop here before they go do whatever it is they planned."

"What's that mean?" he asked.

I regarded Rollo. "I think we're going to find out."

*　*　*

I figured I should do something with Dmitri's heads up. Clearly, we couldn't face hundreds of Lokhar capital ships. Why would the tigers come to the solar system with an armada? Did they mean to annihilate us? Remembering the Shi-Feng, I thought, *Maybe*.

Anyway, I ordered the *Thomas Aquinas* to Earth. Through autopilot, Rollo sank it deep into Lake Erie.

As Dmitri raced from Pluto to Ceres, I gathered my two cruisers. As fast as we could, I had people cart our missile launchers and beam cannons off the big asteroid. I had them bury the ordnance on smaller asteroids. I didn't want the Lokhars to know we'd raided a Jelk Corporation star system.

Why would the tigers care? Good question. They were aliens, and they were coming with far too many starships. Maybe they were here to steal our artifact.

The days lengthened, and finally the first Lokhar cruisers and battleships appeared through the Pluto jump gate. They radioed with the special system, telling us Admiral Saris of Purple Tamika came to inspect our Sol Object.

She'd been here more than seven years ago when I'd returned from hyperspace. In fact, she'd traded us our three cruisers. I asked her what she wanted. She smiled and requested a face-to-face meeting in four days.

What could I do? I said, "Yes. It will be my honor."

***

From the bridge of the *Aristotle*, Ella counted their warships as the mass swarmed toward the Forerunner artifact. Five hundred and sixty-four Purple Tamika vessels moved toward us. The armada had six times the mass of the Starkien fleet that had been here before. There were cruisers, battleships, carriers and missile-ships in abundance. Clearly, we were fleas compared to the elephant.

The bulk of the Purple Tamika armada took up station near Jupiter. Fifty battleships came on toward Ceres. I had Diana and the rest of the Earth Fleet stay near the freighters.

Thus, I waited near Ceres with two former Lokhar cruisers.

Finally, the fifty battleships braked nearby, stopping. The admiral requested my presence aboard her flagship. I went alone, with my trusty .44 beside me. The idea of coming by my lonesome was to shame them and in a sense, give them as a subtle insult. Saris was the great admiral. I was Commander Creed, and I walked alone.

What do you want to hear? I docked my shuttle, walked corridors lined with hundreds of tigers in powered armor. Each held a rifle at port arms and stared with obvious hostility. Finally, I reached a hatch where the biggest tigers I'd ever seen waited. Without a word, the smaller of the two opened the way.

I walked through. Two hundred Lokhars waited for me inside. Most had lined up against the bulkheads. They all wore fancy uniforms with lots of purple, golden braid and medals. A big conference table was in the center of the chamber. Around it sat thirty tigers. Most were fleet officers, with a few robed adepts and some infantry generals. At the head of the table sat Admiral Saris. She was tall for a Lokhar, and she sat as if someone had surgically inserted a steel rod into her spine.

I only recognized one other tiger. He was a bluff combat officer with a White Nebula with purple trim pinned to his jacket. I'd seen him seven years ago.

Halting before I reached the table, I bowed at the waist. There was a stir among the Lokhars, whispering. Finally, Admiral Saris spoke.

"Where is the rest of your entourage?"

"I came alone," I said, loudly.

That brought more whispering. The admiral frowned at the combat officer beside her. Good, I'd upset them. Their armada upset me. I knew it couldn't be good for us.

"Very well," Admiral Saris said. "You will sit here near me," she said, pointing at an empty chair.

"Thank you," I said.

"First, though, you will give up your sidearm."

They must have heard what I'd done to the Emperor's daughter-wife, Princess Nee. I dearly hoped the big dog hadn't come along and just waited for me to be disarmed before he made his appearance.

I handed over the magnum. Then, as if heading for a gallows, I walked toward my spot beside the admiral and across from the combat officer.

After I sat, the admiral offered me refreshments. I nibbled on some Lokhar jerky and took a shot of tiger liquor. It exploded in my belly, spreading warmth. After I wiped my hands on a napkin, I figured it was time to get started. I didn't really care to have all these tigers watching me. Maybe I should have brought someone else along. It's hard being alone.

"I have to admit," I said, "I didn't expect to see you in our solar system so soon."

"Those are my feelings as well," Saris said.

"The Emperor is well, I take it?"

"He is," Saris said. "I'm sure it would make him glad to know you care about his welfare."

"We owe much to the Emperor," I said. Meaning that someday I'd like to slit his throat and watch him bleed to death. I wondered what would happen if I mentioned the Shi-Feng. Nothing good for me was the likely answer.

Saris showed me her teeth in what might have been a smile. I'd never seen the lady do that before. She had to be the gravest tiger I knew.

"This is not a pleasure call," she informed me.

"I didn't think so."

"This is a functional war fleet."

"I hope you're not here to wage war against us."

Saris looked around as if surprised. The room erupted with tiger laughter. I wondered if this was what a gazelle might feel surrounded by snarling lions.

"No, no," the admiral finally said. "We are neither at war with you guardians nor with the humans. Are you surprised at my distinction between the two groups?"

"Not really," I said.

"The Emperor and his advisors view the humans as beasts," Admiral Saris informed me. "You are something different, something higher on the evolutionary scale."

"Is that supposed to make me grateful?"

"Yes," she said flatly.

"Okay then. Thanks."

"Admiral," the combat officer said. "You should not tolerate his sarcasm."

"You are wrong, General," Saris said. "He has entered the hyperspace artifact. He spoke to the Forerunner object, and it told him its name."

101

Halfway down the conference table, a robed adept rustled her garments. She had the most fur on her face of any Lokhar I'd ever seen. Maybe that meant she was old. "I would hear the object's name," the ancient adept said in a quavering voice.

"In a minute," Saris said. She fixed her yellow orbs on me. "Doctor Sant stayed here for many years, did he not?"

Was that what this was about? I cleared my throat, saying, "The good doctor left some months ago."

"In an Orange Tamika vessel, yes?" Saris asked.

"I think so. Why, is that important?"

The admiral's eyes seemed to glitter with malice. "There is evil in the space lanes," she declared. "It came on an ill wind of fate."

The old adept with her purple robe struggled to her feet. She was shorter than any Lokhar I'd seen and her head thrust forward. Trembling with age, she pointed a clawed finger at me. "The ill wind came upon his return," the adept said. "It came as he rode the artifact to the solar system. We must return the object to the Altair star system. It is blasphemy for it to reside in the abode of beasts."

"Your words are blasphemy," I said.

The room grew deathly silent. The adept turned wild eyes onto me. She gnashed her teeth until foam flecked her mouth.

"Who are you to speak against an adept of the third degree?" she asked in a quavering voice.

"I am Commander Creed," I said. "I am he who closed the portal planet and halted the Kargs from invading our universe."

"Lies!" the adept shouted.

"Yeah?" I asked. "What part specifically are you referring to?"

"Lokhars closed the portal planet. This is a proven fact."

"You're dead wrong," I said.

The adept turned to Admiral Saris. "I claim—"

"Silence!" Saris snarled.

"No!" the adept shouted in a reedy voice. Others around her took up her cry.

Admiral Saris pressed a button, and a loud klaxon blared. No one could speak until she removed her finger.

102

"Sit down," Saris said. "I rule here. I will decide the agenda."

The adept looked as if she wanted to argue. Finally, reluctantly, the trembling adept resumed her seat.

The interchange so reminded me of Prince Venturi and his adept on the *Indomitable* that I wondered if this was some sort of ritual the tigers went through during every big meeting.

"Commander Creed," Saris said. "Orange Tamika has raised the flag of revolt against the Emperor. Did you know that was the doctor's intent?"

"I wondered about it, yeah," I said.

"You admit to this?" Saris asked in wonder.

"I have nothing to hide."

"This is a grave breach of trust," Saris said.

"I don't see it that way," I said. "Your lovely Emperor caused my planet's destruction and billions of humans to die. I saved his bacon some time ago. To my way of thinking, he and you Lokhars owe us big time."

Once more, silence filled the chamber.

"You are not very diplomatic," Saris said.

"I figure you're going to do what you came here to do. It hardly matters what I say."

"Force him to tell us the artifact's name," the adept rasped from down the table.

"Yes," Saris said, staring at me. "It is time for you to reveal the artifact's name."

I made of show of looking around the room. The Lokhars seemed to edge toward me, to wait expectantly for the great secret. They hungered for it. Settling back into my chair, I regarded the admiral. Did any of the Shi-Feng sit among them? I dearly wanted to know more about these holy assassins.

"Let's think about this for a minute," I said. "Many years ago, the artifact fled the Altair star system—"

"Listen to me," Saris said, interrupting. "We are not here to relate old exploits. We know what happened at Altair and at the portal planet. It is inconceivable that a human knows the artifact's name. What makes it more galling, is that no Lokhar has shared such a profound knowledge with a Forerunner

103

object before. There are those among us who view this as a grave breach of protocol."

Did she mean the Shi-Feng? Hmm, surrounded by all these tigers, with all these warships ready to attack the last humans, maybe I should speak delicately for once.

"Who am I to decide such things?" I asked. "I'm just a man, as you keep pointing out. If the artifact felt inclined to tell me and no one else, I'm going to keep it that way."

"You must tell us," Saris said. There was something new in her voice. It almost sounded whiny. Was the admiral desperate?

Maybe it was time to try a new tact.

Once more, I cleared my throat. Then I asked, "Do you believe in the Creator?"

Lokhars cowered and cried out, some shielding their eyes from me with their arms.

"I'm taking that as a yes," I said. "If you wish to profane this ground, attempt to force me to speak. Otherwise, quit asking me because I'm not going to tell you. The artifact chose me. It didn't choose anyone else. That must mean something, right? Maybe it's even the Creator's decision."

My words made several adepts cringe. One tiger standing at the farthest wall watched me with hot eyes. He looked tense. I felt certain that Lokhar belonged to the Shi-Feng.

I bet they're everywhere.

"Oh, by the way," I said, "Doctor Sant dearly tried to learn the object's name as well. I didn't tell him, either."

"The doctor claims you did tell him," Saris said.

"I don't believe you."

"Kill him!" the adept screeched. "Boil him in stem oil and eviscerate him."

"Silence," Saris told the adept, "or I will have you removed from the chamber."

The old adept breathed heavily and eyed me with wild eyes. Even so, she held her tongue.

I glanced at the far wall. The tiger I'd seen earlier wasn't there. What did that mean?

"Look," I said. "I think we should work together. We have been for some time, and it has been beneficial for both of us. What kind of alien is attacking the Jelk in the core worlds?"

"Your only concern is in telling me the name of the Forerunner artifact," Saris said.

"John F. Kennedy," I said, promptly.

A gasp went throughout the chamber. Tigers stared at one another in awed wonder.

"This is the artifact's true name?" Saris asked in a soft voice.

I was tempted to say yes. Instead, I shook my head. "Sorry, no, it's the name of a human leader."

The wonder turned to outrage.

"He mocks us," the combat officer said. "Let me kill him. His ways are profane, an insult to the Lokhar race."

"Hey, I'm the object's guardian," I said. "You need to start giving me some respect. I still haven't decided if I'm going to let you view the artifact or not."

"How can you stop us?" Saris asked.

That was the rub. I didn't have a powerful weapon. I needed one, all right. If I had the Purple Lokhar armada, ah, that would be something. Then things would be different around here.

"You do not yet understand your place in the scheme of existence," Saris informed me. "Perhaps it is fortunate for you that I am about other matters at present. We came here for your cruisers and starships. You will return them to Purple Tamika."

"What are you talking about?" I asked.

"The two cruisers facing us and the Earth Fleet warships, we're taking them back," Saris said.

My gut tightened with rage. I had bought those with the most precious commodity in the universe: human lives. It took an act of will for me to refrain from launching myself at the admiral.

In a shaking voice, I said, "We humans earned those warships with our blood."

"Times change," Saris said, pretending not to notice my anger. "Unknown aliens appear to battle the Jelk Corporation. Can the Jelk stop these invaders? If not, the Emperor might have to do so with the might of the Lokhar fleets. I, as the Emperor's representative, will ruthlessly put down the Orange Tamika rebellion before that. Thus, I demand every warship I can lay my hands on. You have ten."

This was a disaster. I had to use my wits, and use them now. Despite the seething inside me, I said, "Nine warships not ten."

"What happened to the tenth vessel?" Saris asked.

"I sent it out on a raid," I lied. The tigers no longer deserved even an approximation of the truth. "The cruiser never returned."

Saris sat utterly still. Finally, she shrugged. "I will take the nine."

"No!" I said. "How am I supposed to defend the Forerunner artifact without warships?" When Saris didn't answer, I said, "What if Baba Gobo shows up again and takes the object?"

"Before that happens," Saris said, "I have no doubt the object will disappear as it did before in the Altair system. It will not allow Starkiens to hold it."

"How will the artifact know what's happening?" I asked.

"You are a dense beast," the adept said. "The artifact knows, of that you should have no doubt."

I sat stunned. Despite my efforts to use cunning, I found it too hard to concentrate. "You're not taking our warships," I said. "We'll fight to the death to hold them."

"Perhaps that is so, Commander Creed," Saris said. "If that is true then you will die, and all humanity will die with you. Is that worth a noble but futile gesture?"

I studied the admiral as wheels turned in my mind. Finally, I concluded she was telling the truth. We'd have to give up our cruisers. That would leave us practically defenseless. Just when we'd begun as Star Vikings, Admiral Saris came and took all our *dragonships*. Was this going to be the fatal handicap that ensured our extinction?

If Baba Gobo returned too soon or some other predator alien then the answer would be yes. Instead of climbing out of the hole, Admiral Saris was putting us as deep down as humanity could go.

-12-

Several days later—after the Lokhar armada had left—Diana informed me that panic threatened the people packed in the Jelk freighters. As the vessels orbited Earth, there were riots, fights and assassinations.

I came to a hard conclusion and loaned her half the assault troopers. It was difficult to think of ourselves as Star Vikings now. In any case, in a Demar hauler, troopers from Mars Base landed on freighters in Earth orbit, breaking heads as they helped restore order.

The Purple Tamika armada had left us defenseless, taking every warship they could lay their paws on. Fortunately, they didn't taken any haulers, freighters or hidden loot on the asteroids. Nor did they hunt too diligently for the sunken cruiser and Demar hauler sitting down on Earth.

What was one more cruiser to their mass anyway? To us, the single warship might mean everything.

I admit it. Depression hit me hard. A single alien pirate ship might annihilate humanity. We had to act fast. But what was the right decision?

In our Demar hauler, I descended through the atmosphere toward Lake Erie. The Great Lakes looked normal from high orbit. No artificial lights shined up from the planet, though. Everything was dark the way only North Korea used to be.

Little had changed on Earth since the nukes and bio-terminator had hit. Winds howled, shoving multicolored

107

clouds. They reminded me of oil slicks in puddles I'd played around in as a kid.

N7 piloted us. I had a skeleton crew along. Most of the troopers were in the freighters, fighting under Rollo and Dmitri. During times of panic, a hard fist with shows of mercy to the defeated often helped quell rebellions the quickest.

The hauler shook as greater winds struck our hull. There were no more trees on Earth, no more grass or lichen, moss or mushrooms. It was a dead world with quickly decomposing skeletons, rusted metal and crumbling brick and concrete structures. The Lokhar decontamination ships had begun their work. After they left, though, the process of de-atomization continued.

Our automated factories worked slowly but relentlessly. It would take them more than a century to clean up the biohazard mess. Humanity needed something quicker.

In any case, Lake Erie had the multicolored glare. It made me sick seeing it. I hated walking on Earth now. The bio-terminator was still strong in places. Four years ago, we'd lost twenty thousand freighter people when someone with the terminator bug returned to the living quarters up there.

After that, Diana's people quit mining the Earth for old junk. It wasn't any wonder the Lokhars hadn't looked too hard here for the missing cruiser.

The Demar hauler shook as it touched down. N7 and I traded glances.

"I'll see you around," I said.

"This is wrong, Commander," N7 told me. "Send someone else."

"No. This is my job."

"You are too important to lose," the android said.

I laughed sourly. "Right. I've brought humanity back to square one. Do me a favor, N7. Tell Rollo the artifact's name if I don't make it back. Promise me you'll do that."

"I give you my solemn oath, Commander. I will do so because you dared to risk taking androids from the Demar Starcity."

We shook hands. Then I headed for the hatch that would take me outside.

***

In my pressurized suit, I walked on Earth. Despite the ruins around me, I felt as if I'd come home again. That was crazy, don't you think?

I saw badly rusting cars, buildings looking as if hungry termites had been eating for a hundred years. The freeways were still intact. They were like the granddaddy of dinosaur bones laid in the Earth. Nothing living grew up through them. I wondered if a thousand years from now the freeways would be all that was left of mankind's rule on Earth.

I have to change this. I have to make the Earth green again. I want children to frolic under our sun.

This sense of purpose steeled my heart for what was to come. I didn't have any right to be depressed. Someone had to drive ahead and make these aliens pay for what they had done to us.

I reached Lake Erie's shoreline. The waves lapped on the lonely Earth. I was the only living soul walking the planet. It made me shudder, and it almost brought tears to my eyes.

I refused to give the aliens the pleasure. This was my planet and they had destroyed it.

"Think, Creed. What are you missing?"

I could feel a hole in my head. No, not a literal hole. But there was something knocking around inside my noggin that I wasn't getting. It plagued me, demanding attention. Was it my subconscious?

With a shrug, I began to wade out into the cold water. I wore a pressurized suit. Forcing my legs, I waded so the water reached my knees, my waist and finally my chest. The harsh sound of my breathing was the only noise in my ears.

"Let's get this over with," I told myself.

Water swirled before my eyes. Despite the queer colors in the water, it was clear down here. I could see easily, rainbows in the water as far as I could look.

For the next hour, I tramped along the muddy bottom. All plant life down here had died. Mud swirled and slowly it became darker. I would look up and see faintly colored light.

109

At last, that stopped and I moved within a world of eternal gloom. How deep had I come?

I didn't have any instruments to measure that. Instead, I had a locating device. It beeped every minute. After two hours, a dot appeared on my HUD. That would the Lokhar cruiser hidden down here.

Okay. Here's what happened. I walked forever and reached the outer hull. I couldn't see a damned thing until I turned on my headlamp. It felt eerie as all get out as the spotlight washed over a Lokhar letter. If something had swum by me then I'd have freaked out and raved. I didn't even have a spear gun, just a knife.

Twenty minutes later, after marching around the craft, I found the hatch. Slowly, I rotated a wheel and tugged. Nothing happened. Had the deep pressure sealed this thing shut for the rest of my life or was that rust doing its trick?

Inside my helmet, which dripped with condensation, I snarled. I recalled Rollo and his one thousand pound bench press. It was time for Creed to play muscleman. I pulled harder, all to no avail.

Maybe I should have sent someone else down here, Rollo for instance.

"Nope, I'm doing this."

The words sounded hollow to my ears. I put my feet up against the hull. I gripped the wheel and I began to pull. The hatch moved so very slowly. I wondered then how I'd prop it open. The frustration made me roar, and I pulled it wider. Quickly, I squirmed between the hatch and the hull. I forced myself through as the pressure of Lake Erie shoved the hatch against me. I bellowed in pain. If the hatch should breach my suit—

I couldn't worry about it now. Water came gushing in with me. Then I slithered through. The hatch clanged shut and water came up to my chin. It was slow work, but I finally opened the inner hatch. The water gushed through with me into the warship's hall, but I was inside the cruiser with contaminated Lake Erie water.

Sealing this area, I found my way to a decontamination area. After a long scrubbing, I shed my suit. Finally, I walked the lonely corridors of the starship. Outside were millions of tons of water pressing down against the hull.

I turned on the engines, flicked on the gravity generators and lifted the Lokhar cruiser. An hour later, I parked the cruiser in orbit.

We had our sole remaining warship.

**

Later, I spoke with Rollo as we inspected the cruiser. The man might have looked like a muscle-bound idiot, but he was anything but.

"You know," I said, as he ducked into engineering. "We have a cruiser, as in one to humanity's name. What do we do with it?"

"It seems to me that sitting on our butts only means it's a matter of time before Baba Gobo or someone like him comes around to kill or enslave humanity," Rollo said.

"So...?" I asked.

"So we must go on more Star Viking raids and rebuild," Rollo said. "Nothing else makes sense to me."

"If we take the cruiser that leaves nothing behind to protect the freighters," I said.

"Well, the freighters do have their mobility," Rollo said. "They can run away."

"That's one possibility, I suppose."

"We also have a few missile launchers and ground-based laser cannons we took from Demar," Rollo said. "We can fortify an asteroid or two so they can defend against pirates. We could set up the weapons systems like German 88s as Rommel did in the North African deserts during WWII. The freighters race for safety to the laser cannons and bam, the rays take out any following pirates."

"I like it," I said. "Yeah, I think you're right. We have to keep raiding. We have to build up to the best of our ability. It's a long shot. But ever since the aliens showed up on our doorstep this has been a crapshoot. It's surprising we've managed to keep the remnant alive for as long as we have."

"I'd agree to that," Rollo said.

"Right," I said. "It's time to get to work."

111

**

Nine days later, we were almost ready to leave the solar system in our cruiser.

The freighter riots had ended. Most of the ringleaders found themselves in the brigs. Murad Bey spaced a few of them. I wished he hadn't had done that. I would have taken the so-called troublemakers with me, if nothing else.

We'd worked overtime getting ready. Ceres bristled with the Demas system weaponry we'd taken. It was a veritable space fortress now.

After long days of work, Rollo, Dmitri and I relaxed in a rec room aboard *Glorious Hope*. We'd rechristened the vessel with its new name.

The three of us played pool on a regulation-sized table. The trick was to beat Dmitri, a real shark. The Cossack didn't spend long seconds eying the billiard balls either. He would chalk the cue stick, step up to the table and put his left hand on the green cloth. Then, as quick as you please, he readied the stick, slid it twice through his fingers and *whacked* the cue ball. The targeted billiard sank like lead into a pocket.

Once again, I didn't get a shot for an entire game. Instead, I watched Dmitri sink all of his balls and then the eight ball.

He straightened with a grin. "Another game?" he asked.

Frustrated, I handed my stick to Rollo.

"This time you're going down," the muscleman told our Cossack.

Dmitri only grinned. With a *crack*, he split the balls, which expanded across the table. This time, none of them fell into a pocket.

"My turn," Rollo said. He proved the opposite of Dmitri, carefully lining up each shot. After a long study, he tipped the cue ball, which rolled and nudged a striped fellow, which ever so slowly rolled to a side pocket and…fell in.

"Yes!" Rollo said, shaking his stick.

"Look at him," Dmitri said with an indulgent smile.

Taking just as long for his second shot, Rollo sank another billiard ball.

"Now you're showing real improvement," Dmitri said.

112

Rollo threw the Cossack an evil grin, and he squinted studying his next shot. He sank the third ball.

Dmitri said nothing this time.

In fact, Rollo sank five balls before missing his sixth shot.

"Fatal are thy mistakes," Dmitri said.

Rollo quietly stepped back, no doubt seething inside but calm outwardly.

Dmitri sank everything, including the eight ball. "Creed?" he asked.

I almost shook my head. Instead, I said, "Yeah, one more time."

Dmitri chalked his tip as I racked the balls. "You know what I think sometimes?" our Cossack asked me.

"What's that?" I asked, stepping away from the table.

"Why you don't use the Forerunner artifact as a ship?"

I hung the billiard rack onto its peg and turned around to stare at Dmitri.

"Do you remember how the artifact disappeared from the Altair star system?" Dmitri asked. He walked to the end of the table, leaning down to take his shot.

I said nothing.

With the cue stick sliding between his fingers, Dmitri said, "And how the artifact vanished from the portal planet with all of us hitching a ride on it?"

I still didn't say a word.

Crack! Dmitri's break did better this time, sinking a striped and a solid. He lined up another solid, sinking it. As he moved around the table, examining the balls, the Cossack said, "I've wondered why you don't go back into the artifact and talk to it. I mean, if it can teleport wherever it wants"—*crack*, another solid went down into a pocket. "Why not convince the artifact to pop around the galaxy for us. Can you imagine what kind of Viking ship the object would make?"

Dmitri straightened, glancing my way. He frowned. "Creed, you okay?"

Rollo had been looking at something on a computer pad. He looked up too. By the frown on his face, it appeared as if Rollo played back in his mind the Cossack's words. Suddenly, the muscleman glanced at me.

"That's brilliant," I whispered.

Dmitri raised his eyebrows. "You think so?"

"I should have thought of it," I said. "Yeah, the artifact just zipped away from the Altair system. It brought us home from hyperspace." I laughed, and even to my own ears, it sounded a little crazy.

"I thought the artifact has gone to sleep for twenty-five years," Rollo said. "It's going to think things through."

"That's what it told us," I said.

"So how can you get it to talk to you?" Rollo asked.

"That would be the first trick," I said. "The second would be to convince it to move around for us."

"Are you serious?" Dmitri asked. "You really think that would be a good idea?"

I grinned from ear to ear. "We're going to postpone our next venture." With a snap of my fingers, I said, "I need to talk to N7." I put away my stick, heading for the hatch.

"Hey," Dmitri said. "What about the game?"

I was too wound up to answer, beginning to run as I moved through the hatch.

-13-

N7 and I used thruster-packs, flying from a Demar hauler to the giant artifact before us.

As I've said before, the object looked like a gleaming silver donut the size of a medium asteroid with an artificial black hole in the center. Whatever anchored the black hole wasn't visible to the naked eye or to our scientific instruments.

In my opinion, the technology of the First Ones was in play. In most cases, their machinery baffled us.

Who were the First Ones anyway? That's what I wanted to know. As the name implied, they were the supposed to have been the first on the scene. The tiger religion said the Creator sculpted the universe, first making the substance, of course. Then He poured the First Ones down as a baker might dribble sugar into a cake mix. The Forerunners—the First Ones—made the artifacts, and in the course of time, the living beings vanished. No one I'd spoken to had given me an explanation as to why the First Ones went extinct. It was a *fait accompli*. The artifact-makers were gone, but they had left behind their impressive machines and the jump lanes between the stars.

The Jelk, the tigers and the baboons all wanted the artifacts for themselves. Heck, even Abaddon had wanted them. Everybody did.

N7 had been inside the artifact on the portal planet with me. Why shouldn't he join me a second time, if it proved possible? Send a thief to catch a thief. Use an android to convince a living machine to help.

The Forerunner artifact had told me its name before, Holgotha. Over seven years ago, N7 and I had been inside one of the squat buildings on the inner portion of the donut nearest the black hole. There, the artifact and I had engaged in an interesting conversation.

As I jetted through space toward the approaching object, I recalled the words we'd spoken together while on the portal planet:

"Did the First Ones see the Creator?" I asked.

"Not to my knowledge," Holgotha replied.

"Is there a Creator?" N7 asked.

Holgotha paused, finally saying, "My designers and builders believed so. I have awaited the cycles and millennia for conclusive proof."

"Is that why you came here?" I asked. I meant to the portal planet in hyperspace.

"I do not understand your reasoning," Holgotha said. "Can you be more specific?"

"Do you wish to unleash an apocalypse on our universe in order to see what will happen?" I asked. "Do you believe that will bring the Creator into sight?" If Abaddon and the Kargs had reached our space-time continuum with all their moth-ships, it would have meant death for everyone else.

"For the first time, I find your reasoning interesting." There was a pause, before Holgotha added, "I wonder if some of my oldest subroutines subscribe to such a notion. I will investigate."

"How long will that take?" I asked.

"Do you mean in your time?" asked Holgotha.

"Sure," I said.

"Twenty to twenty-five years," the artifact said.

"So your internal investigation is going to take quite a bit of your, ah..." I hesitated. Just how touchy was the artifact? "I don't want to be imprecise and I don't mean to demean you by implying you're a computer. But will your twenty-year analysis absorb the majority of your computational abilities?"

"Eh?" Holgotha asked. "Did you ask another question? I have begun to assemble my inquisitor files."

I licked my lips.

116

"Interesting, interesting," Holgotha said. *"There is a new development occurring even now…"*

My head twitched as N7 veered toward me in space. His silver faceplate stared at me.

"Is there a problem?" I radioed N7. The artifact loomed before us, while Ceres was a speck far behind.

"Negative, Commander," the android radioed. "You seemed distracted. I merely wondered if everything was well."

"I'm doing great. Now let's concentrate. We'll have to brake soon so we can land."

I used the familiar throttle controls. We wore ultra vacc-suits, heavily shielded against radiation. We'd soon need every bit of armoring against the black hole.

The trouble, as I saw it, would be waking Holgotha up to us. His subroutines were busy making his computations. What did an artifact of Holgotha's magnitude think about during his many millennia of existence? I couldn't comprehend. Then again, I didn't think I had to. Instead, I would use imagination. That was the great human gift, right? Today, I'd have to employ it better than I ever had.

Commander Creed, the man with the golden tongue. Yeah, right, I didn't see it, but I'd give it a go.

"It is time, Commander," N7 radioed.

Twisting around so the nozzles pointed at the approaching surface, I engaged thrust. White hydrogen particles hissed from my pack. I began to slow down. The giant donut loomed even larger behind me. I could see it in my HUD. The last time I'd touched the ancient metal, I'd left the donut after having escaped Abaddon.

The good news, Holgotha hadn't departed our solar system yet. We really had no idea how fussy the big thing would prove to be. In the Altair star system, the object had disappeared when the Starkiens and we assault troopers had approached too closely during combat. I'd never thought to ask the artifact when I had the chance why he'd done that.

Using even more thrust so my torso trembled, I lightly touched down onto the silver skin. Beside me, N7 did likewise.

I shut off my thruster-pack and began to undo the buckles and seals. Soon enough, I magnetized the propulsion system to the artifact.

With magnetized boots, I tramped my way toward the curve that would take me to the inner portion of the donut. N7 moved in his lurching step beside me. Magnetized walking always took some getting used to.

I saw a long trail of port exhaust up there in space. The hauler moved back from us.

Turning, I waved to N7. He waved back. We wore ultra-dense vacc-suits, carried many days of air with us, concentrates and water and a special system that would help to eliminate wastes. The gear was good, but none of that would matter if we failed to find a way to wake Holgotha to us.

"Ready?" I radioed N7.

"Let us proceed," the android said.

It took a long time to walk around the curve, starting toward the black hole. Light couldn't penetrate it. A ball of deepest darkness hung there in the exact center. I shuddered and wondered how well the ultra-suit would protect my bones and tissues from the deadly rays.

Strange script in golden letters highlighted the artifact's inner surface. Then I spied them again; the low buildings huddled together. While back on the portal planet—in the exact center of it, to be precise—N7 and I had walked through the walls of one of the ancient buildings, bringing us to a place where Holgotha had communicated with us.

I imagined for a moment that Holgotha wasn't a space artifact, but one of the Creator's rings. Did a creator exit? Had aliens concocted the idea simply as a useless space religion? No. The artifact couldn't be a ring. Why would the squat buildings be there then?

Once again, N7 aimed his faceplate at me. I tried radio reception. All I heard was harsh static on my earphones. Making an exaggerated shrug, I continued toward the buildings.

It's hard not to get loopy with odd feelings while trudging on Holgotha's inner surface. The artifact had been around longer than humanity had existed. Yet I walked along the

118

surface. Beings called First Ones must have welded hull plates together. Could any of the builders have realized their machine would continue for such a vastly long age? It seemed doubtful.

In time, the squat buildings loomed before N7 and me. The highest stood two stories tall. There was nothing grand about them. Together, they looked little more than boxes of varying sizes shoved near each other. The streets were the same as the rest of the artifact's surface. The buildings were dark, looking like chalk.

With my gauntlet, I rapped against a wall. The side felt like metal.

N7 pointed at a particular wall.

Chinning my headphones on again, all I heard was static. Here, the black hole was our enemy.

I turned my microphone on. "Holgotha," I said. "There is danger in the solar system. We request a quick counsel session to learn your wishes."

Nothing happened.

I banged the flat of my gloves against the wall. Once, the gauntlets had sunken through. Then I'd walked through a wall to the other side. It wasn't happening today. Could the artifact even hear my words?

"Something attacks the Jelk Corporation," I said into the microphone. "The Jelk have summoned Saurian fleets from our frontier to help them closer to the center of the galaxy. The balance of power is shifting around us. We need some help."

N7 faced me. I looked around. This was such a bleak place. I felt lonely and more than a little useless. What would budge the artifact? I had no idea.

As I opened my mouth, I sensed a word in my mind. "*Go.*"

Did Holgotha communicate with me in some strange manner I didn't understand? It seemed more than likely.

Seconds later, N7 tugged at one of my arms. I glanced at him. The android pointed toward the nearest edge. I had the feeling N7 wanted to go.

"No," I said. "I'm not leaving."

N7 tugged harder. I disengaged my arm from his grip. The android's shoulders deflated.

"Holgotha!" I shouted, slapping my palms against a wall.

119

"Go now while you are able."

The artifact seemed to be able to put thoughts into my mind. Holgotha possessed super-advanced technology. Maybe telepathy was one of its forms.

Stubbornly, I shook my head. The Shi-Feng had tried to kill me. Doctor Sant had pumped me full of poison. The Starkiens made a bid against us. And now, the Purple Tamika Admiral Saris had taken all but one of my warships. I needed this ancient machine's cooperation.

"Holgotha," I radioed. "You're in Earth space. We're down to one spaceship. I need to discuss your defensive situation with you."

Fear hit me then. I cringed, wilting away from the building. A howl lodged in my throat. This was a terrible place. Ghosts must inhabit the artifact. What kind of fool had I been to return to this holy place?

Even as I felt this, I realized Holgotha must be manufacturing the emotions. The artifact beamed the feelings at me. I refused to let them sway me.

"Forget it, bud," I said between clenched teeth. No machine was going to out-mule me. I drew a sidearm, one gained during the battle on the portal planet. Aiming at the wall—

"Wait."

I hesitated. Had that done the trick?

On impulse, I put my free hand against the wall. It sank into the substance. A giddy sensation bloomed within my gut. Holstering the sidearm, I shoved my shoulder against the wall. Ever so slowly, I sank into it. Maybe I should have waited to see what N7 did. Instead, I pushed through the solid yet wavering wall. As if pushing against a raging stream, I fought my way through the material.

A few moments later, I staggered through into a small chamber. The walls gleamed white as brightness shined down from the ceiling.

I didn't remember this place from last time. Then again, that had been over seven years ago.

A second later, something staggered against me. I turned around and found N7 couched low.

"You may remove your helmets."

120

The words sounded muffled. They came from the vibrations of the farthest wall. Like last time, I thought of the trick as a super-larynx.

Hesitantly, I reached up and twisted. With a *click*, I removed my helmet. Chemically harsh odors made my nose twitch and me to jerk.

"What is the problem?" Holgotha asked.

"The odors in here are burning the inside of my nose," I half-choked in reply.

"A moment," the ancient artifact rumbled. "There. Is that better?"

I sniffed experientially, expecting an even worse assault against my nostrils. Instead, a spicy scent made me sneeze.

"What is wrong now?" Holgotha said in his deep voice, the wall continuing to vibrate.

"Nothing," I said. "Don't mind me."

"On the contrary," the artifact said. "You have allowed me nothing less than to mind you."

I glanced at N7. The android had removed his helmet, holding it in the crook of his arm. He appeared calm. I knew better.

"Do you have a place to sit?" I asked Holgotha.

A stretching noise heralded substance oozing up from the floor. The sight increased the unreality of this place. The moment the substance stopped stretching, I sat. My knees had become weak. I realized we had gravity in the room. My magnetized boots no longer worked on this floor. That was interesting.

"Hurry," Holgotha said. "Tell me why you found it necessary to aim a weapon at one of the monitor stations."

"Truthfully," I said, "I aimed it out of frustration. Perhaps I also hoped it would get you to respond."

"I am busy in my analysis," Holgotha said. "This talk wastes time. Something I deplore."

"I'm with you there," I said. "That's another reason I wanted to talk with you."

"You are tedious, Commander Creed. I prefer your companion, N7."

"That doesn't surprise me," I said.

121

"Your inflection," Holgotha said. "You mean to imply…a joke with that comment, do you not?"

"Maybe," I said.

"Explain your humor."

"N7 is a machine. You're a machine."

For a time, Holgotha said nothing.

"You may have insulted him," N7 whispered. The android had quietly moved up behind me.

"That is impossible," Holgotha said. "I have passed far beyond threats from such as you."

I filed it away that Holgotha viewed insults as threats. Was that a glitch in his communication program or something more troublesome?

"If you're far beyond insults," I asked, "why did you just stop talking a moment ago?"

"I am busy in my analysis," Holgotha said. "This conversation is a waste of time."

He seemed to be speaking like a machine, with conversational limitations. I realized we knew precious little about Holgotha or any of the other artifacts.

"I'm afraid it could get much worse for you," I told the machine.

"Explain your statement."

I told Holgotha about the Purple Tamika armada talking nine of our warships, leaving us defenseless.

"I fail to perceive why any of that matters to me," the artifact said.

"There are several problems," I said. "And they're interconnected. Before I can explain them, I have to know why you fled the Altair star system eight years ago."

"Fled implies fear," Holgotha said. "I lack the sensation."

"You don't have emotions?"

"Do I sensate like a biological creature?" Holgotha asked. "In no way is that accurate. I have sensation centers that compel me in one direction or another. To forestall another spate of simian questions, I will inform you that my present perception is one of curiosity."

"Concerning the Creator?" I asked.

"Among other factors, yes," Holgotha said.

"And these curiosities are no doubt tied in with Abaddon and his Kargs."

"That is incorrect."

"Oh." Did that mean my dream about Abaddon meant nothing? Would Holgotha automatically know if the Kargs had invaded our space-time continuum?

"Uh," I said, "I still don't understand why you left the Altair star system as the assault troopers and Starkiens closed in upon you."

"Your implication is that I feared either species in some manner. To halt your chatter, I will inform you that I deplore Starkiens."

"Do you have a reason?" I asked.

"It would be a non-sequitur if I did not."

"What is the reason?" I said, "If you don't mind me asking?"

The wall that had vibrated grew still. Finally, Holgotha spoke once more. "The Starkiens failed in a sacred charge. Namely, an artifact in their possession perished."

"What happened?" I asked.

"Just like humans," Holgotha said, "Starkiens have simian inquisitiveness. They swarmed their object, testing, probing and questioning it. Finally, they tore into the subroutines and processing centers, attempting to understand Forerunner technology. In their quest, they destroyed what they did not understand. A machine of the ages perished while in their possession. A stellar-wide alarm pierced each of us. We understood. We altered our defenses, and we made the other races aware of the sacrilege. Since that moment, the Starkiens have become outcasts to the noble races. The others scoured Starkien planets, turning them into smoking cinders. The last of the artifact-destroyers took to the stars in their ships, a wandering remnant of those who would profane the works of the First Ones."

"You have a pretty high opinion of yourself, don't you?" I asked.

Holgotha said nothing.

"Perhaps we should leave, Commander," N7 said.

"I second the suggestion," Holgotha said. "Leave before I eject you."

"Wait a minute," I said. "No one here suggests we're going to try to probe you. One of the reasons I'm here is to tell you that the Starkiens made a play for you in our solar system. You do realize that, don't you?"

"Of course I am aware," Holgotha said. "The Orange Tamika Lokhar handled the situation in a salutary fashion."

"Doctor Sant has left the solar system, stirring up rebellion in the Lokhar Empire. I'm wondering if a religious crusade has started in the Jade League."

"War brews everywhere," Holgotha said. "That is one of the signs of an approaching apocalypse."

That was ominous sounding. *Concentrate on the issue, Creed. Don't let the artifact sidetrack you with rabbit holes.* Right, I had to be like a pit bull, refusing to release my grip. Even so, the topic intrigued me enough to say:

"World War II didn't bring the end of Earth," I said.

"Your allusion escapes me," Holgotha said.

"Just because everyone goes mad with battle fury, doesn't mean God is going to show up and end existence. It means everyone has lost his cool. Now the blood is going to flow."

"One of these times, it does mean the Creator will approach to judge existence," Holgotha said. "That is one reason the Forerunners constructed us."

"You really believe that?" I asked.

"I have no habit of lying, no programs to guide me in the dark art. I leave that to your kind, Commander Creed."

The artifact's insult helped clear my thoughts. I noticed the spicy scent had departed the room. In its place, I detected a faint body odor, my own leaking up from my suit. I sweated hard inside.

First clearing my throat, I said, "My point is the Starkiens came to the solar system. They might have wiped us out before swarming onto you."

"I will not let Starkiens swarm me," Holgotha said. I noticed his voice deepened as he spoke the words.

"You'd kill them?" I asked.

"That is not my way. No. I would depart."

124

"But only after they wiped out humanity?" I asked.

"Why would that make any difference to me?"

"Don't you care if humanity is wiped out?"

"No," Holgotha said. "Many species have perished throughout the millennia. It is one of the natural processes of existence."

I jumped up and began to pace within the small chamber. To give me room, N7 backed against a wall.

"Look!" I said. "Let's make this mutual. You help us, and we'll help you."

"How can you possibly help me?" Holgotha asked.

"The lion shouldn't mock the mouse."

"Explain your reference."

I stopped in front of the vibrating wall. "A man named Aesop once told this old tale. A lion walked through the forest and happened to step on a mouse. The lion looked down, and opened its jaw to devour the tiny beast. The mouse squeaked, 'Have mercy on me, O King. In time, I will return you a favor.' The lion laughed. 'What can a little mouse do for me?' 'Some day,' the mouse squeaked. 'You will find out.' On a whim, the lion lifted its paw and watched the mouse scamper away.

"In the course of time," I said, "the lion became ensnarled in a net. The king of beasts thrashed and struggled, all to no avail. As the moon rose and the lion waited for the hunter to come and kill him, a tiny mouse ran along the rope. 'I have come as I said I would,' the mouse told the lion. 'You once showed mercy to me. Now, I will help you.' As the lion watched, the little mouse gnawed the rope. Before dawn appeared, the last rope fell away, and the lion shook himself free. He thanked the mouse, glad he'd shown mercy when he'd had the chance."

"The tale is supposed to stir me?" Holgotha asked.

"It should cause you to reflect," I said. "In helping us survive, we might in some manner aid you in a time of need. How that would occur, I have no idea. As an extra benefit, if you aid us, you would also get to observe a desperate species taking on the entire galaxy."

"Do not strain my computational innocence," Holgotha said. "You are too few to take on anyone."

125

"There you're wrong," I said. "If you provide the motive power, we'll show you a spectacle such as none of you artifacts has ever witnessed."

"This is vain boasting," Holgotha said.

"You claim to have curiosity circuits," I said. "In all your varied existence, don't you long for something new to see?"

"There is nothing new under the stars," Holgotha told me, as if he spoke a maxim.

"Have you ever spoken to someone like me?" I asked.

Holgotha said nothing. Time lengthened. Finally, the artifact said, "There was one like you long ago. It was during the last days of the First Ones, just before their disappearance. His rashness changed the complexity of the galaxy, causing the terrible loss of the Forerunners. We wondered if the Creator would appear to rectify the situation. During the next few centuries, we realized he had caused irreparable harm. Yes, I remember. He died brutally. Few mourned his passing. As I consider you, and given regular probabilities, you should have already died a vulgar death."

"I lead a charmed life," I said. "I'm difficult to kill."

"I fail to see why that should be."

"And yet, I'm here," I said. "Stick that in your pipe and smoke it."

From the far wall, N7 attempted to gain my attention. I ignored the android.

"You have aroused a modicum of interest," Holgotha told me. "What is your plan?"

"I want to use you as a mobile platform," I said, promptly. "You'll appear inside a planet's atmosphere. From you, the assault troopers will launch their attack. If things go badly for us, you can simply transfer back to the solar system."

"What is this spectacle I'm supposed to see?" Holgotha asked.

"A daring Star Viking raid," I said.

"What is that?"

"Agree to this and see," I said. "You won't regret it."

Holgotha fell silent, no doubt computing. Finally, the artifact said, "I see no benefit for myself. Worse, this will interrupt my investigation. Now, you must leave. I have grown weary of your incessant chatter."

"Wait a minute," I said, casting about for an angle. "You said there was one like me long ago. He changed many things, including the disappearance of the First Ones. Maybe I'll also change many things, but this time it will be for the better."

"I find that doubtful."

"The evidence says you're wrong."

"Explain this," Holgotha said.

"We humans were instrumental at the portal planet. Our actions halted Abaddon's invasion, which would have been a monumental event in the galaxy."

"This is startling to me," Holgotha said. "There is truth to what you say."

"Maybe humanity is the component the Forerunner artifacts need to shake things up. That shaking will bring about the appearance of the Creator."

"You spout sheer sophistry," Holgotha said. "It is time for you to depart."

"Wait," I said. "Let me finish. Nothing else has worked for you artifacts, right? I'm suggesting you try something new. I bet you've never been part of an assault before."

"That is true," Holgotha said. "I have not."

"For this trial run, you'll play the part of a military machine. Look, we Earthers have hit rock bottom. My envisioned raid will give us the tools we need to stand up again. Consider what happened last time we had the means. I'm speaking about our assault at the portal planet. We kicked ass. You do realize that the Lokhars fear us, right? Why otherwise did they strip us of our latest weaponry? The Jelk fear us. Abaddon and his Kargs rue our existence. If we only had the means—which this single raid will give us—there is nothing we might not accomplish."

I was stretching big time. But a sales pitch should be over the top. We needed this. Without a rich raid, I couldn't see how we'd build up in time to face the return of Baba Gobo, for instance. Never mind what else was coming our way.

"Yours is an interesting proposal," Holgotha said in what seemed to be a grudging manner. "There is a unique aspect to your puny race. I am curious to see what your rash mind has conceived. It is fitting that I warn you, though. If I am destroyed, your race will be blotted from existence. You are aware of that, yes?"

"I'm willing to roll the dice. Are you willing to try something new?"

"I am intrigued enough for a single venture," Holgotha said. "Afterward, I may well depart to a place far from you inquisitive humans. I find you to be an annoying race."

I don't know who was more surprised at my success, N7 or me. We had a shot, and we had to make it count. That meant we'd better pick the right target. After that, we'd unleash ourselves against the galaxy.

"Okay," I said. "You won't regret this." Turning to N7, I said, "Let's go. We have a lot to do to get ready."

-14-

With Holgotha's provisional acceptance to try the plan, we no longer had to worry about slinking through the jump lanes in our lone vessel. We would move directly to target. That meant we could leave the cruiser in the solar system if we wanted. It was time to decide what and how to do this exactly.

"I suggest we use every trooper we have for the raid," I told the others.

We stood in the conference room on Mars Base. A huge window showed the interior dome outside the chamber. Assault troopers jogged by in their zaguns across an asphalt running track.

Rollo, Dmitri, Ella, N7 and I debated policy. We had drinks in our hands. Rollo sipped beer, Dmitri and Ella wine, while N7 held a bubbling mixture only an android could love. I cradled a shot glass with a splash of whiskey at the bottom.

"I figure it like this," I said, setting the glass on the table. "We have to maximize the strike. Likely, it's the only one where we'll have the artifact. Therefore, we should take every assault trooper, grab a horde of ships and rush back with them to Earth. Then we can think about our next target."

"Shouldn't we leave a few assault troopers behind to garrison Mars Base and our equipment on Ceres?" asked Ella.

Before I could answer, Dmitri said, "Since the artifact is our transport, it seems senseless to fortify Ceres. There's nothing to guard out there anymore, at least while we're gone."

"Good point," I said. "Where should we fortify?"

"The only place that matters," Rollo said, "Earth. And that means the Moon. Take all the hardware at Ceres and set it up there. Let the Earth Council decide who runs it."

"Do the rest of you agree?" I asked.

The others nodded or murmured their assent.

"Okay," I said, "next order of business. What do we do with the *Glorious Hope*? Do we take it with us or leave it behind for the Earth Council."

"Better to take it with us," Dmitri said.

"Depends on where we're hitting," Rollo said.

"If we perish," Ella said, "wouldn't it be better for humanity to have at least one warship with its Moon fortress?"

"I'm inclined to agree with Ella," I said. "What do you think, N7?"

"What happens to the androids in storage?" N7 asked. "The ones we took from the Demar Starcity."

That was a good question. We hashed it out and decided to unpack them. They would help fortify the Moon.

We decided to hold off on making a decision about the cruiser. First, we'd have to know the target. That was going to take some thinking. Before that, we had to ready the solar system for our absence.

Work revved up after the meeting. We hauled the defensive equipment from Ceres to the Moon. Then we dismantled parts from Mars Base. During our absence, humanity would porcupine around the mother planet. It was poisoned, but it was still home.

I spoke to Diana and Murad Bey. With our coming absence, their power would increase, but so would their vulnerability. They asked questions. I supplied few answers. I wondered if the Shi-Feng had sleepers among the last survivors in the freighters.

Finally, we had to decide on the target. I secreted myself with N7, deciding to thrash it with the only person who knew more than I did about the region of space around us.

N7 had begun existence as a Jelk mining android. When the assault troopers had been under Shah Claath's employ, the Rumpelstiltskin devil had used androids as our drill instructors. Because of that, the N-series androids gained upgrades. N7 had proven better and more successful than his fellow machines, and he had consistently won more improvements. During the Sigma Draconis campaign, N7 decided to cast his lot with us. He helped us gain our freedom as we attacked Claath's battlejumper.

N7's memory cores never forgot anything. Even better, he could retrieve the memories. He did so now as we stood on *Glorious Hope's* bridge.

"You ask me where we should attack," N7 said. "That depends on your requirements."

"That's simple," I said. "I want warships, better light arms for assault troopers, haulers to carry it back, anti-bio-terminator scrubbers and better planetary missile and ground-based beam systems."

"One requirement makes the choice obvious at least in one regard," N7 said.

"What would that be?" I asked.

"For anti-bio-terminator scrubbers, you will have to attack a Lokhar world. The Saurians lack such hardware, at least in any abundance."

"So be it," I said.

N7 observed me. "You do not mind declaring war against the Lokhars?"

"Who said anything about that? I just want to grab what I need. There's no declaration of war."

"The Lokhars might view it differently."

"I'm thinking they have enough on their hands with a civil war brewing. Besides, how will they know it's been us? If we strike deeply enough, they'll absolutely *know* it couldn't have been us humans who struck."

N7 appeared dubious. "Eventually, the other races will learn that an artifact aided humanity."

"I don't see why that's a given. We'll have to take great care after the assault. During the Vietnam War, the NVA soldiers usually dragged away their dead after a firefight. It made it seem as if the U.S. seldom slew that many. We'll expand upon the idea."

N7 become thoughtful. "That would imply you don't plan to leave any survivors to report on our attack."

That was a good point. I mulled it over, finally saying, "The Lokhars nuked the Earth and sprayed the survivors with a bio-terminator. They started this. They can pay for it. I have no problem grabbing what we need from a Lokhar world and ensuring no tigers survive the attack. In fact, the more I think about it, the better I like it."

I was also thinking about the Shi-Feng. They would be out there.

"Emotions are not the best guide in these matters," N7 told me.

"You're wrong," I said. "The heart is everything. Without it, logic means nothing. You have to *want* something in order to fight for it and that desire comes from in here," I said, tapping my chest.

"Perhaps you are right. In this area, I will not dispute you."

"Great," I said. "Given our requirements, do you know which system we should raid?"

N7 turned toward the viewing port. In its reflection, I saw the android's eyelids fluttering. At last, N7 turned back to me.

"The Sanakaht star system seems ideal for your needs," N7 said. "It possesses a small world with vast abundance. There are many mineral asteroids in the system and heavy metal moons. Sanakaht the planet is so small that many freighters land to load and unload cargo. My cores tell of surface shipyards building warships that would otherwise be constructed in space."

"Tell me more," I said.

N7 did.

Afterward, I pondered the information. I needed a situation where I could employ the bio-suited assault troopers. I thought hard, finding difficulties in the location. Holgotha couldn't very well teleport onto the ground. The artifact would have to appear in the atmosphere. Getting everyone off the giant donut would be the problem. The assault troopers would have to jump, maybe use parachutes, parasails or—

I snapped my fingers and pointed at N7. "I have it. I know how we're going to this." I laughed as I envisioned the attack. It would be wild, wooly and maybe the most exhilarating ride of my life.

"What is your idea?" N7 asked.

"Do you remember the air-cycles we carted from the Demar Starcity?"

N7 froze a moment, before nodding. "Of course I recall. They are the DZ9 air-mobile attack cycle. The originator—"

"Yeah," I said. "I don't need those kinds of details. Tell me what they can do."

"I am not familiar with them in that aspect."

"Then it's time to become familiar. We'll test them on Mars."

"How many cycles will we use" N7 asked.

"All of them," I said.

"All?"

"Yeah. That's right."

***

Before I unpacked all the air-cycles, I took several to Mars. A few trial runs showed a problem. After several passes, the fine sands of the Red Planet clogged the air-intakes. This wasn't a desert flyer.

Even so, the DZ9 air-mobile cycle was an interesting vehicle. The closest equivalent Earth craft would have been a bulked-up jet ski that was able to fly through the skies.

Taking several to Earth, I did some trial runs. They flew well enough. The trouble was scrubbing everyone afterward. Finally, I took a few air-cycles out to Titan with its molecular nitrogen atmosphere. That proved the right decision.

N7 said Titan was closer in size to our targeted world than any other planetary body in the solar system. That was good to learn, as it would solve the biggest problem: how to get four thousand assault troopers down to the surface in a hurry.

The air-cycles were big enough so troopers could double up on one. On Titan, we practiced dropping from a Demar hauler. With two troopers, their suits and equipment, that meant squeezing onto the seat. It also meant more than normal weight. With Titan's thin atmosphere, the loaded air-cycles dropped fast.

We lost seventeen of them to crashes. Five troopers died. I hated that. For two weeks, we practiced so we could get it right against the Lokhars.

Four mingans of assault troopers were going to hit Sanakaht. Likely, that was too few. The small planet boasted big shipyards. That would mean protection, right?

"We don't have a choice in this," I said, bringing up a tough subject. "We're going to have to deploy missiles from the artifact. We need to take out the areas too far to hit with our troopers."

"If you do that," N7 said, "you're risking return fire."

"I realize that."

"What kind of warheads will we use?" Rollo asked.

Here it was: the tough choice. "Thermonuclear," I said.

Silence reigned. Ella grew pale. "Creed—"

"Stow your complaints," I said. "We have to use nukes. We're too weak to play fancy." I stared into their eyes. "Look, people, this is the big strike. We have to win huge this time. If we don't, it could be over for our race."

"The Lokhars will retaliate against us," Ella said.

I snorted. "This is our retaliation for what they did to Earth."

"The tiger Emperor has helped us since then," Ella said.

"Has he really?" I asked. "Who do you think sanctioned the Shi-Feng attack in Wyoming?"

"All indications show they are a holy order," Ella said.

"Holy my ass," I said. "They're assassins. I bet they're tight with the Emperor. Besides, he reneged on his deal and took away our warships." I pounded the table with a fist. "You'd better believe we're going to use thermonuclear weapons. We're smashing Sanakaht flat and taking its goodies."

"Is that how old-time Vikings did it?" Dmitri asked.

"We're Star Vikings, Earth's last hope. Not only do we have to win, but we'd better do it so they don't know who hit them. That means we flatten their planetary defenses, strike, grab, get back up to the artifact and disappear before the space assets arrive."

"That isn't going to give us much time," Ella said.

134

"No, it isn't," I agreed.

"I'm not sure this is the best idea," Ella said. "Perhaps we should strike another Saurian-guarded star system."

I stood up and walked to the viewing screen. With the click of a switch, I turned it to Olympus Mons. Fiddling with the controls, I scanned up to the top cone.

"The Lokhars put their flag up there," I said. "That's claiming territory."

"It may have a different purpose in Lokhar culture," N7 said.

"I'm guessing you're wrong about that," I said. "My point is that they came to our star system and planted their flag on our biggest mountain. Was that a Freudian slip?"

"What does that mean?" N7 asked.

I ignored the android's question. Turning to the others, I said, "Look at this another way. Doctor Sant has gone on a walking tour, spouting religious rebellion. It's frightened the Purple Tamika Emperor. He's gathered an armada, maybe to squash the rebellion. Our strike way out at Sanakaht might aid Orange Tamika, and that could possibly aid us in the long run."

"How do you reason this?" N7 asked.

"If we do this right," I said, "Sant might point to Sanakaht as the judgment of the Creator. Let's suppose a few tigers survive. They'll talk about an artifact appearing. The Lokhars are crazy concerning the Forerunner objects. Many tigers swayed by Sant might view the attack as just deserts for the sins caused by the Purple Tamika Emperor."

"That's silly," Ella said, "and it's really reaching."

"No," Rollo said. "I think Creed has a point. You don't see that, Ella, because it doesn't mix with your world-view. The way a tiger looks at the universe, yes, the attack might help Sant's theological rebellion."

"If Lokhars survive on Sanakaht and report on an artifact," N7 said, "that might give away our involvement. Surely, the others would consider us the primary culprits."

"Yes," Ella said. "They know Creed is unbalanced enough to attack them and would suspect him of having suborned our artifact. He knows its name, after all, which they consider vital. For that reason alone, we must pick a different target."

135

We went around and around with the debate. In the end, I put it to a vote.

Ella turned her thumb down. She wanted to hit the Saurians again. "We have a proven method for dealing with the lizards," she said. "It worked last time. It's always best to use what has actually succeeded."

"Nope," Rollo said, aiming the open end of his beer bottle at her. "I say we follow Creed. We're all free because he had the balls to try outlandish feats, beginning in Antarctica. I say we should hit Sanakaht."

"The tigers sent assassins at Creed, blowing themselves up to get him," Dmitri said. "I think we should blow *them* up with thermonuclear weapons. I say we raid Sanakaht for supplies and then stomp them flat afterward."

We all turned to N7.

"I began as the Commander's adversary," the android said. "Since then, I have learned to marvel at his ploys. Let us attack Sanakaht as he wishes."

I faced Ella, raising an eyebrow.

"Yes," she said tiredly. "Let's attack Sanakaht."

"Your wish is my command," I said. "In five days, seven at most, we strike back at the tigers."

136

-15-

It ended up taking thirteen days to coordinate everything. As D-Day approached, my fears increased.

We were about to transfer hundreds of light years into a planet's atmosphere. I couldn't conceive the technology such an event would take. The coordination was beyond phenomenal. It was the next thing to supernatural.

I wondered if I was getting religion. Wasn't that crazy? But a small part of me wondered about the ethics of using such a spectacular machine as Holgotha in such a bloody, murderous venture.

Most of the time, endless work submerged my qualms. I preferred that to worried pondering. The rest of the days, I used my imagination, stretching it to its utmost.

N7 and Ella helped me. We had to envision the situation with gravity present. Holgotha would have to stay airborne. The day I'd spoken to him, he hadn't seemed concerned about the problem. I didn't know if that meant he hadn't considered the situation in detail or if he simply already knew what he needed to do.

I'd find out on D-Day when everything was in place. The hour rapidly approached.

Finally, the missiles, the planetary beam cannons, the air-cycles and a Demar hauler moved into position. In the Asteroid Belt, we unloaded everything but the hauler onto the artifact's surface. The spaceship would remain in the vicinity. At Altair, we'd seen that everything in a nearby radius left with the

137

transferring artifact. Once the hauler reached Sanakaht with us, it would lift into a low planetary orbit, deploying drones to act as a temporary space force.

It took hours arranging everyone in the proper location. Before I trudged off to speak with Holgotha again, I wanted to make certain everything was ready for battle conditions.

We had a command center on Holgotha's surface. We had missile launchers to strike outlying areas on Sanakaht and planetary beam cannons to hammer in a direct line of sight whatever would need it. Finally, we had Star Vikings. The former assault troopers wore their bio-suits, shouldered their light arms and waited beside the air-cycles.

With everyone waiting, I began the journey in my heavy vacc-suit. Walking alone, I headed for the curve that would bring me in sight of the black hole and then the small city on the inner circle.

In time, I waited before the wall. Would Holgotha be too immersed in his computations to remember the plan? Would I have to go over everything again?

No. I put my hand against the wall, and it went through. A vast sense of relief swept over me. I laughed aloud in my helmet. Then, I began the final trek to see Holgotha.

Soon enough, I stood in the same white chamber as before. It felt different without N7. The fantastic age of Holgotha impinged upon my senses. Who was I to try to trick an ancient Forerunner artifact? I felt like a bullfrog who had puffed himself up so large he might end up exploding.

"Why have you returned so soon?" Holgotha asked in his deep voice.

I stood, holding my helmet. I tried not to think how easy it would be for the artifact to snuff out my life.

"I've gathered the troops," I said.

"A moment," the artifact said. "Ah. I see. Time has elapsed since we last spoke."

I reminded myself that Holgotha's perception of time was different from mine.

"Yes," I said, trying to sound more confident than I felt. "The assault troopers are in position."

"You have other machinery on my surface areas."

138

"A few missile batteries," I said.

"They are of grossly inferior design compared to me. I do not want them on my surface lest some come to believe they are mine."

"As soon as we're at Sanakaht, the majority of the hardware will leave."

"You will remove the inferior machinery off me at once," Holgotha said.

I stood there blinking. "We, need the machines."

"That was not part of the bargain," Holgotha said.

"Why are you being so stubborn?" I asked. "Those items were implied. We're not like you, Holgotha. Humans need their tools to amplify their abilities."

"Inferior equipment breeds inferior results," the artifact boomed.

"Don't you think we know that?"

"Not necessarily," the artifact said.

"That's why we're making this run in the first place. We need superior equipment."

"Why do you seek Lokhar weapons then? You should espouse for the best Jelk equipment."

"We've made our plans," I said. "For us, they're quite elaborate tactical ideas. We've trained for Sanakaht. Now, with the entirety of our equipment, we're hoping to get started."

"When?"

"Now," I said. "When did you think?"

"I see. Very well, give me the galactic coordinates of your destination point."

Closing my eyes in frustration, I realized I should have brought N7 along. The android waited at the command center. I wanted him ready to make decisions the instant we appeared in the planet's atmosphere.

"Are you familiar with the Sanakaht star system?" I asked.

"By the entomology, that sounds like a Lokhar name."

"Right," I said.

"I am unfamiliar with Lokhar galactic coordinates."

"Come on," I said. "You're trying to stall. I thought your given word meant something."

"Holgotha does not stall," he said. "You are besmirching my honor with such words."

My facial skin turned cold with fear. I sensed his anger, and I didn't like it. What did I really know about the artifact? The answer was practically nothing. I hadn't expected a sense of advanced computer honor.

"You're taking my meaning wrong," I said.

"I have correctly analyzed your words. They have incensed me."

"You know, the trouble is I expected you to act like me."

"Me respond like an animal?" Holgotha asked.

"There you go. I'm a biological being. Therefore, I expect sentient objects to act in a similar manner."

Holgotha grew silent for a time. Finally, "Yes. My memory files agree that many creatures act in the way you describe. I do not act in that manner, however. I am Holgotha, a thinking machine of the First Ones."

"So, what I'm suggesting is that you take the Lokhar name and correlate it with your ancient star coordinate name."

"What does that have to do with your accusation of my stalling?"

"Very little," I said. "I'm trying to drop the subject because it has made you angry. I don't want to offend you."

"This is your attempt at an apology?"

"I'm sorry I insulted you," I said. "Just so you know. No one else has gotten that much from me."

"I accept your groveling," Holgotha said.

I almost shook my head in annoyance. Instead, I sighed. Very well, let him think I'd been groveling. Let's just get started already.

"Where is the star system Sanakaht?" Holgotha asked me.

I told him the best I could figure it.

"A moment while I correlate," he said.

I waited twenty minutes, which surprised me at first. Then, it made me nervous. I began to sweat. That made my symbiotic skin shift in delight under the heavy vacc-suit.

"I have the old galactic charts," Holgotha said.

My head snapped up, and I chuckled nervously. His talking after being silent so long startled me.

140

"That's great to hear," I said.

"I cannot find the Sanakaht star system, though."

"That's what the Lokhars call it," I said. "You should be able to find what the First Ones named it."

This time it took the artifact twenty seconds. "You mean the star system—" He gave me an unpronounceable name.

During our attack on the portal planet, I'd had a chance to view what might have been First Ones. They had looked like giant centipedes. I hadn't liked the thought of that at the time. Could what I'd seen have been a representation of a serpent?

I knew which side snakes were supposed to be on, and it wasn't the side of the angels. Now, hearing the ancient unpronounceable name, I shifted my shoulders uneasily.

"Where on the planet should we land?" Holgotha asked.

"Not on the surface," I said. "You're going to appear in the atmosphere."

"That is acceptable," the artifact said. "Now give me the coordinates for the exact location on the planet."

"You're kidding me, right? I don't have that kind of information."

"How will I know where to appear, then?"

Then it struck me. I wondered how any of us had missed it. How indeed would a machine know where to transfer hundreds of light years away?

"Can you see where you're going before you move?" I asked.

"Of course," Holgotha said. "It would be foolish to travel in this manner otherwise."

"Can you show me a map of the planet as it is now?"

"I can," Holgotha said.

"Right," I said. "Let's do it then, and I can tell you."

A minute later, I viewed Sanakaht through Holgotha's screen. The world had green continents and big lakes, no oceans that I could see. I didn't ask him how he could scan this distance. Frankly, I doubted I would have understood the technology that did it. Since I saw the effect of the tech, I figured that was good enough.

"Can you give me a closer scrutiny?" I asked.

141

He did. I examined several cities and finally fixed upon a shipyard. There were tigers and machines everywhere. I counted the missile batteries and the orbital platforms, trying to memorize everything. Next time—if there was one—I'd bring N7 along with me.

Finally, I showed the artifact the spot to transfer.

"When do you wish to relocate?" Holgotha asked.

"Can you give me an hour to leave here and reach my people on your surface?"

"Yes," the artifact said.

"Well. That's it then. I'm going to leave. An hour after I exit the building, transfer to the atmosphere of Sanakaht."

"When will you wish to return?"

I blinked several times. Why hadn't I thought of that before? Been too busy, I guess. "I'll walk back here and tell you."

"And if you die on Sanakaht?" Holgotha asked.

"Then N7, Rollo, Dmitri or Ella will come and ask you to return to the solar system."

"Noted and accepted," the artifact said. "I will be observing your action on Sanakaht. Afterward, I will make my decision whether I will remain among your savage species."

"Sure," I said. "I look forward to your decision."

"We shall see," Holgotha said.

"Yeah," I said, mainly so I'd get the last word in instead of Holgotha.

***

I reached the mobile command post on the surface of Holgotha. A thought kept troubling me. Would the artifact keep the right side "up" when he appeared in the atmosphere? Gravity would pull at us then. If the donut-shaped artifact transferred the wrong way, we'd all fall off onto Sanakaht. That would end the Star Viking raid right there.

For the next twenty-three minutes, I fretted over the problem.

"You should have set up a communication system with the artifact from here," Ella radioed me.

142

I should have done many things differently. Thinking myself imaginative, I'd failed to consider too much. Humanity wouldn't survive on luck, although we needed it.

"Ella," I said. That was as far as I got.

Space began to blur. At first, just the edges seemed fuzzy. Soon, everything became blurry and indistinct. Then colors flowed out of the darkness of space. The pin-dot stars swirled, spinning faster and faster.

I heard a garbled message in my headphones. Then, sounds dwindled into nothing. The space merging became painful to look upon, so I closed my eyes. Vertigo hit me. Nausea caused stomach acid to burn the back of my throat.

Last time—seven years ago—I'd blanked out as this happened. Now, I fought to remain conscious. I wanted to man the guns right away on Sanakaht.

Around me, assault troopers began thudding onto the metal surface. Some of them thrashed about. What if the nuclear warheads went off accidentally?

If they did, that would be game-over. Since I'd be dead then, I wouldn't have to face the shame. So, I quit worrying about it.

At that point in my thinking, a yawning abyss seemed to grow before my strained senses. What mechanics did the artifact use to make the transfer?

The First Ones knew so much more than we did. What had made them so smart? Could the tigers be right about the beginning? Had a creator formed everything? Wouldn't those in the beginning be the best, with everything running down afterward? That was an old ontological argument: the wound-up clock. God set it up, all wound-up, and since then the universe wound down toward entropy. Things went from extreme order to disorder, taking a long time to do it in.

Ella didn't buy any of that. She believed random chance plus long time-periods created order.

At that moment, I didn't care. I hurt. My symbiotic suit squirmed. Then everything changed. Something dragged against me, pulling down, clawing at my atoms. Finally, I realized what had happened. I'd come to a place with gravity.

I opened my eyes. I spied blue above along with faint images of stars and two moons.

Why am I seeing two moons?

It troubled me for ten harrowing seconds. I began to panic. Then, I realized we'd transferred, traveling hundreds of light years in the blink of an eye. Our asteroid-sized Forerunner artifact hovered high in Sanakaht's atmosphere.

-16-

Around me, assault troopers stirred on the silvery surface.

No, I told myself. *We're Star Vikings. We have to think of this as gathering loot, not conquering an enemy.*

"Ella, can you hear me?" I said into my helmet microphone. When she didn't respond, I said, "N7?"

"Yes, Commander," the android said.

"Where are you?" I asked, looking around.

Air-cycles lay clumped nearby with Star Vikings beginning to drag themselves to a sitting position. Farther away, large beam cannons aimed targeting apertures in various directions. Bigger generating systems hummed quietly beside them with thick cables linking the two. Beyond them, like waiting attack-dogs, leaned the thermonuclear-tipped missiles. We'd literally packed tons of deadly ordnance in one small area.

The only non-symbiotic-suited trooper raised his arm. He wore a cyber-suit. It was similar to Lokhar powered armor. N7 would stay up here on the artifact at the mobile commander center.

"Come here and give me a hand," I said. "I want to pinpoint the outlying targets."

The command center was composed of heavy tables with computers, targeting systems and drone equipment. We sat under the open air with a few high clouds above. Far below so everything merged together was the Sanakaht surface. It was bright green like a fairy tale with a ribbon river to the left.

145

As others began to stir around me, N7 and I sat on swivel-seats, tapping screens.

Large-winged drones buzzed with noise. The mini-planes sped on the surface before lifting sharply. They had hypervelocity settings, but each needed a target before we engaged the high-Mach speeds.

Trying to remember what I'd seen inside Holgotha, I told N7 about the different tiger defensive establishments.

The two of us sat side-by-side. We played the part of drone pilots. Soon enough, our boards lit up. The sniffing drones picked up radiation and Lokhar radar signals.

Tap, tap, tap.

One after another, the drones kicked into hypervelocity. They sped to check out the various military installations. Most of them were over the horizon.

Sanakaht had ten percent greater mass than Titan possessed. Saturn's moon had a diameter of 5120 kilometers. It meant we were light and strong here, and that the horizon was much closer than it would be on Earth or even Mars.

As the drones dwindled into dots and disappeared from my naked eyesight, I had time to ponder the situation.

A monster asteroid had just appeared high in Sanakaht's atmosphere. One would think such an occurrence would have freaked out everyone on the planet. I'm sure that's what happened. We must have achieved surprise, complete and total shock. How could it be otherwise? Giant metal donuts with artificial black holes don't just appear in skies. Yet here we hovered, bearing a brutal life lesson for the Lokhars below.

I believe we achieved bewildering surprise over the Lokhars. It gave the assault troopers time to stir and gather their wits.

As Star Vikings righted their air-cycles, my first drone reached its destination.

On my screen, I observed closed silos. No tiger technician ran across the grounds. No Lokhar cars screeched, sending up smoke. The place lay placid and serene.

A glance at N7's screen showed me similar complacency. No. I take that back. As the android switched to another drone,

I saw big circular plates in the ground dilate open. A focusing mirror rose to do battle against us.

"It's time to launch, boys and girls," I said.

N7 glanced at me.

"Yeah," I said. "I mean you and me, just boys this time."

With quick precise taps, N7 did the honors.

Around us, the artifact trembled as two dozen missiles took flight. They roared with spewing fire, leaving thick smoky trails in the sky.

I had to close my mouth and let my eyes blink several times. The missiles gained velocity fast. Much quicker than the drones had done, the missiles dwindled out of sight.

"Get the beam cannons lined up!" I shouted. "We want to knock down all the defensive satellites upstairs."

Others now began to sit down at their tables, adjusting computer screens. Chatter increased between them.

The big focusing systems swiveled. Some aimed up. Others watched the horizon for tiger attack-craft. Soon, stabbing rays reached up from Holgotha.

I'd moved behind the new command team. On a screen, I watched a laser beam eat into an armored defensive satellite in orbit. The ray burned white-hot substance, turning the rest of the outpost into vapor. As predicted, Lokhar satellite weapons system had their cannons aimed into space not down at the planet.

Craning my neck, I watched the Demar hauler. Smoke poured from its exhaust ports. Flames flickered through it at times. The spaceship climbed for orbital space. There, it would unload its missile-drones. Their task was to knock down any approaching starships.

"We're doing it," I said.

For the next few minutes, I stood content. Rollo, Dmitri and other commanders gathered their attack teams. On the radio-nets, they gave last minute instructions.

A woman cursed softly in horror.

I looked up. Someone grabbed my bio-suited triceps and pointed to the left. I saw what had made her curse.

Checking a helmet chronometer, I realized that ten minutes after Holgotha's appearance in Sanakaht's skies, the first thermonuclear warhead went off on the planet's surface. Given the mushroom's size, this one had to be fifty kilometers away. The cloud kept growing, rising and expanding as it radiated dirt. There wasn't anything pretty about this. Yet in its own way, the atomic cloud had a horrible majesty.

I saw another, a third, fourth, fifth—

With an oath, I turned away from the explosions. We were doing to the Lokhars what they had done to us. Part of me exuded savagery at the act, but another part felt small and dirty. Nuking planetary structures just seemed wrong. I wondered if I had let my hatred and my need get the better of me.

First breathing deeply, I asked, "Ella, N7, do you have everything under control?"

"Affirmative," N7 said.

"Yes," Ella whispered. She stared into the distance at the biggest mushroom cloud.

"Don't look at them," I told her.

She aimed her visor at me.

"We had to use them," I said. "We have to knock out their retaliatory ability in order to win this fight."

"I know," she whispered. "It doesn't mean I have to like it."

I swallowed down a snappy retort. Maybe sticking to business was the best way to play this.

"Keep everything off our backs," I told her. "I don't want any Lokhar spacecraft, star fighters or even balloons in the air. Knock down everything. We're going to hit the spaceyard."

Ella's visor moved up and down in acknowledgement. "Be careful, Creed. The tigers hate you."

"Some of them at least," I said.

"There could be Shi-Feng on Sanakaht."

Thank you, Ella Timoshenko. Her words snapped me out of my brooding. We nuked them because we had no choice. This was their fault, not ours.

"I'm hoping there's some Shi-Feng," I said. Spinning around, I sprinted for my air-cycle. The time for contemplation and planning had passed. It was time to rock and roll.

***

148

As if an internal switch had flipped, my outlook changed as I ran from the command center to my cycle. Worry about unleashing nuclear holocausts dwindled just as the drones had done from my sight. I found myself grinning.

Then I leaped onto my Saurian-built DZ9 air-cycle. Sometimes, life could be glorious and sublime. A few like me rode alone without a back-sitting passenger. Twisting the throttle gave me power. With a hum of energy, I rose into the air. All around me, troopers lifted above Holgotha's gleaming surface.

Over my headphones, I heard radio chatter, commands and grid coordinates. I heard bubbling engines and saw airborne troopers bobbing several centimeters up and down.

I gunned my machine, speeding away from the artifact. For a sick moment, fear curdled my gut. I zipped past the silver donut surface and hung over a vast abyss of air. Far below me spread out Sanakaht's green surface.

The fear evaporated as I shouted, "Here were go!" The sound reverberated inside my helmet. I loved it.

Then, as if I were in the middle of a cartoon, my air-cycle dropped. I plummeted toward destiny. Around me, other air-cyclists dropped likewise.

I could feel my lips stretch into a wild grin. This was too awesome. Today, I had become Superman. Titling my air-cycle's nose downward, I gave it more power. I sped down for the spaceyard like a bullet.

Whooping like a berserk Hell's Angel, I lead the pack down upon the Lokhars. This had to be the greatest moment of my life.

"We're the Star Vikings, baby!" I shouted. "We're here to rock your world and bust your balls!"

As my velocity built, my machine began to shake. I loved it. Hunkering lower, I sledded down like a madman. A quick twist of my head backward showed me a horde of Star Vikings hot-dogging it after me on their DZ9 cycles.

Maybe the tigers had AA guns and missiles. Stolen Saurian beam cannons lanced their rays down from Holgotha. They burned defensive equipment out of existence.

I'll spare the sensitive and anti-poetic among you. Riding the air-cycles, we swooped toward the spaceyard. It might have been a little after lunchtime Sanakaht-time.

Buildings soon came into focus. Smashed missiles and jumbo-jet craft burned crazily on the ground. Most of them sent up thick oily smoke. Things like bus-sized dune buggies raced away from the spaceyard. Other tigers sprinted for cover. A few took potshots at us with hunting weapons.

At that point, I don't know what everyone else did, but I can tell you how I enjoyed my visit over Sanakaht. Rocketing like vengeance, I chased several dune buggy buses. They rocked up and down on the road and swayed side to side. The vehicles had some springs. The path looked like a steel highway. It reflected the harsh sunlight, forcing my visor to darken.

In the nearest buggy, ten tigers turned around. A few pointed with their fingers. I couldn't tell if they'd exposed their claws. One cocked his arm and tossed what must have been a grenade. It exploded in the air far before me, leaving a black mark. I dodged it just in case. Only two tigers seemed to have guns, and those were stubby like carbines.

As I closed the distance, the carbines bucked upward. Did the tigers fire bullets? I couldn't see any laser or particle beam.

With both hands on the bars, I swooped down after the bus like a hawk from Hell. None of our air-cycles boasted integral ordnance. These things were as innocent of weaponry as the first biplanes in World War I on Earth. Yet just like the first observers in those biplanes, I carried a handgun. Mine did not pop weak slugs. I had a heavy laser pistol specially selected for this.

A coil linked the pistol to an energy pack strapped to the air-cycle.

Guiding the cycle one-handed, I drew smoothly. The tigers kept shooting. A bullet might have hit my cycle. It rocked. Another slug definitely struck my bio-armor. I felt a sting of pain in my side. Soothing coolness smothered the sensation almost instantly.

I pulled the trigger. The beam lanced down, visible on my HUD. It rayed beside the buggy. As I closed the final distance,

I adjusted. The beam cut down several tigers, including one of the rifle-Lokhars.

My HUD schematics showed me the buggy's fuel pod. I held the ray there for two seconds. Then my cycle passed overhead by ten meters. Behind me, I heard a terrific explosion.

I twisted around and had the distinct pleasure of watching the bus flip. Tigers spilled out, raining onto the road and the soft ground beside it. Then the buggy crashed, shedding metal. And it exploded again, flipping and twisting the thing.

I turned forward, holding the air-cycle's bars with both hands. The concussions from the bus made it a bumpy few seconds.

After turning the DZ9 around, heading back at the buggy pack, I found myself roaring with laughter. I'd been waiting to do something like this for a long time. I remembered seeing my dad—Mad Jack Creed—dying from a tiger beam. I remembered the cities of Earth igniting, including my hometown. I could also remember little penguins keeling over and spitting black gunk.

The laughter changed to snarls of savagery. With each pass, I took out another dune buggy. *Whoosh*, I'd rush over the vehicles, beaming. Then I'd turn the handlebars, swinging around, heading back—*whoosh.*

Big old dune buses burned on the steel highway. Dead tigers bled. It had become their personal Highway of Death. The U.S. military had done the same thing to the soldiers of Saddam Hussein in 1991.

Here on this alien world, we taught a few Lokhars why their brethren shouldn't have nuked the Earth.

After the sixth pass, it finally dawned on me that I'd let my symbiotic suit get the better of me. For once, I'd gotten carried away with battle-madness and bloodlust.

It took a minute of intense internal dialogue to head for the spaceyard. Killing Lokhars had its own appeal. Coming home victorious to Earth trumped that.

It was time for me to go tactical and remember the victory conditions. That was to bring home as many assault troopers as I could, along with prime loot.

151

Killing tigers didn't count in that. Grabbing territory didn't matter at all, either. But I needed to ensure we brought back as much stuff as possible.

Turning the air-cycle, I sped above the gunmetal-colored road. The spaceyard was in the distance. Behind me spread out a Lokhar city. This one had tall steel towers like old science-fiction posters. Big block buildings glittered with sunlight. I saw a tiger air car take off one of those. It raced away.

That didn't seem good, but I wasn't going to worry about it now.

Facing forward, I saw Star Viking cycles dipping and darting above the spaceyard. As I neared, I heard tiger roars, screams of agony and machine gun chatter. An air-cycle broke apart, its two riders falling a hundred meters, no doubt to their deaths.

The high-pitched whine of lasers focused my vision. I saw bright rays stabbing down from the back riders. Tigers curled on the ground like bugs burning beneath a child's magnifying glass on a hot August day.

The heavy machine gun quit firing. Then it started up again. Other Star Vikings killed those Lokhars, too.

A new squadron of cycles from Holgotha roared toward an empty tarmac. Rollo shouted orders. I heard them on my headphones.

The spaceyard had big skeleton girders. Inside most of those cradles sat spaceships. A few were mere skeletons themselves. Other half-completed jobs showed pleasure yachts and military patrol craft. Several big warships looked finished to my eye. Seeing them made me grin.

Then one of those ignited. Geysers of metal and electrical wires fountained into the air. Tigers raced away from the damage.

Sabotage. They wrecked the warship.

I gunned my cycle, heading for the other completed cruisers and missile-ships. We needed those, all of them we could grab.

I landed hard, running before my cycle had quit humming. Yelling at an arban of troopers to follow me, I began hunting for saboteurs.

152

We flushed three Lokhars trying to plant a bomb on the side of a cruiser. As we approached, one of them leaped to his feet and raced nearer, igniting into a fireball, taking two Star Vikings with him.

"Get down!" I shouted.

The next Lokhar sprinted at us. He moved fast with smooth rhythm.

The rest of the arban reacted beautifully, hitting the deck. The second tiger exploded harmlessly. That left the last one.

They work in triads, I thought to myself. *These tigers were Shi-Feng.*

The last Lokhar's gaze locked with mine. He began to squint, which I recalled was the firing mechanism. I beamed him in the head; to the side, it turned out. Yeah, I should have hit the ground like the other troopers. Instead, I waited for the explosion. It didn't come. The tiger slumped onto the ground and didn't ignite. Had my headshot shorted whatever mechanism made him blow up?

I debated beaming his body into a crisp. We couldn't take chances with the Shi-Feng. Then, I reconsidered. I'd like to get my hands on one of the holy Lokhar warriors.

"Get up," I told the troopers. "Back away from his body."

"Sir," their leader said, a woman named Zoe Artemis. "You should back up, too. We can't afford to lose you."

"I have to check something."

Zoe glanced at the remaining arban of troopers. Something passed between them. They rushed me.

"What are you doing?" I shouted as they grabbed my arms. They dragged me farther from the downed tiger. Smoke trickled from his wounded head.

"What we *should* do, sir," Zoe said, answering my question. "We're keeping you out of danger. Henry, check the tiger."

I struggled, but there were several of them and only one of me. "I just want to know if he's still alive," I said.

Gingerly, the selected trooper bent over the obvious Shi-Feng Lokhar. "He's still breathing," Henry said.

Zoe aimed her silver visor at me. "What should we do with him, sir?"

I thought fast. "Do you have any bomb detectors?"

"Yes, sir," she said.

"Check the tiger for explosives."

"Where does he carry them?" she asked.

"In his body is my guess."

Zoe stared at me a moment later. Then she snapped her head around, facing the trooper. "Henry," she said, "back away from the tiger."

He did, fast.

Soon, with the others still holding my arms, Zoe approached the unconscious tiger. The Lokhar had a hole in his head that leaked blood onto the tarmac. Zoe had a boxlike device aimed at the Shi-Feng.

She adjusted dials and turned to us. "He's definitely got explosives in him," she reported.

"Can you remove them?" I asked.

"Are you kidding me?" Zoe asked. "According to this—" she raised the detector— "the junk is in his stomach."

"I realize that. Can you take it out of him?"

Zoe didn't stare as long this time. "There's only one way to find out, Commander."

"He might blow up if you try," I said. "Let me do it."

She motioned to her troopers. They dragged me farther away.

With her Bahnkouv, Zoe Artemis beamed the tiger's stomach, slicing open his stomach with a deft touch. Then, she knelt and reached in with a bio-suited hand. A second later, she yanked out a bomb with bloody wires. Cocking her arm, she hurled the warhead, doing it none too soon.

With a terrific blast, the bomb exploded in midair. A zagun of troopers turned and stared.

Zoe re-aimed her detector at the Lokhar. "He's clean now, sir," she said. Her head jerked. It must have been a signal.

The four troopers released me. I hurried to the tiger.

"No hard feelings, sir," Zoe told me. "We were just following orders."

I said nothing. Instead, kneeling beside the defused Shi-Feng, I took out a medikit. With it, I began to patch him the best I could.

154

"Are you trying to keep him alive, sir?" Zoe asked behind my back.

"As of now," I said, "your task is to bring the tiger back alive. I want him upstairs with us when we leave."

Zoe aimed her visor at the sky.

I stood, looking up too. The vast silver donut gleamed up there. It seemed obscene somehow, and it struck me as very like the science fiction stories I'd read in my youth.

"Is he important, sir?" Zoe asked.

"I don't know. It's possible."

She nodded, motioning to her troopers.

I could see that Zoe Artemis ran a tight ship. That was a good sign. Soldiers like her were one of the reasons we'd won so many of our encounters.

After watching Zoe and her arban hustle the unconscious tiger to their cycles, I went back to mine.

Lifting into the air, I searched for Rollo. It took me a few moments to find the right channel. He stood with a clot of Star Vikings near the biggest spaceship.

I landed beside him.

For the next few hours, Rollo and I toured one spaceship after another. Those we could take rose upstairs to Holgotha. The rest we rigged with explosives.

At this point, I discovered a problem with using the artifact as the central attack platform. On Sanakaht, Holgotha remained stationary. I would have liked to hit the opposite side of the planet and do the same thing there as we'd done here.

"From what I can tell," Rollo said, "the outskirts of the city are where they keep the warehouses."

I gazed at our new warships floating beside the artifact. The raid was supposed to be a rich one for us, the big daddy payday.

In World War II, at the start of the Pacific War for America and Japan, the enemy had struck at Pearl Harbor. Everyone knows the story. Japanese planes destroyed docked American capital ships and parked aircraft, although they missed the carriers. The U.S. flattops had been out at sea on maneuvers. On the return to their own carriers, some of the Japanese pilots begged for one more strike. They wanted to hit the big oil tanks

155

onshore and blow them up. The Japanese Admiral Nagumo wanted no part of that. He wished to bring the Japanese fleet home intact. They'd done enough. It was time to scram. So, they sailed away, leaving the oil tanks intact. If they had made one more strike, it would have crippled American recovery efforts even further. Without those oil tanks in Hawaii, the American Navy would have had a much harder time striking the Japanese Empire as soon as it had.

This was our Pearl Harbor. I had to grab as much ordnance as I could, not rush out too soon.

"Gather your troopers," I told Rollo. "We're hitting the outskirts of the city."

-17-

From the spaceyard, we rose like a swarm of angry wasps. Gunning our DZ9 air-cycles, we sped for the city warehouses.

As we approached, the Lokhar urban area took on a more distinct shape. Some of the steel towers looked rusted, which seemed strange. I saw chips in the big block buildings. Had there been fighting here recently?

A few tigers stood on the roofs with heavy machine guns and handheld RPGs. The rockets flew as slugs and beams struck us. They took out several cycles. Then we closed, slaughtering the Lokhars on the roofs.

We landed and killed every tiger we saw on the ground. It became a massacre. The warehouses stood several stories high. Each held military hardware, much more than we could carry away on our cycles.

I made a call. Haulers rose from the spaceyard and landed here. On the double, troopers loaded the grounded spaceships. We packed the cargo holds, raced to the next warehouse and emptied it as well.

For me, time sped up. Several hours passed in a flash. There was so much to do and no time to do it.

Then, tiger tanks rumbled out of the city. The cannons on Holgotha put on a laser light show, destroying them all. Death from above, baby.

Later, power-armored tigers tried to surprise us, bounding like maddened grasshoppers, desperately trying to close. The artifact-perched lasers hit them too. By that time, three

157

captured Lokhar pinnaces joined the fun. They slid above like air-sharks. Particle beams destroyed tiger combat cars sweeping from the west.

We were the Star Vikings. We smashed the local tiger forces and filled up hauler after hauler. Each one rose up to Holgotha, waiting to leave.

Those who remained on the surface went to another spaceyard fifty kilometers away. There, we repeated the sequence. At that point, the resistance *on* Sanakaht ended, although we didn't know it yet.

Could we have looted the entire planet? It's possible. A surprise against us halted our operations.

After a solid seven hours of fighting, looting and laughing, I called up to N7. A soldier had told me they really wanted to speak with me.

"Commander Creed, where you have you been?" N7 asked.

"Just tell him," Ella said in the background.

"Tell me what?" I asked. From where I stood, I watched troopers entering a hauler, stowing away hardware as if they were African army ants.

"We have to leave Sanakaht, Commander," N7 said. "A flotilla of Lokhar warships is headed from the heavymetal moons toward us. They've already wiped out our space-drones. The Demar hauler is heading back to Hol—" N7 almost spoke the artifact's name. "The hauler returns to—" He probably realized he shouldn't call it *the artifact* either. Not if Lokhars could hear him.

"I understand," I said.

"We must leave, Commander," N7 said. "The approaching warships will have the high ground against us. We can send up five patrol boats, but we still haven't shaken down our own cruisers and missile-ships. If the enemy attacks us from orbital space…"

"Okay," I said. "Start packing. I'll talk to Rollo. We'll lift up to…the platform. I want you to be ready to leave at a moment's notice."

"Someone will have to go see our pilot," N7 said.

"Roger," I said. "I'm coming upstairs."

Our android meant I should go see Holgotha in the inner chamber. It was time to let my troopers finish their tasks and scram. Rollo and Dmitri could take care of things down here. I had to get the artifact ready to transfer back to the solar system before the dreaded Lokhar cavalry arrived on the scene.

***

My air-cycle used the last of its power source to climb upstairs. Stolen Lokhar cruisers, missile-ships and patrol boats hovered around the artifact. Seeing them made me feel good inside.

From the direction of the faintly appearing stars, I saw the Demar hauler descending. What had N7 told me? The approaching Lokhars had already destroyed the hauler's space-drones.

Yeah. It was time to go.

I grounded the DZ9 on Holgotha's metallic surface. Sprinting to a waiting locker, I threw it open. Yanking the heavy vacc-suit inside, I put it on. Afterward, I jumped onto the cycle again and floated toward the inner curve. Halfway there, the cycle shorted out. I would have to hoof it the rest of the way.

After ten minutes of walking, my headphones crackled. I chinned a response.

"Commander," N7 said. "I have a message from the Lokhar flotilla admiral."

"Why would I care?" I asked.

"He wishes to speak with you. He asked for you by name, Commander."

"Come on, N7. Did you forget to turn off your video when you addressed him?"

"I followed procedures, sir. He demanded to speak to Commander Creed."

"Do you personally know the Lokhar admiral?"

"No," N7 said.

"All right," I said. "Patch him through to my HUD."

I trudged along Holgotha, using my magnetic boots at full strength. I didn't want to fall off. As I walked, an old tiger appeared on one half of my HUD. The other half let me see where I was going.

The old guy had a wide face for a Lokhar with too much white fur. This tiger had jowls like a bulldog. I'd never seen that before on one. I suspected he was fat. He wore a heavy purple garment with a fringed purple robe. His eyes were bright orange. I wondered if drugs had caused the color.

Naturally, I kept my face from his sight.

"You wanted to talk to me, so talk," I said.

"Commander Creed?" he asked in a rich voice.

"Don't know who that is," I said. "But it's true I lead the expedition."

"You are the one known as Creed," he said with finality.

"Is this Creed a legendary space pirate?" I asked.

The tiger snarled. It brightened his already orange eyes. It also made the white fur stand out. "Do you not realize who you address?" he asked.

"Nope," I said. "Don't have any idea."

"I am the Emperor of the Lokhar."

Oh, I thought to myself. *You've got to be kidding.*

"I am Felix Rex Logos," he said. "I have heard of you, savage. Know, the Imperium of the Lokhars shall hunt you down to the ends of the galaxy. There is no place you can hide."

"The worst part is that I bet you think that's an original threat," I said.

He snarled again, spraying spit.

"Got a bit of an anger issue, do you?" I said.

"You have bitten off more than you can swallow, beast. You have awakened my wrath against your species."

"Turn that around, and you'll get some idea of how I feel about you, Mr. King-bro."

"I accept your declaration of war," Emperor Felix told me.

"Great," I said. "I accept as well. Destroy these others you speak about as I laugh all the way to the bank."

He leaned toward me with his eyes widening. "You consider yourself clever by hiding your visage, beast. Yet, I know it is you, Commander Creed. We have images of the Forerunner artifact in Sanakaht's skies. All aboard my flagship

160

know it as the Altair Object. I know every mark on the holy relic."

For a moment, I closed my eyes. I hadn't thought about that. "I don't have any idea what you're talking about, King-bro," I said.

He snarled a laugh. "Do you not realize yet? Once, during the reign of my mother, I commanded the Lokhar Fifth Legion as it guarded the holy artifact in the Altair star system."

I scowled. If he'd led the Fifth Legion once...

"I served the artifact and gazed upon its beauty," the Emperor said. "Many times, I walked upon it as I considered the holiness of the Creator. You, beast, attacked the Fifth Legion. You and your Starkien scum used nuclear weapons to kill my brothers in arms. I know you, Creed-beast. In an arcane, vile fashion, you have suborned the noblest of the artifacts. It sickens me. Yet I have heard you know the relic's name. How this can be so is a mystery. But for your reckless killing on Sanakaht—"

"Hey, you know what, Mr. Big Shot," I said. "Why don't you shut the Hell up? You ordered my Earth destroyed. You tried to take humanity down."

"Yes. I knew from the beginning that you were savages beyond the pale of civilization. I indeed ordered your species' destruction. My only remorse was that some of you survived the attack. Orange Tamika has much to answer for in failing to do as I bid them."

"That's it," I said. "By your own words you've sealed your fate."

"No. You have sealed yours."

I almost told him, "No way, man. I said it first." But this wasn't a pissing contest. This was the game of races.

As I trudged across Holgotha, I considered what the Felix Rex Logos Purple Tamika Emperor had just told me. He'd once been a legionary of the Fifth. I'd helped slaughter the legion. He knew Holgotha by sight. Yeah. I could see this was bad.

Instead of a Star Viking raid so humanity could grab some extra stuff, I'd just ensured we were in a war to the death with the largest battlefleet around. The Jelk didn't seem to be interested in this part of the Orion Arm just now. They had their own problems. Instead of improving mankind's situation, I'd just made it a whole lot worse. Great.

"What are you doing in the Sanakaht system anyway?" I asked.

"Vain beast, I shall capture you."

It was time to throw him a curve ball. "Are you going to do it with the Shi-Feng?" I asked.

On my HUD, the Emperor recoiled. "How have you come to learn the holy name?" he asked in a higher voice.

"Secrets, secrets are no fun," I answered. "Secrets, secrets hurt someone."

He gnashed his teeth and sprayed more spit. "Know, you foul beast, that I shall begin a holy crusade against humanity. You will not be able to hide among the Jelk. No. You cannot run far enough to escape my wrath. I will track you and slice your belly open myself. Then, I shall pull out your intestines and feed on them to my court's delight."

"I'm not that fancy, King-bro. I'm just going to blow your head clean off and piss down your neck."

"Enough!" he roared.

"That's right," I said. I clicked off the connection. I'd had enough of his royal majesty.

I stalked across Holgotha, getting angrier by the moment. This was just great. This—I had to warn the others.

"N7," I radioed.

Static answered me. Our radio equipment didn't seem to be as good as what the Lokhar Emperor possessed. I'd have to wait until I was farther away from the black hole to communicate with the others.

Why was the Emperor in the Sanakaht star system? I shook my head. It didn't matter how Felix Rex Logos had come to be here at this time. I wondered if Holgotha had known. Would the artifact even care? Maybe.

I began to wonder why the artifact had agreed to my request to transfer to Sanakaht. Had Holgotha computed the present situation between the Lokhars and us? At this point, did he wish to see humanity gone forever?

If true, that had ominous implications.

162

Shaking my head again, I realized I couldn't worry about any of that now. We needed to get out of here before the tiger flotilla reached its operational range. Surely, they would have T-missiles.

I increased my pace across Holgotha.

An eternity later, I stood before the wall of the building. It looked different in daylight. I'd never realized before how pitted the surface was. Raising my right gauntlet, I curled the fingers, getting ready to strike the wall with my knuckles.

"You are ready to return to the solar system?"

"Yes," I radioed.

"You do not need to come inside. Instead, return to your people. I will transfer in thirty of your minutes."

"How about doing it right now?" I said.

"That would kill you. Knowing that, do you still wish for me to leave instantly?"

"Can you sense the approaching Lokhar ships?"

"I am aware of them, of course. I have been the entire time."

"Can they attack us within thirty minutes time?"

"No."

"Then give me those thirty minutes to get out of the black hole's range."

"Good-bye, Commander Creed. Do not ever attempt to speak with me again. I find myself sullied by today's murders."

"Why would you care? It is the way of the universe, things dying out. You told me so yourself."

"Heed my words, Commander. I am sick of your voice, your thoughts and your ways. Do you seek to speak with me again. I will finish my analysis in your solar system. Then I will leave."

"That gives us eighteen more years, right?" I asked.

"You are deluded. Your species does not even have three years left. The Purple Emperor will annihilate every human in existence before the triple years run their course."

I didn't know what to say to my own private oracle preaching doom. So, I turned around and headed back toward the outer surface.

Thirty-nine and a half minutes later, the vertigo struck again. Everything blurred and the Forerunner artifact transferred from the atmosphere of Sanakaht back to the middle of the Asteroid Belt.

We returned to the solar system with our captured starships, patrol boats, missiles, container-loads of small arms and bio-terminator scrubbers. The Star Viking raid proved a smashing tactical success and a bitter strategic loss.

Now what were we going to do?

-18-

Due to our form of travel, we had some time to decide on our next maneuver.

Felix Rex Logos Purple Tamika Emperor raced in a warship within the Sanakaht star system. That happened to be three hundred and thirty-seven light years away from the solar system. Even with his fastest scouts, it would take time for the news to travel throughout the star lanes.

Before we did anything, though, we needed to count losses and gains.

The Star Viking raid onto Sanakaht cost us one hundred and seven dead. The wounded hardly mattered because we could heal them back to full health in the Jelk tank.

We lost a little over double that number in air-cycles.

The reward went beyond my fondest hopes. We reaped five patrol boats, four cruisers and three missile-ships, along with a good supply of missiles and planetary particle beam cannons. That didn't include a horde of small arms, mortars and grenades.

We had newer and more modern starships compared to the ones we'd lost. We also had patrol boats. They could enter a planetary atmosphere or race through the jump gates and watch.

If I kept everything together in one group, humanity possessed a modest flotilla. True, it couldn't face Baba Gobo's fleet or Admiral Saris', but it was a beginning.

Unfortunately, I didn't have enough assault troopers to man all the spacecraft and have a viable ground fighting force.

Therefore, I summoned Diana and Murad Bey to Mars Base. They brought their sole cruiser together with an armed escort of bodyguards. The guards cooled their heels in a holding area under the dome, far away from the meeting chamber.

In the conference room, Diana studied me and Murad Bey tried to smile.

He was a square-shouldered giant of a Turk. Even after eight years in power, he had the blackest hair I'd ever seen. These days, I had the feeling he dyed it. Murad Bey combed the mass straight back. Plastic surgery had taken away an old burn scar on his neck.

As the two Earth Council members listened, I gave them a rundown of the raid, including my conversation with the Emperor.

Diana grew pale. Murad Bey's jaw muscles, the ones hinging them, bulged out and in.

"It is to be a war to the death," Murad Bey declared in his slow voice.

"No," Diana said. "If the Lokhar Emperor comes to Earth, it means extermination for us and nothing bad for them."

"By Allah," Murad Bey said, his dark eyes shining. "It will not be so."

I've said it before, and I think it bears repeating: the humans left were the tough, willing to scrap against anyone. It didn't matter from what race or religion our enemies came. The last one percent were the rawest sons and daughters of bitches our planet had ever borne.

"Do you have a plan?" Diana asked me.

"Not yet," I admitted.

The Amazon Queen put her hands on the table, staring at me. "Your madness gave us our chance. Now, your insanity has taken it away again."

"We have options," I said.

"I would dearly like to hear them," Diana said.

Standing, glancing at Ella, who pretended to take notes, I strode toward the viewing screen. It showed the asphalt of Mars Base, our empty sidewalks.

Staring out of the viewing port, I said, "First, we could do a Starkien."

"Leave our solar system?" Diana asked.

"It is the optimal choice," I said.

"No. We need a home base," Diana said. "You may have patterned your troopers off the Mongol nomads. The rest of us need a place to call home. Otherwise, we'll become demoralized."

"I do not know if I agree," Murad Bey said. "The Prophet Mohammad journeyed from Mecca for a season. Perhaps we must emulate his example."

My head snapped around. I'd been staring at Zoe Artemis as she walked on a sidewalk outside.

"What did you say?" I asked Murad Bey.

He had a wooden face with almost no expression. The skin looked leathery.

"In the beginning," the big man said, "the people of Mecca did not believe the Prophet's words. Thus, he took his followers and traveled to Medina. There, he gained more servants of Allah. With them, he raided his accusers. Unable to bear this, the merchants of Mecca gathered an army to do war against them. Allah granted the pagan army into the hands of the true believers, giving them to Mohammad. The rest you know, as Islam spread throughout the world."

The Amazon Queen glanced from Murad Bey to me. "What are you thinking, Creed?"

"What?" I asked, lost in thought again.

"I know that look," she said. "You have an idea. You're not really considering following Mohammad's example, are you?"

"Doctor Sant did," I said softly.

Diana blinked those big eyelashes at me.

"Think about it a moment," I said. "I know the artifact's name. I rode it from the portal planet to the solar system. Seven years later, I rode the artifact again. This time, I did it to chastise the Lokhars. I did it in the system where the Purple Tamika Emperor happened to be."

167

"That was a coincidence," Diana said.

"Do you really believe that?" I asked.

Ella set down her stylus. She couldn't keep silent but asked, "Did the artifact tell you the Emperor would be there?"

"The relic didn't have to," I said.

The two women traded glances.

"Are you saying you planned this?" Diana asked.

I had to chuckle. "No. I'm not saying that at all. I'm talking strategy. Look, the Jelk Corporation is out of the present fight. That leaves the Jade League. Why did the various races form the league in the first place?"

"To protect themselves from the Jelk," Diana said.

"That's right," I said. "They also did it to protect the Forerunner relics. For most of them, the league has taken on religious significance."

"So?" Diana asked.

"So we have to fight fire with fire," I said. "The Purple Tamika Emperor told me he'd build a massive crusade against humanity. Well, we have to counter that. How do you battle an idea?"

"With a better idea," Ella said.

"Exactly," I said, pointing at her.

"I don't think you've thought this through," Diana said. "The aliens think we're beasts. They're not going to listen to you, a talking animal. They wouldn't even let the Forerunner Guardians join the Jade League."

"Yes," I said with a laugh. "Don't you see? That's why the artifact acted on our behalf. The relic righted the injustice of keeping us out of the Jade League. Who paid for the insolence of keeping us out? The Purple Tamika Emperor, that's who. Doctor Sant preaches against him. Now, I'm going to preach against Felix Rex Logos myself."

Diana folded her hands together, keeping them on the table. She stared at the multitude of rings she was wearing. Finally, she looked up. "There's a problem with your logic. You just told us about it, remember? Since the raid, the artifact doesn't want anything to do with you."

"*You* know that," I said.

"What are you suggesting?" Diana said.

168

"That *they*, the aliens, don't know that. Look, as far as they're concerned, I'm the man when it comes to our artifact. This latest exploit will seal it. The aliens aren't going to come around, asking to see me enter the artifact to prove myself. Word will sweep near-space about our venture to Sanakaht. The Emperor is going to make sure of that. He's giving us free publicity."

"In all likelihood," Diana said, "he'll call you a devil."

"The merchants of Mecca spoke evil words against Mohammad," Murad Bey said.

Diana sat back as she eyed her Earth Council confederate. "I'm surprised you're agreeing to this," she told Murad Bey. "Creed isn't religious. You know that. He's simply doing this as a strategic ploy. He's going to play a part."

Murad Bey turned his inky eyes on me.

"He's sullying Mohammad's ways with his idea," Diana said.

"What are you trying to do?" I asked her. "Put a wedge between Murad Bey and me?"

"I don't think you fight fire with fire," Diana said. "What you're suggesting is too dangerous."

"No," I said. "It's our only chance."

"I insist on one thing," Murad Bey told me. "You must not call yourself the Prophet."

"No one is suggesting I do," I said.

"But you are claiming to start a new religion," he said.

"Not at all," I said. "I'm claiming to clean up the oldest one. These aliens have been worshiping the Creator for a long time. They've done so at the artifacts, right?"

"What will you tell them?" Murad Bey asked.

I could hear the anger in his voice. If anything, his reaction proved the soundness of my idea. Few things moved people like religion. For some people, their politics was their religion. For some, football, soccer or bowling became their most sacred belief. On Earth in the past, communism became the religion of Karl Marx, Lenin and hundreds of millions of true believers. In the United States, feminism had become a religion. If you spoke out against it, certain people went ballistic. The same

169

held true for gun rights and a host of other issues. It seemed to be the same for aliens.

If the Purple Tamika Emperor stoked aliens' passions against us through religion, we humans would soon all be dead. I had to find a like passion to pit against his idea. That meant I had to go into the holiness business. Fight fire with fire or a crusade with a crusade.

"You are not the Prophet," Murad Bey said stubbornly.

"No I'm not. I'm Commander Creed, a plainspoken man who entered a Forerunner artifact. I make no special claims, but an ancient relic did tell me its name, and it took me to a Lokhar star system to wage war against the heretic Purple Emperor."

"Will you try to speak words of Truth?" Murad Bey asked.

I held my hands palm upward. "I am a man, the one who entered a Forerunner object. Why the ancient machine admitted me and not another is not for me to discern. I only know that the named artifact took me to the planet Sanakaht. There, I punished those who followed the heretic, Felix Rex Logos. Now, the Purple Emperor tries to slay the one the machine of the First Ones chose to converse with alone."

"The humble route doesn't fit you," Diana said. "Your plan smacks of gross hypocrisy."

"I'm not being humble," I said. "I'm inserting a new idea into the game. I'm doing it in the only way the aliens might be able to hear the idea."

Diana disengaged her hands, using a finger to curl several strands of hair. "Your idea is so brassy that maybe it will work."

"If it was just me alone," I said, "I don't think it would fly. But given Doctor Sant and his message, I think there's a possibility some aliens will listen."

"Let's suppose that's so," Diana said. "How will you get your message across?"

"Yeah," I said. "That could be a problem. Let me think about it for a couple of days."

"What do we do until you come up with a workable scheme?" Diana asked.

"We train," I said. "I'm giving the Earth Council three quarters of the new ships. I'll also forward you a goodly amount of missile launchers and particle beam cannons. You should turn the Moon into a fortress."

"That fortress won't last long against Admiral Saris' fleet," she said.

"Let's build one strongpoint at a time," I said. "That's better than sitting on our thumbs doing nothing."

We talked longer, but didn't come up with anything more. Before I proceeded with my plan, I needed more information about the Emperor. Ella had a machine, and I had a tiger whose mind I'd like to open. It was time to chat with my Shi-Feng captive.

***

Several days later, I walked down a steep set of rock stairs. The Lokhars who built Mars Base had jackhammered the steps and the subterranean chambers out of the Red Planet.

"Why did you put your equipment way down here?" I asked.

Ella walked ahead of me. I liked the sway of her hips and the tightness of her garments. Our scientist must have turned heads back in the day. She carried a heavy flashlight, the beam jostling ahead of us.

Ignoring my question, Ella came to a thick door. She withdrew a small box from a pocket, pressing a red-lit switch.

With a *click*, the door swung open. We entered a sterile area of white corridors and red rock walls. Mats lined the floor.

"Is this a dungeon?" I asked.

"Don't let your imagination get the better of you," Ella said over her shoulder.

First clicking her red button again, she pushed against a door. It was heavier than the first. I followed her into the room.

The odor struck me right away. A sour rancid smell permeated everything. I saw the tiger. Two attendants watched him.

The Lokhar leaned forward in what looked like a tilted, backward-facing chair. They had stretched his arms in front, securing each to an arm-long rest. His chin rested in a groove

171

and steel bands kept his head in place. Other restraints held his torso and legs, which were stretched out as far as they could go.

"That looks uncomfortable," I said.

The two attendants snapped up, staring at me.

Ella spun around, scowling. She put a finger in front of her lips.

Slowly, the tiger stirred. Maybe squirmed would be a better word.

I didn't like this place. It made me wonder what the Lokhars would do to me if they managed to get their paws on me.

Ella moved to the attendants, whispering something into their ears. Soon, the three of them went behind what looked like a lead curtain. The biggest attendant reappeared and drew it aside. Ella and the woman attendant pushed a big machine on wheels toward the tiger.

The machine looked like a big refrigerator. There were lights sparkling up and down one side. The two pushed the "refrigerator" near the tiger. Ella nodded. The woman attendant bent low, locking the wheels into place.

Ella opened a small hatch in the box. She withdrew what looked like a portable lamp a college student might have used over her desk in the dorm. She adjusted it so the shade aimed at the tiger. Returning to the refrigerator, she slid open a panel. Her fingers tapped against a pad.

A light clicked on under the shade. It centered a green dot on the tiger's forehead.

Ella went to the shade, manually adjusting it. She moved the dot until it beamed between the tiger's eyes.

His eyelids fluttered and he twitched and groaned.

The sound put goosebumps on my arms. I hated this place.

The green light continued to shine on his fur. Slowly, his eyelids fluttered more. He relaxed. I thought he would fall asleep. Instead, he practically slumped. The restraints held him in place, though.

With a forefinger, Ella motioned me nearer. I stepped beside her in front of the tiger. She pointed at his eyes. Bending

172

low, putting my hands on my knees, I peered into his orbs. They were glazed as if he were hypnotized.

Ella picked up a stool and set it down to his left. The woman attendant took another stool, sitting to his right. She clipped leads to his nostrils and another pair to his furry ears.

Now, don't get me wrong. I didn't have any sympathy for the Lokhars. This tiger was Shi-Feng. The being would gladly give his life to explode others to death. Yet, I didn't like to see anyone in such a situation. It seemed inhuman.

Remember the ninety-nine percent who died to the Lokhars. The only reason he's strapped down like this is so mankind can climb out of oblivion.

I sighed. Ruthlessness didn't sound so noble now. It seemed grubby and dirty, which was exactly what it was.

Ella began to speak to the tiger. He didn't respond right away. The last attendant stood behind the others. A big finger tapped a switch now and then. It sent shocks to the Lokhar, jerking his furry head. He yowled more than once, sounding like a wet cat.

Finally, the tiger began to answer Ella's questions. He did it haltingly, with many stubborn moments of silence. I stayed, forcing myself to witness this.

Later, I sat with Ella in a side room. I felt soiled.

"Is that what you did to Doctor Sant?" I asked.

Ella stared at me. We sat at a big table with snacks and drinks to the side. Neither of us ate or drank anything.

"Do you really want to know the answer?" she finally asked me.

My stomach tightened a little more. I shook my head.

Ella's nostrils flared. Her mouth grew firm. She nodded.

"This is a dirty business," I said.

"Is your killing any better than what I do down here?" she asked.

I wanted to tell her yes.

"You leave people dead, Creed. You have no compunction slaughtering Lokhars. I'm merely drawing out some information. Afterward, they're very much alive. How can what I'm doing down here be worse than what you do in the open?"

173

"Easy," I said. "It's called the Golden Rule."

"He who has the gold makes the rules?" she asked. "I don't understand what you mean."

"I'm talking about the other Golden Rule," I said. "Do unto others as you would have them do unto you."

"So you'd like to be gut-shot on a battlefield?" she asked.

"I don't mind dying a warrior's death," I said. "Getting mind-raped in a dungeon, no, not so much."

"Once you're dead, life is over," Ella said. "Those who live still have hope. No. Killing is worse than torture. It is an order of magnitude of difference. You're squeamish because of the social sensibilities you've accepted. If you strip those away—"

"Strip those sensibilities away and you become a devil," I said with heat.

A faint smile touched her lips. "You don't realize how antiquated you are. The real wonder to me is how fossilized the aliens are in their mindsets. Our superior outlook allows us to survive where any other race would have already perished."

I might have argued with her. In the end, I told myself this was her inner armor that allowed her to do these things. Humanity needed them done. Could I look down on her then for doing them?

"What do we know so far?" I asked.

Ella stared into my eyes half a second longer. Then she reached for a reader, tapping the screen, bringing up her notes.

"Ras Claw, the name of our Lokhar, believes himself a holy warrior in an ancient fraternity," Ella began. "It appears the Shi-Feng have close ties with Purple Tamika. The sacred warriors help to keep the other Tamikas in check."

"They assassinate other Lokhars?" I asked.

"Oh yes. I believe they concentrate on their own kind much more than against aliens."

"Did the Emperor sanction the strike against me?" I asked.

"I wondered the same thing," Ella said. "Ras Claw didn't know. He suspects so, though."

"That means the Purple Emperor would have already decided against us," I said. "Our attack against Sanakaht didn't really change anything then."

"Exactly," Ella said. "Along with that line of inquiry, I asked him about Admiral Saris. When Ras Claw heard about the Purple admiral taking our warships, he hissed in appreciation."

"Do you know why?" I asked.

"I queried him on that. He surmises the Emperor set humanity up for failure. This would come in two varieties. Without any self-protection, a greedy species might attack us in order to gain the artifact. We would die under their guns. Or mankind would fail to protect the artifact, possibly letting it be destroyed. In that case, righteous fury would stoke the rest of the Jade League. Soon, races would demand our deaths as blood payment for our failure."

I thought about that. "Yes. The Emperor would have kept his hands clean. In either of those cases he could say he'd kept his oath with us."

"Yes," Ella said.

I scowled. What a bastard. Even before the Sanakaht raid, Felix Rex Logos had plotted humanity's destruction. Helping the Lokhars against Abaddon seven years ago had merely given us a little more time. It hadn't bought us good faith from the Lokhars."

"Does Ras Claw know why the Emperor hates humans so viciously?"

"No," Ella said.

"You asked him?"

"Oh yes."

I grabbed a package of spice sticks, but didn't tear open the alien cellophane. Shaking my head, I tossed the package back among the other goodies.

"The Emperor wants to annihilate us," I said. "I wonder if even now a fleet races toward the solar system."

"According to Ras Claw, the Emperor will come in person. Felix Rex Logos will want to make an example of us."

"No. I bet it's more than that," I said. "Doctor Sant began his metamorphosis here. If the Emperor annihilates us and retakes the artifact, won't that negate Doctor Sant's truths?"

"I'm not sure I follow you," Ella said.

I reached out, taking the spice sticks again, opening the package. Putting one in my mouth like a cigar, I sucked on it thoughtfully.

"It seems simple enough," I said. "If humanity becomes devilish, anything learned in our star system becomes suspect. That would mean Sant worked with devils. It would nullify his words and likely destroy any credibility Orange Tamika gained in stopping Abaddon and the Kargs."

Ella blinked thoughtfully. "Yes, I see what you mean."

"If the other alien races and the other Tamikas believe we're vile, they'll vie to destroy us. That means it won't matter how big we become. We'll be evil. Thus, we're forced to enter the religious fray."

"I doubt you'll make a persuasive spokesman to the other aliens," Ella said.

Taking the spice stick from my mouth, I pointed it at her. "Then we have to find ways to increase our persuasiveness."

"How?"

"Well," I asked, "did Ras Claw tell you anything useful in that regard?"

Pursing her lips, Ella peered at her reader. She began to tap the screen, scanning her notes. A few minutes later, she said, "Here's something interesting."

"Let's hear it."

"The Shi-Feng has an elite guard at Purple Tamika's Hall of Honor."

"So?" I said.

She looked up. "The Lokhars view the Shi-Feng as a holy order in much the same way as humans viewed monks during the Middle Ages."

"Got it," I said.

"A hall of honor is something else. According to Ras Claw, each Tamika has one."

"So?"

"You're looking for an edge," Ella said. "To gain one, you need to know how Lokhars think. Here's my point. Why would the Shi-Feng send an elite guard to the Purple Tamika Hall of Honor? They're a holy order and they've sent their holiest to

176

the hall. Maybe if you knew why, you'd know the Emperor's thinking better."

"I want to speak with Ras Claw," I said.

"That could be a problem," Ella said.

"Why? Is his mind damaged?"

"No," Ella said, "at least not how you're thinking. We worked him hard under the machine. He needs his rest before we put him under again."

"Forget about the machine. I'll talk to him one on one."

"Old-fashioned persuasion techniques?" asked Ella.

I almost told her I wasn't a torturer. I doubted she thought of herself as one, either. So it wouldn't help if I implied she was.

"One on one," I said. "It will be just the tiger and me sitting across a table. Sometimes, a straight talk is the best way to see how someone thinks."

Ella appeared dubious. "Well, in that case, I can have him ready to speak in...hmm, ten hours."

"Good," I said. "It's a date."

-19-

"He's more dangerous than you realize," Ella told me.

She and I peered through a two-way mirror. The tiger in question—Ras Claw of the Shi-Feng—sat on a chair behind a table. It looked like an old-fashioned police interrogation room.

The tiger was taller than average, about seven and a half feet. He had wide shoulders and narrow hips, an athletic looking Lokhar specimen. A bare line in his stomach showed stiches where Zoe Artemis had sliced open his gut with a laser. He stared at the two-way mirror.

Ella pointed that out to me. "Whenever the door opens, he becomes tense. It's as if he's waiting for you."

"I believe that once he realizes who you are in particular, the tiger will attempt to kill you."

I nodded absently, realizing I could use that to my advantage.

"You're not listening to me, Creed. The Lokhar is a killer, one of their fighting specialists. He's a hand to hand expert."

"So what?" I said.

Ella Timoshenko knew me better than most people did. She might have divined my thinking.

"Do you really believe you can defeat him that easily?" she asked.

I nodded.

"Sometimes, you're not realistic," Ella said. "With his internal bionics, he's probably stronger than you are."

"Do you even know how much I bench?"

"He weighs more, too," she continued, ignoring me. "Worst of all, he has his claws."

"I'm faster."

"If that's true," Ella said, "it's not by much."

"He's been drugged lately and badly cut. How good can his condition be?"

Ella waved her hand dismissively. "In his mind, we've dishonored him. Losing the stomach bomb—you can't understand his shame. He'll do just about anything to wipe away his humiliation. Assassinating humanity's leader—"

"Whoa, whoa, whoa," I said. "I'm not humanity's leader."

"I know you keep giving the Earth Council spaceships. For some reason, you don't like the idea that you're the one who wins or loses it for us. But for good or bad, Creed, everyone knows you're leading us to victory or to destruction."

I swear I could feel the weight of that pushing down on my shoulders. I was just the chief Star Viking, though.

"Whatever you do," Ella said, "don't let him know who you are."

"Yeah, okay," I said.

"Are you really sure you want to go through with—"

"Enough already." I motioned to the attendants to open the cell door.

"I wish you'd let me handcuff him first," Ella said.

"Oh," I said, "before I forget. There's one thing. Whatever happens, don't enter the room to help."

Ella gave me a hard look.

"Those are my orders," I said.

"What are you planning, Creed?"

"Watch through the mirror," I said, "and you'll find out."

***

The bigger attendant opened the door, although the man stayed out of sight of the Shi-Feng assassin.

I stepped into the doorway, stopping to stare at the tiger.

He grew tense, glowering, but making no move to get up.

I moved into the room and listened to the door shut with a heavy *whomp* and a *click*. Finally, I put my hands on my hips.

"What's your problem?" I asked in Lokhar.

179

His eyebrows rose in surprise. I don't think he expected me to know his native tongue.

"I'm Commander Creed, the leader of the Forerunner Guardians. When I enter a room, you need to stand in respect."

The tiger stiffened. I could almost hear Ella cursing outside the chamber. I wasn't supposed to let the tiger know I was important. Well, I had a different agenda. This was warrior to warrior. Let him come at me if he wanted. I'd kick the stuffing out of him and earn his respect in the process.

I waited, but he remained seated.

"Fool," I said. "Don't you know that your Emperor once served in the Lokhar Fifth Legion?"

"I am not a fool," he rumbled.

A normal person would have respected his obvious deadliness. I was anything but normal.

Laughing, I pointed at the shaven line on his belly. "Do Shi-Feng warriors normally lose their gut-bombs?"

The tiger moved with startling speed. With a roar, he hurled the table. It was heavy, made for abuse. Even so, the table splintered against the wall. Almost before the breaking sounds reached me, the tiger assassin leapt.

Ella had told me about his bionic strength, that he was stronger than me. Because the mechanical parts had been embedded so deeply in his muscles, to remove them would have killed him. Thus, we'd left them intact.

The juggernaut of a killer sailed at me. Titanium-tipped claws appeared out of his fingertips. He slashed as he landed, his eyes blazing rage.

I'd already decided to be elsewhere, spinning away like a galaxy-class kung-fu artist. The claws left streaks in the metal, ripping steel like tinfoil.

The tiger whirled around to face me. "You have erred, human. I am Shi-Feng." The titanium tips of his right hand touched the fur of his chest. "Today you will learn what Shi-Feng means," the tiger finished.

"I already know."

He tilted his head as if questioning me.

"Jack squat," I told him.

"You speak alien words. What do they mean?"

180

"That you won't do a thing."

His roar hurt my ears. All over his body, the fur stood on end. He launched himself, moving like a bullet.

It was the deadliest game of tag I'd ever played. I dodged, twisted, threw myself backward, forward and once smashed a right cross against his snout. That snapped his head back and made him stagger, giving me the opening to slide away from those claws.

Gingerly touching his nose, he hissed, "I do not understand. Why can't I cut you?"

I turned my left side to him. The cloth showed rips with blood dripping from them. "You touched me," I said. "If you keep trying, you might do it again."

"You *want* me to attack you?"

"I get it now," I said. "You're one of those bright tiger boys, aren't you?"

"Is this another insult?"

"Wow. You're a real Einstein."

He cocked his head.

"That means a smart human," I said.

After that, Ras Claw kept coming. Soon, he panted so froth shot from his snout and blood trickled from the stitch-holes in his gut.

My chest heaved. But I was in better shape than him. I'd rested these past days and eaten well. He'd had his mind probed after sustaining heavy wounds.

"You will die," he said.

"Don't tell me about it. Show me. Otherwise, I'm going to believe all Shi-Feng are hopeless braggarts."

He did try. His leaps had less force, and his swipes came more slowly than before.

Then I decided to go on the offensive. With carefully controlled attacks, I hit him in the face, in the chest and against his arms.

In retaliation, he slashed a single claw across my forehead, drawing blood that dripped into my eyes.

"You are a clever fighter," he said. "But I am the superior warrior."

Backing up, ripping off my shirt, I shredded it and bound my forehead with a strip. Then we fought some more. With a hammer blow, I broke his right wrist. Flipping him, I darted in fast and stomped on his left ankle, listening to it crunch.

He never made a sound. Slowly, he stood, balancing on his good one.

I panted with sweat covering my skin.

"You are a warrior," he said grudgingly.

"I am the Forerunner Guardian of the artifact that has told me its name."

He blinked several times, finally nodding. "I have seen the impossible. Yes. You *did* transfer with the artifact. Why has it done this for you? I cannot understand."

"Because your Emperor has dishonored his name," I said.

"I do not believe this."

"Why then has an animal learned the name of the former Altair Object?"

"This is a mystery. I…suspect Kargs had a hand in it."

"You are a fool who lost his bomb," I said. "You know nothing."

For the first time, I saw defeat in his eyes. He hung his head. "I have lost my honor," he said. "Today an animal has defeated me in honorable combat."

I believe that I'd finally reached the needed psychological moment. "Ras Claw," I said, "you're an even greater fool than I realized."

He studied me, finally asking, "Why would you say this?"

"Because I'm not an animal," I said. "I'm a man, superior to any Lokhar. The reason the artifact told me its name is that the machine of the First Ones realizes my superiority."

He scowled. "This…this cannot be."

"It is," I said. "My victory proves my righteousness. That you have lost your honor proves you served a heretic."

His head dipped lower. "I am shamed," he whispered.

Stepping closer, I saw the movement of his eyes. Ah, Ras Claw had a final ploy in mind. I would have to let him try it before I could proceed with my plan.

"A new era has come to the galaxy," I said boastfully. "The Lokhars are losing their place of privilege. That is why the Shi-Feng have failed to slay me."

"Ah," he said. "You must be right."

I took another step closer. Raising my arms, I looked away. He must not have realized I watched his reflection in the mirror.

With a howl of agony, Ras Claw launched himself at me a final time. My hands blurred as I shifted. Using his momentum, I flipped him hard, hurling him against a wall. He hit and crumpled to the floor. Then I rushed in, stomping on his other ankle until I heard a *crack*.

He groaned.

"Sleep, Ras Claw," I said, moving in, hitting him as hard as I could in the head.

He slumped unconscious onto the floor.

***

When Ras Claw came to, he lay in a bed in a sealed chamber. Ella's people had set his broken bones and put intravenous-tubes in his arms. A medical monitor watched over him, beeping from time to time with flashing lights.

At his first groan, I looked up from my chair. I'd been reading reports. Dmitri had spotted Starkien scouts in the Epsilon Indi system. That put them several jumps from the solar system.

What were the Starkiens doing so close to Earth? I had a good suspicion as to their motives. Too bad Dmitri couldn't have told me their leader's name. Was it Baba Gobo or someone else?

"You," the tiger said in a soft voice. He glanced at the tubes in his arms, noticing the casts. "Why have you done this for me?"

"Because that's what a warrior does," I said.

"You claim warrior status?" he asked.

"Who's lying in the bed, and who is sitting in the chair?"

He cocked his head in what appeared genuine puzzlement. "A warrior helps his defeated foe?"

"A warrior honors another warrior, particularly when the defeated foe gave the victor a worthy fight."

Ras Claw watched me with an unblinking stare. "No. I have lost my honor. I am no longer a warrior."

"Do you mean you did so by losing the bomb in your belly?"

"You speak crudely," Ras Claw said, "but accurately."

"I think you're wrong. You fought valiantly. You have retained your honor."

On the pillow, he moved his head from side to side. "I am bigger, faster and stronger than you are. I should have won."

"There is no *should have* in a fight," I said. "There is only what is. You are taller. I am both stronger and faster. More importantly, I am smarter than you are."

"This may be true," he said.

"Yet, I'm supposed to be an animal."

Again, with his unblinking stare, the tiger watched me. "No. An animal would not have put his defeated foe in a hospital bed."

"This may be true," I said, mimicking his former words.

He stiffened, saying, "I must warn you, human. Once my bones mend, perhaps before that, I will attempt to kill you. If you come too close now, I will try it here."

"The warning does you credit, Ras Claw of the Shi-Feng. I respect you more because of it."

Frowning, he said, "You are not like the others who toy with my mind."

"I am Commander Creed. I am the human who rode in the Forerunner artifact to bring ruin to Sanakaht."

"This is something I do not understand," he said. "Why should you have picked my planet to attack?"

"Because the Purple Tamika Emperor was in the star system," I said.

"How could you have known he was there?"

"I am the one to ride the artifact. I know many things."

His eyes widened as if with superstitious fear. Finally, he nodded. "You have ridden the artifact. It is a great mystery. Yet, who can speak against the one the artifact has chosen?"

184

"The Purple Tamika Emperor speaks against me," I said. "It will cost him dearly."

Ras Claw grew thoughtful. He turned away, mumbling to himself. Then he peered at me sidelong. "The Emperor has great honor, the greatest among all the Tamikas of the Lokhars. It is why Purple Tamika choses who will wear the crown."

"This is no doubt true," I said.

"Do you claim I lie?"

"No. You fought too well to be a liar." I laughed. "I would not honor you if I believed you lied."

Ras Claw shifted on his pillows, sitting up, regarding me solemnly. "When I take your head, Commander Creed, I will clean every tissue from it. I will polish the skull with gorgon oil. After carving your name onto the bone, I will present it to the Emperor as a gift. I am sure he will set it in Purple Tamika's Hall of Honor."

"I've never heard of this hall," I lied. "It is important?"

Opening his fanged maw, Ras Claw laughed hoarsely. "It is only the soul of Purple Tamika. Within the hall lies the great purple tapestry, woven from the fur of past emperors. In the hall are the many ancient trophies, the sacred fetishes: Pre-Space armor, a thousand tattered banners, scrolls and declamations, fragments of rock, bone, steel and charcoal, vials of dried black blood commemorating battles and Purple Tamika valor. In the center of the hall lies the undying fire. For ten thousand years it has burned."

"Huh, how about that," I said.

Ras Claw refused to let me deter him. "Your skull will reside in the hall throughout the ages. Because of the mighty deed of gifting it to the Emperor, I will regain my honor and my soul before I die."

"Your soul?" I asked.

"Without honor, no Lokhar is anything. With honor, any feat may be attempted."

I backed away from Ras Claw, sitting in the room's single chair. "I plan to keep my head," I told him.

"Which will make my feat all the more singular," he assured me.

185

I gave the tiger a wintery grin. "While keeping my head on my shoulders, I would like to see this Hall of Honor. It would surely be a sight."

"You will never see it," Ras Claw declared.

"Because you'll kill me before that?" I asked.

"That is one reason. The other is that no one but high-ranking Purple Tamika warriors and vestals are allowed inside the wooden walls."

"You're telling me the hall is old?"

"Ancient," Ras Claw said. "After the Forerunner objects, it is the most heavily guarded place in Purple Tamika control."

"Oh," I said. "In that case, maybe I'll have to force my way into the hall."

The tiger shook his head before wincing and closing his eyes. "It would sully the honor of Purple Tamika if you set eyes upon the trophies and fetishes. The present Emperor would be forced to step down for one of his brothers. No, Commander Creed, you will never see these things, but your skull will sit there."

It was my turn to give the Lokhar an unblinking stare.

He opened his eyes and bristled under the scrutiny. "Have I dishonored you by speaking these truths?" he asked.

With a start, I shook my head. He'd given me an idea. "No," I said. "You have given me many sad thoughts to reflect upon."

"Why sad?" he asked.

"Because we humans lack a hall of honor of our own," I said.

"I am not surprised to hear this. You are Earthlings, little better than beasts of the field. You lack a single Tamika. How then could you have a hall of honor?" He yawned, and I could see that he was exhausted.

"Sleep, Ras Claw. Regain your strength. You are going to need it soon."

"We will fight again?" he asked hopefully.

No, I thought to myself. *You'll need your strength so Ella can discover from you the location of this Hall of Honor*. It sounded like just the place for a Star Viking raid. That meant

186

the tiger would have to go under the Jelk machine at least one more time.

-20-

I left Mars Base to inspect the Luna defenses. For the journey, I went in a new patrol boat, *Achilles*.

The warship had narrow corridors but a large enough cargo bay to hold a gym. There, I met the new captain, a woman upgraded from an arban leader to a patrol boat commander.

Zoe Artemis had dark hair and darker eyes. She was slender with small breasts, boyish hips and a deadly quickness. She was lithe like a lynx. Her beauty rested in her eyes and the shape of her triangular chin.

One of my command maxims was to reward initiative and thought. Both were too rare. In having her troopers restrain me on Sanakaht, Zoe had shown both in large quantities. Humanity only had a handful of warships. Therefore, I wanted proven doers in charge of them.

We needed every force multiplier we could get.

After finishing my calisthenics, I toweled my face and watched Zoe hit a heavy bag. Her *thuds* rocked the bag. Her snap-kicks made it swing.

"Nice," I said.

"I hope you don't want to spar, sir," she said.

I shook my head.

"I'd like to thank you again, Commander, for this chance."

"You don't have to thank me," I said. "Your initiative won you the opportunity."

"Well...can a woman be grateful?" she asked.

Did the look in her eyes offer me more? It was possible.

188

"Why don't you show me around the ship," I said.

We talked about Sanakaht as we toured the engine room, the particle beam generator and finally ended in the control room.

It had five people in a semi-circle facing a viewing port. Zoe's chair was behind them. Outside in space were a thousand stars with Earth and Luna among them. To the left, the Sun blazed.

Zoe turned to me. The top of her head reached as high as my shoulders. "Can I ask you a question, sir?"

"Please," I said.

"Do you think we can hold the solar system?"

"You need to be more specific," I said.

"No. That's my question. Can we hold Earth against invaders?"

"Probably not," I admitted.

"Will you fight here no matter what?" she asked.

"What's on your mind, Captain?" I noticed the others at their stations listening carefully.

"What's more important, sir?" Zoe asked. "Holding and possibly dying at our home or surviving as a people?"

"Surviving," I said.

"Like the Starkiens survive?" she asked.

"If we have to," I said.

Zoe pursed her lips. "I tend to agree with you, sir. Then I think about Admiral Saris bringing her battlefleet or the Starkiens swarming here again. It makes my blood boil thinking of them chasing us from our home."

"I agree," I said.

"We need more warships, sir."

"We need more people. We need our planet back. It will be generations until we're anywhere close to having billions again."

Zoe scrunched her brow in thought. Then she brightened. "The Jelk stole enough humans in the past. Why not open up the Earth to those outcasts and let them settle here?"

Her words struck in my heart. My lost girlfriend, Jennifer, hadn't been born on Earth, but in Jelk space. The alien abductors had taken her mom and dad during World War II.

189

There were countless others like her. The Jelk had visited our world for centuries. The little red aliens had millions of tame Earth-descended humans. The Jelk had come to Earth the last time to pick us wild people, the barbarians that would make good soldiers. Maybe with training, we could turn the tame, civilized slaves back into fighters. For sure, their children would learn the hard arts needed for remaining free.

Laughing, I squeezed Zoe's shoulder. "That's an excellent idea. If we win through all this, that's exactly what we'll do."

The patrol boat captain grinned. She looked even prettier as she smiled.

I noticed several of the bridge crew still watching I hadn't taken my hand away. Zoe raised an eyebrow. Before I released her, I squeezed her shoulder a second time.

Yeah, I know. I shouldn't have done that. Jennifer remained Abaddon's slave. Until I'd freed her, how could I love another woman? Yet, that had been seven years ago. How long did I have to mourn Jennifer?

With a start, I removed my hand. No one spoke for a time.

Finally, Zoe cleared her throat. "Can I ask you another question, sir?"

"You bet," I said.

"What will we do when Admiral Saris shows up? I mean, you do think she'll show up, don't you?"

"The Emperor threatened us with a crusade. Eventually, the Lokhars are going to want a pound of flesh for what we did on Sanakaht."

"Will the artifact help us again?" Zoe asked.

"We shouldn't count on it," I said, remembering what Holgotha had told me.

"So either we need more warships or allies."

"That about sums it up," I said.

She thought about that, soon asking, "Who among the Jade League will fight against the Lokhars?"

That was the question. I'd been racking my brain about it for some time. Ras Claw had given us a possibility. If we raided this Hall of Honor and stole all the loot, would Felix Rex Logos make a deal with us to get it back?

Did Orange Tamika have any warships left? If they did, would they be enough combined with our paltry numbers to make a difference? I had a feeling Orange Tamika did not have enough. That's why Doctor Sant walked the worlds, trying to drum up aid through his preaching.

I left the bridge, feeling worse than before. The Lokhar had a crusade building against us. How did we build one of our own against them that mattered?

Half a day later, the *Achilles* braked as we neared Luna.

Two Earth Council cruisers and a missile-ship orbited the dead planetoid. At the Lunar North Pole waited ex-Saurian missile launchers and laser cannons. Intermingled among them were shorter-ranged Lokhar particle beam accelerators. This was our fortress. It possessed greater firepower than any three of our starships.

I bid Zoe good-bye and used a thruster-pack down to Luna. Floating in the void gave me time to think. I set my course for the Lunar North Pole. Afterward, I studied the blue-green ball of Earth in the distance.

Look at our homeworld. It was so beautiful, like the greatest gem in the universe set off by the blackness around it. The automated factories down there churned every hour. Diana had a crew using the scrubbers we'd taken off Sanakaht, burning away bio-toxins. Given enough time, we'd make our sweet home habitable again.

That was one of my great goals. Then, I had to defend Sol. How could we do that? I liked Zoe's idea to bring all the human waifs back home and train them to think like free people. Most of them were presently slaves or servants of the Jelk, as Jennifer used to be.

Who exactly did the Jelk Corporation fight a thousand light years away from here? I would have liked to know. With a shrug, I realized I'd have to save that for another day, another war. First, mankind had to survive a holy tiger crusade.

We need numbers. We need hordes of warships. I grimaced, shaking my head. It was an impossible problem.

No! I told myself. *That's BS. You have to think, Creed. You're missing something vital. What is it?*

191

Maybe I needed to consider this logically. We were few and faced many. The other aliens thought of us as animals. We needed allies, but who would join us?

Other desperate aliens might throw in their lot with us. But why would they do so if we were weak?

The Forerunner artifact is the key, I thought to myself.

Felix Rex Logos had once been the commander of the Lokhar Fifth Legion. We assault troopers had helped to decimate them. Holgotha had transferred rather than letting Starkiens reach its surface. All the artifacts hated the baboons. That was funny, because the Starkiens desperately wanted their own artifact. One of the reasons was to wipe away the ancient shame of losing theirs. Thus, Baba Gobo—

My jaw hung open. I had it. I knew the answer to one of our problems.

Chinning on my helmet radio, I hailed the *Achilles*. Soon enough, Zoe appeared on my HUD.

"Captain," I said.

"Yes, Commander?" she asked.

"Hold your position," I said. "I'm coming back up."

"Sir?"

"Once I'm aboard, we're heading back to Mars Base. Commander Creed, out."

I chinned off the link and throttled my thruster-pack to full acceleration. Instead of floating down to the Moon, I shot back up to the waiting patrol boat.

***

Several days later, I strode through Mars Base with Zoe hurrying to keep up. I'd kept to my own quarters during the trip back, carefully considering every angle.

At a three-meter fountain in the middle of the dome, I met Ella and N7. Dmitri and Rollo were both out on patrols. The orange-skinned dome spread out over us with squat buildings pressed together on the ground. Sunlight shined through the shielding material. I could feel the heat on my neck. The geyser of water sprayed down onto the main basin. Goldfish swam in the water. It was good to see them, reminding us of better days.

"I have an idea," I said in lieu of a greeting.

192

Ella looked tired with bags under her eyes. "I'm sorry, Commander. I have bad news for you."

"What is it?" I asked.

"Ras Claw is dead," she said.

"What? How?" I realized it truly saddened me losing him. Maybe fighting Ras hand-to-hand had caused me to gain respect for him. "Did the Jelk machine kill him?"

"No," Ella said. "He did it, strangling himself."

"Why?" I asked, dumbfounded.

"He didn't want to confirm the coordinates to the Purple Tamika Hall of Honor."

That left me blinking. Ras Claw must have realized I'd tricked him. I should have known he'd figure that out in time. Well, I couldn't do anything about it now. He'd simply become another causality in the Human-Tiger War. I had to concentrate on victory, which meant steeling my heart one more time.

"Did you get the location?" I asked.

"Maybe," Ella said.

"No. You have to know. It's vital for my plan."

"I have *a* location," Ella said. "Since Ras Claw slew himself, I don't know if it's the *right* planet. Either he killed himself in shame, realizing we'd tricked him, or he lied about the location and killed himself to keep us from forcing the true location from him."

That could be a big problem. But I didn't want to thrash it out this second. "Okay," I said. "That might put a serious kink in my plan. I still have a new idea. Are you ready for it?"

The others nodded.

"Simply put," I said, "our problem is a lack of numbers. We don't have enough warships to give a big fleet pause. That means we need more. We need allies."

"We've been over all this before," Ella said.

"Right," I said. "Now I realize I've been looking at this the wrong way. I've been thinking about how to persuade Jade League members to join us. But I doubt any of them are going to listen to humans."

"You finally realize that no alien cares you rode inside the artifact," Ella said.

"You're dead wrong," I told her. "They're going to care, but maybe not enough. We need more persuasion. Usually, a person has to have a great desire. That's the fulcrum you use to change their key ideals."

"Are you speaking about Orange Tamika?" N7 asked.

"That's one group," I said. "We have to find Doctor Sant and tell him the situation. Yet there's another large group of aliens with a desperate desire—the Starkiens."

Ella stared at me a second before she laughed. "You can't seriously mean them. Everyone hates the Starkiens."

"Exactly," I said. "And why do they hate Starkiens? Because the baboons destroyed their artifact. The Forerunner objects all hate Starkiens, too, and won't let them near any of them."

"What is your idea?" Ella asked.

"To find Baba Gobo and make a deal with him," I said. "If the Starkiens will gather their flotillas, I'm betting that would make a tremendous fleet. If it's big enough, that might slow down Admiral Saris when she shows up. And that might give us enough time to raid the Hall of Honor."

"Commander," N7 said. "The Starkiens are notorious double-dealers. If you allow them in the solar system—"

"They can never enter the solar system in any depth," I said. "That would risk having the artifact depart and spoil everything."

"Then what good is your plan?" Ella asked. "The Starkiens want to win an artifact, and you can't give them one."

"No," I said. "That's exactly what I *can* give them."

"You're not making sense," Ella said.

I turned to Zoe. "Would you be willing to take me to Epsilon Indi?"

"Yes," she said quietly.

Ella glanced from Zoe to me. "You're likely sealing your deaths doing that. I suspect you want to speak directly with the Starkiens in that star system."

Ignoring Ella, I said, "N7, I want you to come with me. This will be just like old times when we went to see Naga Gobo aboard his flagship."

194

The android dipped his head in acknowledgement. Good. He would come. I didn't want to do this without him.

"This is a bad idea, Creed," Ella said.

"Those kinds of ideas might be all we have left," I said. "A Lokhar crusading fleet is likely going to hit us soon. We have to meet it or we're all dead anyway. Doesn't that mean taking risks?"

Ella said nothing.

"I think it does," Zoe told me.

I grinned at her. "It's settled then. N7, get your kit. We're going to leave in an hour."

-21-

It took three jumps to reach Epsilon Indi, which translated to eight days of travel. The longest parts—the light years between gates—took the least amount of time. Moving from one gate to the next in a star system took the most time, accelerating and decelerating.

In a straight line, Epsilon Indi was twelve light-years from Earth.

The system had an unusual feature. Epsilon Indi was a K Spectral Class star, about three-fourths the mass of the Sun with a slightly higher gravity. What made the system interesting were the companions. Binary brown dwarfs—objects with a mass of fifty Jupiters—orbited Epsilon Indi at 1,500 AUs. They were both T class brown dwarfs with a separation between them of 2.1 AU.

We stayed far from the star and the brown dwarfs. So did the Starkien fleet. Yes. They were in the Epsilon Indi system. That made this easier as we didn't have to hunt them down.

An hour had passed since I'd spoken with Baba Gobo via screen. Almost gleefully, the chief baboon had given us permission to fly out to meet him on his flagship. Since assurances for our safety seemed superfluous, we went without them.

N7 and I wore vacc-suits with thruster-packs spewing hydrogen spray. We sailed toward a large shark-shaped vessel sliding closer toward our patrol boat.

The majority of the Starkien fleet waited in orbit around a nickel-iron planet. Bright lights showed shuttles lifting from the surface. They must have been mining boats, bringing the ore to one of their giant starships. N7 had told me before those were the factory vessels.

In time, N7 and I passed through a bay door into a Starkien ship the size of Manhattan Island. I felt like a flea landing on an elephant. With our packs vibrating, we came down onto a deck. Various star fighters were parked nearby, but no baboons were visible.

Behind us, the bay door slid shut, closing with a *clang*. It told me an atmosphere already hissed into place. Otherwise, we wouldn't have heard the sound waves. A hum began, and I stumbled. The place had gravity again, the deck plates turning on.

Just like the last time I entered a Starkien vessel eight years ago, no one greeted us. N7 removed his helmet. I did the same with mine. The air stank like a monkey's zoo cage. Some things never changed.

"Ah, we're home," I said.

N7 gave me a quizzical glance.

"A joke," I said. "Let's get started." My gut roiled with unease. I was more than nervous.

We marched to a bank of hatches. The middle one dilated open. Despite my resolve, I took a deep breath. I shouldn't have done that. The stink seemed to lodge down near my throat.

Coughing, with my head bent, I followed N7 along narrow corridors better suited to Rottweilers. The bulkheads seemed to close in around us and the corridors turned much too sharply at times. As before, there were fist-sized portholes along the bottom of the walls like giant mouse holes. I still didn't know what they were for.

The blinking dots leading N7 brought us to a small hatch. It opened, and a greater stink wafted out. That increased my coughing.

N7 glanced at me. I forced myself to stop hacking, nodding for him to go. He led, I followed, both of us ducking in order to enter a far too low-ceilinged chamber filled with Starkien commanders.

This time I could tell. They grinned like predators, each of them gleeful. As before, they wore harnesses and tubular guns. Instead of a table, they sat on low daises, seven important-looking lords. Each had gray or a white-streaked mane. The biggest Starkien had a shiny white mane with horribly red-rimmed eyes.

I walked toward Baba Gobo. That started the baboons hooting and flailing their arms. Two reached for their tubular guns.

I halted beside N7, switching on my translating device.

With a slight bow of my head, I said, "It is good to see you again, Baba Gobo."

The mighty, high lord baboon took his time answering. He was an alien, but I could tell he dearly loved the situation. I would have liked to know Starkien beliefs concerning torture. It didn't help that I'd recently watched Ella torment Ras Claw. Was I going to get exactly what I'd given? I hoped not.

"Commander Creed," Baba Gobo drawled. "This is a welcome surprise," he said. "You do realize that you shall never leave this vessel?"

For once, I restrained myself from speaking too forcefully. I found that difficult.

"I know that you have a hard decision to make," I said.

"Me? Hard?" The high lord baboon showed off his yellow canines, glancing at his elders.

They hooted with the best of them. A few jumped up and down on their daises. It was quite a sight. As they grew quieter, Baba Gobo turned back to me.

"I believe today's decisions will prove easy and enjoyable," he said. "It is not often that a Starkien's enemy freely places himself in our hands. My only curiosity is why you've become so foolish?"

"Need," I said. "Hope."

"Yes," he said, "to be needy is bad. To hope for the best often leads one into traps he cannot escape. All Starkiens know this. That is why we are the most cunning race in the Orion Arm."

"Well, that's why I'm here. Actually, your cunning has become a cul-de-sac for your species. It's the reason you're the gypsies of space."

His brows thundered. "What are these gypsies?" he asked.

"Wanderers, nomads, people without a settled abode."

"Oh." He shook his head. "You are wrong, human, in thinking we are forced into this. It is a survival trait, our way. We Starkiens do not wish to hamper ourselves by settling into any one particular place."

"No, *you're* wrong," I said. "That's exactly what has happened. Others have forced you into this wandering existence. There's no other reason for it."

The good humor vanished from Baba Gobo. He leaned forward, stabbing a dirty finger at me. There was dirt impacted under the fingernail. "What does an animal only recently allowed into space know about the great Starkien people?"

I glanced at each elder in turn. "You're kidding me, right?" I asked.

"Vain beast," Baba Gobo said. "You are not safely aboard one of your warships. You stand with a mobile thinking machine before the elders of our fleet. Your hours of life are quickly dwindling. A single word from me will end your existence. Ponder that instead of spouting your vulgarities."

"Holgotha," I said.

Baba Gobo scowled worse than before. "What does that nonsense word mean? It does not translate into a Starkien meaning."

"How interesting," I said. "I've just told you the name of the Forerunner artifact in the solar system."

It took him a second to understand my meaning. When he did, his red eyes squinted with suspicion. "You lie," he said.

"No. I'm telling you the truth."

"Are you that foolish? The evidence does not support the idea. Why would you give me the name, beast, knowing as you must that it is a marvelous treasure?"

"For some it's a treasure," I said.

"For *any* who possess the name," he said.

"Tell me, Baba Gobo. What will you as a Starkien do with your newfound knowledge?"

199

He glanced at his silent fellows before regarding me again. "Do you truly not understand? I will go to your solar system and lay claim to...*Holgotha.*" He said the artifact's name slowly, tasting it with joy and satisfaction.

"I would advise against such an action," I said.

Baba Gobo hooted with Starkien laughter. "Why would I care what an animal advised me to do?"

"Let's consider the question, as it's an important one. Suppose I'm an animal, as you claim. Why would a Forerunner artifact tell me its name then?"

Several of the elders glanced at Baba Gobo. He pretended to ignore them, although he frowned at me.

"You've just received the name of a Forerunner object: Holgotha. But if you're right, that I, an *animal,* gave it to you, won't the other races laugh when you tell them how you came to learn the name?"

Baba Gobo closed his eyes and rested his snout on a fist. He sat like a statue for several seconds. Then his eyes snapped open. He looked upon me with wonder.

"You are not an animal," he said.

"Correct."

With the same dirty finger he'd pointed at me earlier, Baba Gobo stroked his lower lip. At last, he asked, "Why have you told me the sacred name?"

"Before I answer that, you should know that we used Holgotha to transfer to the Sanakaht star system. That's deep in the Lokhar Empire."

"I am quite aware of the location of the Sanakaht system."

I nodded. "We raided the planet of Sanakaht, dropping nuclear warheads onto the surface."

Baba Gobo gave a start. Several elders murmured in wonder. "Why would you do this?" he asked, sounding amazed.

"For a simple reason," I said. "The Purple Tamika Emperor was in the system. I wished to teach him a lesson."

The baboon scowled. "*You* teach the great Lokhar Emperor a lesson? No, not even you are that rash. You are spouting lies to me."

200

"Think well, Baba Gobo," I said. "If you truly believe I lie about our Sanakaht attack, then Holgotha is not the artifact's name."

For several seconds, he stared at me in silence. I could see his mind spinning. Soon, he nodded. "You are cleverer than I realized." It was a grudging admission. Then his eyes widened. "Ah, I believe I understand now. The artifact must have found you unworthy. That has angered you, yes? To gain revenge on the object, you have run to the Starkiens."

"That's not even close," I said. "I came to you because Holgotha told me the ancient history. He explained how the Starkiens once possessed a Forerunner artifact of their own. They lost it, however, and the other races attacked your ancestors because of it."

Their delayed reaction startled me. It seemed as if it took the words time to percolate into their skulls. Then, as one, the Starkiens lifted their snouts toward the low ceiling. They howled in despair. It was a mournful noise.

Soon, Baba Gobo lowered his snout, and said, "You must die. It is our custom to kill any who repeats the wretched story of old."

"You want to kill me even as I offer you the chance to redeem your race?"

"What do you mean?" Baba Gobo asked hoarsely.

"It's simple," I said. "The Emperor of the Lokhars comes to Earth. He preaches a holy crusade against us and wishes to annihilate humanity in person."

"Then you are as good as dead."

"No, I'm not," I said. "The Emperor is a heretic. Thus, his crusade is doomed to fail."

"What folly do you spout?"

"It's pure logic, Baba Gobo. Think about it. Holgotha brought us to the Sanakaht system. There, the assault troopers slaughtered Lokhars. There, the Emperor himself witnessed our daring. Now, you have to ask yourself the question: Why did the artifact take us to the place where we could fight the Emperor? The answer is simple. Felix Rex Logos called humans beasts. He would not admit us into the Jade League. Yet, the Forerunner object has told me its name. It has shown

201

we belong. The Emperor has sullied himself with his heresy. Now, the ancient artifacts move against him."

Slowly, Baba Gobo nodded. "That is an interesting argument. It might actually sway some."

"Doctor Sant of Orange Tamika preaches against the Purple and thus the Emperor," I said. "This is an opportunity for those with eyes to see."

Baba Gobo glanced at the elders. One of them nodded. Regarding me, the chief baboon asked, "If we helped you, you will give us full control of the artifact?"

"Baba Gobo of the Starkiens," I said in a ringing voice, "I am about to tell you the ancient history of the universe. It is the truth. This is what Holgotha told me about the Starkiens."

I then repeated the story in all its details, particularly the part where the Forerunner artifacts decided that no Starkien would ever walk on them again. That caused the baboons to howl longer and with more misery than before.

"This is a lie," Baba Gobo whispered.

"Your despair shows me you know better."

His entire body sagged. Several of the elders crouched low, covering their heads.

"Go," Baba Gobo said, hoarsely. "Leave our vessel and leave the Epsilon Indi system. Never return."

"No. I came here for Starkien aid, and that aid I will get."

"You are mad, Commander Creed. There is nothing you can offer to entice us to help a doomed species."

"You should listen to me first. I can help you gain redemption in the eyes of the other races. They will think the Forerunner artifact approves of you. Then, the Starkiens will no longer have to wander the star lanes as gypsies."

Baba Gobo studied me for the longest time. Finally, he raised a baboon hand, groping in the air as if he was a baby. I had struck upon the great Starkien desire: to have an artifact, to win their way back into the good graces of the others. Could he dare trust me? Would his hatred and despair be too great?

"How..." he said. "How can you do this for the Starkiens?"

In that moment, I knew I had him. Hiding my excitement, I took a step closer.

"Would you know our great secret?" I asked.

"Yes."

"We will fight the Emperor's fleet a jump before the solar system. We will mass such numbers of ships that he will pause in bewilderment."

"Can you know what route the invasion fleet will take?" he asked.

"I won't have to," I said. "Starkiens are the Orion Arm's greatest scouts. They will seek the Emperor's fleet and report back so our mass can intercept them."

"Who told you we are the greatest scouts?"

"It's obvious," I said. "You're the nomads of space. Back on Earth, our nomads always made the best light cavalry."

"This is not Earth."

"But you are nomads," I said. "Your existence relies on speed and knowledge. If you had to fight at the other races' whims, the Starkiens would have already been dead. That you have survived this long shows me you know how to maneuver out of the way of stronger forces. That implies speed."

"You are cunning," Baba Gobo said. "And it is true. None can match us as scouts. Yet we speak about the Purple Tamika of the Lokhars. They are fierce soldiers, enjoying head-to-head battle. Few dare to stand in the path of a Lokhar battlefleet."

"That's not my plan. We'll raid the crusading fleet the entire distance, striking like Plains Indians of the American West."

"I do not perceive your meaning."

"Hit and run," I said.

"That I do understand. We might bloody them, but it won't stop the Lokhars."

"You're going to buy us time," I said.

"In order to do what?" he asked.

I grinned. "The Star Vikings are going to save the day by producing the soul of Purple Tamika."

"Who are these Vikings?" Baba Gobo asked. "What do you mean soul of the Lokhars?"

"Star Vikings," I said, thumping a hand against my chest. Then, I bowed at the waist.

"You?" he asked. "How can you acquire the soul of the Lokhars?"

"You weren't listening close enough," I told him. "I'll bring the soul of the Purple Tamika Lokhars to the battlefield. There, they will not dare to risk its destruction."

Baba Gobo scratched his baboon chin. "If you can do as you say, I fail to see how that will win the Starkiens their redemption."

"I want to save the solar system. If I achieve that, I'm not worried about who gets the credit for stopping the Lokhar Crusade. If the Emperor races to Earth, and then he and his fleet reels back in defeat, people will demand to know how that happened. I will say, 'The Starkiens outfought the Purple Tamika Lokhars. They did it to defend Holgotha, the Forerunner artifact. As Holgotha's spokesman, I will say the machine has forgiven your old mistake. This is a new era where Starkiens have honor.'"

Baba Gobo scowled. "We already have honor."

"No you don't."

Several of the elders hooted with outrage.

"Hey," I said. "Get real. I'm the one who walked alone onto your flagship. I did it without assurances. You must have wondered how I could have been so foolish."

Baba Gobo glanced at the elders. Several nodded. "Yes," the old baboon said. "We wondered why you'd taken leave of your senses."

"Clearly, I had a plan. You even like my plan. It turns out that I knew exactly what I was doing."

"So it would appear," Baba Gobo admitted.

"I'm the man who told you the name of Holgotha. I asked for nothing in return."

"Yes," Baba Gobo said. "That is strange."

"I'm Commander Creed," I said. "I do things my way, and I kick ass. If you want a piece of the Purple Tamika Lokhar, you have to listen to me, and you have to learn to trust me."

"Trust is not the Starkien way," Baba Gobo said.

"And look where that's gotten you," I said.

"We have survived the ages."

"Yeah, on the run, hated and despised by all. Oh yeah, that's really impressive. In case you can't tell, I'm being sarcastic."

Behind me, N7 poked a warning finger in my back.

"Look, Baba Gobo," I said. "Prince Venturi of Orange Tamika came to me for Earth troopers. He wanted the best fighters in order to save our universe. Well, the prince didn't survive. But I did. We smashed Abaddon and defeated his Kargs on the portal planet. I have a track record of defeating whoever faces me. If the Starkiens want in this time, join up and reap the rewards."

"Will there be others beside us to fight the Purple Tamika Lokhars?" Baba Gobo asked.

"Of course," I lied, hoping I could find others. Where was Doctor Sant? "This is the Holgotha Crusade," I said. "We're going to gather the biggest fleet ever seen and smash the heretics who thought to stamp out humanity and ostracize the Starkiens. You're going be in the limelight, my friend."

"That isn't the Starkien way," Baba Gobo muttered. "We have worked from the shadows for a long time."

I nodded vigorously. "Can you imagine how many Starkien flotillas there are?"

"No Starkien ever wonders about that," he said. "Once, we had many fleets. Now, only seven remain."

"Okay. That's your first assignment. You gather the Starkien remnants into one place. I'll grab the Orange Tamika Lokhars and snatch the soul of the Purple."

Baba Gobo stared at me for a time. "Would you wait outside, please, as we confer on this?" he asked.

"With pleasure," I said.

Together, N7 and I walked into the corridor. The hatch closed behind us and the elders must have begun to talk.

"I don't understand how you hope to achieve your goal," N7 whispered.

"How can you say that? You've been with me the entire time?"

"The Starkiens have never done as you suggested."

"Right," I said. "That's what I'm bringing to the table: new ideas. Haven't you learned yet that's the most powerful thing in the universe?"

"I am learning," N7 said.

We could hear their voices through the sealed hatch, but not their individual words. Traveling up the corridors to us were internal ship clangs and hisses. There was a surprising amount of those noises.

"There is a thing that troubles me," N7 said.

"Yeah?"

"Why does Baba Gobo listen to you? I would not have believed it unless I saw it."

I grinned. "I gave him something incredible for free. That baffled him. It threw him off his normal pattern. That made him susceptible to my confidence."

"Why would this be?" N7 asked.

"Because he can't understand the source of my confidence," I said.

"Neither can I," the android said.

I made a soft sound and frowned down at my boots. "It's called balls to the firewall."

"I lack human reproductive organs."

I nodded.

"Why would testicles make the difference?" N7 asked.

"Smoke and mirrors," I said, "fast-talking and atomic self-assurance. That persuades people. Besides, I've been lucky a few times. People start to wonder about that. They figure there has to be a reason for my successes. What could be the reason? It baffles them. Finally, they figure, 'He must be something special, maybe a battle genius or something.' Now, I don't believe that myself. This entire episode began in Antarctica when I grabbed a rifle and stormed a space lander. Basically, I've been doing the same thing only on a grander scale each time. The gall throws people off."

"Extraordinary," N7 said.

"Maybe," I said. "Growing up, I used to read about a guy called the Charles the XII of Sweden. He was the Berserker Knight-Errant, constantly fighting three to one, five to one and even eight to one odds battles and winning."

"Charles could do anything?" N7 asked.

"No. In the end, he lost the Swedish Empire. The king was crazy and his lopsided battles finally caught up with him on the field of Poltava."

206

"Did he die there?"

"No. He escaped to the Sultan of the Ottoman Empire, waging war against Russia from the court of another ruler."

"What happened to the Berserker Knight-Errant in the end?" N7 asked.

I took my time answering. "At a siege in Norway, he was shot in the head, from behind. Most commentators speculate that one of his own troops finally had enough of his endless wars."

"Is that what will happen to you?" N7 asked.

"I don't see how it couldn't," I said, shrugging, pretending I didn't care. "But it doesn't matter. I plan to be the Berserker-Star Viking, doing whatever I have to in order to give humanity its place among the stars."

The hatch opened before N7 could respond. The smallest elder beckoned us within.

In silence and under the starting eyes of Baba Gobo and his elders, N7 and I walked before them.

"Commander Creed," the white-maned baboon said.

I dipped my head in acknowledgment.

"We are impressed with your courage," Baba Gobo said. "And you are a cunning military officer. But we cannot agree to face the might of a Lokhar crusade, one bent on destroying humans. The Starkiens will sit out this battle and war."

"What?" I said. "But, but..." *What had I done wrong? I'd been sure they would agree to my plan.*

Baba Gobo shook his head. "We are decided on this. Yet, I have this to say. For your gift of the name Holgotha, we grant you your life. Good-bye, Commander Creed. May the Creator have mercy on your soul and on the lives of your people. I do not think any of you have long to live."

-22-

Depressed, I returned to Patrol Boat *Achilles*. This should have worked. If all the Starkiens had gathered their warships and used their speed, we could have harried the Emperor's fleet.

"They lack courage," I told N7 as we took off our helmets in the patrol boat's locker room.

The android nodded. I wondered if he thought I lacked foresight. I'd been so sure Baba Gobo would join us. It had been obvious to me.

After leaving the Epsilon Indi system, I sat morosely in my cabin. The odds against humanity had turned horribly long again.

Several hours later, I stalked through the corridors into the cargo hold. There, I wrapped my fists. I began to smash the heavy bag, thudding blow after blow.

What do you what to hear? I bet I know—*Zoe Artemis came to talk to me, we made passionate love, everything cleared up in my head and I saved the day*. No such luck, I'm afraid. Real life doesn't often work like that.

I hammered the heavy bag until my arms hung at my sides. Sweat soaked my t-shirt. My hands ached.

Standing in front of the swaying bag, I realized this was *our* problem. Humanity had to gather its paltry number of ships and hightail it elsewhere. For a time in his life, Genghis Khan had done exactly that.

No. That wasn't quite right. He'd become a sneaky young man, but he'd kept the nucleus of his Mongols on their ancestral lands. Some things were worth dying for. Ras Claw had shown me that. The tiger strangled himself rather than reveal the location of the Purple Tamika Hall of Honor. Or had our Shi-Feng captive slain himself out of shame? Maybe he had given us the right location though.

Raising my fists, I whacked the bag another few times. Then, I stood flat-footed and began to wail on it. I did so until I staggered backward and slammed down onto my butt. I sucked down air. Sweat dripped from my face.

Slowly, my breathing evened out.

The Shi-Feng had started this mess. The exploding tigers had tried to take me down in Wyoming. I closed my eyes, listening to my heart thud.

Maybe that's how this one had to go down. We were in a game of commando raids. The Lokhar Emperor had used the Shi-Feng. I planned to hit back with the Star Vikings. I'd done it once already, and it had given us more ships, more guns and more information through Ras Claw. It had also given us a more direct problem: a genocidal Lokhar holy crusade.

Climbing to my feet, I began to unwrap my hands. Maybe I'd lost my touch. How long could someone continue to pull a rabbit out of the hat? I wasn't a stage magician, but a combat soldier.

No, you're a Star Viking now. If one avenue fails, you try another one. The Starkiens aren't going to help you. That means everything rests on raiding the Hall of Honor.

Grabbing the bandages, using a forearm to wipe sweat from my eyes, I headed for the exit. It was time to closet myself in my room and come up with a better plan.

***

A week later, I sat with Rollo, Dmitri, N7 and Ella around a dinner table in Ceres Asteroid. We ate steak kabobs with rice pilaf and pineapple slices. Afterward, we watched an old Avengers movie in the next room.

The credits finally played and I said, "Lights."

We sat in big easy chairs, sipping our favorite alcoholic beverages.

"It's time to decide," I said.

"Do you mean what to do against Purple Tamika's Hall of Honor?" Ella said.

"That's right."

"You realize Ras Claw may have given us false directions?" she said.

"That's coloring my idea on how we should attempt this," I said.

"Oh?" she asked.

I rattled the ice cubes in my glass and sipped the last of the Scotch whiskey. "I don't know if Horus is the Lokhar planet of origin or not," I began.

"I don't believe it is," Ella said. "But for reasons we haven't divined yet, the planet Horus is important to Purple Tamika."

"What can you tell us about it?" I asked N7.

The android shrugged.

"You don't know?" I asked him.

"I do not, Commander. I am sorry."

"I've discovered a little," Ella said. "While under the Jelk machine, Ras Claw gave away a few hints. Horus is a swamp world, dismal with thick fogs and giant snake-creatures. Vast trees grow there. Chopped down and cured, the wood is almost as tough as steel. From what Ras Claw said, the hall is fashioned from such lumber."

"Did you learn anything more?" I asked.

"After that, no, nothing concrete."

I tilted the glass to my mouth, sucking on an ice cube. After crunching it, I said, "Tell us what you surmise about the place. What seems likely?"

Ella swirled the wine in her goblet, staring at it. "There will be war-pickets in orbit and surely ceremonial guards on the surface. I suspect the Shi-Feng will guard the hall. They will no doubt prove deadly."

"This is going to be a commando raid," I said. "That means stealth is going to count for as much as hard fighting."

"How many assault troopers and ships will you use?" Ella asked.

"One transport," I said, "along with one hundred Star Vikings."

"Why so few?" Rollo asked.

"We're not going to fight our way down because I think we'd fail if we tried it like that. We have to slip into the hall, steal what we can carry and run away as fast as we can. That's why we're taking a patrol boat along."

"Won't that look suspicious?" Ella asked.

"The patrol boat will be in the transport. After the strike, we unship it and run back for Earth as fast as we can."

"Patrol boats are fast," Dmitri said. "But that's about all they are."

I nodded.

"I want in," Rollo said thoughtfully.

"Me too," Dmitri said.

"You'll need my expertise," Ella told me.

I pointed at each of them in turn and said, "No, no and no. Someone has to stay here in case my plan backfires."

Rollo scowled in an angry way. In the old days, I wouldn't have cared. These days, the big guy had become scary. "You're not thinking this through," he said. "In the past, you've grabbed the dice of fate and placed everything on one wild gamble. And you've won big."

"I know," I said. "That's why you're staying back this time. Sooner or later, the dice are going to roll against me. Look at what happened aboard the Starkien flagship. I failed. If I fall on my face out there, I want you people to carry on back here."

"You're wrong about this, Creed," Rollo said. "We're staking everything on grabbing the articles in the Hall of Honor. If we fail, humanity has to run away from the solar system. Practically speaking, we'll have to flee to the Jelk Corporation and hide there."

"That would probably mean the end of our freedom," I said.

"Which is why I'm coming along," Rollo said. "If this is our only chance, we have to front load the dice."

211

"I'm going too," Dmitri added. "On this, my mind is made up."

"I already lost Jennifer," I said. "I don't want to lose any of you too."

"That is touching," Ella said. "It is also uncharacteristic of your decision making. You cannot use your heart in this. You need us because we have worked as a team for a long time. No one is better than the five of us together."

"She has a point, Commander," N7 told me.

Maybe the whiskey did the thinking. Maybe I didn't realize how beat down the Starkien refusal had left me. I didn't have enough fight left to disagree with the four of them.

"Okay," I said. "You're all in. It's probably just as well. I have a feeling we're going to have to do a lot of on-the-fly-thinking if we're going to pull this one off."

"I have a question," Ella said.

"Shoot."

"Do we have enough time to reach Horus, loot the hall and return to Earth before the Emperor's fleet arrives in the solar system?"

I snorted quietly. That was yet another problem. Even if we got the needed articles, we might not make it back in time to save humanity.

"I don't know," I said. "Let's call it a night so we can start first thing tomorrow morning. We should have left a week ago already."

***

Storing *Achilles* in the transport took longer than I expected. Then I had to choose the one hundred Star Vikings.

I debated skimming the heroes from each zagun. Soon I realized that was the wrong way to do it. I studied the records and decided on one of Dmitri's zaguns. It had the best combat record. Unfortunately, it only had eighty-seven effectives. Still, they would be the commandos, the Star Vikings I used for the strike.

Zoe would have a zagun of troopers to run the transport. Dmitri's led the assault team. I wanted a unified battle group where the members implicitly trusted one another. A well-led combat team became greater than the men and women in it.

Three days later, the *Peru* jumped through the Neptune gate, beginning our expedition against Purple Tamika's Hall of Honor.

-23-

Until this mission, I hadn't needed precise information regarding the size, shape and extant of the Jade League. It was going to make a great deal of difference now.

In broad terms, the Jade League and Jelk Corporation touched the solar system at one of their far corners. The bulk of the league was in the direction of Rigel, while the bulk of the corporation was in the direction of Deneb.

What I hadn't realized was the extent of the unease among certain Jade League members. With the removal of the main Saurian fleets from the border regions, the old quarrels among league members had reignited. We found out that meant a lack of Jade League guardians at the jump gates nearest Jelk territory.

Maybe that's another reason Baba Gobo's Starkiens had been at Epsilon Indi. As nomads, they moved into power vacuums. They went where enemy warships were thinnest.

We had occasion to speak with other trading crews and a few picket officers at a key jump gate. Four years ago, a league race known as the Ilk had begun an accelerated warship-building program. They controlled twelve star systems behind the border region. The Ilk had longstanding grievances against the Eiljanre and the Gitan. Several "incidents" had already taken place: ships firing on other vessels. Maybe as telling, the Ilk had purchased large numbers of troop transports.

In the worsening atmosphere, and with the removal of Lokhar warships from the border, the Ilk, the Eiljanre and the

Gitan had pulled the bulk of their battle cruisers from jump gate duty. Those vessels now guarded their home systems and key colony worlds.

For us, it meant we had to answer a few questions at some jump gates, but that was it. Since we were a trading vessel, and a small one at that, it was clear we presented little danger to anyone. Fortunately, for the time being, the Jade League remained intact. That was important because the pickets could have acted as pirates, hijacking the *Peru* and stealing our cargo. Instead, the questions directed at us implied a desire for a continuation of interstellar trade.

For fifteen days, we made headway toward our destination of Horus, which was deep within the Jade League. With the relocation of the Saurian fleets, we dared to use several Jelk Corporation jump gates. That allowed us to enter the league at a different angle than if we'd headed straight from the solar system.

On the sixteenth day after leaving Earth, we had our first crises. The *Peru* jumped into the Octagon star system.

On the bridge, I toweled my face with a wet rag. I'd found it the quickest way to get me thinking again after a jump.

Using a clicker, I studied the system on the main screen. A bloated red giant sat in the center with three terrestrial rock-balls orbiting it, making up the inner system. The outer had a single Jovian planet with swirling green cloud cover. The gas world was one hundred thousand kilometers from the jump gate.

"Star fighters," Ella said from her station.

"What's that?" I asked.

"I'm picking up a trio of star fighters," Ella said. "Let me give you higher magnification."

She did something to her board. On the main screen, three triangular-shaped fighters leaped into view. I sat forward, squinting. Lokhar pilots sat under bubble canopies. Each of them wore a red-crested helmet.

"Those are tiger fighters," Ella said.

My spine turned cold. Had we jumped into a trap? "Is there any indication as to their Tamika?" I asked.

"Look!" Ella said, tapping her panel. A yellow circle highlighted a red fireball beside the Lokhar numbers 312 on the side of the closest fighter.

"I recognize the symbol," N7 said from his station. "The fighters belong to Crimson Tamika."

"Do we know if Crimson stands with Orange or with Purple Tamika?" I asked.

"Oh-oh," Ella said. "This isn't good. I'm counting nine spaceships heading for us. Let me try the recognition codes so I can tell you what kind of warships they are."

I disliked the wait. I wanted to know now why Lokhar warships headed for us on an intercept course. From my conversations with other freighter captains, I'd learned the Lokhar didn't own any star systems in this region. They had fleet outposts, but most of the flotillas had abandoned them. The *Peru* had swung wide around the only known Lokhar-manned station. Two captains had spoken about the tigers choosing sides in what appeared to be a possible civil war. The growing rumor was that Orange Tamika led a secret rebellion against the Emperor.

Would the heightened tensions make our raid impossible? Maybe the brewing insurrection would keep the Emperor from Earth. I doubted it, though. It seemed the source of Doctor Sant's authority came from Holgotha and his ride on the artifact. If Felix Rex Logos could discredit Sant by annihilating us and regaining control of Holgotha, might that cause Orange Tamika's rebellion to fizzle?

In the here and now, Ella looked up with worry in her eyes. What had she discovered?

"Four Lokhar battle cruisers and five frigates are heading straight for us, Commander," she said. "The ships are accelerating from a habitat orbiting the Jovian planet."

I nodded, asking, "Are there any more star fighters?"

"Yes," Ella said. "I'm picking up six more. Oh-oh, it looks like there's a carrier out there, Commander."

There went my notion of turning around and running away through the gate before the Lokhars reached our ship. Nine fighters would nail us before we could escape back the way we'd come.

216

"Give me a wide angle view of everything," I said. In a few seconds, I studied the six new fighters. Tigers piloted them, too. I assumed the nine warships would also have Lokhar crews.

Turning my chair, I regarded N7. "This is bigger than a picket but much smaller than a fleet."

"Given our data," N7 said, "I do not understand why a force of this size is out here."

"Commander," Ella told me. "We're being hailed." She listened to her earbud. "Sir, a Crimson Tamika Lokhar demands to speak with our captain."

"Put the tiger on the main screen," I said.

A moment later, I faced the gaudiest Lokhar I'd ever seen. He was normal sized, which was to say seven feet tall. He wore a military cap with an ornate red badge on the bill. Crimson stripes ran up and down his black jacket. He had rows of medals on his chest. If he'd been an old-time Earther, I'd have figured him for a staff officer or a general trying to prove his manhood through the amount of tin he could pin on his chest. I'd never trusted such types.

On the spot, I decided on some playacting. What else could I have done? Letting my shoulders deflate, I lowered my head as if awed by his presence.

"Great war-leader," I said in Lokhar. "This is an amazing honor. I am too dim to withstand the glory of your presence."

N7 stared at me in astonishment.

"You know the great tongue," the Lokhar said haughtily.

"Yes, yes," I said, bobbing my head. "It is good for trade."

His magnificence scowled. "Our noble tongue is used for *war* and to describe acts of *valor*. It is not used for *trade*."

"Yes, yes," I said. "You are most assuredly correct. Please forgive my error."

The Lokhar raised an ornate baton, waving it imperiously. "You will prepare your ship for boarding," he said. "Once my flotilla reaches you, I will send inspectors to check your holds."

"O Great One," I wailed. "This is not good. No. It is bad. I have a priceless cargo. I fear some of your soldiers might steal from me."

217

The Lokhar became outraged, bristling. "Do you have any idea who you address?"

"I am at a terrible lack, lord. I do not know. No, no, please forgive me."

"I am Senior Razor Dagon, the Lord Inspector of Crimson Tamika."

"You are allied with Orange Tamika perhaps?" I asked meekly.

"By no means," he declared. "We are in league with Purple Tamika. A vile species of…" He squinted at me. "What is your race, trader?"

"I am from Alpha Centauri, Great One."

"You look like these humans we have come to destroy. Have you heard of Doctor Sant?"

"Who?" I asked.

"He is a renegade Lokhar of the vilest sort," Dagon said. "He tells feeble lies that ensnare the simpleminded. During his stay with them, the humans warped Sant's mind. By the species description, you appear to be human."

I gathered saliva in my mouth and spat on the floor. "I despise the humans. Yes, I know about them. They are a wicked race of upstarts. No, Great One, to our bitter shame we of Alpha Centauri resemble these filthy mongrels. I am glad you Lokhars have decided to capture them all."

"Foolish trader, we crusaders will *annihilate* the vermin."

"Genocide, Great One?" I asked.

"We must cleanse these imps before they become demonic servants of the Jelk. How else can one explain their ability to warp a Lokhar of the oldest house?"

I was beginning to see the Emperor's propaganda angle. Sant's contact with devilish human had deranged him.

"Ah," I said. "I had not realized humanity's crime was so grave."

"Yes," the Lokhar said. "The Emperor himself comes to sit in judgment of them. He will lead us to glorious victory over the vermin."

"He leads Crimson Tamika?" I asked.

The tiger's eyes narrowed. "We have allied with Purple Tamika. That is true. Yet I wonder about you. Where did a simple trader come to learn about the Lokhars in such detail?"

On my chair, I cringed before him. "Please, my lord, all know about the mighty Lokhars. You are a valorous race, defending the artifacts with your blood."

He nodded, but still seemed suspicious. I had to distract him with something else. What could I say, though? Then I thought I had it.

"I see your medals, lord. You must have an amazing war record."

His eyes narrowed even more tightly than before. "I understand your tactic. Flattery will not help you, trader. We are guarding the league from all possible contact with the Earthlings. Prepare your ship for boarding. My soldiers will search your cargo and check your logs, insuring you have not secretly aided the targeted savages."

"Please, Great One. Have mercy on me, a trader. I fear your soldiers will pilfer my rich goods. Perhaps if you came yourself, lord…"

I felt N7 watching me closely.

"I would gladly honor your visit by gifting you with precious gems from my rarest collection," I said.

From Ras Claw, Ella had learned about the Lokhars' love of jewelry. I was testing that lust.

Senior Razor Dagon, the Lord Inspector of Crimson Tamika, regarded me closely. A crafty smile slid across his face.

"Yes, I think I shall make this a personal inspection," the tiger said. "You will of course, as a matter of protocol, send your highest-ranking officers aboard my flagship."

"But of course, Great One. We will honor you in whatever way you deem necessary."

"We will make the exchange in three hours," the Lokhar said.

I smiled in the oiliest manner I could summon. Then the screen went blank as he broke contact.

"I do not understand, Commander," N7 asked. "Once the Crimson Lord Inspector boards our ship, he will realize you're human. Then he will kill all of us."

"Tell Dmitri and Rollo they're going over to the tiger flagship," I said.

"What are you thinking, Creed?" Ella asked me.

I glanced back at N7 before studying Ella. "We're going to have to work fast," I said. "You brought the Jelk mind probe, right?"

"What?" Ella said. "I don't know what you have in mind. I would need hours to prep him and study his psychology before I could begin to tamper with his mind. That is what you're thinking, isn't it?"

"That's right," I said. "We'll subdue him once he's on board and put him under the machine. You'll have ten minutes to condition him."

"Didn't you just hear me?" Ella asked.

"I did. That's why I'm telling you that you have ten minutes."

"That will be long enough to scramble his brains, nothing more," she said.

"If you don't succeed," I said, "Dmitri and Rollo will die, along with all of us under Lokhar lasers. That will mean the Lokhars win the crusade against Earth."

"This is a rash plan," Ella said.

I spread my hands. "Under the circumstances, I don't see what else I can do. Senior Razor Dagon strikes me as an arrogant pretender. Our only hope is to get him to come aboard ship where we can condition him. At least we knew they love gems, so we were able to entice him with a bribe."

"I am surprised he is so foolish," N7 said.

"I'm not," Ella said. "He has all the warships. He knows he can order our destruction with a snap of his fingers. Such a situation often makes humans overconfident. Creed's guess was to believe it would do the same thing for Lokhars."

"We don't have him yet," I said. "So let's get ready."

***

220

Three hours later, I shook Rollo and Dmitri's hands before watching them enter a hatch. They would board a three-man flyer and head to the Lokhar flagship. I wondered if I'd ever see either of them again.

I hadn't expected anything like this. The Emperor had moved quicker than I'd thought he would. It appeared that he had ordered a blockade around our region of space. It seemed like a wide and rather porous net. I wondered on the Emperor's reasoning. I knew too little regarding the many factors an Emperor would have to take into account for his crusade. Maybe the wide blockade had more to do with halting the efforts of Orange Tamika than catching humans. Maybe catching humans was simply a pretext for the flotilla being here. That made more sense.

Whatever the real reason for the warships, it showed me that at least one other Tamika had joined the crusade. It showed, too, the Emperor had kept good on his threat. He meant to wipe us out.

Standing in the reception area, I exhaled. Zoe and Ella waited with me.

"I hope you know what you're doing, Creed," Ella said.

"Don't I always?" I asked.

Ella snorted softly.

On a hand monitor, I noticed the arrival of the Lord Inspector Senior Razor Dagon. He came in a rakish shuttle with several star fighters flying guard. The procession reminded me of a parade more than a military exercise.

Soon, outer locks *clanged* and pressure gages *hissed*.

"Remember," I said. "We're traders. That means we cringe and act awed toward them."

"I just want to kill," Zoe said.

"Finesse," I said. "It's all about finesse."

"I like that coming from you," Ella said.

"Good."

A louder hiss told me it was time. I straightened, pasting a fake smile onto my face. I wore a red silk shirt, fluffy green pants, a green cape and boots. It made me feel like a Christmas ornament.

The hatch opened and three big Lokhar guards stepped forth. They wore body armor but lacked exo-skeleton strength. Good. They underestimated us. Each guard cradled a big machine gun, looking as if he wanted to unload his weapon into our bodies.

Another impressive Lokhar stepped up. He wore gaudy red garments and swept the floor with a broom. The last Lokhar appeared, Senior Razor Dagon. His fur had good color, but he stooped. That meant he was older than I'd realized. I suspected the Lord Inspector used fur coloring.

Stepping forward, I went to one knee, bowing my head.

"You are the trader?" Senior Razor Dagon asked.

"I am, lord."

"Rise," he said. "Show me to your storeroom and these precious gems you spoke so highly about. I am eager to select my gift."

I stood, keeping my head bowed before him. "Would you like to see the rest of the vessel first, lord?"

"No," he said, sounding irritated. "I told you my desire. Now attend to it."

"Yes, great lord. I obey." Turning, I swirled the cape and pointed at Ella. "Hurry wench, open the hatch for the mighty Lokhar of Crimson Tamika."

Struggling to keep from rolling her eyes, Ella tugged the hatch open. I strode through. Next, the three guards followed, the other with his swishing broom and finally Senior Razor Dagon.

As he moved through the corridor, the chief Lokhar sniffed aloud. "I detect a taint of oil in the air," he said. "On the outside, this looked like a new vessel. Within…I am displeased at the state of the recycling unit."

"I will beat the chief engineer, lord. Of this, I assure you."

"Never mind about that," he said. "Let's hurry to your storeroom."

I took them on a long walk through the corridors. As I'd guessed, the chief Lokhar wasn't in as good a condition as the guards. Soon, he panted. Out of the corner of my eye, I saw him open his snout to complain about the length of our trek.

"We're almost there, lord," I said.

222

Senior Razor Dagon nodded brusquely.

"There, wench," I said, pointing at the selected hatch. "Hurry, open it for his magnificence."

Ella opened the hatch.

"Out of the way," I said, pushing her onto the deck plates. "This way, lord. This is my inner sanctum of gems."

I jumped through. The three Lokhar guards followed, each of them ducking his head.

I spun around, having slipped a sap from my pants pocket and into my right hand. As the first guard straightened, I swung. The sap connected against his forehead. He dropped hard onto the deck. The second guard I caught under the chin. His fangs clicked together, his head lifting. On the next swing, the sap caught him on the left temple, and he, too, dropped onto the deck plates. The last guard got off a single shot. The bullet smashed against a bulkhead. I swung. He blocked with his rifle, catching my forearm.

With a yell—my forearm bone throbbed—I ducked. He swung with the butt of his machine gun. The hard wood swished over me. Charging him, I hit his midsection with my shoulder and hammered his back against a wall. He grunted, dropped his weapon and struck my head with the bottom of his fists. That staggered me so I stumbled away from him. The guard growled, picking up his fallen machine gun. I hurled the sap. It hit his face and gave me a moment's grace. I whipped out a force blade and thrust. The powered knife hissed as it cut through armor and buried into his chest. Blood jetted from the wound and he gaged on the gore bubbling in his mouth. I barely moved aside fast enough to escape most of the blood and his falling body that thudded onto the deck.

I found myself staring into the eyes of Senior Razor Dagon. Ella had taken down the sweeper.

"You're mad," the tiger said in a hoarse voice. "All of you are as good as dead."

First flicking off the force blade, I jumped through the hatch and wrestled the old Lokhar around.

"Unhand me," he demanded.

He'd have been better off fighting instead of jabbering. In seconds, I had his arms pinned behind him. Ella snapped plastic ties onto his wrists. Forcing his head down, I pushed him into the room with his deceased guards.

"You are dead," he said. "You're all as good as dead."

"Give me a hand," I told Zoe.

She rushed in. Together, we manhandled the protesting Lokhar into a chair, strapping him into place, immobilizing his head with steel bands.

"This will never work," Ella told me. She slid a lead curtain out of the way, revealing the refrigerator-sized Jelk machine.

"What is that?" Senior Razor Dagon asked. He was stretched out belly-first like a pinned butterfly in a boy's collection, with his chin resting in a groove.

With a grunt, Ella rolled the machine closer. Then she opened a slot and took out the lampshade-shaped focusing device. Fiddling with it, she aligned it with the tiger's forehead.

"You aren't from Alpha Centauri, are you?" Dagon asked.

"Don't answer him," Ella said. "It will only make this more difficult."

She clicked on the device. The main machine hummed with an obscene sound. A light appeared between the tiger's eyes. She adjusted the dot of light.

"He's right about one thing," Ella said. "This is madness."

I backed away, pulling Zoe with me. Once outside the room, I shut the hatch.

"You killed the Lokhar guards," Zoe whispered.

"I didn't want to."

"It can't work now, can it?" she asked. "Dagon will have to go back without his guards. How can he explain that to his officers so we're not blasted out of space?"

I looked into Zoe's eyes. "Give it a little while and we'll find out."

***

Fifteen minutes later, the hatch opened. Through the opening, a dazed-looking Senior Razor Dagon peered quizzically at me.

"Hello," he said.

"Don't speak to him," Ella said from out of sight.

224

Senior Razor Dagon cocked his tiger head. He appeared more confused than before.

"Get out of his way," Ella said.

I backed against a bulkhead. Zoe did likewise.

"Aren't you going to speak to me?" Senior Razor Dagon asked.

I stared at the floor.

A moment later, the tiger stepped through the hatch. "I must return to my ship," he said to no one in particular.

Ella appeared behind him. She looked haggard but determined. She didn't say anything more.

Slowly at first, the Crimson Tamika Lokhar headed back the way he'd come. When he turned the wrong way, Ella called out to him.

The Lokhar stopped. In slow motion, he faced her.

"Commander Creed," Ella said. "Show the great lord the way."

"A moment," the tiger said.

Glancing at Ella, I saw her nod. Therefore, I faced the Lokhar.

"You are the notorious animal, Commander Creed?" he asked.

"Don't answer that," Ella warned.

I expected Senior Razor Dagon to glance at her. He did not. Instead, the most puzzled expression of all appeared on his furry face. Finally, he motioned for me to walk ahead of him.

I did, all the way to the exit.

He donned his spacesuit. Without a word good-bye, he entered the airlock and closed the hatch.

I whirled around to Ella. "What did you tell him?" I asked.

"A form of the truth is always the easiest to sell," she said. "I told him this ship carries the notorious Commander Creed. We're on a secret mission in regards to the crusade."

"That's a big risk?"

"Do you think so?" Ella asked.

I didn't like the look in her eyes. She seemed frazzled. "What about his dead guards?" I asked. "How is he going to explain them and the sweeper?"

"They're to remain here and ensure our success," Ella said.

225

"Do you think the Jelk conditioning will hold once he's back on his flagship?"

"I give that a fifty percent chance of success," she told me.

I thought about that. "Well, it's better than what we had when he first hailed us. All right, you two did well. Let's get back to the bridge."

***

Like many of these affairs, the ending proved anticlimactic. Ten minutes after returning to his flagship, Senior Razor Dagon sent Rollo and Dmitri back. Twenty minutes after his return, the Lokhar hailed our ship. He spoke to Ella.

"Do you require an escort to the next jump gate?" he asked.

"No," Ella said. "You must treat us as a regular trader. That will arouse the least suspicions regarding us."

"I understand," he said. "And yet...it feels as if I'm forgetting something vital."

"Don't you remember?" Ella asked. "The Emperor himself will reward you once this is over."

"Ah..." he said. "Good. This is good. Good-bye, and may the Great Maker bless your enterprise."

Ella nodded. The screen went blank.

I sucked in air several times before I managed to say, "Head for the next jump gate at full acceleration. I want to get the hell out of this star system as fast as we can."

226

-24-

It would have been so much easier if Holgotha had simply transferred us to the planet Horus. We could have completed the mission already and returned home to drink beer.

Instead, the days merged into weeks. The farther we left the border region behind, the easier the receptions became toward us. Once we left Ilk territory far behind, it became like moving through the old United States. A few border guards asked a question at some crossings. At others, a sign told us we entered a new state.

Finally, the weeks merged into a month and a half. Shipboard life had become monotonous. We drilled to remain sharp, but I believe we lost some of our skills.

This wasn't like the attack upon the portal planet. We'd had space on the Lokhar dreadnought. The *Peru* proved cramped, and I began to wonder if I should have brought half the number of troopers along.

The sheer size of the Jade League began to dawn on me. It was one thing to study a star chart. It was another to actually make jump after jump, heading ever deeper into league territory.

The extent of the league and the number of different races caused me to wonder why the aliens cared so much about Earth. How had an emperor come to worry what the Jelk did with us?

In ancient times, had our ancestors been active in space? Was there some terrible, lingering memory that propelled the aliens against us?

I've always thought it strange how human history just appeared almost full blown onto the scene. The greatest culprit in that regard had been Ancient Egypt. Even the early pharaohs had pyramids, while the culture had math, skull-drilling medicine, all kinds of technology including batteries. It seemed as if everything had simply leapt from Horus' brow full grown instead of painfully climbing through stages.

I happened to remember that some of earliest Ur had roomier and richer houses than later Ur. That's what archeologists had dug up. It meant the first ones on the scene had been wealthier than the latter. Just like in Ancient Egypt, Sumer also seemed to have simply begun with a high culture as if the people were colonists from a different time and place.

Could the story of Noah and the Flood, Gilgamesh and the Deluge have cosmic implications? Maybe old Noah had been a spacefarer kicked out of the void. Maybe the aliens had conveniently forgotten to tell us the true history of humanity. Then it would make sense why human history just seemed to pop up with advanced technology. Why did recorded history only date back to around 4000 B.C.?

I'm not talking about prehistoric times, but written, historical events. If modern Homo Sapiens had been around for one hundred thousand years as some of my teachers had taught, you'd expect to find ancient civilizations fifty thousand years old, thirty thousand. No. It never worked out like that. Around 4,000 B.C. everything seemed to appear as if with the snap of someone's fingers. Was that when the other aliens had driven humanity from the stars?

I had no idea. But the size of the Jade League daunted me. Why would an emperor start a crusade to wipe us out? Why not just bring several hundred warships and get the job over with? Why make such a production out of it?

Even after eight years in space, I knew far too little concerning the aliens, the Forerunners and their artifacts and our place in all of this.

228

***

After seven weeks of travel, armed pickets began to appear again at the jump gates. We were stopped twice, endured inspections and hard questioning. I asked several trader captains about that. Their hints implied what I suspected. We passed Lokhar worlds now, and tigers were busy choosing sides for what appeared to be a brewing civil war.

On the ninth week after our encounter with Senior Razor Dagon, we neared Horus. Then, we finally had a breakthrough in a critical area.

I shot pool with Dmitri. Let me rephrase that. I stood beside the pool table with a stick in hand, watching Dmitri school me on the game.

Ella walked through the hatch. *Crack.* Dmitri shot, and I heard another billiard ball drop into a pocket. I'd hoped her appearance might have disrupted his concentration. No such luck.

"Ella," Dmitri said, as he walked around the table.

"Dmitri," she said, before giving me a significant glance.

"Is there a problem?" I asked.

"We're a day out from the second to last jump gate," she said.

"Uh-huh," I said, watching Dmitri sink another ball.

"N7 finally hacked a planetary data core," she said.

"What?" I asked. "The packet didn't self-erase?"

"No," she said.

I put up my pool stick. That finally got Dmitri's attention.

"Where are you going?" he asked, looking up.

"Didn't you hear Ella?" I asked.

He shook his head.

"Two more jumps and we're at Horus."

"We already know that," Dmitri said, shrugging. "That still gives us plenty of time to finish the game."

"Not me," I said. "N7 finally hacked a data core. It's time to plan."

"After the game, yes?" Dmitri asked.

"Go," I told Ella, making shooing motions. She raised an eyebrow. I made urgent shooing motions.

229

Finally, she headed out of the hatch. I followed as Dmitri *cracked* another billiard ball.

"What was that all about?" she asked.

"I'm tired of watching him win all the time."

Ella rolled her eyes and continued down the corridor. "Humanity's future is at stake, and you're worried about losing another game of pool?"

The way she put it, that sounded childish. Just once, though, I would have liked to beat Dmitri.

Ten minutes later, I stood with Ella in the chart room. N7 had hacked something called *A Jade League Catalog of Planets and Customs*. In essence, we googled the information from a hijacked alien computer core.

If some are wondering why, after eight years ,we had so little interstellar information on the Jade League, the answer was simple. In many ways, the Lokhars ran the league just as the Soviets had run the Russian Empire called the USSR. In those days, good maps had been the next thing to state secrets. We'd been having a bear of a time getting real data on the inner Lokhar worlds.

Ella and I used separate readers, ingesting the information. Twenty minutes later, N7 showed up. Our android began to sped-read files.

We discovered a few interesting facts about Horus and its star system. It possessed a G-class star with a single planet. There were no asteroids, meteors, comets, nothing, just the planet and its star. Despite its being a swamp world, the planet had desert poles with huge cracks in the rocky surface. Hot oceans separated the poles from the central continent. There, life thrived in marshy abundance. Steam rose constantly and thick fogs drifted everywhere. A high mountain range provided the living area for the Lokhars. In that region grew giant trees and large predatory snakes.

The compendium didn't say why Purple Tamika had chosen Horus as their shrine planet. I would have dearly liked to know. A single short entry suggested the Shi-Feng used Horus as a training center.

I set down my reader. Hadn't Doctor Sant told me no one spoke about the Shi-Feng? Why did this data chip have

230

information about them then? Shrugging, I stretched my back and continued reading.

The planet lacked mineral resources, manufacturing centers and did not appear to produce art of any kind. So what good was it?

"Maybe it used to be a prison planet," Ella said. "Long ago, the elders of Purple Tamika were exiled on the mountains. They rose up and came back to win the empire. Hence, they turned Horus into a shrine planet."

"Maybe," I said.

"I have a different theory," N7 said. "The planet appears to have religious significance."

"How do you know that?" I asked.

N7 tapped his reader. "I just read about an ancient Forerunner city. Eons ago, it sank into the world ocean."

"Ah," Ella said. "It appears they have an Atlantis myth. This is interesting."

"Pardon?" N7 asked her.

"Forget about Atlantis," I said. "What about this sunken city?"

N7 blinked twice before continuing. "Purple Tamika excavates the underwater city. Yet the procedure is perilous. Water monsters constantly attack the submarines. Underwater volcanoes spew hot mud and ash on the finds. Still the priests search through the watery ruins for clues to the First Ones."

"Okay," I said, "Horus appears to be a religious shrine planet. I seem to recall Shah Claath talking about a shrine planet before."

"You refer to the Sigma Draconis system," N7 said. "Shah Claath and his brethren wanted something from the planetary shrine. That is why we attacked the Planetary Defense Station."

"That's old news," I said. "I want to know where this Hall of Honor is located. Have you found out yet?"

N7 pointed at a screen chart. It showed the small habitable area on the central mountain plateau. "The hall lies in the city of Zelambre," he said. "It is the largest metropolitan center on Horus, complete with a spaceport."

"Give me a magnification of Zelambre," I said.

N7 did, showing us a dismal place. Mist drifted over wide canals crisscrossing a city built of log cabins, log palaces and log stadiums. Big motorized dugout canoes traversed the waterways as they used to in Venice, Italy.

"Seems primitive for a spacefaring race," I said.

"Since Purple Tamika could presumably build any type of city they desired," Ella said, "we can surmise they raised Zelambre this way for a reason."

"Sure," I said. "It's still primitive."

"That might make sense for a religious center," she said.

"No," I said. "The Forerunner city is underwater in the ocean, not perched in the mountains. Zelambre houses the Hall of Honor. That's not religious."

"Maybe the two are related," Ella said. "Maybe honor is part of their religion."

"Whatever," I said. "In the end, it doesn't matter for our strike. What are their orbital defenses like? Have you found anything about that?"

"The compendium did not specify the planetary defenses," N7 said.

With my elbows on a table, I bent my head, rubbing my temples. "It's strange when you think about it. We've come all this way to hit them in the heart, and the planet turns out to be a primitive place stuck in a swamp."

"It is Purple Tamika's origin point," N7 said. "Clearly, they wish to preserve it in its original state."

"Well, parts of it are primitive," I said. "The oceanography shows us they're willing to use modern technology to search the ancient city."

"That is an astute observation," N7 said.

"Yeah," I said. "Well, it looks like we'll have to wait to make our final plans until we see how well they guard the planet."

"Another three days should bring us to Horus," Ella said.

I stared at the orbital shot of the log city. It must have been taken on one of the rare clear days. Clouds normally covered every inch of the planet. It was strange. The Emperor brought a crusading armada against the poisoned Earth. Many hundreds of light years away, we readied to strike a primitive swamp world.

If we won here, could we get back home in time to stop the Emperor? I had no idea. I just knew I was going to try with everything I had.

***

That sleep period on my cot, I wondered just how sacred these shrine planets were to the Lokhars and to the other Jade League members. The aliens had formed their league to halt the depredations of the Jelk Corporation. The league races protected the artifacts. I'd been with Claath when he attacked a shrine planet at the Sigma Draconis system. The Jelk fixation on the planetary shrine had helped to give us assault troopers time to make our play for freedom.

The historical Vikings had struck at Christian monasteries in the Dark Ages. Among the Christian princes and kings of England, France and Germany, such places were held in reverence. The Viking raids against the Church had shocked the Christians of that era. Since the Vikings had originally been pagans, worshiping Odin and Thor, they hadn't given a fig about insulting God or Christ.

How would the Jade League races react to our attack against the Purple Tamika Hall of Honor? Would it outrage the Lokhars? Would it outrage other aliens to such an extent that they would unite even more vigorously against humanity?

I had no idea. If we were lucky, the Lokhars would guard their Hall of Honor with as much force as the medieval Christians had originally guarded the monasteries, which was to say, not at all.

We were the Star Vikings, and we planned to hit Purple Tamika where it hurt the most.

-25-

Coming out of the Horus jump gate, we found ourselves half a million kilometers from the planet.

A picket ship twice the size of the *Achilles* hidden in the belly of the *Peru* moved leisurely toward us.

"His particle beam cannons are activating," Ella told me.

"Hail the ship," I said.

Ella did so, finally saying, "He wants to know why we're here."

"Can you put the speaker on the screen?"

"He won't agree to that," Ella told me, "says it is against Horus custom."

"Tell him we're gem traders. We had a good season of trade. In order to show our appreciation, we are going to place our three best gems in the planetary shrine."

Ella relayed the message. Putting a forefinger onto her earbud, she listened to his reply. Finally, she told me, "He likes your story, Commander. The particle beam cannons have gone offline. We're to proceed to the planet."

"Is he giving us an escort?" I asked.

"Negative, Commander. I imagine he trusts us."

I eyed Ella, wondering if that was supposed to be a barb. In any case, the *Peru* headed for the planet.

It soon became apparent that many spaceships orbited Horus, more than we'd expected.

"I'm counting three hundred spacecraft all told," Ella said.

"Are they all military vessels?" I asked.

"No. Traders, what I take to be yachts, system craft, escort vehicles and a few large battle cruisers and carriers."

I exhaled sharply, watching the screen, studying the strange world. The desert poles with their visible cracks reminded me of the old Martian canals. There weren't any on the Red Planet, but in the good old days, people thought Mars did have canals. Some of the oldest pictures showing the planet had them, with artists having penciled them in.

Now, I viewed a world that seemed to have a massive drainage system. The more things changed, the more they stayed the same.

For the next several hours, the *Peru* headed for Horus.

Ella began picking out the orbitals. They were ugly constructs with heavy armor and big plasma cannons. The Lokhar meant to protect this world.

Soon enough, the largest space station hailed us. The operator gave us a flight schedule to bring us into low orbit. Horus might have old-fashioned log cities, but there was nothing ancient or decrepit about the planetary defenses.

Too soon, the *Peru* braked. In another three hours, we would be in orbit.

"Do you still think we can do this?" Ella asked me.

"It doesn't matter what I think. We're going to try."

Ella nodded.

I stood. "I'm going to get ready."

"Good luck, Commander," she said.

Nodding tersely, I stalked off the bridge.

***

As such things went, the *Peru* was a small trader, well able to land on a gravity surface.

Ella asked the space station commander for permission to land at Zelambre's spaceport. The operator told her we would have to wait several days. Health inspectors would have to board the ship first and clear us.

By now, we knew regular Lokhar customs and had expected this. Fortunately, we had ten stealth pods. They were military grade insertion devices stolen from Sanakaht. Made for bigger and heavier Lokhar maniples, it gave each arban enough space to bring their DZ9 air-cycles.

The *Peru* orbited Horus five times before Zoe brought the *Achilles* out of the transport's belly. The patrol boat's sides showed Lokhar lettering. The vessel's computer held Purple Tamika codes from Sanakaht. We'd been saving that, along with a trick I'd learned in hyperspace from Shah Claath.

The two ships orbited side by side in order to show one radar signature. Finally, zero hour approached. It was night in swampy Zelambre, with first light still hours away.

One by one, we maneuvered the stealth pods out of the *Peru's* cargo hold and into space. In low orbit over Horus, Star Vikings using thruster packs glided their air-cycles into the drop pods.

Soon, it was my turn. I secured my DZ9 to a rack and then settled into one myself. I wore my symbiotic skin and carried my Bahnkouv along with a Lokhar machine gun and a satchel of sonic grenades.

N7, in his cyber-armor, sat webbed in at the drop pod's controls.

"Ready, Commander?" the android asked me.

"What does Zoe say?" I asked.

"Everyone is in position, Commander."

My gut tightened into a tiny ball, squeezing harder and harder. Man, I had to go to the head and take a piss. My stomach seethed, and I found myself trembling with anticipation. I had a bitter surprise for the tigers. Not only would we act like Star Vikings, but the worst sort of vandals, which seemed just in a way.

The word came from an old German tribe called Vandals. In the bad old days of the failing Roman Empire, they had raided the borders. Eventually, the Vandals crossed into Spain and forded the Strait of Gibraltar into North Africa. There, they marched on the Roman city of Carthage. They took it, and became the worst sort of pirates—the Vikings of their age. Anyway, a day came when their greatest king, a man named Gaiseric, sailed upon Rome and sacked it. His warriors looted in such a thorough and savage fashion that people coined the

236

phrase, "Looting like Vandals." In time, the word *vandal* came to mean "wanton destruction."

I planned on some wanton destruction down on Horus but for a tactical reason. Maybe future generations would curse me, but I didn't care. I wanted to save humanity, and for that, I would do just about anything. I didn't give a damn if the Horus tigers had to pay for what other Lokhars had done to Earth. They should have left us alone. That's all I care say about that.

"Let's do this," I told N7. "Let's show the Purple Lokhars that payback is a bitch."

***

The stealth drop reminded me of my days with the Jelk Corporation in one particular. We couldn't see a thing going in.

With cold jets of propulsion so we didn't give ourselves away with a heat signature, the black drop pod maneuvered for the atmosphere. Internal anti-gravity chutes whined inside the pod. The plunging sensation reminded me of Great America as a kid. I'd ridden the Drop Zone hundreds of times. The ride had gone straight up. Then, it released, and you dropped straight down. Maybe it wouldn't have been as bad in the pod if I could have seen outside.

Around me, assault troopers groaned. Others clenched their teeth. We fell and fell toward Horus. Time lost meaning. The plunge seemed to go on forever. Then, with a lurch, the dropping sensation departed. We floated, and the high whining inside the pod ceased.

A ragged cheer went up from the troopers.

"Has anyone spotted us?" I asked N7.

"No radar has touched the outer surface," he said, with his face pressed against the view plate.

That brought another cheer.

The minutes ticked by. Finally, N7 said, "Landing in thirty seconds. As desired, we're headed for a vast body of water."

I waited, and the stealth pod struck the surface. That caused the entire structure to tremble. One air-cycle fell out of its restraints and hit the deck with a crash and raining of parts.

The entire compartment surged upward as if carried by a huge swell.

"There are waves," N7 said needlessly. "The sides will blow away in three, two, one…"

A sudden shudder caused the sides of the stealth pod to explode outward. I watched one big piece tumble end over end. One hundred meters away, it struck the dark waters with a splash.

At the same time, a wave rolled into our compartment, soaking three troopers.

"Get on your cycles!" I shouted. "Start them up. Get airborne."

I yanked the release cord and guided my DZ9 in a controlled descent onto the sloshing deck. The entire pod had already begun to sink. More waves rolled toward us. With a jump, I crashed onto the saddle. My thumb pushed the starter. Nothing happened. Around me, other cycles sputtered into mechanical life.

The waves seemed to get bigger and faster the longer we were in the water.

I shoved my thumb against the starter and told the cycle some choice words. That must have done it. My air-mount hummed with sound. I twisted the throttle and the machine rose just in time to avoid the wave.

Unfortunately, two troopers failed to do what the rest of us had. The wave catapulted a DZ9 over the deck and into the soup. It plopped out of sight, sinking. The other cycle slid for the edge but the trooper grabbed it. Using steroid-68 strength magnified by her symbiotic armor, she stopped the machine from reaching the ocean. Straddling the bike, she started it and rose into the air.

The arban leader shouted orders. An air-cycle dipped low, and the stranded trooper climbed aboard as a passenger.

Around us in the storm-tossed sea were other stealth pods. From them rose the wasp-like Star Vikings. In all, ninety-three DZ9s made it. Only one trooper drowned.

"Rollo," I radioed.

"I know what to do," he said. Gunning his air-cycle and taking three other troopers with him, Rollo headed for the underwater excavation. Between them in a mesh net, the

238

machines carried a present for the tigers. It was part of our escape plan.

The other ninety cycles hummed as we sped low over the water toward the mountains in the far distance. On one of those plateaus was the city of Zelambre and the selected Hall of Honor.

We'd made the space drop. Now it was time to see if we could hit the city before anyone knew humans were on Horus' surface.

***

This strike was different from Sanakaht in a number of ways. The biggest difference was the need to travel three hundred kilometers before we struck the first blow.

I led the pack, an air-cycle gang from Earth. The image made me grin for thirty kilometers. Opening the throttle, I flew until my craft shuddered. Below, the ocean whizzed past. Soon, we hit a sandy beach, climbed above plants that looked like palm trees and made the cycles throb with strain as we rode up steep slopes.

It was dark, and thick cloud cover meant no stars. We passed monsters the size of city blocks, slow-moving slug creatures. Lava pits roared with flame fifty meters tall. Darting bat things swooped at me like gnats. Two struck my suit, flopping away as each gave their death-screech. Stupid bats.

"Slow it down," I ordered.

We were forty kilometers from Zelambre. Horus time, it must have been two o'clock in the morning. Dense cloud cover protected the surface from the star's harsh radiation. This system's sun gave off more bad rays than Earth's did.

The DZ9s skimmed a swamp. I saw the scummy water ripple. Once, giant coils like a Loch Ness monster spun into sight and disappeared just as fast.

"Snakes," Dmitri said. "I hate snakes."

I smiled. The Cossack loved old movies and repeating his favorite lines from them.

"No mercy," I reminded my bikers. "Kill anyone getting in the way. This is one raid that must succeed."

No one argued. Everyone knew the score. Still, I felt it was good to remind them.

The last ten kilometers showed farmland and bizarre structures. The latter reminded me of the funky statues I used to see on American college campuses. I know. I'm a philistine when it comes to art. I had a simple rule of thumb. Anything I could do wasn't art. I could fling paint on a canvas. I could twist girders and cement them into the ground. I couldn't paint like Rembrandt or chisel marble and make it look like a beautiful naked lady. Those things were art. The crap at the end had been the ugliness that the last American upper class had shoveled onto the rest of us and called it beauty.

It seemed like the Purple Tamika Lokhars had the same mental disease.

I gripped my handlebars. On my HUD, the dark log city rose into view. Well, *rose* might be the wrong word. It appeared as a cold, sleepy town with a few of the bizarre artwork statues thrown in.

In the center of town was the biggest log palace that I'd ever seen. If I had to compare it to anything, it would have been the Kremlin in Moscow. The Russians had known how to build with wood. They had those crazy domes and cool spires. Sadly, these days, Moscow was a radioactive crater.

I grabbed a sonic grenade from my pouch. Activating it with my thumb, I dropped it onto the first street. Other Star Vikings did likewise.

Our helmets would stop the debilitating, and in some instances, killing noise. As the DZ9s buzzed Zelambre, we dropped our tiny bundles on a clearly unsuspecting metropolitan suburb.

"Dmitri, now," I said.

The Cossack ordered his arbans. Almost immediately, missiles roared from under the belly of selected cycles. The small rockets hissed with hellish speed and blasted against the Hall of Honor.

Explosions rocked the log palace. Wood shot into the air. Flames jetted. Fires blazed into existence. More missiles struck.

240

Tiger guards appeared on untouched wooden parapets. They wore absurd plumed helmets and hefted long sticks with blades on the end. This was getting better and better. They must have been ceremonial guards.

With my Bahnkouv, I shot one of them in the chest. The Lokhar crumpled around the beam, with his fur smoking. Another, I pierced in the head, which vanished under the hot laser.

Then, I dropped the rifle and used both hands. I flew through an exploded opening into the Hall of Honors. Before me flashed the ancient prizes Ras Claw had described.

Standing up as if riding a jet ski, I skidded across the floor until I reached a blazing fire. Tigers roared, shouting what sounded like obscenities. Were these the vestals? They didn't have weapons, but they did charge with their claws extended.

I thought about my dad. He'd never had a chance against the Lokhar dreadnought. Yeah, everyone wants war to be fair and honorable. It never has been, and it never will be. That's just my opinion, for what it's worth.

With a Lokhar machine gun, I put every tiger on his back. Blood and guts blew everywhere. I'm a savage. I'm an Earther. I'm not making excuses. I'm not proud of what I did to them. Could I have done it another way? Yeah. If I'd been thinking more clearly, I might have used another sonic grenade. I didn't, though. I got off my cycle and slaughtered them.

Then I proceeded to beat out the fire. Why would any tiger care about these flames? Ras Claw had told us about the Eternal Fire of Purple Tamika. An old Lokhar prophecy said that if it ever went out that would be the end of the tribe. Well, I beat out the fire except for one precious coal.

Three troopers ran near with a hot box. Using tongs, I grabbed the last coal and dumped it into the container. A different trooper put in the special tinder for the coal. Great stacks of wood lay nearby. In the box was the last of their Eternal Fire. If Purple Tamika wanted it back, they were going to have to be nice to me.

"Go," I told the three. "Take the fire and guard it with your lives."

They raced back to their humming cycles on the floor.

I rotated in a slow circle, watching my people at work. Dead Lokhars lay everywhere. We ripped tapestries off the walls. Those were made from the fur of kings and emperors. Ancient tiger armor tumbled into our carrying carts. Swords, knives, kick boots filled our boxes. Black blood, skulls and banners twelve thousand years old fell into special sacks. Smooth gold coins and stone talismans clattered against each other.

"Lokhar military or religious police are on their way," Dmitri radioed me.

I ran to my air-cycle, lifted and shot through an exploded opening. With five other Star Vikings, I flew at lights bobbing along the widest canal.

Big log boats with mounted weapons sped toward the middle of Zelambre.

"No you don't," I said. "Follow me," I told the troopers.

I flew down their throats. I mean straight at those mounted weapons. There wasn't any swerving or darting. Locking the direction of my cycle, I stood and blazed away with the Lokhar machine gun. Tigers tumbled from the dugouts.

A red beam from one of the boat cannons hit a cycle. The DZ9 exploded in a fiery blast. A helmet hissed past me. It carried the head of a dead Star Viking.

The machine gun trembled in my hands as I hammered tigers and their boats. Bloody chunks mingled with smoking wood. Then, everything went crazy as two red beams struck my cycle. They chewed metal, and I immediately began to drop.

With a bellow of rage, I leapt from my DZ9. Luckily for me, I struck water. I plummeted and hit bottom almost right away. Using my legs and the enhanced power of the symbiotic suit, I leapt again, this time for the surface.

My head broke the surface with big dugout canoes all around me. Blades slashed at my helmet. Several struck like gongs, making my ears ring. It's hard to remember exactly what happened next. In a red haze, I recall grabbing a pole and yanking myself toward the surprised tiger. He braced his feet to keep from tumbling into the water. For his sake and that of his

242

fellow guards, he would have been better off letting go of his pole.

Like a monster from a swampy lagoon, I climbed into his dugout. Tearing the halberd-thing from a Lokhar, I hacked with demented strength. They roared and rushed me. I mowed them down because I had a pure heart and wore living skin of Jelk design.

When I cleared the first dugout, I leaped, rocking the next as I landed. With fury, I chopped furry bodies. For as long as I lived, I planned to kill and destroy the enemies of Earth.

Even with the symbiotic suit, I began to grow weary after the third dugout. The skin had taken cuts and oozed, attempting to heal.

A red beam slashed past me.

That revitalized my energies. I dove, hiding on the bottom of the boat, crawling for the front of the craft. I never made it. Using beams, the tigers sawed and hacked my dugout. Instead of dying to their weapon mounts, I slithered overboard, sinking into the murky water.

Aiming my visor toward the surface, I used my HUD to make out the dugout bottoms. Some of the fury departed my brain as I stood down there. I recalled my sonic grenades and the force blade at my side.

Right, I knew how to play this.

With a leap and a bellow inside my helmet, I shot up, latched a hand onto a gunwale and pulled myself aboard a new dugout. Tigers roared and hacked.

My suit had hardened and fended off the first round of blows. Before the second cut my living skin, I rolled a sonic grenade onto the sloshing bottom.

It must have gone off. The tigers dropped, with blood pouring out of their ears. Some clapped their paws over their ears and dove overboard.

I stood and began lobbing sonic grenades into other dugouts. Soon, I stood alone, bobbing in the canal.

On shore, the big Hall of Honors burned nicely. I watched with professional appreciation and saw air-cycles burst out like a swarm of bees. They flew for the ocean. I waved to them, and I would have used my helmet's radio to call. Unfortunately, it

243

had shorted out. Must have happened because of all those halberd slashes to the head.

I breathed deeply. How long would it be until the tigers brought power-armored soldiers to take me down?

I shrugged.

Then, I noticed three cycles skimming the water. I waved again, more vigorously than before. One of the riders must have seen me. He turned, and in less than thirty seconds, he hovered just above my head.

Gratefully, I climbed onto Dmitri's cycle. The Cossack hadn't given up on me. I owed my friend big time.

Slapping him on the back, I let him know I was okay. He gave me the thumbs up. Then Dmitri gunned his DZ9, heading out of Zelambre with our sacred loot.

We'd made it in, always the easier part of a raid or an assassination. Getting out alive was going to be the challenge.

-26-

As Dmitri drove, I worked on my helmet radio. When we flew over the sandy beach, I finally managed to reconnect by using a secondary emergency pack.

N7 had already arranged the timing with Ella upstairs in the *Achilles*. I confirmed that everyone was ready.

"The orbitals have gone onto high alert," Ella told me.

"It's time for our surprise, then," I said.

"Are you sure you want to do this, Creed?" she asked.

I didn't mind that she used my name on the radio. Let the Purple Tamika Lokhars know I'd done this. Let them crap their drawers over me.

"I'm sure," I said. "Do it."

"Roger," Ella said.

I waited behind Dmitri. He skimmed over the dark waves. Around me, the Star Vikings flew in a tight formation.

After another thirty kilometers, I swear I felt a shudder coming from the planet. That was impossible, of course. First, I was airborne. Second, how could Horus tremble?

Then, I saw it. My heart went cold. Far out on the watery horizon, a giant mushroom cloud rose higher and higher.

I swallowed uneasily. Had I done the right thing? I had a feeling I'd have to pay for giving this order. Maybe not right away, but someday.

At my orders, Rollo and his team had carried a hell-burner, dropping it over the ancient Forerunner city. The fantastically powerful explosive must have sunk onto the sea bottom before igniting. Could the blast have made the planet rumble? No. It must have been a guilty subconscious on my part.

I'd destroyed a great archeological dig. The site had held history from the beginning, ruins from the fabled First Ones. What did I care, right? Why fret over it? The Lokhars had nuked and poisoned the Earth. Screw the old digs. The tigers had messed with humanity. I wanted them to gnash their teeth and pull out their fur over us. Maybe just as importantly, I wanted something to occupy their thoughts. Let them wonder what we would strike next. Let them focus on the terrorist attack instead of the Star Viking raid, at least for a few minutes, in order to let us execute our last maneuver.

The mushroom cloud grew as a brilliant flare of noonday light expanded on the horizon. Hell-burners have that effect. We only had the one, though.

Heaviness squeezed my chest. Despite my hatred for the Earth-destroying Lokhars, I felt bad for the order to drop the nuke. Still, I didn't think my personal payback would happen today. That meant I had to concentrate on the here and now.

"Let's do it," I said. "Go!"

All around me, DZ9s shot upward into the sky like old-time Blue Angel jets. We attempted to rendezvous with the *Achilles* in the upper atmosphere.

***

By the time we reached our limit, the light from the hell-burner had long since died down. I imagine every orbital and its sensors watched the sea. I also figured that many of them would be blind for a little while longer.

When the explosion first blasted in the Horus Ocean, the *Peru* and the *Achilles* plunged down into the atmosphere. They came for different reasons.

As the *Achilles* hovered in place with its anti-gravity pods whining at full power, Star Vikings drove to an open bay door. This was the tricky part. The cyclists didn't drive in. Instead, they hovered in place and pitched their cargo through the door. Then, they leaped into the patrol boat. Afterward, the DZ9 fell toward the ocean.

Soon, it was our turn. The larger *Peru* hovered beside the *Achilles*. We lifted between the spaceships as Dmitri maneuvered the cycle to the open door.

"Go, Commander," he told me.

I stood and made sure not to look down. Instead, I focused on the open bay. With a leap, and the cycle dipping under me, I shot through the gap into the waiting arms of fellow Star Vikings. A second later, Dmitri followed. His cycle plunged down.

We lost three troopers who misjudged the distance or were wounded or too tired. I would have liked to rescue them. We had no more time, though. They dropped with the falling DZ9s.

The bay door closed, and the *Achilles* headed for low orbit. Beside the patrol boat, the automated and quite empty *Peru* did likewise.

Zoe's patrol boat had a special feature, a cloaking device. It didn't need to work long, but it needed to hide us from scanners for a few critical hours.

I shed my symbiotic skin, depositing the quivering blob into its heated cylinder. After capping the unit, I literally ran down the ship's corridors, reaching the bridge as the boat entered the darkness of space.

"Commander," Zoe said from her chair. She rose to move aside for me.

"No, sit down," I said. "You're running the *Achilles*. I'm just here to watch."

She nodded, sitting down and all business again as she rapped out commands.

The two vessels rose together almost side by side.

"Now," Zoe said.

A terrific hum vibrated the deck plates under my feet. The boat's pilot slowed our climb. On the main screen and in the view port, I watched the *Peru* accelerate into higher orbit.

Over our speakers, harsh Lokhar voices uttered orders.

We ignored them. So did the *Peru*. Did the orbital operators know about the looting of the Hall of Honor? It would appear so. No plasma cannons fired on the transport. If I had to guess, the tigers didn't want to destroy the precious cargo they thought rode in the hauler.

On auto, the *Peru* headed for deep space.

I stared at the main screen. It showed a passive sensor image of what happened. Twenty Lokhar military vessels peeled out of orbit, accelerating after the *Peru*. Clearly, they must have known about the sacrilege to the Hall of Honor. They must have known that whoever had attacked had stolen precious items. The tigers obviously wanted those items back.

In the *Achilles*, we tiptoed the rest of the way up from the planet. With the cloaking device, we slipped past orbitals and big Lokhar battle cruisers.

As a kid, I used to read war novels and history. War World II had always held a special place in my heart and imagination. I recalled the tale of German Lieutenant Commander Gunther Prien.

On October 14, 1939 in U-47, a German submarine, Prien snuck into Scapa Flow at night. The British home fleet was concentrated there. Slipping past antisubmarine defenses, steel nets for instance, and negotiating treacherous riptides, Prien fired two spreads of four torpedoes. He scored several hits against the battleship *Royal Oak*. In two minutes, the British capital ship went down, taking 786 officers and men with her. Afterward, Prien slipped out of the harbor and away, making the most gallant exploit of the sea war between the two nations.

Standing on the *Achilles'* bridge behind Captain Zoe's chair, I felt a thrill similar to what Commander Prien must have felt back then.

How long could our cloaking device hold? Maybe no longer than it took the tigers to storm aboard the *Peru*.

In the end, it took the Lokhars forty-three minutes for a battle cruiser to speed beside the transport. Power-armored tigers made the small voyage between the two ships, landing on the *Peru's* hull.

We'd been waiting for that. The transport exploded into a massive fireball. The battle cruiser's shield held for a tenth of a second. After that, it went down, and the *Peru's* debris smashed through the armored hull, destroying the Lokhar capital ship. There wouldn't be anything left of the boarders.

It was a dirty tactic, I know. I planned it that way. I wanted the horror of the situation to dull their reactions. Later, rage

248

would consume the tigers. For now, I wanted them drugged with dazed disbelief at the loss of the precious cargo the *Peru* supposedly carried.

For the next several hours, we headed cloaked for the distant jump gate.

By that time, radio traffic raged with accusations back and forth. Priests called for an hour of silent grief. Lokhar scientists begged for decontamination units.

A psychic force seemed to build over Zelambre. I could sense it aboard the *Achilles*. It felt as the unified fury and tiger grief reached out to our patrol boat. No one cheered here. No one clapped each other on the back.

I made the rounds through the corridors and cabins. Relieved assault troopers stared at me with huge eyes.

"Are we going to make it, Commander?" a man asked.

"We're doing it," I said. "But we're far from out of it yet."

I wanted to tell them to wear slippers and keep their voices down. It wouldn't make any difference, but in our hearts, we must have all felt that.

Finally, I returned to the bridge.

Zoe turned to me. She shook her head. The woman looked exhausted. "Please, Commander, take over."

I nodded.

She got up, moving like an old woman.

With a sigh, I sank into the command chair. I could feel the weight of responsibility descend upon me.

Maybe this was why I loved riding the cycles so much. I'd felt free hours ago on the planet. This…it strained my nerves and curdled my gut.

"The enemy sensor sweeps are getting stronger, sir," the comm operator told me.

A hatch opened. I turned my chair. Ella walked to me and leaned against an armrest.

"Maybe we should just make a dash for it," she said.

"Look at those battle cruisers heading for the jump gate," I said. "Their beams would spear us in a moment."

"They're going to know we went through the gate."

"We'll see," I said.

Time ticked by with agonizing slowness. Was this how Prien had felt on the way out of Scapa Flow? The Germans had sunk a mighty British battleship. Their lives would have been mud if they failed to slip away undetected. Ours would be scrambled atoms in the void of a Lokhar star system if we failed.

How could we beat the Lokhars? What would Gunther Prien do in this situation?

For the next ten minutes, I thought furiously, and I drew a blank. We weren't U-47. We were the Star Vikings. Yeah. What would a Viking captain of old have done in this situation?

Our cloaked patrol boat would never make it past the star fighters beginning to spread out in front of the jump gate. Two battle cruisers already waited there. Three more came, with even more heading out.

Did they know we'd made it off the planet? Maybe they suspected a trick. How would a Star Viking react?

My eyes widened. I turned to Ella.

"What's wrong?" she asked.

"I know how we can escape the Horus star system," I said.

"Tell me," she said.

I did.

After listening to the idea, she told me I was a lunatic. Maybe she was right. We had thirty minutes to get ready. Then it would be time to attempt the craziest attack of the mission.

***

I pulled my blob of symbiotic armor out of the heat unit. Stepping onto it, I let the warm substance slide up my legs. Soon, I put on a helmet and shouldered a thruster pack onto my shoulders. Around me, assault troopers did likewise.

With Zoe's people added in, I had one hundred and seventy-three effectives. That left the bridge crew to run the *Achilles*.

The three battle cruisers from Horus had already begun braking maneuvers. The two in front waited, with the wall of star fighters behind them at the jump gate.

I had another Bahnkouv, a souped-up weapon we called Hot Shot. It would burn out after ten or eleven intense laser blasts. Usually, a laser rifle would fire for a long time. Each of these laser bolts had the ability to burn through Lokhar powered armor. Soon, if everything went right, we would be facing power-armored legionaries again.

"All right, people," I said over the short-speaker. "Probably, only half of us are going to be alive an hour from now. This is balls out to the firewall. I don't see any other way of getting home, though. Kill every Lokhar you see, no exceptions. Don't give the engine crew time to blow their ship. This is a blitzkrieg attack plus ten thousand. Any questions?"

No one had any.

We waited in the cargo bay, the one we'd entered not so long ago above the Horus Ocean.

"Hang on," Zoe said over the ship speaker.

I grabbed a crash bar. Others did likewise. A period of hard maneuvers took place.

"One more minute," Zoe said.

My palms became slick with sweat. Would the patrol boat remain cloaked long enough?

"Thirty seconds," she said.

I would have liked to say something more to my troopers. My mouth had turned too dry.

"Now," Zoe said.

The bay door began to slide open. Stars appeared. Then I saw the underbelly of a big Lokhar battle cruiser. It, too, had an open bay door. Fighters launched down from it.

That was our one stroke of luck. It might be all we needed.

"Hang on just a moment longer," Zoe said. "I'm taking us closer."

She maneuvered the patrol boat. A Lokhar fighter barely missed us as it flashed past. The wash must have hit our cloaking field in same manner. An electrical discharge flared between the two vessels. Ours was a toy compared to the battle cruiser.

"Someone spotted us," Zoe said. "Go!"

I let go of the crash bar. With my magnetic boots, I ran along the deck plates. When I reached the open bay door, I cut their power and jumped. At the same moment, I turned on the thruster pack. At maximum acceleration, I rushed the battle cruiser's fighter launch bay.

Behind me, other Star Vikings did likewise. It was a race, all right. We were going to board and storm the vessel and try to take it over as our own.

I expelled hydrogen spray, a white misty trail behind me as I strained to reach the open bay door. If I failed, humanity would never make a comeback. My teeth ground together as rage consumed me. I envisioned the Emperor himself aboard the craft. My head began to beat in time to my heart. A hazy red nimbus surrounded my vision.

A cool, detached part of my mind, a little citadel buried deeply in my brain, watched as berserker-gang overcame me. Maybe the suit pumped the drugs. Maybe I did it on my own. For once, I couldn't tell the difference.

Raving, I closed the distance and the bay doors began sliding shut. I came like a cannonball, readying my Bahnkouv. Ten shots to win a species—mine—another extended bout at life.

I flashed past a giant door and pulled the trigger. Eighty meters away, a clear surface shattered so shards glittered in the hangar bay. A Lokhar officer backed away from his controls. I shot again, and he exploded in fur, blood and bone.

Speeding fast, I twisted my torso, readied myself and struck a bulkhead. Cannonballing off it, pushing with my legs to guide my direction, I shot at the wrecked control chamber. I swiveled my torso once more and blasted a roar of hydrogen spray from the thrusters. I had to slow down.

More armored Star Vikings flew into the hangar bay. Their laser bolts took down floating tigers and others running away with magnetic boots clanking along the deck plates.

Swiveling around again, I pulled the trigger three times. The shots blasted within the chamber. The closing bay doors halted, frozen with ten meters of space between them.

Then, I hit a gory wall within the control chamber, bounced and floated out.

A big hatch deeper in the hangar bay opened and power-armored Lokhars poked their rifles through.

I emptied my Bahnkouv at them, dropping three tiger legionaries. Before they murdered me, I landed behind steel cylinders, activating my boots. My head still beat with a savage pulse. Instead of sonic grenades, I had proton hand-bombs. Pressing a thumb on the igniter, I hurled one so it sped like a bullet. Two tigers shot at me. One missed. The other hit symbiotic skin, making my suit quiver with pain.

The berserker-gang evaporated from my brain, making me realize the suit had been giving me the madness.

At the big hatch leading into the interior of the battle cruiser, a proton explosion took out the legionaries.

"Follow me," I radioed. In leaping bounds, I moved to the wrecked portal into the ship. Grabbing a Lokhar rifle, slipping on a power pack, I charged down the corridor. It had gravity so I moved like a freight train on meth.

Star Vikings rushed behind me.

We had surprise and murdered every tiger we saw. More power-armored legionaries appeared. We killed them, losing ten troopers to their weapons.

Dmitri split off, leading a team for the bridge. Rollo likewise went another way as he fought to reach the T-missiles. I battled my way to the engine room.

Instead of playing a skilled game of maneuver and countermove, I lobbed proton bombs and rushed to close quarters. There I stabbed with my force blade. If I'd tried for perfect tactics, I'm afraid we would have traded shots from around corners. That would have slowed everything down. Time counted more than ensuring we didn't take casualties.

It meant the headlong attack cost human lives. We traded them for time. Then, the Lokhars must have run out of power-armored legionaries, at least the ones facing all died.

Our last gamble turned into tiger butchery. Twenty-two Star Vikings, along with me, burst into a huge chamber. It contained silver-colored, throbbing fusion cells. I shot sprinting Lokhar engineers trying to get away. Then, I blew away the heads of three tigers madly tapping at controls. I assumed they attempted to build a fusion overload.

Star Vikings rushed to those panels. Three minutes later, my techs turned to me and popped up their thumbs. They had the engines under control.

In my helmet, I flipped onto a different channel. "Dmitri?" I asked.

"We have control of the bridge, Commander. But I have bad news. The other battle cruisers are turning to engage us."

"Are the ship's shields at full power?" I asked.

"Yes, Commander," Dmitri said.

"Is the *Achilles* in the main hold?"

"Yes, Commander," the Cossack said.

"Then hang on. I'm coming up to you."

"We cannot defeat the enemy fighters and the battle cruisers about to engage us," he said.

"You don't think so?" I asked.

"No, Commander," Dmitri said.

Once more, I switched onto a different channel. "Rollo, are you ready?"

"Give me ten more minutes, Creed," Rollo said.

"You have five. Then it's go time."

"That's cutting it too close," Rollo said. "It's not going to work if you don't prepare properly. Five minutes isn't enough time to rig everything perfectly."

Through the comm-line, I brayed with laughter. "No battle is perfect, my friend. It's all about winning. Nothing else matters."

"You think we can win through to the jump gate and beyond?" Rollo asked, sounding dubious.

"We're about to find out," I said. "Now quit jabbering and get those T-missiles ready for launch."

-27-

I stood on the bridge of our captured battle cruiser. It was a big ship, an engine of destruction, although unequal against a Jelk battlejumper. This vessel must have been a fifth the size of Shah Claath's former flagship, which gives some indication of a battlejumper's power.

Ten Star Vikings stood on the bridge with me, Dmitri among them.

The rest of the boarders had returned to the *Achilles*. The patrol boat waited in another cargo bay, the armored doors sealed shut.

I still breathed hard from the tremendous exertion.

"Commander," Dmitri said. "The enemy wants to bargain with you."

"Put him on the side screen," I said.

"Her, Commander, the Lokhar admiral is a female."

"Whatever," I said. My helmet sat on the former battle cruiser captain's chair. He lay sprawled on the deck plates, half his head a gory ruin.

A tiger appeared on the screen. She must have sprinkled ash over her fur, because it was dull gray color. Her red eyes squinted at me.

I used a technique on her that Shah Claath had played on us during our attack on the portal planet. With Dmitri at the comm-controls, I had him transmit a fuzzy image of me and deepen my voice.

255

During the portal planet attack, the Jelk had pretended to be Abaddon. It had scared the crap out of us at the time. Maybe I could pull something like that here.

"I am Admiral List Mocker," the tiger woman said. "Who are you?"

"Abaddon," I said.

The Lokhar recoiled, her eyes widening. "You lie," she whispered.

I forced a laugh. "Why do you think I struck the Purple Tamika Hall of Honor?"

"I have no idea. It was barbaric and sacrilegious."

"First, I will stamp out your honor," I said, trying to sound like the devil himself. "Then I will demand your lives in payment for your crimes."

"What crimes?" the admiral shouted.

"That of living in the same space-time continuum as me and my Kargs," I said.

She became visibly emotional, breathing hard as she wrestled with her superstitious fears. Finally, she pointed a clawed finger at me. "Whoever you are, I demand you return our sacred articles of honor. If you do, we will let you depart with your life. If not, you will die."

"You are wrong," I said. "It is you who are about to die."

"You have one crippled battle cruiser. We have a flotilla of star fighters and four battle cruisers with fifteen more on the way."

"Prepare to die," I said, and I nodded to Dmitri.

The Cossack cut the connection. "Did she buy it?" he asked.

I had no time to answer him. Instead, I told our pilot, "Full speed for the jump gate." Then, I radioed Rollo in the T-missile quarters, "Send the first one," I said.

"I'm as likely to ignite it in here," he said over the helmet radio, "then get it out there."

"Then do it right," I said.

"Like I have a choice in the matter," Rollo said. "You'll get what I can get."

I would have preferred more confidence from him. This was stressful enough. I stared at the screen, watching, waiting.

256

Star fighters raced at us, about two hundred space vessels readying their particle beam cannons. A battle cruiser stood in our way, heating its considerable number of heavy weapons. The other battle cruisers came up fast from behind.

"They're waiting for our move," Dmitri said. "They don't want to destroy us because they still think they can get their precious items back."

I blinked hard. Why was waiting such a difficult thing to do? My plan was simple. A T-missile was a teleporting missile. It was an ingenious weapon. Special tubes launched them. I didn't have time for that. Nor did I have time to make precise calculations for each missile. N7 would have been needed. He was on the patrol boat. Instead, Rollo would cause one missile at a time to teleport outside our battle cruiser.

From within my helmet on the headphones, I heard Rollo shout, "Fire one!"

Inside our battle cruiser, nothing extra happened. Outside, it was a different story. A T-missile appeared behind the approaching star fighters. That meant the missile was close to us, too. Its thermonuclear warhead ignited, creating a blinding white flash.

"Fire two!" Rollo shouted.

As the small attack fighters vaporized in the atomic blast, a second T-missile appeared. This one ignited between two approaching battle cruisers and us.

From this close, our ship took the blast and hard radiation. Our screens buckled.

"Keep them popping," I shouted at Rollo. "Saturate the battlefield with nuclear fire."

"Roger that, Creed," Rollo said in a hoarse voice.

This was like lobbing grenades a few yards from oneself and hoping the body armor held. It decimated the star fighters and hammered the enemy battle cruisers. Unfortunately, we started taking a pounding from our own weapons as we headed for the jump gate.

***

In slow motion, like a dying destruction derby car near the end of its existence, our battle cruiser glided past the wreckage

257

of hundreds of star fighters. The nearest Lokhar battle cruiser slammed point defense shells into our ruptured hull. The force screen had died several minutes ago. From behind us, enemy particle beams shredded our ship.

Then another T-missile popped into existence beside a Lokhar battle cruiser. Because of the thermonuclear blast, I lost sight of the enemy. The particle beams stopped, though. Seconds later, our bridge shuddered. More of the ceiling crashed down onto the deck plates. Electrical wiring writhed like angry snakes, hissing and showering sparks. Lights flashed and klaxons wailed.

"Get to the patrol boat," I ordered.

"You'll need help up here, sir."

"No! I'm coming with you. Just give me a few more seconds."

"Creed!" Dmitri shouted. "You cannot stay."

"Go," I said. "Hurry."

Dmitri stubbornly shook his helmeted head.

"Look—"

Another thermonuclear explosion shook our vessel. Everything went dark except for a side, viewing screen.

"I only have two T-missiles left," Rollo radioed me through harsh static.

"Save them for the other side," I said.

"Don't you think I know that?" he bellowed.

Dmitri and I watched the screen. Our battered vessel slid past the last star fighter. The enemy battle cruiser no longer peppered us with its point defense cannons. Behind us by several thousand kilometers, another battle cruiser slid into view. Its particle beams stuck our battered vessel.

Sloughing off like ice from an iceberg, more of our craft fell away. Internal explosions made it hard to stay standing on the buckling deck.

At that point, our battle cruiser reached the jump gate, sliding through toward the other side.

***

Groaning, I pushed myself off the deck plates where I'd fallen. This jump had been particularly bad.

I floated up toward the ruined ceiling. The anti-gravity plates had stopped working.

The flu-like symptoms of jump left me achy and dull-witted.

"Dmitri?" I asked in a hoarse voice.

"There has to be better way for star traveling," the Cossack said, his voice weak.

"Tell me about it. How are the rest of you feeling?"

"We're ready, Commander," one of the other troopers said.

"Rollo?" I radioed.

He coughed before saying, "I'm all set."

Pushing against the ceiling, I floated down to the only working screen. It showed the jump gate behind our vessel. So far, no one else had followed us through.

"Now," I told Rollo.

Seconds passed and turned into a full minute. I hated this damn waiting. What was wrong? Why couldn't Rollo—

Just then, a T-missile appeared by the jump gate. Its fusion engine burned. These missiles could move in the normal manner as well. A blue tail appeared behind the exhaust port. It grew longer by the second, accelerating the missile.

Our gift to the Lokhars went through the jump gate back to the Horus star system. Would the timer function? Would the warhead explode, smashing nearing enemy craft at just the right time?

"Go," I told Dmitri and the others. "We have to get back to the patrol boat."

Before they could argue with me, I leaped for the corridor. The hatch onto the bridge had blown open some time ago. With my HUD giving me visibility of the dark hall, I propelled myself off the sides. I "swam" faster and faster, taking the corners at a dangerous speed. Behind me, the others did likewise. We were old hands at these kinds of zero-G maneuvers.

In less than five minutes, we vomited out of the last hatch, shooting for the patrol boat sitting in the big bay.

From a different hatch, Rollo flew for the boat, meeting us at the *Achilles*. We scrambled inside. My last glimpse of the inner battle cruiser was the bay doors lurching open.

Thank God, they still worked after the pounding this vessel had taken.

Before I reached the bridge, Zoe Artemis guided the *Achilles* out of the battle cruiser's belly. She built up speed, moving away from it.

I entered the bridge, still wearing my symbiotic skin.

"Turn on the cloak," Zoe said.

A member of her crew did just that, tapping her board. That caused a high-pitched whining sound throughout the patrol boat.

"Captain Artemis," a man said, pointing at me.

Zoe swiveled around and grinned hugely. I wanted to hug and kiss her.

"Commander, you made it," she said.

"Captain," the sensor operator said. "Lokhar fighters have just come through the jump gate."

"Put it on the main screen," Zoe said.

I steadied myself, holding onto the back of her chair.

"I don't know if the cloak will hold," she whispered to me. "The star fighter earlier damaged our field generator."

I didn't say a word. I watched the screen, wanting to know what the Lokhars were going to do. As I did, a big battle cruiser appeared in our star system. That was bad.

"The admiral is hailing our old battle cruiser," the comm operator said.

"Let her do it as much as she wants," Zoe said.

I couldn't tear my eyes away from the screen. Would the tigers fire at the empty vessel? I didn't think they would. They didn't dare.

Several minutes passed. My gut tightened all the time. Another Lokhar warship entered the system.

Shuttles left the first tiger battle cruiser. Those looked undamaged. Six of the assault shuttles gathered under the wrecked and empty battle cruiser. Once ready, they moved in a flock toward the battered hulk. One by one, the shuttles entered the ship.

At that point, Rollo's last T-missile ignited inside the vessel. Even on the screen, I could see it shudder. A microsecond later, it expanded like a slow-motion grenade. The sides blew off and a white explosion grew. Coils, fusion engines, hull parts, dead tigers and humans, water, concentrates, mass of junk blew apart in an expanding ball of destruction.

"Let's hope that blinds their sensors for a time," I said.

Our bridge crew turned to stare at me. I guess my words sounded inappropriate. I couldn't help it.

Anyway, long story short, we made it by playing the same trick twice against the Lokhars. Hey, if it ain't broke, don't fix it, right?

As the surviving Lokhars began to search the debris, we tiptoed away in the cloaked *Achilles*.

The good news was that this system had several jump gates to choose from. We slid toward the nearest. If we could get some real separation from the Lokhars, we wouldn't have to worry about our damaged cloaking device lasting any longer.

"Captain," the comm operator said. "The Lokhar admiral is placing a system wide message. Should I put it up?"

Zoe turned to me. I nodded.

In a moment, the tiger with the ash fur appeared. She seemed tired beyond anything I'd seen.

"You are not Abaddon," she said. "I know that for a fact. Never fear, we will learn who you are. We will find you. Then we will destroy your race limb from limb. I don't know how you did this or why, but you will never gain from your vile deed."

The cloaking whine increased within the patrol boat.

Zoe looked worried. "Our invisibility isn't going to hold much longer," she whispered to me.

"Race for the nearest jump gate," I told her.

"They might see us if we accelerate too fast."

"If we want to win, we're going to have to risk it."

Reluctantly, Zoe gave the order. The *Achilles* built up velocity. That made the cloaking device labor overtime. It sounded worse than before.

On the bridge, we watched the main screen and listened to the sensor operator give a minute-by-minute report.

"I think you're right," Zoe told me. "The last T-missile hurt the enemy's sensing systems."

Afraid of jinxing our good luck, I didn't say anything else about that.

Ten minutes later, Zoe asked, "Why aren't they splitting up to search the different jump gates?"

"Good question," I said. "Despite the admiral's words, maybe they wonder if we really are Abaddon. The possibility terrifies them, making them afraid to go off alone." I grinned. "It doesn't seem they know if we're even alive or not."

Zoe frowned. I don't think she accepted my explanations. The truth was I didn't know why the tiger admiral didn't race ships to each jump gate. By the time they decided to do anything else, it was too late.

We entered the next gate, and it looked like we had raided Horus and gotten away with the loot. Now we had to see if we could reach home in time to stop the Emperor's armada.

-28-

The comedown after the daring assault brought depression to the survivors. Instead of cheering wildly at what we'd done, we remembered the friends who died at Horus and during the deadly battle getting out of the star system.

The small size of the patrol boat didn't help matters. To make sure no one went stir crazy, I began training exercises three days after leaving Horus. Bored troopers were harder to handle than exhausted, recovering soldiers. As the trip lengthened, I increased the intensity of the drills.

Even so, we had our problems the next few weeks. They had to do with the ship itself. Despite our best efforts to keep the *Achilles* out of the fighting, the patrol boat had taken damage. Most of it had come from our own T-missiles.

The cloaking device shorted out for good. We weren't going to be able to use it again until the ship went through of month of repairs at a dockyard. Worse for us, the anti-gravity plates had taken a pounding. Much of our trip, they didn't work. Extended time in zero-G wasn't any fun.

There was another problem with that. Without the anti-gravity dampeners, hard acceleration strained the crew. I ordered Zoe to push the ship anyway. We had to keep ahead of the news. I could imagine the shockwaves hitting the Lokhar worlds, particularly those belonging to Purple Tamika. A league-wide manhunt must have already started against us. Certainly, the Lokhars on Horus were going to find human

263

corpses. How long would it take the tigers to reach the right conclusion?

Our engineers worked overtime on the ship to keep it running. There were fights among the crew. The people using their fists I could understand. Then, two troopers fought over a man. One of the women killed the other with a force blade. I debated executing the victor. I couldn't afford to lose any more fighters, though. So I put her in a closet, calling it a brig.

Afterward, for five miserable days, I ran everyone but the bridge crew and techs through savage calisthenics. Maybe I took the guilt gnawing at my conscience out on them.

Rollo warned me. "If you don't ease up, you're going to have a mutiny on your hands."

I ignored him.

A day later, Dmitri told me the same thing. I knew why I couldn't hear them. I kept thinking about the hell-burner. Had I really needed to explode it? I wondered if I'd destroyed half the planet. First Sanakaht and now Horus—how many Lokhar worlds should I pulverize? My bloodlust against the tigers must have been waning and I found that hard to deal with.

What saved me from munity, I believe, was running into an Orange Tamika warship in the Sargol star system.

The place swarmed with asteroids and heavy metal meteors. It was supposedly neutral territory and a miner's playground.

"We have to fix our anti-gravity systems," Ella told me. We floated in a corridor while hanging on to side-rails. "Too many troopers are on the edge, Creed. If you continue to push everyone…"

"Okay, already," I said. Their combined nagging had put *me* on edge.

After some tough haggling, we put the patrol boat into an asteroid dockyard called Rill 7. Squat-bodied Ilk ran the place. I paid them in platinum. They sent two tech teams aboard, dragging their equipment on sleds. Dmitri watched the one, Rollo the other.

I kept N7 with me and toured the interior asteroid. The Ilk were busy hollowing it out, using the heavy metal ores for their trade.

We went to the main bazaar. The Ilk held it in a vast underground hall several kilometers in circumference. All kinds of league races bartered and dickered with each other from metal-walled booths. A few of the "booths" were the size of old Safeway stores with floating forklifts to bring down the big items. Fortunately for us, we'd traveled fast enough from Horus that no one had heard about our raid yet.

As we explored the marketplace, N7 pointed out five Lokhars in body armor. The tigers argued with a squat Ilk over combat weaponry.

"What Tamika do you think they are?" I shouted at N7. The bazaar thrummed with noise, making talking a chore.

The android stood for a time, watching the tigers. Finally, one of them must have felt the scrutiny. He turned and scowled at N7.

"I believe they are Orange," N7 informed me.

"Let's find out," I said.

N7 put a restraining hand on my forearm. "If I'm wrong, it could mean trouble."

"It could mean it anyway," I said.

As I brushed past aliens, I slapped away the slippery tentacle of a thief trying to pickpocket me. No matter how far one went from Earth, nothing ever really changed in a fundamental fashion.

The biggest Lokhar watched our advance. He was a good seven and a half feet tall, a towering individual. Even better, he had the widest and deepest chest I'd ever seen on a Lokhar. Was he a wrestler or a combat specialist?

"Who are you?" the Lokhar growled at me, with his ears laid flat against his skull. I knew that was a bad sign.

"We are friends of Orange Tamika," I said, in the tiger tongue.

The Lokhar's head swayed back. The others talking to the Ilk pulled away, coming closer to us, with their hands drifting to the guns and knives on their belts.

"Are you bounty hunters?" the big Lokhar growled.

The way the other tigers readied themselves made me wonder if the big guy had reason to fear hunters. I decided to take a chance.

"I personally know Doctor Sant," I said.

The big tiger hissed and stepped back among his friends.

"You're being rash," N7 whispered to me.

I was too busy watching the Lokhars to worry about that.

The big boy nodded, it seemed to himself, as if he'd made a decision. He muttered at the others. Then he stepped toward me. "Once, Sant was a doctor."

"I know," I said. "Eight years ago, I journeyed with him to the portal planet in hyperspace. Prince Venturi led the mission."

"Who are you?" the tiger asked in a hoarse voice.

"Are you of Orange Tamika?" I asked.

He watched me with his cat eyes. What was he thinking? Finally, he pushed aside the bottom of his torso armor, revealing an orange shirt underneath.

"I'm Commander Creed," I said.

N7 shook his head as if he could take back my words.

Once again, the tiger hissed. "You lie. Creed is in the solar system. I have heard the seer say so many times."

"Do you mean Seer Sant?" I asked.

"You just called him doctor. Now you name him correctly. What treachery do you plan, human?"

"Me?" I said, jamming a thumb against my chest. "Look, buddy, the Shi-Feng tried to assassinate me on Earth. They failed."

As one, the Lokhars roared and went into combat stances, two of them drawing hook knives.

The noises of the bazaar lessened. Many aliens turned to stare at the Lokhars and then at us.

The big tiger looked around. He noticed others watching us. Even so, he said so only I could hear, "I must slay you, outlander. You have spoken words that should have remained silent."

"Wrong," I told him. "I just proved to you that I'm Commander Creed. If you've heard Sant talk about me, you know that I do and say whatever I want."

"This is true," one of the other Lokhars said. "Maybe he is who he claims to be, baron."

"Baron...?" I asked.

266

Slowly, the big tiger straightened. His friends put away their knives. The regular loud sounds of the bazaar quickly resumed. The other aliens must have realized there wasn't going to be a fight.

"I am Baron Visconti," the tiger said in a deep voice. "Prince Venturi was my third cousin on my father's side."

"Venturi never had your size," I said.

"No," Visconti said. "The prince took after his mother's people, not his father's."

"Sure," I said.

"Come this way," Visconti said. "It is not proper for us to speak of these things in the open where any ear can hear."

I glanced at N7. He shook his head. Good. I wanted him paranoid so he'd stay alert. Then I indicated for Visconti to lead the way.

The baron guided us to a tent on an open grassy area to the side of the bazaar. Bright sunlamps provided the greenery with light. They also made it hot. Other Lokhars stood guard around the tent. Two outposts held heavy machine gun teams, with barrels poking past piled sandbags.

"Come inside," Visconti said.

Inside the tent, a tiger opened a flap into an interior sanctum.

N7 and I headed toward it.

"No," Visconti said, putting a big paw on N7's chest. "The machine cannot enter."

N7 and I traded glances. "Forget it then," I told the tiger.

Baron Visconti looked down at me. "It would not be seemly if he came within."

"Hey," I said, "we can talk just as easily out here."

The big guy thought about that. He nodded, and the trace of a grin might have appeared on his face. "Now I truly know that you are Commander Creed. It has been said you drive Lokhars mad by your arrogance. Experiencing your vanity for myself, I begin to understand how hard it is to work with you. The stories are true after all."

"Yeah, I'm a real head case."

"Yet, it is said you are a mighty warrior."

"Not just mighty," I said, "the greatest."

He eyed me. I think he wanted to test my mettle, see if he was tougher than me. Finally, he laughed. "Bring your machine. For the great Commander Creed, I will make an exception."

We went into the sanctum, sat on mats and sipped a hot Lokhar drink called task.

"Look," I told him, after lowering my drinking bowl. "I'm sure you're in love with your customs, but we don't have time to indulge in all of them."

Visconti brushed his paws together and waved off a server. The baron leaned his head toward me and spoke in a whisper.

"It will be as you say." He seemed to compose himself before adding, "I wonder at your presence, Commander Creed. At first, I believed you an assassin from Purple Tamika. I recognized you as human, but…" He shrugged.

"Why do you wonder?" I asked.

He laughed before saying, "I am bringing my House troops to the fleet. I have decided to cast my lot with Seer Sant. He heads to the solar system, there to stop the Emperor from destroying your people."

"Sant's headed for Earth?"

"I have just said so," Visconti said, with a bite to his voice. "I am unaccustomed to having my words questioned."

"Yeah," I said, "sorry about that. Do you know how close the Emperor's armada is to Earth?"

"Several weeks away, maybe as much as a month," Visconti said.

I made some quick calculations. If we continued the journey at a little more than top speed, we might just make it home in time to face the Emperor.

"How far is Doctor Sant from Earth?" I asked.

"He is called Seer Sant," Visconti said.

"Of course," I said. "That's what I meant to say."

The baron stared at the ceiling in seeming annoyance. Finally, he said, "The forward elements of the Orange Tamika fleet should already be approaching your world. We will attempt to ambush the Emperor's leading elements before they reach your star system."

268

That had been my original plan. Was that a coincidence? I decided to find out. "Too bad the Starkiens didn't agree to join us," I said.

"The contractors?" the baron asked with distaste. "I do not understand your meaning."

I gave him a quick rundown on my offer to Baba Gobo.

Visconti sat back, stroking his furry chin. "That was an interesting offer, if lacking honor."

"Surviving a crusade has an honor all its own," I said.

The baron chuckled as he shook his head. "Your way of thinking is difficult for me, but I can understand your point, Commander. You must know, though, that Starkiens have hired themselves to the Jelk before. That placed them beyond the pale of righteousness."

"I used to fight for the Jelk Corporation," I said. "But here I am on the side of the angels."

Beside me, N7 stiffened, closing his eyes as if in pain.

Visconti studied me, once more stroking his chin. "Do you have a point in saying that?"

"I do," I said, thinking on the fly. "Lokhars destroyed my world and nearly wiped out my people. I've been told that was to save me from Jelk slavery."

"That was only partly the reason," Visconti said.

"What was the other part?"

"The Emperor fears your race."

I'd never heard that before. It put a new complexity on the situation. "Why would that be?" I asked.

Visconti shook his head. "I do not know. Perhaps the Emperor heard an oracle about you. If he did, he should have shared the knowledge with the other Tamikas. He has flown alone in regard to the human problem."

"Now we're a problem?"

Visconti spread his paws. "The Lokhars are about to wage a bloody civil war. Two opposing armadas race for Earth, heading toward a collision. Yes, you are a problem."

"Can Orange Tamika win the battle?" I asked.

Visconti looked away. "I cannot see how," he said. "Orange, Yellow and Green have joined forces. Several outlawed Tamikas have added their paltry number of vessels to

269

the rebel fleet. The Emperor must have two to three times our fighting craft."

This was highly interesting news. "Why are the fleets headed to Earth exactly?" I asked.

"Because of the Forerunner object," he said. "Surely you realize it is the most venerated in the league, perhaps in the Orion Arm."

This was news. Why hadn't Sant told me? Frowning, I realized the Emperor had let that slip when we'd talked in the Sanakaht system. Felix Rex Logos had once served the Lokhar Fifth Legion as its commander. Where would a prince-to-be-emperor serve? In the most illustrious post, of course. Our artifact near Ceres was critical, drawing the Lokhars to us. It would appear that a victory in the solar system had even greater importance for the tigers than I'd realized.

"You need the Starkien ships to help you even the odds," I said.

"There is merit to your words. But you already offered them a chance to regain honor. Just like a Starkien, Baba Gobo refused."

"That's one way to look at it," I said. "Still, if they had all their vessels in once place, maybe it would give them and you a fighting chance. I expect Baba Gobo thought this was a lost cause. It's not if you rebels have enough warships."

With a huge hand, Visconti picked up his tiny porcelain cup. The two looked incongruous together. He sipped and lowered the cup to his lap, sitting thoughtfully for a long time. Twice, he gave me sharp glances.

The baron was clearly working something out in his mind. I decided silence was my friend, as I wanted that something to mature.

"You are too hopeful," Visconti said at last. "That means you know something more. I believe you have a secret."

"It's true, I do," I admitted.

"Can you tell me your secret?"

"Sorry. I would be unwise to let you know."

Visconti scowled. "Are you suggesting your secret would bring harm to the Lokhars?"

270

"Harm to Purple Tamika," I said. "My secret would most certainly strengthen Orange Tamika."

"Then you must tell me."

"I'm afraid not," I said.

"What if I told you I will not allow you to leave this tent unless you tell me?"

I wanted to tell him, "Then I'll have to kill you." This time, however, I decided on tact. "Where would be the honor in that?" I asked. "We're drinking task together in friendship. Would you bring dishonor to your House?"

"Not willingly," he admitted.

"Then, I am safe talking to you."

"Yes," he said, nodding. "You are safe—for the moment."

"Sant should seek out the Starkiens," I said. "He should ask for their aid."

"No," Visconti said gravely. "In the past, Starkiens hired out to the Jelk Corporation. Starkiens lack honor. They are untrustworthy as allies."

"That was my point a few minutes ago. I once worked for the Jelk Corporation and rebelled. Why did I work for them originally? In order to save my people from extinction. The Starkiens are a dwindling race. Now, they seek to save their race."

"They are unworthy of saving," Visconti said flatly.

"To you, maybe, but not to them. They seek survival. Use that for Orange Tamika's good."

"What will a few more warships matter anyway?" Visconti asked with a shrug.

"Perhaps they're the edge Orange Tamika needs for victory. Or would you prefer to let your bigotry doom your House to death? Will you let Purple Tamika destroy you and your kind?"

"You killed Princess Nee on an Orange Tamika dreadnought," Visconti said. "The Emperor wants revenge against you. Maybe I could buy my Tamika's survival by handing you over to him."

"Maybe," I said, locking stares with the tiger.

After a second, Visconti shook his head. "I will not dishonor my House in such a manner. You went to the portal planet and won existence for our universe. I owe you a debt of gratitude. In doing as you did, you heaped praise and glory onto Orange Tamika."

"The Orange should rule the Lokhars," I said.

"Yes."

"To do so, you must defeat the Emperor's armada."

Visconti raised his cup, sipping once more. He inhaled, expanding his chest. "I have decided," he said. "You must return to Earth as quickly as possible. If you wish to contact the Starkiens, that is your task, not mine or any other Lokhar's. To help you in your secret quest, I will give you my fastest warship. In exchange, I will accept your patrol boat."

"My boat is already fast," I said.

Visconti shook his head. "Not nearly as fast as the *Quarrel*. It is our latest advancement, able to reach twice the velocity as your craft. Besides, your boat is in a dockyard. I know the Ilk. They will delay repairs and force you to pay more until they have drained you of exchange units. You would be wise to accept my offer, Commander."

Did he know what the *Achilles* held? Did he suspect? Baron Visconti was one big tiger. He also seemed sharp. Did I dare trust him? How did he know so much about our patrol boat? It would be a risk unloading and then reloading the relics from Purple Tamika's Hall of Honor. Yet, I didn't see the utility of getting back to Earth a week after humanity had perished.

"Yes," I said. "I accept your offer."

-29-

The exchange went flawlessly. A day later, we left the Sargol star system, accelerating toward the jump gate.

Three days into the journey, a tap came at the closed hatch to my quarters.

It was a Spartan chamber with a cot, desk and view screen. Slapping a switch, I saw N7 standing at the portal. He looked uneasy.

"May I speak with you, Commander?" he asked.

"Come in," I said.

I sat on the cot. N7 leaned against the desk. The android refused my offer of a drink.

"Why are you looking so confused?" I asked.

"You sense it?"

"Would I ask you if I didn't?"

"Ah, an interesting point," N7 said. He stiffened against the desk, becoming formal. "Commander, I have been uneasy for several days. At first, I could not fathom the reason. Finally, I ran a probability analysis."

"An analysis regarding what?" I asked.

"That is an astute question. At first, I made it a broad analysis as I attempted to pinpoint my unease. I could not accept that I had intuition or an instinct as you humans perceive. Those are illogical concepts filled with emotion. I still struggle with those."

I waited, saying nothing. I'd seldom seen N7 so agitated.

"After six hours of inquiry, my analysis finally reached a conclusion. Our meeting with Baron Visconti was too coincidental for it to have occurred at random."

"Why do you say that?" I asked.

"Several times before the meeting you spoke of the need to reach Earth faster than our craft could achieve. What did Baron Visconti offer us? Just what we needed: a faster ship."

"You have a point to this?" I said.

"After the meeting, you said it was odd that the baron knew so much about the *Achilles*. I pondered your statement and ran another analysis. It seems clear that the baron was privy to the facts before our encounter."

"Are you saying the baron played us?"

N7 cocked his head as if puzzled. "Ah, I see. You are asking if he maneuvered us into doing what he wished us to do."

"Yes, only I said it in a pithier way."

"Please, Commander, let me continue with my analysis report."

"Sure," I said.

"Probability factors led me to the conclusion that Baron Visconti wanted to meet with you in order to give you his speedster. Why would this be? Because he or his superiors wanted you on Earth sooner rather than later."

I said nothing.

"I believe the baron wishes you to contact the Starkiens," N7 said. "Yet, even after reaching this conclusion, I was troubled. I allowed the analysis to probe deeper. Three hours later, I reached a new and startling conclusion."

"Yeah?"

"Doctor Sant watched our proceedings with Visconti," N7 said.

"What?" I asked. "You can't possibly know that."

"I can and do," N7 said. "During the meeting, I detected a hint of a familiar odor. Only after these labored analyses did I allow my brain core to match the scents. It was that of Doctor Sant. I also saw the claw-patch the doctor usually wears on his left sleeve. It is conceivable the doctor removed it and forgot to take it before we entered the inner tent."

"So…you're saying Sant was hiding on Rill 7 and through Baron Visconti he maneuvered us into heading back to Earth faster?"

"Exactly," N7 said.

"Why?"

"In order to aid Orange Tamika in the coming battle with the Emperor," the android said.

"That seems like a mighty big stretch," I said.

"No. Doctor Sant has attempted a risky political tactic, rebellion against the governing authority. He has allies, as Baron Visconti related. I believe Doctor Sant wants you to convince Baba Gobo to join the rebellion so Orange Tamika has a greater chance for success."

"That's not how I meant a *big stretch*," I said. "How could Sant possibly know the *Achilles* would come to Rill 7?"

"I asked myself a similar question," N7 said. "The answer lies with the Forerunner artifacts. During our stay with Prince Venturi aboard the dreadnought, we learned the Lokhars have an oracle."

"I remember," I said.

"Can Forerunner artifacts foretell the future?" N7 asked. "I do not believe so. Yet we have learned that Forerunner objects can communicate with each other. Perhaps as interesting, they are able to scan remarkable distances. Could the artifacts inform each other on particular occurrences? With enough information and computational ability, the artifacts could make astute guesses on future events. That information might fool lesser beings. The Lokhars would take the data as an oracle."

I frowned as I followed his logic. "So…you're telling me a Forerunner object told Sant about us?"

"It is a possibility," N7 said.

"That would mean the artifacts are interested in what happens among us."

"That, too, is possible."

"I'm not sure I like that," I said.

"It does add a new layer of complexity to our situation," N7 said.

"Why would Holgotha have gone to the portal planet eight years ago? Did the artifact have a greater ulterior motive than it has already admitted to us?"

"I give that a high probability," N7 said.

That got me thinking. Just how meddlesome were the artifacts? Why had Holgotha agreed to transfer us to Sanakaht but no more?

"I'm glad you ran your analyses," I said. "You did good, N7."

"Thank you, Commander."

"But about Baba Gobo joining us, the baboon already said no."

"You have added new factors, Commander: the articles of Purple Tamika honor, for one. The approaching rebel fleet is another element. Perhaps those new additions will sway the Starkiens."

"I doubt it."

"My probability analysis reached a similar conclusion. Yet I cannot fathom any other reason as to why Doctor Sant gave us the speedster."

"Given that you're right about all this," I said.

"Yes," N7 said.

I stood up and began to pace. "Well," I said. "Talk is cheap, and whiskey costs money."

"Commander?" asked N7.

"The proof will be in the reality once we reach home. Soon, one way or another, we'll have to test our theories on the field of battle."

***

Our speedster, the *Quarrel*, proved itself many times over. The vessel was fast, had an extraordinary amount of anti-gravity plates and lacked much in the way of shields, armored hull or weapons. This thing was meant to run fast, run long and outmaneuver enemies. It wasn't meant to fight in any but the lightest engagement. That allowed us to zip through star systems. Time after time, we acted like a rabbit darting into its burrow, escaping any perusing vessels by beating them to the next jump gate.

In time, we left Jade League territory and raced through no-man's land toward the solar system. Then our luck ran out in the Wolf 359 star system, which was in the Leo Constellation. The star was a cool red dwarf, one of the faintest known. The star's photosphere was a mere 2800 K. Wolf 359 also happened to be a flare star, throwing off sudden bursts of X-rays and gamma ray radiation. In a straight line, the red dwarf was only 7.8 light-years from Earth. We were almost home.

After shaking off the symptoms of jump, we accelerated toward the next gate. The alien ships didn't begin appearing from behind the various planets until we were four hundred thousand kilometers from the entrance gate.

"Commander," Ella said. "You're not going to believe this."

The bridge was small and cramped, with barely enough room for Ella, our present pilot, N7, Zoe, Rollo at weapons and me in the center. I sat above them and could stare down at their panels.

"Look," Ella said. She typed on a holopad, the keys visible in the air. Her effort produced another holoimage.

The red dwarf system has two inner planets and five outer gas giants. From every world, ships began to swing around into view. The smallest and fastest shark-shaped vessels raced for the two jump gates: the one behind us and the one we aimed at.

"Starkiens," I said.

"Correction," Ella said, "hidden Starkiens."

I nodded. Their appearance in these numbers and precision meant they had been hiding before we appeared. That would indicate one of two possibilities. Either they could see into another star system many light-years away or these ships had kept hidden for days and more likely weeks. Had they been expecting us?

I didn't like the implications.

"Incoming message, Commander," Ella said.

"Go ahead," I said.

The holoimage shimmered as the star system disappeared. I found myself staring into Baba Gobo's ugly face.

"I can't believe it," Rollo said.

"Who did you expect?" I asked.

"What?" Rollo said.

I pointed at the waiting holoimage of Baba Gobo.

Rollo looked up at it. "Oh. No. I wasn't talking about him. I mean the number of Starkien ships."

"How many are you counting?" I asked.

"One thousand, five hundred and twenty-three," Rollo said.

My gut tightened. "I don't want you to count star fighters," I said.

"I'm not," Rollo said. "The number includes anything above a frigate, nothing smaller."

My stomach pain increased. I scowled down at Rollo. "Did Baba Gobo call all his Starkiens together?"

"Foreign vessel," Baba Gobo said, finally deciding to speak. "You have entered Starkien space. I demand that you cease acceleration and begin braking procedures. You must comply at once, or we will destroy you."

I thought about it for all of two seconds. With over fifteen hundred starships, there was no way I could outrun every missile and beam.

"I'm going to talk to him," I told Ella.

"I thought you might," she said.

Clearing my throat, I sat up. "Baba Gobo," I said, "this is Commander Creed speaking. Please explain your presence here."

I waited for the transmission to reach him. It didn't take long. That would indicate the Starkien leader was in one of the nearest warships.

"Commander Creed," the baboon said. "This is a highly pleasurable experience. It appears the Orange Tamika doctor is a Lokhar of his word after all."

"What are you talking about?" I asked warily.

"He did not inform you?" Baba Gobo asked.

"Inform me of *what*?"

"We must talk in private, which means in person," he said.

"You can forget about that," I said. "If you remember, I came to your flagship once before. I don't plan on doing it again."

"If I wish," he said, snapping his fingers, "I can destroy your vessel like that."

"If you do, you have no chance of gaining a new lease on life for your dying race."

"How can you say dying?" the baboon asked. "Do you see the number of warships I possess?"

"Once your race had millions of vessels," I said. "Now you're down to just this few. Your species lost out because you played the wanderers too long. I have a plan, though. It will save the Starkiens, Orange Tamika and humanity."

"Interesting," Baba Gobo said. "Seer Sant said this would be so."

"When did he tell you this?"

"Not him in person, but Seer Sant's emissary, Baron Visconti."

I found myself blinking at the baboon. I didn't understand what was going on.

"What are you talking about?" I asked.

"Meet with me," he said.

"I'm meeting with you now."

Scratching his nose, Baba Gobo seemed to consider that. Finally, he said, "Very well. Time is critical. We shall proceed. First, you must know that the Emperor's armada approaches Earth. Second, I will give you the broadest outline as to why I am here.

"After you left us in Epsilon Indi, I began to consider your words. You have the gift of persuasive speech, Commander. Few fighting men like you possess the ability. We are dying out; you are correct is saying that. Many years ago now, my nephew Naga Gobo went to the Jelk Corporation in order to prolong his fleet's existence. Instead, he brought about its destruction. My elders discussed this with me. We agreed that perhaps it was time to die with honor.

"I know," Baba Gobo said, holding up his slender fingers. "You and the Lokhars do not believe in Starkien honor. Yet, Seer Sant does. But I leap ahead of the tale. The elders suggested that perhaps we should return to our old ways. You called it *hit and run*. In the oldest days, we lived as open predators. That brought about the beginning of the Jade League."

"Wait a minute," I said. "I thought it was to stop the Jelk."

279

"That came later," Baba Gobo said. "In the early years, the others feared us. We battled for many centuries, winning often but losing numbers. Then we made a critical error. Many elders have come to believe that the Forerunner artifacts had an agenda. The ancient machines aided the league with intelligence."

"They made the Lokhars, Gitan and Ilk smarter?" I asked.

"No. The ancient machines gave out information; the artifacts informed the Lokhars, the Gitan, Ilk and others of our movements. Jade League fleets ambushed us many times. Our numbers rapidly dwindled. Finally, we disengaged from open predation, suing for peace. The league members never gave it to us, but in time their depredations lessened as they began to strive against the Jelk Corporation."

"Are you saying the Forerunner machines are helping Doctor Sant?" I asked.

"After listening to his emissary," Baba Gobo said, "I believe the artifacts are divided among themselves. They have relayed intelligence to Seer Sant. I think they have also told the Emperor choice bits of information."

"That's all very interesting," I said, stunned by these revelations. "Now, what are we going to do about it?"

Baba Gobo leaned forward. "You have a secret weapon, do you not?"

"That's right, I do," I said. "It's called my brain."

"We have no more time for your boasting. You have something other than your arrogance."

"Well, why don't you tell me what you think I have," I said.

"I do not know, but I would like to."

"If I did have such a weapon," I asked, "why would I tell you?"

"It should be obvious," Baba Gobo said. "To give me a reason to throw in the Starkien lot with Orange, Yellow and Green Tamikas."

"And fight the Emperor?" I asked.

The baboon actually straightened, holding his head high. "Yes," he said.

280

"You'll have to give me a minute," I said. "I need to talk this over with my people."

"I grant you ten minutes," Baba Gobo said, trying to sound generous. "After the time limit, my fleet will begin to maneuver to net you so we can capture your vessel and take your secret if we must."

"Right on," I said. "Until then, Commander Creed out."

Ella cut the connection so the holoimage vanished.

Bemused, I exhaled and sank back into my cushioned chair.

"We didn't see that one coming," Ella commented from below.

I scowled at her. "I thought you did something to Sant's brain on Mars. He's supposed to help us, not throw us curve balls."

"Sant has helped," Ella said. "My original effort has yielded great dividends. To begin with, through the baron, Doctor Sant gave us this speedster."

I ingested her words before looking at each of them in turn. "Okay. I'm open to suggestions. What should we do?"

"If the Starkiens join Orange Tamika," Rollo said, "we might have the numbers to beat the Emperor in a straight up space battle."

"Even if we convince the Emperor to leave us in peace," Ella said, "humanity is going to need allies to survive. This sounds like a golden opportunity for us."

"N7?" I asked.

"I foresee several problems," the android said. "What does Doctor Sant know? What does the Emperor know? If we win, the battle will likely decimate both fleets."

"And why would that be bad?" I asked.

"There will come a time when the Jelk defeat or lose to the present invaders?" N7 said.

"Okay," I said. "I see your point. If the Jelk win, they'll send the Saurian fleets back to the border."

"And if the Jelk lose," N7 said, "the invaders will likely come to the border."

"So what are you suggesting?" I asked.

"That we win the present struggle without mass destruction of warships," N7 said.

Rollo laughed. "That would be a mighty fine trick. How do you propose to do it?"

"With our secret weapon," N7 said. "We bargain with the Emperor. That has always been the plan. It is still the best one."

"Let's say we force the Emperor to back off," Rollo said. "That still leaves Purple Tamika with a massive fleet. As Ella has suggested, that creates problems for us in the future."

"We must take one step at a time," N7 said.

"What do you think, Creed?" Rollo asked.

"That both Ella and N7 are right," I said. "Humanity needs allies, and we can't afford to decimate ourselves, knowing the Jelk or the invaders will come in time. Before we do anything, though, we need the Starkien fleet. We have to have enough numbers to make the Emperor and his admirals pause long enough to listen to me."

"Can you trust Baba Gobo with our secret?" Ella asked.

I flexed my fingers and rolled my shoulders. That was the question, wasn't it? "Let's put the baboon back online," I said. "We're about to find out."

***

"Ah…" Baba Gobo said, as if tasting a rare and wonderful vintage. His dark eyes glowed with lust. "This is amazing. You are a scoundrel, Commander Creed, an interstellar rascal," he said, heaping Starkien praises upon me.

I sat in my command chair, watching his holoimage. I'd just informed the baboon that I held the key articles from the Purple Tamika Hall of Honor in Zelambre on Horus.

"You are a thief," Baba Gobo added.

"Star Viking," I said, correcting him.

"I am unfamiliar with the term."

"When you look at me," I said, "that's what you're seeing."

Baba Gobo rubbed his hands. "Yes. You hold a powerful secret weapon. For safe keeping, you will now deliver it into my keeping."

"Is that what you think?" I asked.

"Your vessel is fast, but it is under-armored and possesses few weapons. Anyone can take the articles from you."

"When you say *anyone*," I said, "I hope you realize that doesn't mean you or any other alien."

"Yes, yes," he said. "You are a vainglorious beast—"

"Man!" I said, interrupting him. "I'm a vainglorious man, human, person of high intelligence. You'd do well to remember that."

"Don't goad him," Ella whispered to me.

I made a slicing motion with my finger at her. She got the message and zipped her lips.

On the holoimage, Baba Gobo became oily in his manner. "Commander Creed, you must be reasonable. The Starkiens hold the key to victory."

"Wrong," I said. "Commander Creed and his Star Vikings hold the key."

"No!" he said, angrily. "Have you counted the number of my warships?"

"Sure have," I said. "It's an impressive amount."

"We can easily destroy your vessel."

"That's true," I said.

"Since you understand this, you realize that you must bring the articles of honor to me at once."

With a smirk on my face, I leaned back in my chair, staring at him.

"What is this you're doing?" Baba Gobo asked. "I disapprove of your leers and grimaces. We have serious business at hand."

"Creed," Ella pleaded, "please don't goad him."

This time, I ignored her altogether.

"I am ordering my ships to ready their weapons," Baba Gobo told me.

"Let me ask you a question," I said.

"There is no more time. Decide."

"If you destroy my ship, what happens to the articles of honor?"

Baba Gobo blinked several times. Then his scowl deepened.

"Good," I said, "I see you're finally thinking about this."

"The articles will be gone," he said, "and you will be dead. Then, we Starkiens shall leave his part of the Orion Arm."

"Good luck with that," I said. "You must realize the Purple Tamika Lokhars will know what you did."

"Who will tell them? You? I do not think so, as you shall be dead."

"Yes. I'll be dead."

"That's my point," he said. "How will the Purple Lokhars ever learn of our deed?"

"How do they learn many things?" I asked. "In time, the Forerunner artifacts will tell them. Then, nothing will protect the Starkiens from the vengeance of the Lokhars."

"Because of your present stubbornness," Baba Gobo said, "humanity's fate is death."

I shook my head.

"The Purple Tamika Lokhars will never forgive you your raid on Horus," Baba Gobo said.

"I don't care about their forgiveness. I just want their words of honor that they'll leave humanity and Earth alone."

Baba Gobo stared at me. Slowly, he began to nod. "You are a clever—" I'm sure he almost said, "Beast," but he stopped himself. "You are very clever, Commander."

"Coming from you," I said, "that is high praise indeed."

"I'm glad you can recognize that."

"Good. Now let's get down to it. We're keeping the articles of honor. You're coming with us to just outside the solar system. Let's make it Alpha Centauri."

Baba Gobo pursed his lips in a baboon-monkey manner. Then he looked away, sighing deeply. Finally, he shook his head before regarding me once more.

"Yes," Baba Gobo said. "We will do as you say. The Starkiens have entered the lists once more, ready to do battle in order to win our rightful place in the Orion Arm."

It was the grandest speech I'd ever heard a Starkien make. Afterward, the *Quarrel* headed for the jump gate. Behind us, the Starkien fleet began to maneuver into its battle formation.

***

Two days later, we made it to the solar system. The crew cheered, and everyone slapped each other on the back.

To make N7 feel like he was part of us, which he most certainly was, I made sure to pummel the android's back until he finally asked me to stop. Both Ella and Zoe gave him hugs.

Soon, the *Quarrel* orbited Mars. Diana and Murad Bey waited down there in the dome.

"I'll tell you what this is going to be," I told the assembled people, both assault troopers and Earth Council delegates. "This is like the Sea Battle of Lepanto in 1571. Back then, the Ottoman Turks tried to smash the assembled Christian fleet. The Turks had been making sweeping conquests, and this was Europe's answer. Papal ships, Venetian and Spanish combined to face the dreaded enemy."

"Face the glorious conquerors," Murad Bey declared.

I glanced at him. "Yeah, I get it. You have a different outlook on the event. My only point is that the Papal commanders, the Venetians and the Spanish all quarreled with each other like crazy up until the cannons began firing. On the day of battle, they put aside their differences just long enough to win a smashing victory. We have to figure out a way to get Lokhars and Starkiens to listen to us so I can talk sense to the Emperor."

"That may be more difficult than you realize," Diana told me.

"Probably," I said. "But that's our goal. I also think we humans will have to take all our warships to the battlefield. We're going to be the final reserve—that's if it comes down to a slugfest. It's all or nothing for us. It's too late to run away. If we tried that, the Emperor's approaching armada would just chase us down."

"Can you really make the Emperor see reason?" Ella asked.

"If not, I'll destroy the Purple Tamika articles of honor," I said.

"That will only enrage them," Murad Bey said. "They will boil with fury at humanity and seek vengeance."

"That's how you would react," I said. "It might not be what a tiger will do. Maybe it will dispirit them. They'll fight listlessly afterward."

"We must not destroy each other," N7 said. "The Jelk or the invaders will eventually return to the border region."

"Why is that a given?" Diana asked him. "Maybe the Jelk and the corporation invaders will destroy each other just as you're worried we'll do here."

"Good point," I told Diana. "Anyway, Baba Gobo sent us a message a day ago. The Emperor's battlefleet is two weeks out. It's massive, likely fifty percent bigger than our combined force."

"The Starkiens will run away for sure," Rollo said.

"I'm not finished," I said. "We have to buy time. The bulk of Orange, Yellow and Green Tamikas is three weeks out. I have to convince the Starkiens to engage in hit and run raids in order to slow down the Emperor's armada. I suggest all Earth's warships go out and help in this task."

"Risky," Diana said.

"It is that," I said. "It's also our only hope. Is anyone opposed to the idea?" I scanned the strained faces staring at me.

No one opposed.

"Very well," I said. "I'm giving us two days to get ready. Then, our fleet moves out to Alpha Centauri to link with the Starkiens."

"What is to prevent them from rushing into the solar system and holding our freighters hostage?" Diana asked.

"Not a damn thing," I said, "other than Starkien integrity."

"You can't be serious," Rollo said.

"If they lacked honor," I said, "they'd never fight in the first place."

"So you hope," Rollo said.

I studied my massive friend. Nodding, I said, "Yeah, I hope."

Rollo crossed his arms but didn't say anything more.

"Is that it?" I asked. "Or does someone else want to add something?"

No. The meeting ended on the sour note. The struggle against the Emperor's crusading armada was about to begin.

-30-

Rollo, N7 and Zoe Artemis stayed aboard the *Quarrel*. Their task was to keep the Purple Tamika articles of honor in human hands. They parked the ship in lunar orbit near the weapons systems of the Moon fortress.

I went out with a Starkien strike force. Baba Gobo had decided to deploy three hit-and-run flotillas. Our task was to slow down the crusading armada's advance. We had to gain time for the rebel fleet to maneuver between Earth and the Emperor.

Earth didn't have much to add to the flotillas. But what we did have we used. I brought three Sanakaht attack cruisers, joining Kaka Ro's strike force.

Our attack cruisers were teardrop-shaped vessels with powerful particle beam generators. These had heavy mounts, giving the particle beams extra range. Because of our low speed, we joined the strike force's reserves, thirty-seven Starkien beamships.

Strikers composed the force's main element, one hundred and fifty-three Whale Shark-shaped vessels. They were bigger than the beamships and bigger than our attack cruisers. The strikers carried drones and moved fast, with amazing acceleration and deceleration abilities.

Eight days and five jumps brought us to the Beta Tarn system. A G-class star pumped out normal light. A thick interior asteroid belt gave us the perfect ambush site. Starkien scouts had returned with news. One of the main arms of the

287

Emperor's armada was on its way. It would be coming through the jump gate near the star. The problem for our attack cruisers and maybe the accompanying beamships would be the exit, the jump gate we'd used to reach Beta Tarn. The gate was near a Pluto-like world in the distant outer system. Two Jovian gas giants provided the only terrain between the inner asteroid belt and the Pluto-like rock.

The strikers raced for the asteroid belt. My attack cruisers lagged behind the faster beamships, following the forward elements the best we could.

Thirty-eight hours later, Ella told me, "There's a signal coming through."

I nodded.

"It's Kaka Ro, sir," she said. "He's ordering the beamships to hide at the outer edge of the belt. Lokhar warheads just went off near the inner star gate. Kaka Ro believes the enemy will be coming through soon in force. If that is so, he plans to bring the Lokhars to us."

"Signal our acceptance of the order," I said. For the present, I was content to listen to the Starkiens. They helped the last humans. So, I'd do my part the best I could.

Along with the beamships, our attack cruisers braked hard, slowing our velocity. Five hours later, my three ships waited behind an icy asteroid the size of Australia.

Before I relate what happened next, I should point out that space battles were much different from old naval wars on Earth. There, even in fights between carriers, planes were hours away from their targets, not days. Here, one made a plan and executed it, and waited a day or three to see if it would work or not. The stellar distances mandated the time delay.

Fed with data from the forward strikers, we watched the Starkien warships spew their drones. The drones were slender needles, dark as sin, made of a composite materiel hard to spot. The missiles used cold propellants, which meant they lacked speed until a final hot burn. That was clever, as the cold propellants would help keep the drones invisible from enemy sensors.

Three hours later, as I studied the main screen, the advance arm of the crusading armada began to pour through the gate. Warship after warship entered the system.

The Lokhars had mobs of attack cruisers, big carriers and masses of pursuit destroyers. In a short amount of time, four hundred and twenty warships deployed.

"That's too many," Ella said. "Kaka Ro should order us to run while we have a chance."

"No," I said. "One way or another, we have to buy humanity a chance. Unless Sant arrives in time, the Earth freighters are doomed."

"*You* have to bargain with the Emperor, Creed. You won't be able to do that if you die in this star system."

"N7 can bargain with the Emperor just as well as me, and Rollo can take my place for the other task. I'm no longer invaluable."

Ella didn't respond to that. She watched the main screen. We all did. The Lokhars were good, maneuvering their numbers with precision. That made us even queasier than before. Our Starkien allies didn't move like that. Clearly, we were going against the best, personnel who obviously knew what they were doing. Finally, en masse, the large enemy fleet began to head for the asteroid belt.

Even with their numbers, the strikers managed to remain hidden among the asteroids near the inner edge. They reminded me of American colonials fighting the British Red Coats on the road to Concord.

As the Lokhars approached, the Starkiens maneuvered stealthily, heading deeper into the rock field. The striker pilots used intervening objects to mask their movement from the enemy. Then something gave them away, likely an old-fashioned heat signature.

The Lokhar admiral reacted, sending a wide-beam message. I recognized her. It was Admiral Saris, looking as stiff as ever.

"Foreign vessels," Admiral Saris announced, "we are here under Jade League orders. The Emperor and his Court has decreed the humans a walking plague. We will annihilate them from existence. Whoever stands against us will share their fate."

I wondered if Kaka Ro would answer. He didn't. Neither did I.

The pursuit destroyers led the way, followed by the Lokhar attack cruisers and then the carriers. It took hours as they accelerated for the belt.

We waited behind our asteroid as the other reserve vessels waited behind theirs. What could twenty-seven Starkien beamships and three Earth cruisers do against the Lokhar fleet? The strikers needed to whittle down the enemy.

Hours later, Kaka Ro's first move paid dividends. Cold, dark Starkien drones burned hot. Because of the Lokhars' acceleration, the missiles were almost on top of them.

Even so, the Lokhars were ready. Saris had seen enough to know that something was up. Beams and destroyers' point defense cannons took out ninety percent of the first wave. The trouble for the tigers was the Starkien missiles kept coming. Kaka Ro clearly believed in a hard first strike.

Enough drones struck Lokhar warships to cause massive detonations all along the line. Seventeen pursuit destroyers exploded. Nineteen more took damage. Five of those kept coming. Something inside them no longer worked. Escape pods jettisoned from those five. The other damaged destroyers began to decelerate.

I expected Admiral Saris to order the rest of her warships to attack vigorously. These were Lokhars, the headlong attack artists. Maybe Kaka Ro knew a few things about Lokhars. The cold needle drones had proven a clever tactic.

Faced with unknown and unseen assailants, the Lokhar fleet slowed its velocity. Our sensors showed them scanning hard. Tiger drones burned brightly, racing ahead of the main fleet. In such a fashion, Saris crawled into the rock field.

The battle changed demeanor then, turning slow motion as the Starkiens played drone games with the Lokhars. This wasn't like our asteroid belt in the solar system. This belt had an incredible mass of rocks and debris. Because of that, stealth counted for as much as speed and firepower. Ambushes constantly occurred. The Starkiens retreated, leaving hundreds of dark missile surprises. The Lokhars destroyed most of the enemy drones, but kept taking hits nonetheless. This went on for an amazing two days.

We waited back here to do our part with the beamships when the time came.

Finally, Kaka Ro sent us a pulse message. I expected the Starkien lord to demand our firepower. The Lokhars kept pursuing. Instead, the lord said, "Run for the distant jump gate. Try to lure the Lokhars after you."

"Smart," Ella said.

I shook my head. "I came here to fight."

Ella swiveled around to face me. "You came to slow down the Emperor's advance. We're doing that."

"The Starkiens have done it, not us," I said.

"We're here. We're part of the effort. Maybe the Starkiens wouldn't have come if you'd hung back at Earth. Well, now we need to save our ships for the next star system. Kaka Ro must realize that as well."

I could see Ella's logic, and I wanted to live. Finally, along with the beamship captains, I acknowledged the message by accelerating at full speed for the distant jump gate.

Kaka Ro was clever. I'd never seen the Starkiens in their element before, making plans their way.

Twenty-seven beamships fled for the distant gate. Three attack cruisers did likewise. I shouldn't have been surprised Admiral Saris singled us out.

She hailed our accelerating cruisers. I refused to speak with the Lokhar.

After a time, Saris sent a wide-beam message. "Renegade Lokhars, we have marked your ships' registries. I am putting you on the Emperor's proscription list. Even if you reach the jump gate, you are doomed."

Yeah. I could see what was going on. Our attack cruisers had been built on Sanakaht, the reason for Admiral Saris' mistake about who we were. After the message ended, a mass of T-missiles appeared near us and the running beamships. Our particles beams destroyed some. We'd been waiting for the tactic. For just such a reason, I'd also seeded proximity mines

291

behind us. Some of those detonated, annihilating T-missiles, but not all. Three thermonuclear warheads exploded.

"Get ready!" Dmitri shouted.

Our shield went dark as the electromagnetic field around the attack cruiser absorbed the heat and deadly X-rays and gamma rays.

Admiral Saris wasn't through with us or with the beamships. For over two days, her vessels had faced dark drones streaking from cover. Lokhar rage must have built during the time. Maybe Kaka Ro had counted on that. It was a big asteroid belt, meaning the Lokhars were already at far teleportation range from us.

In any case, more T-missiles appeared, but the beamships and our cruisers kept raying them. As another thermonuclear detonation flared nova-white on our screen, I began to see another aspect of Kaka Ro's cunning. Our attack cruisers and the beamships had heavier armor and better shields than the strikers did. If we took the brutal hits now and depleted the Lokhar stocks of teleporting missiles, afterward, the strikers could flee without worrying about the same thing happening to them.

Fortunately, we had a few critical advantages in this contest. T-missile technology was chancy at best. The longer the teleportation range, the less likely the warhead would appear in the exact targeted location. We tried to put more separation between Admiral Saris and us, as we were already near their operational limit. The other thing was this: before a T-missile appeared, it created a hazy image in space. Then, its form became distinct and finally it solidified into existence. The first haziness—like a heat wave on blacktop—was a telltale giveaway. It allowed our gunners to fire before the warhead could ignite.

Then, all our advantages vanished as a T-missile exploded a mere three kilometers from one of our vessels. Given the admiral's present distance from us, that was a fantastically lucky break for the Lokhars.

At the blast, the nearest attack cruiser's shield buckled and overloaded, going down. The rest of the nuclear discharge tore the ship's armored hull apart. It must have also done something to the vessel's core. A furious internal explosion sent a geyser of light and radiation out of the craft's exhaust ports. Then, the attack cruiser began to tumble end over end, heading away from us.

Ella tried to raise the stricken crew. They must have all been dead already.

"Expend our mines!" I shouted. "Seed them everywhere."

The Lokhar T-missile assault continued. Two Starkien beamships blew apart, another took crippling hits, its accelerating rush slowing down. Another round of T-missiles finished it off.

Our particle beams rayed. Mines raced outward in all directions. Another round of exploding warheads poured massive doses of radiation against our shield, enough leaking through the armored hull to affect us. Fortunately, we wore our symbiotic suits. The living skins seeped anti-radiation drugs into our bodies.

My attack cruiser still functioned, although several ship systems began to go offline.

We accelerated, but so did our Lokhar tormenters. That meant Admiral Saris' warships in the asteroid belt came after us. That was their mistake. The Lokhar vessels raced smack into waiting Starkien needle missiles. The drones burned hot and detonated. Twenty-eight Lokhar warships blew apart. Others took damage.

For the next several hours, Admiral Saris turned her attention onto the nearby snipers. An eighth the number of T-missiles popped near us. The mines helped destroy most of them. Our gunners had also become expert now, recognizing the telltale shimmer sooner than ever. As the objects solidified, particle beams already chewed into them.

Nine hours later, our two attack cruisers and the surviving beamships gained enough separation that no more T-missiles appeared.

Far back in the inner asteroid belt, the Starkien strikers burst into open space. Kaka Ro made his run for the portal.

"Are any T-missiles attacking them?" I asked.

Ella watched her panel. "Not yet," she said.

By the time we reached the jump gate, she hadn't seen any more of the deadly Lokhar T-missiles strike the Starkien vessels. It looked as if Kaka Ro was going to make it to the next star system with us.

We'd hurt Admiral Saris' fleet more than she had hurt us. Unfortunately, the Lokhars still outnumbered us.

***

We accelerated through the next system. It possessed many jump gates, branching off to various stars. We raced for the gate that would take us into the Wolf 359 system.

In time, we entered Wolf 359. Advance guard Orange Tamika battle cruisers waited there, one hundred and ten altogether. We signaled them. Seven hours later, the strikers came through. Kaka Ro told Baron Visconti, who commanded the advance guard, that Admiral Saris was hot behind them.

The Starkien lord proved right. Purple Lokhar warships began to appear in the Wolf 359 system. With T-missiles, Visconti hit the entering warships, obliterating all nine enemy vessels.

Time passed as we waited for more of them. Five and a half hours after the slaughter, enemy drones slid through the gate. They exploded with thermonuclear warheads. Thirty minutes after that, more Purple Tamika drones appeared.

From three hundred thousand kilometers away, Visconti let them advance.

Finally, another group of Purple Tamika pursuit destroyers came through. Once more, the baron saturated the jump gate area with T-missiles. It was a devastating tactic. The advancing Purple drones used heavy jamming equipment, but it didn't matter this time.

Soon, Starkien needle missiles destroyed the ECM drones.

We were doing it.

For two more days, Baron Visconti and Kaka Ro held off Admiral Saris. The Purple Lokhar commander must have feared to send the bulk of her fleet through the jump gate into the Wolf 359 system.

Then a messenger ship came through our back gate, signaling us. The messenger brought news. Using other gates and star systems, the Purple Tamika fleet had gained reinforcements from the Emperor. Using different jump gates, Saris worked her way around. It appeared she was trying to trap us in the Wolf 359 star system by coming in from behind.

We saw the danger. Every ship accelerated for the exit. As our ships left Wolf 359, the last trooper on my attack cruiser recovered from radiation poisoning. Unfortunately, some of our vessel's weapons systems no longer worked.

I learned that the trick to this kind of jump gate battle was to funnel the enemy's advance. If you stopped her too cold at one particular gate, she would go around a different way. Then, it became a guessing game. Our strategy called for hit and run attacks. We tried to whittle them down just enough so they took longer. We didn't want to damage their flotilla so much that the fleet came at us from a different set of jump gates.

Maybe Visconti had miscalculated by hammering them too hard at the Wolf 359 entrance gate.

At this point, the baron played a hunch. He met with Kaka Ro. I attended the battle meeting. Visconti told us his father had once been Admiral Saris' chief of staff. That had been many years ago. Saris used to eat at the Visconti home and discuss tactics with the young baron-to-be. After having studied a star chart, Visconti assured us Saris would try to sneak through by going around to Ross 128.

Instead of splitting off and guarding each gate with minimal force, we rushed our beef-up strike force to Ross 128. The system possessed three gates. The red dwarf star was faint to the naked eye. It had fifteen percent of the Sun's mass, but it generated energy so slowly that it only had 0.036 percent of the Sun's visible luminosity. Ross 128 was 10.89 light years from Earth in a straight line, but not part of the closest jump routes.

"Saris would rather travel farther for a better position than battle head-to-head," Visconti said. "She is an artist of maneuver."

It turned out that the baron knew his opponent. Saris entered the system a mere three hours after we did. That put us too far from each other to attack right away. Her reinforced fleet had far more warships that we did. But if Kaka Ro's escape from the Beta Tarn asteroid belt was any indicator, the admiral's ships likely didn't have *masses* of T-missiles. Of course, she might have received more from supply ships.

Visconti didn't think so. Saris used speed whenever she could. The problem was that our side only had a minimal number of T-missiles left. The baron had used most of them in the Wolf 359 system.

After gaining Kaka Ro's agreement, Visconti decided to bluff the admiral. He teleported every T-missile he had left, sending them as far as he could. Then, the drones accelerated for Saris' approaching fleet.

None of our T-missiles had a chance of doing damage, of course. That hadn't been the point. Before the flock of T-missiles reached the enemy fleet, Admiral Saris' ships maneuvered, turning hard. She wasn't going to brake and accelerate back to the gate she'd used to enter. Instead, she headed for the third gate in order to escape us.

"Amazing," Dmitri said. "Admiral Saris has more ships, yet she flees."

"That is sound tactical doctrine," N7 said. "The baron would not expend his T-missile like that unless he had a vast supply. Visconti's strike also predicates a lack of T-missiles on the admiral's part. Saris does not wish to sustain massive T-missile damage from us before entering beam range. Thus, she retreats until such time as she can replenish the number of her T-missiles."

"It seems too elementary a tactic to work," Dmitri said. "I would realize the baron was trying to bluff, close in and smash us."

"Saris' actions tell us that she is not Dmitri Rostov," N7 replied. "She wishes to preserve her ships for the great battle."

In order to seal the bluff, Visconti had us accelerate after the fleeing enemy, increasing our strike force's velocity. Only after the last enemy warships departed the Ross 128 system did we begin braking. It was time to go back the way we had come.

Baron Visconti's hunch had paid off. Even better, our strike force had slowed down the enemy advance to Earth. Had the other strike forces done likewise? Or was the crusading armada knocking on Earth's door. It was time to find out.

-31-

It turned out that two taskforces fought masterful delaying actions. The third perished but gave a hard fight. Three strikers from the destroyed force raced back to give an account of the battle.

The senior captain believed the Lokhars had been surprised at Starkien ferocity. Although the way had been open for the Lokhar flotilla, they had paused and sent messenger ships back to the main armada.

"I believe the admiral wished for new instructions," the senior striker captain told us. "One last ship remains at the farther gate. It will arrive to tell us when the Lokhars enter the star system."

Another day passed in anxious waiting. Finally, the forward elements of the rebel fleet reached Alpha Centauri.

After that, all hell broke loose. Elements of the Emperor's main crusading armada crashed into the rebel fleet in the Wolf 359 system.

For a day, it looked as if every ship we had needed to race there. Baba Gobo readied the Starkiens. Kaka Ro suggested a surprise rush to take the Emperor from a back system. Baron Visconti had other ideas.

Before anyone could implement one of the plans, Lokhar pride and honor changed the equation. The Emperor sent messenger ships to the rebels. Soon enough, Sant listened to the request and agreed.

The Emperor's forward admirals backed out of Wolf 359. The rebel fleet poured through, rushing to bring everything to Alpha Centauri.

"That's no way to run a war," Rollo said. "The Emperor should have pushed his advantage."

"Agreed," N7 said. "Undecipherable Lokhar honor is one of the reasons the Jelk Corporation has successfully waged war against the Jade League for these many years."

Only later did I learn what had happened. It came out during the grand meeting on Sant's flagship, a gigantic mauler.

The Emperor made a deal with Sant. Felix Rex Logos would let Sant bring his entire fleet through Wolf 359, if later the seer agreed to let the crusading armada through into the Alpha Centauri star system."

"We will wrestle our differences with honor," the Emperor had said. "The winner will rule the Lokhar Empire."

Sant had agreed to the deal. He brought the rebel fleet to Alpha Centauri, the massed might of Orange, Yellow and Green Tamikas, along with lesser Houses. Combined together with the last Starkien fleet in existence, it made for a vast force.

The next several days saw hurried deployments, last minute repairs and the great meeting between the leaders.

I went, taking Ella with me. The Lokhars didn't like N7. So for once, I left him behind.

Sant had eight maulers. Orange Tamika loved giant vessels. The round ships lacked the dreadnought's sheer mass. Nothing had ever matched the hyperspace vessels. But a mauler was five times bigger than a Jelk battlejumper. The super-ship boasted immense laser cannons, and it could deploy hundreds of star fighters.

The great meeting took place on a stage for Lokhar plays. I sat in the front row. Baba Gobo crouched nearby on a low seat.

After the seats filled up, Doctor Sant walked onto the stage. He'd changed since I'd seen him last, looking older, more weighed down with responsibility. He wore an orange toga and moved with serene authority.

I won't bore you with the long-winded speeches. Lokhars loved to talk. They loved it even more at big meetings where everyone should have discussed strategy and tactics. Sant

298

launched into a monolog that lasted hours, talking about ancient history, religion, customs and seemingly everything but the coming battle.

After Sant's introduction, others talked.

Finally, Baba Gobo glanced at me. I shrugged. What could we do? The tigers blabbered endlessly. Only toward the end, as even Lokhars began to nod off, did Sant stand up again. He finally opened it up to military suggestions.

I pinched myself, waiting to hear about subtle maneuvers and clever tactics. Shockingly, most of the Lokhars talked about courage and standing at one's post to the bitter end.

"We must trick them!" Baba Gobo shouted. "We must whittle them down with cunning."

At the Starkien's outburst, the auditorium grew silent.

Seer Sant stood up once more. The acolyte who had been talking sat down. "Baba Gobo," the Lokhar said. "This is a matter of honor. Hard fighting will win the day, not sly ruses."

"The Emperor's forces outnumber us," Baba Gobo said.

"Yet, we will still win," Sant said. "This I know."

"How will we win?" the Starkien asked.

"Through valor," Sant said.

The Lokhars roared and pumped their fists into the air.

Baba Gobo shrank back against his chair.

In that moment, I feared the Starkiens might leave the grand fleet. I stood up and motioned to Sant.

"Commander Creed," the Lokhar said. "Do you wish to add a word?"

"I do," I said. "I think we must find a way to defeat the crusading armada without destroying their ships or ours."

"How can you do this?" Sant asked. "Will you threaten to destroy the Purple Tamika articles of honor?"

The auditorium of Lokhars strained to hear my words.

"If I must," I said.

A low groan went through the chamber.

Sant held up his hands. The noise died down. "We will fight with honor. It is to be seen if the Emperor of Purple Tamika can fight without a soul. Once Commander Creed brings the wrath of the Creator down on his head, then we of

299

Orange, Yellow and Green Tamikas will destroy the beasts among us."

Again, the Lokhars roared with approval.

"Who do you mean by beasts?" I asked, bristling.

"Those formerly of Purple Tamika," Sant said, sounding surprised by my question.

"Oh," I said. Once I destroyed the articles, Purple Tamika would lack a soul. By Lokhar logic, they would become beasts. "Yes, of course," I said. Sitting, I leaned past Ella and whispered to Baba Gobo, "It sounds like a clever plan."

"The Lokhars are seldom clever," Baba Gobo whispered. "But they do like to fight."

"Will you fight?" I asked the Starkien leader.

He stared at me with his red eyes. "Yes. I will fight."

Sitting normally again, I thought about Sant's overall plan. It had seemed foolish to grant the Emperor the opportunity to freely enter the Alpha Centauri system. Yet, the two Lokhars had given their word to each other. Felix had let Sant race through Wolf 359. Now Sant would let the Emperor set up here.

It reminded me of the old-time chariot lords of Ancient China. The nobility of that era had fought on their state-of-the-art, horse-drawn battle carts. Just like medieval French knights, the Chinese of that time had set great store by chivalry. In the story I'm referring to, a noble with a tactical advantage behind a river had thrown away his gain. The opposing king told him it wouldn't be chivalrous to attack him while he forded his chariots across the river. The noble graciously allowed the king to bring his host across and deploy. They fought a righteous battle, and the honorable noble lost the fight and his life.

I hoped we weren't making the same mistake.

Sant ended the so-called strategy session by telling everyone that in a battle for the Lokhar Empire, we had to adhere to the ancient traditions.

I could see what he was doing. Sant wanted to keep his hands clean by having me do the dirty work. He said I'd make the Creator angry for destroying Purple Tamika's articles of honor. I hoped that was just an expression.

Even as Sant made his last, long-winded monolog, a high-ranking official raced into the auditorium.

The seer stopped talking. Every eye turned to the official.

The Lokhar said in a higher voice than normal, "The first ships of the Emperor's armada have entered the star system."

A combined sigh went through the chamber. Afterward, it only took Sant another hour to finish his talk.

-32-

In a straight line, Alpha Centauri AB was 4.37 light years from Earth. It was a binary star system, as two stars orbited a common point. Alpha Centauri A had 110 percent the mass of the Sun, while Cen B had 90.7 percent the mass. A third star, Proxima Centauri, had some gravitational effect upon the system. It was in an orbit four hundred times the distance that Neptune circled Sol. That meant Proxima Centauri had a negligible effect upon the coming encounter.

The sheer gargantuan size of the Emperor's crusading armada caused me to question his sanity. Surely, Felix Rex Logos had called in Lokhar warships from all the provinces of the empire. He must have stripped defensive frontiers of every mobile formation he had. No wonder he'd allowed Doctor Sant to bring the rebel fleet through Wolf 359. By fixing his enemy's location, the Emperor could crush him permanently, not having to worry about pirate formations in the years to come from those who had escaped. The Emperor's only fear might be rebel sneak attacks as his ships came through jump gates. By his nobility, Sant had thrown away that possibility.

The Emperor must have had three times our numbers and four times our tonnage. This was going to be a slaughter. Yet, the vast numbers on our side meant the rebels would inflict telling damage to the imperial fleet.

The Emperor's commanders brought the mass forward in three distinct sections. As if the fleet was a legion, the commanders had separated it into three waves.

Huge bombards lumbered toward us. Bigger than Orange Tamika maulers, the bombards had massively armored hulls and double-strength shields. They could take a pounding and deal one. Their weakness was a lack of speed. In such a mass battle as this, though, I doubted they would need quick acceleration.

Surprisingly, the Emperor's commanders had spread out the bombards, each ship hundreds of kilometers from its neighbors. If we launched T-missiles at them, we wouldn't be able to take out clusters of vessels, just one big vessel at a time.

The next square had battle and attack cruisers in daunting numbers. Thousands approached behind the bombards. That square could have faced our fleet alone and likely come out victorious.

Carriers and pursuit destroyers made up the final square.

Taken all together, it was far too much for us to face and win. Three times the ships meant the Creator sided with them, didn't it? The old quip said that God fought on the side with the biggest battalions. Well, that would be the crusading armada.

We approached the enemy in a vast globular formation shaped like a teardrop. The bulbous part faced the Emperor's bombards.

At our lengthy council of war, we had decided to use massed counter-fire to destroy any teleporting missiles. It was riskier than our enemy's plan, but could prove superior if we could wipe out the appearing T-missiles before they detonated. Then, we could strike the bombards with our concentration and supposedly defeat them in detail.

Counting the amazing numbers, I realized that a space war shouldn't ever come down to such a grand encounter in one star system. Yet, here were most of the Lokhar military vessels, representing over eighty percent of the tiger empire's firepower. If we fought, it would surely cripple Lokhar fleet strength for decades, maybe forever, depending on who struck next and with what strength.

Maybe the Emperor could see that. Maybe he thought the armada's size would astound us. Doctor Sant understood that a battle here today would cripple Lokhar military power. It would probably also mean our annihilation. Baron Visconti understood, as did the other rebel leaders. Baba Gobo dreaded the coming fight, yet the Starkien had become too proud to flee.

This was a historic moment, and it occurred right next door to Earth. Wasn't that awesome?

No. It was horrible.

The two fleets moved through the Alpha Centauri system. Seen one way, it was majestic. Looked at another, it could mean doom for millions of combatants and then the final death of humanity.

It was time to make my play. Our side counted on it. I was back in the *Quarrel* with my people. The speedster stayed in the tail area of the globular formation.

With the permission of Seer Sant and his leaders, I now radioed the Emperor's flagship.

As I sat in my command chair above the bridge crew, I tried to compose myself. For once, I wanted to be formal and correct. What if Felix Rex Logos refused to speak to me, a supposed animal? Would I have to destroy articles of Purple Tamika honor on a wide-screen for everyone to witness? I didn't want to, but if I had to, I would most certainly do it.

"Get ready, Creed," Ella said. "The Emperor's comm officer has agreed to our request."

I told myself to relax, breathing in and out. All our hard work, all our fighting and dying—it concentrated into this single moment.

Before me, the holoimage wavered and then solidified. I stared into the face of Felix Rex Logos. He had wide features but no longer had white fur on his face.

Fur coloring, I thought to myself. *He wants to look spry and powerful.*

He hadn't done anything about his bulldog jowls. He wore a large device on his head. Oh, it was a purple crown with red jewels sparkling on the points. His orange eyes shone with purpose, and a purple collar jutted up to his chin.

"Greetings, Emperor of the Purple Tamika Lokhars," I said.

"I am the Emperor of *all* the Lokhars," he said in a ringing voice.

We broadcast to everyone. I guess Felix had his reasons for doing that, and we had ours. Maybe he wanted to show his tigers what a beast I was, a raving monster. Did he know yet that I'd raided his Hall of Honor? He had to, right? Why otherwise agree to speak with me?

"You *were* the Emperor of all," I said. "Then, you made terrible decisions. One of those was to send others to do your dirty work of nuking and poisoning my planet. For that, you're about to lose your crown."

"Who is this beast I see before me?" he asked with a royal sneer.

He'd seen me before. This was playacting on his part. "Whatever you think I am," I said. "at least I'm not the reigning monarch who let his Hall of Honor fall into a Star Viking's hands."

He stiffened and his orange eyes shined with murder-lust. "You lie, animal," he said in a hoarse voice.

I could have taken this a number of different ways. I decided on a direct approach. With a lazy move, I picked up an old spearhead. Using it, I scratched my cheek. The twelve thousand year old weapon had a distinctive mark on its metal, a stamp with a Lokhar flower that looked like a claw.

Upon seeing the spearhead, Felix Rex Logos roared. After he finished showing off his wrath, he leaned forward with his eyes blazing. "What is that you're holding?"

"Oh. This?" I asked, holding up the ancient spearhead. "It's something I picked up in Zelambre during my touchdown on Horus. It was quite an evening. Lots of fire and screaming vestals. We had a jolly old time, you can believe that."

"YOU!" he raved, pointing at me with a wicked claw. "You dared enter our scared Hall of Honor?"

"You'd better believe it," I said, remembering how Lokhars had beamed my dad's shuttle. This was payback, even if it didn't bring back the dead. I wanted to prolong this moment forever, but I knew I had to strike while Felix's emotions raged hottest.

"I'll tell you what, Mr. Emperor," I said. "If you like, you can send over a team of representatives to examine our loot. Let them see if we have your precious articles or not. I imagine

305

everyone is willing to wait before we start the bloodshed. Come and see just how much of your honor I'm holding."

Felix Rex Logos stared at me. I could feel his fury, his rage and impotence. I loved it. I wanted to shove his face into it and say, "Bad kitty, bad, very bad," then kick him in the ass and send him sprawling onto the carpet before I hacked him to death.

As if it had been rusted shut, he opened his mouth. Slowly, his lips moved. Like a dead man, he asked, "If I halt our advance, will your ships halt, too?"

"Yes," I said.

He stared at me longer. "You...a *man*...can speak for the rebels?"

"In this instance, I can speak for Seer Sant, the Orange Tamika Lokhar who rode the artifact from the portal planet to the solar system. I can speak for him because I know the artifact's name and rode *inside* the ancient construct."

The Emperor's eyes bulged outward. He strove to speak. Finally, he said, "I will send Purple Tamika acolytes to see these articles."

"Just make sure there isn't any Shi-Feng aboard," I said. "I'm tired of killing your exploding assassins."

Felix Rex Logos' mouth went slack. He shuddered, I think with fury. A moment later, their comm officer cut the connection.

"Why did you have to add the last bit, Commander?" Ella said. "You're risking too much."

"Maybe," I said in a thick voice. "We'll let the outcome decide whether I went too far or not."

***

As the massed fleets waited on either end of Alpha Centauri, a single Purple Lokhar shuttle accelerated from their side. It was a big craft. It took the vessel twenty-two hours to reach the globular and slow down.

Three hours later, we matched velocities. A boarding tube snaked between the two craft. Three dignitaries marched through it and entered our airlock.

I waited to greet them, with N7 on one side and Rollo on the other. My gun hand rested on my .44. If they played us false, I wanted to blow their bodies apart the old-fashioned way.

The hatch opened, and three old Lokhars stared at me. The first was big with hunched shoulders, wearing an admiral's uniform. The second looked like a Lokhar scholar with a tall collar and square hat. The last was the acolyte with a long purple robe. He trembled from age and had rheumy eyes.

"You are the beast Creed?" the acolyte asked in a brittle voice. His name was Divine Griffin.

"Let's get one thing straight right away," I said. "You don't call me 'beast' or 'animal' and I won't call you stupid before I knock you to the floor."

"We are here under truce," Divine Griffin said. "Would you dare to break such a solemn compact?"

"I won't break the truce," I said.

"Then you must not threaten to strike us," the acolyte said.

"I won't strike you."

"Therefore, if I chose to correctly name you a beast, you will accept it."

"No. I'll have this man here," I said, jerking my thumb at Rollo. "Throw you down onto the deck plate. Then I'll unzip my fly and piss on your head."

"Barbarian!" Divine Griffin hissed.

"Just so you and I have an understanding on how things will go if you can't smarten up, got it?"

The old admiral stepped in front of Divine Griffin. "We will refrain from insults. We ask the same in return from you."

I could have told the tiger the old acolyte had started it, but what would have been the point.

"I will say no more," I told him. "Come. It is time for you to see our loot."

We took them down the corridor to the largest chamber in the speedster. There, laid out on tables and under glass, lay the articles taken from the Hall of Honor in Zelambre.

The three Purple Lokhars moved woodenly to the tables. They gazed in shocked horror. Divine Griffin hissed, shaking

307

his head, clenching his paws into fists. The admiral glanced at me.

I didn't stare back. This must have been difficult for them. As much as I wanted to destroy Purple Tamika, I needed to make a deal with them more.

Ten minutes later, the scholar said, "We have seen enough."

I opened my mouth to ask him the key question.

He must have known what I would say. Surely, none of them wanted to hear my voice again. The scholar raised a furry hand. "These are from Zelambre, from the Hall of Honor. There is no doubt. This is what I will tell the Emperor."

That's all I wanted to hear. In silence, we escorted them to the airlock. They made the trek through the tube back to their waiting shuttle. Afterward, the vessel began its journey across the star system, back to the crusading armada.

∗∗∗

A day went by as the two fleets stared at each other across the star system. What did the Purple Tamika Lokhars say to each other? If they attacked, would they attempt to surprise us?

Tensions grew on our side. Five Starkien vessels left the globular formation, making a run for the jump gate to Earth. Baba Gobo broadcast to Seer Sant. Sant openly instructed Baron Visconti. One last time, Baba Gobo ordered the fleeing Starkien vessels to return.

They did not.

T-missiles popped before the running Starkiens. Thermonuclear explosions destroyed the shark-shaped ships.

The Emperor's crusading armada had just witnessed the event. Had that given them heart to fight it out? Did the Emperor say, "Forget the old articles of honor? Today, we will acquire new ones from their corpses."

Another three hours passed before the Emperor's comm officer broadcast a message to our fleet.

"The Emperor wishes to speak on an open line to the human called Commander Creed."

I agreed, of course. Then, I put on a uniform, a dark outfit with silver trim, with the .44 visible on my hip. Sitting in my commander's chair on the *Quarrel*, I readied myself for a talk that would surely go down in interstellar history.

"He's ready," Ella informed me.

"Put him on," I said.

Seconds later, Felix Rex Logos appeared on the holoimage before me. His presence was regal. I knew that every Lokhar, Starkien and human watched the exchange.

"Commander Creed," the Emperor said, speaking first. "I would address you."

"I'm listening," I said.

"You have perpetrated a heinous and monstrous deed," he said. "You took what did not belong to you. I demand that you return our articles of honor."

"I'll gladly do this," I said, "the moment you return all the billions of humans you ordered to death by your initial attack on Earth."

His manner grew heavier, more solemn. "You know that I cannot do this."

"Oh. Well, then neither can I."

"We will fight and destroy you."

"That's a possibility," I said. "Before that happens, though, I will personally obliterate the soul of Purple Tamika, snuffing out your eternal fire."

"That is too evil an act even for you."

I grinned at him. "That's where you're wrong. But the choice is yours. Personally, I'd keep your soul and forgo the pleasure of trying to wipe out humanity. You can make this a win-win situation for the two of us."

Slowly, he shook his head. "You do not understand, Commander Creed. I possess the old knowledge. Purple Tamika knows that humanity is the great plague to life in the universe."

"I thought that was supposed to be Abaddon."

"He is long gone, eons ago driven from our space-time continuum."

"Because of what the assault troopers and Orange Tamika warriors did on the portal planet in hyperspace," I said, "the Kargs failed to return here. You should be thanking us, not trying to make war."

"You are the ancient plague, the soldiers of Death. You have also named those who must remain unnamed."

"Do you happen to mean the Shi-Feng?" I asked.

The Emperor shuddered. Below me, I heard Ella inhale sharply.

"Vain human," the Emperor said in a hoarse voice. "Do you not realize yet? Once, eons ago, enemies of life fashioned humanity. You are a malleable species, easily led into waging war. In the ancient days, many spoke of annihilating your species. Others said to let you remain for the fateful day of Abaddon's reappearance. They won the debate and set the surviving humans onto Earth. There, your kind has warred savagely against each other, keeping your ancient battle-skills alive. Now, for the good of the Jade League, you must die."

"And the soul of Purple Tamika with it," I said.

The Emperor closed his eyes as if in pain.

I sat stiffly in my chair. Could Felix be right about humanity? I doubted he just made that crap up. Yet, it didn't seem right. There seemed to be something missing from the story.

His eyes flashed open. "You are the desecrator. You are the ancient plague. You—"

"I'm the one who rode inside Holgotha," I said.

"What?" he asked.

"Holgotha," I said. "I've just given you the name of the ancient Forerunner artifact. If we were the ancient plague, the machines of the First Ones would have remembered that. Yet, I convinced Holgotha to leave the portal planet and come to Earth. Later, the artifact transferred us to Sanakaht. We raided the Purple Lokhar world and took many weapons of war. Holgotha returned us to the solar system. Are you saying the ancient machine is in league with the ancient plague?"

"You have named the Altair Object," he whispered.

"No. I've named the Sol Object."

Felix Rex Logos began to pant and his eyes glazed over. What went on in his mind? He stiffened suddenly and hissed.

"I know the name of the Altair Object," he declared. "I challenge you, Commander Creed. Come with me to speak to *Holgotha*. We will enter the great machine. The artifact will

310

tell you I am right. Then, Holgotha will sentence you to die and obliterate your race. Afterward, Doctor Sant will return the articles of honor to me, or he will show every Lokhar alive that he is without chivalry. Then the crusaders shall fight the battle we were meant to wage."

"Do not agree to his," N7 told me.

I glanced down at the android. "You think he's right about humanity?"

"Shah Claath had large plans for your people," N7 said. "I believe the Jelk knew more than he told others."

"Do you have the honor to accept my challenge?" the Emperor asked.

"Our fleets will wait for the outcome of our venture?" I asked.

"I have already agreed to that," the Emperor said.

I knew Holgotha had warned me never to come back. But how could I refuse this challenge? Besides, I was curious as to the truth of the Emperor's so-called ancient history.

"Sure," I said, "why not? Let's go see if we can make the artifact talk to me one more time."

-33-

The Emperor of the Lokhars *clanked* beside me. We moved along the inner curve of Holgotha. The artificial black hole in the center of the donut-shaped artifact radiated its harmful rays against us.

Felix Rex Logos' shuttle waited on the artifact's outer edge. The *Achilles,* under Zoe's command, did likewise for me.

No other Lokhar or human walked on Holgotha. It was just the two of us. The Emperor wore powered armor. I had my heavy vacc-suit. He towered over me and possessed greater girth and mass. I was Creed the Killer, born from a race of fighters, if one believed the Emperor's tale.

Strange how it came down to this, eh? Yet, it was fitting. I'd been right to give everyone the artifact's name. It had cemented my authority to these religion-besotted aliens. I found it interesting that the Emperor hadn't rejected my knowledge of the object's name.

Could I have played this differently?

With a shrug, I continued to trek toward the alien city on the inner edge.

Once, the Emperor stopped and stared. I checked to see what he looked at. It was the city. Back in the Altair star system, he used to guard Holgotha. Now, he had the possibility of going inside. Did it excite old Felix? I imagined so. This must have been a dream come true for him. But he must also fear going in with me.

With my thoughts jumping from one topic to the other, I advanced with the Emperor to the low buildings. Soon enough, we stood before the wall.

I took a deep breath. Holgotha had warned me never to return. Yet, here I was.

"*I knew you would come,*" I heard in my head. "*It is finally time for the testing. Come, Commander Creed.*"

That had been the last thing I expected. First motioning toward the Emperor, I made sure he looked at me. I couldn't see his eyes, but I saw the chrome color of his visor. Then, I pushed through the wall and began to wade through to the other side.

I quickly popped through. This time, I found myself in a larger room, about the size of a youth-league soccer building with a high ceiling.

I checked a wrist monitor and found the air was good for breathing. With a twist, I removed my helmet and breathed deeply.

Beside me, the Emperor did likewise. After he took off his steel helm, Felix glanced at me. His cat eyes were wide with awe and wonder.

"Here we are," I said in Lokhar.

"Yes," he said. "At last, I am in...Holgotha."

"Greetings, Emperor of the Lokhar," Holgotha said. The artifact spoke through a vast vibrating membrane along the far wall. The talking screen showed bronze coloring with little red pyramids tumbling across it.

Without another word, both the Emperor and I approached the pulsating screen.

"I ask that you remove your spacesuits," Holgotha said, with the screen vibrating more rapidly.

At once, the Emperor began to unbuckle his power-armor suit. He did it so quickly that it seemed as if he'd expected the request. Or was it a command?

I began to open the magnetic seals of my suit. What did the Emperor know about the artifact that I didn't? I would bet a great many things. For too long, I'd been playing a game where I didn't know all the rules. As per our agreement, neither the

Emperor nor I possessed weapons. Before making the trek, each of us had undergone a scan by the other side.

"It is well today that the Emperor of the Lokhars and the Commander of the humans stand within my speaking chamber," Holgotha said.

"I just run the assault troopers," I said. "The newly coined Star Vikings, if you prefer."

"No," Holgotha said. "That is false. You have allowed Diana to assume leadership of the Earth survivors. In essence, however, you are humanity's leader."

"He just leads Purple Tamika," I said, pointing at the Emperor.

"Again, you are incorrect," Holgotha said. "Until he entered the speaking chamber, Felix Rex Logos was the true Emperor of the Lokhars and the de facto lord of the Jade League."

"You're saying he isn't any longer?" I asked.

"You are clever, Commander Creed," Holgotha said. "You use every opportunity in an attempt to acquire knowledge. Few species possess such a rabid curiosity as yours. Today, though. I will only grant one answer."

"Okay," I said. "I want to know—"

"A moment," Holgotha said. "I suspect you do not understand the parameters of the meeting. I will answer one question from the two of you. That means only one of you will leave this chamber alive."

"What happens to the other?" I asked.

"As I have already implied," Holgotha said, "he will be dead, and his faction will lose the argument."

"What argument?" I asked.

"Since I am about to explain, I will not count that as your single question. Two modes of philosophy are in conflict in the Alpha Centauri system. On the one hand is the dictatorial rule of Emperor Logos. On the other is the chaotic flux of Commander Creed and Doctor Sant. If the Emperor leaves me, his forces will undoubtedly defeat the upstart Sant. If you leave me, Commander Creed, I foresee Sant's elevation to the Lokhar throne."

314

"Sant will then rule with dictatorial power," I said. "That doesn't sound like flux to me."

"We both know that is wrong," Holgotha said. "Ella Timoshenko will know how to address Sant, modifying his behavior to suit humanity."

"I take it you mean because of our use of the Jelk machine?" I said.

"What machine?" the Emperor snarled at me. "What did you do to Doctor Sant?"

"Ask Holgotha if you want to know so badly," I told the tiger.

The big Lokhar scowled, and he began to roll his shoulders in a way that told me he was about to fight. That was odd because the tiger seemed too old for hand-to-hand combat.

"Did you purposely set up this meeting?" I asked Holgotha.

For a time, the tumbling pyramids silently moved across the screen. Finally, the artifact said, "I cannot accept that as your question. If you consider it, the answer is obvious. You two have come today to wrestle an old question. We Forerunner artifacts have not been able to agree on the correct procedure for the next phase. Thus, in Earth terms, we have decided to flip a coin."

"I do not understand," the Emperor said.

"We have decided to spear the fish barrel," Holgotha told him.

"You would leave your decision to random chance?" the Emperor asked the artifact.

"I have already given you the truth," Holgotha said. "Are you so dense that you must ask for a confirmation?"

"I withdraw my question," the Emperor said.

"You show a modicum of decorum," Holgotha said. "In these recent years, I have grown unaccustomed to it, as I have principally addressed the impulsive Commander Creed."

"*Touché*," I said. "When are you going to tell us the rules of this little mortality play?"

"I am flipping the coin, spearing the fish barrel," Holgotha said. "Perhaps the Creator in His hidden wisdom will allow the correct procedure to take place by aiding the one who then goes on to win."

315

"You're going to stick to the story that you're serving Him?" I asked.

"I have not made that claim," Holgotha said. "I have said that we artifacts await His appearance."

With greater vigor than before, the Emperor rolled his shoulders, trying to loosen them it appeared.

I faced the Lokhar. "Do you know what's going on?"

"We have come to fight," the Emperor declared.

"Are you kidding me?" I asked. "You're too old to want to face me in this battle cage."

Instead of roaring with rage, Felix Rex Logos showed his fangs. "I am not just any Lokhar," he said.

"Yeah?"

"I am the chief of the Shi-Feng."

"So...you're going to blow yourself up?"

"You see an old Lokhar before you. It is an illusion, human. According to the ancient traditions of the Shi-Feng, I have taken body modifications."

"You have bionic strength?" I asked.

"Together with speeded reflexes and titanium-tipped claws," the Emperor told me.

"I thought no one was supposed to utter the name Shi-Feng. If you hear someone say that, you're supposed to go crazy with rage."

"Under normal circumstances that is so," he said. "However, I am speaking to the dead. One may say anything he wants to them."

I'll say this for the old tiger. The Emperor had confidence. Could I have made a mistake in coming here? The idea troubled me. The Emperor must not have wanted to see Lokhar warships destroyed. Felix must have figured this was the easiest way to defeat the rebels.

I faced the bronze screen, asking Holgotha, "What kind of weapons do we get?"

"None," the artifact said. "This is not a battle of technology but of brawn, bravery and what you might term as brass balls."

I took several steps away from the Emperor, giving me some separation. Old or not, I respected those retractable claws.

316

"Seems like I have should have an equalizer in lieu of his natural armaments," I said.

"Lokhar meets human," Holgotha said. "It is a fitting contest. There will be no equalizers, for none are required."

"Why do you say that our meeting is fitting?" I asked.

"Is that your singular question?" the artifact asked.

"I withdraw the question," I said. Afterward, I waited for the machine to tell me I had decorum. Holgotha never did.

"Now," the Forerunner object said. "You must each compose yourself and ask your question. Emperor, as the longer-lived species, you will ask first."

The Emperor sat down cross-legged. He bent his head, no doubt thinking hard.

I walked away from the Lokhar and went to a bulkhead. Sitting as well, I learned against the cool substance. What should I ask the ancient machine? A number of questions tumbled in my mind. I finally settled on what I wanted to know most. Then I really began to think. I had to construct the question in such a way that the machine gave me several answers. Yet, if my key assumption was wrong, I might be throwing away a priceless opportunity. No. I had to ask this the way I planned it.

"I'm ready," I said.

The Emperor looked up, but said nothing. After a moment, he studied the floor again. Fifteen minutes passed. Finally, the old Lokhar stood up.

"I am decided," Felix told Holgotha.

"Ask," the machine said.

"What is the true purpose of the Forerunner artifacts?" the Emperor asked.

I stared at the tiger. That was a good question. It showed me the Emperor had his doubts about the ancient machines. Had he begun to feel manipulated by Holgotha as I was feeling?

"Commander Creed," the artifact said. "What is your question?"

I cleared my throat before saying, "Why are Abaddon and his Kargs beating the Jelk Corporation?"

The Emperor studied me, and I wondered if he wanted to change his question.

"Your queries are lodged," Holgotha said. "Now, it is time to fight. There are no rules. You will continue the match until one of you ceases to live."

Felix Rex Logos roared. As the echoes died, the years seem to shed from him. Had the roar unlocked chemical reactions in his bionically enhanced body? That certainly seemed to be the case.

The big tiger crouched. Slowly, titanium-tipped claws eased from his fingertips. His dark eyes glowed with vitality. He took a combat stance. It must have been a Shi-Feng move. I figured that must be like tiger kung-fu, only twelve thousand years old instead of hundreds.

I would have liked to have been carrying my .44. A simple draw and fire would have ended this farce. Still, the conflict had started with the Shi-Feng attacks against me in Wyoming. Maybe it was good to end it with the Grand Master.

"Do you think you can beat me, old son?" I asked. "I've taken out every Shi-Feng triad that tried to kill me. I only see you, Emperor. Where's your triad backup?"

He raised his right hand and lowered it. He raised his left hand and lowered it and he snapped his head back.

"I am the *living* triad," Felix said, "with my claws and teeth making three. In me is the essence of Shi-Feng. Since you are already dead, you cannot sully the moment with your crudities. Know that I will lead the Lokhars to victory over the great enemy. We will survive until the hour of the Creator's reappearance. Thus speaks Shi-Feng Ultrix."

I clenched my fingers into fists, cracking several knuckles. I had to kill a bionic kingpin, a chemically altered superstar trained in the ancient art of Lokhar clawed combat. Clearly, the Forerunner machines had too much influence in our affairs. If I survived, I planned to change that. Yeah, I'd change a good many things. First, though, I'd have to win this match.

Felix Rex Logos had claws and teeth. I had fists and speed. He had reach, size and maybe even strength. I had my cunning. What had Holgotha said? There were no rules.

I nodded sharply, went into my own combat stance and began to circle the tiger. He watched me. I saw his eyes drinking in everything I did. I had the horrible experience of a master combat artist judging things I didn't even know I did.

"Ah," the Emperor said. "I see what you're attempting. You wish to maneuver me onto the other side of your spacesuit. No doubt, you will attempt to use it like a net."

I halted, stunned. That's exactly what I'd been planning. How could he have known that?

The Emperor chuckled dryly. "Truly, Commander Creed, you do not understand what it means to be Shi-Feng. I will kill you."

"And lose your empire and the league to Abaddon," I said. "I'm the better strategist between us. Without me, your race is doomed to defeat."

"I will stamp out the ancient plague of humanity," he said. "The Others never should have made your kind. Finally, I will right an old wrong."

"Who are the Others?" I asked.

Felix Rex Logos smiled. I wanted to smash the smirk from his face. "It is good to see you yearn to know," he told me. "How miserable you will feel, Commander, going down to death with all these unanswered questions pulsating in your skull."

I gathered saliva in my mouth and spat on the floor. Then, I dashed to the spacesuit, grabbing it in one hand and the helmet in the other.

The Emperor moved fast, charging me. I flung the helmet like a missile. He swatted it away so the helmet shattered against a wall. He moved fast and delicately, with total economy of motion.

I twirled the spacesuit over my head, flinging it low at his shins, hoping to trip him. He leapt so the spinning suit went under him. Without a sound, his padded feet touched down. Then he came at me, swinging those deadly claws at my face.

I retreated. He followed, swishing the titanium-tipped claws. For the next fifteen minutes, we twirled faster than dancers, employing moves and counter moves. Once, he put three cuts in a row on my left inner forearm so crimson drops fell onto the floor. Another time, a slash ripped open my shirt and blood spurted from my chest to splash onto the fur of his left cheek.

By then, we both panted. He looked winded as he retreated, breathing hard as he tried to wipe away the blood on his face. I just stood there waiting, with my heart jackhammering in my chest. After half a minute, the Emperor appeared revived. That was too fast of a recovery, as my heart still thudded.

"Interior chemical injections," I said. "He has an unfair advantage."

"No rules," Holgotha said in his deep mechanical voice.

"Do not whine, Commander Creed," the Emperor said. "Die with whatever dignity you can muster."

I gave him the finger. It made me feel better, as the bastard had tricked me. We weren't supposed to bring weapons. He had. Himself. Chalk one up for the Lokhar Emperor.

Still giving him the finger, I said, "Here's what you can do with your dignity. At your orders, I lost my father, my family and my planet. You have a lot to answer for, Mr. Emperor, dude-bro."

He nodded. "My office is a heavy burden. I admit it. Yet, I carry the weight for the good of my people."

"Oh yeah," I said. "You've done a real bang up job of it too, haven't you? The Jelk Corporation has been kicking your ass for decades. It would be far better for you to commit suicide like your bomber-boys and let a real strategist like me take over. I saved the universe at the portal planet. What did you do? Nothing but try to stop me with your daughter-wife, Princess Nee."

"She begged to go," he said.

"She begged to die, you mean?" I said. "If she'd had her way, the Kargs would be in mass force instead of just engaged in a somewhat even fight against the Jelk."

"You are making guesses about them."

"You think?" I asked.

The Emperor straightened. Making a production out of it, he brought his hands together in front of his face like a kung-fu master. For a second, he held himself perfectly still. Then, he unfolded his arms and took a new stance, one that looked uncomfortable for such a heavy Lokhar.

"Our duel is at an end," he said in a formal way. "I am ready to commit the coup de grace. Know, Commander Creed, that I will detach your head from your shoulders. I will peel away the skin and keep your skull in our Hall of Honor. As long as worlds exist, Lokhars will speak about this day and my glorious victory inside Holgotha."

I watched Felix Rex Logos as he spoke. It occurred to me then that I couldn't survive the fight. He had what was probably the ultimate training, natural armaments, bionic strength and chemical endurance. The Emperor was right. I *was* a walking dead man. That meant I had to decide on the manner of my death. It was time to gamble. Did Holgotha need a victor?

I didn't know. Yet, if I was as good as dead, I might as well grasp at a straw. I would act as if the ancient machine needed one of us. That meant I simply had to outlive Felix Rex Logos.

Okay. Now I understood what I needed to do.

The Emperor attacked, and he moved faster than any feline I'd seen on Earth. Luckily, I was quicker than any human who had lived before the assault troopers. Had Shah Claath foreseen this possibility? I doubted it.

I charged the Emperor, moving at neuro-fiber heightened speed. We closed. His hands flashed, and the titanium-tipped claws shredded the flesh of my chest and gut. It hurt like fire in my belly. At the same time, I delivered a knockout punch against the tiger's jaw. It catapulted his head back, and I heard a crack that might have been neck bones snapping.

Felix Rex Logos slumped unconscious to the gory deck. Blood poured from my ripped belly. Worse, some of my intestines flopped out. Does that sound gross? It most certainly was. I saw rib bones through my sliced chest muscles.

With one hand trying to keep the rest of my guts inside my stomach, I stood beside the Emperor.

Look, I'm not going to get graphic. Well, not too graphic anyway. I wore heavy boots, and I stomped on his face with all the force I could muster.

321

He struggled. I kept stomping, cracking his skull and breaking teeth. It was ugly and bloodier than you can believe. I became dizzy and disoriented. I'd like to tell you it was quick and clean like a laser to the head. Nope. I'd seldom killed like this, and I never wanted to do it again. I lost my hatred of Felix Rex. In the end, I kept going as long as I could.

Finally, I toppled to the deck beside him. I had no idea if I'd won or lost. Everything in me felt numb. The Emperor had as good as killed me. The question was whether I'd taken him with me when I left the land of the living. If Holgotha didn't need either of us, I would never breathe again.

Still not knowing, I fell unconscious, so I can't report on what happened next...

-34-

What I can tell you is that a lifetime later I woke up on my back. I didn't move, just peeled my eyelids open. There wasn't any pain. I took a breath. That didn't hurt, either. Finally, I sat up.

I was in Holgotha's speaking chamber. The Emperor was gone, and so was his powered armor. The floor was clean.

With a start, I yanked up my now uncut shirt. The skin was smooth, without scars.

"Commander Creed," Holgotha said, the bronze-colored screen vibrating.

"Did I lose the fight?" I asked.

"No," the artifact said. "You are the victor."

"I outlived the Emperor?"

"That is a needless question. You are here. He is not."

"You healed me," I said.

"If that is the concept you wish to use, yes,"

Climbing to my feet, I noticed my spacesuit in a neat pile. The helmet was on it, and it looked as good as ever. Something or someone had reordered everything in the chamber. On impulse, I lifted a boot, inspecting the sole. It was clean, baby. I lifted the other boot and saw something. With a fingernail, I scraped away a tiny piece of gristle. I had stomped the Emperor of the Lokhars to death. It had been real after all.

"Are you satisfied?" Holgotha asked.

First flicking the gristle from my fingernail, I regarded the screen. I decided I was done answering the ancient machine.

"I had a question for you," I said.

"Yes," Holgotha said. "It was a cunning question. In the end, humans are more dangerous than Lokhars. It is fitting you won the fight."

I refrained from commenting. I no longer trusted the Forerunner artifacts in any way.

"Your question assumes that Abaddon has reached our space-time continuum," Holgotha said. "It also assumes he brought Karg vessels with him and that he is busy defeating the Jelk Corporation."

I stood before the pulsating screen, waiting for my answer. I wish I'd asked the Emperor's question.

"Abaddon, along with the Kargs he managed to bring through from hyperspace, is defeating the Jelk Corporation because of two factors," Holgotha said. "One, Abaddon possesses superior technology. Two, Abaddon is a loftier strategist."

I found it interesting that Holgotha didn't say Abaddon had more ships. "So Abaddon managed to bring *some* Kargs through but not *all*?" I asked.

"I have answered your question," Holgotha said. "I will not give you another."

"Don't you want to defeat Abaddon?" I asked.

The Forerunner machine did not respond.

"You're a frustrating artifact," I said.

"That means there is balance between us, Commander Creed."

The object must have meant that I frustrated it as well. That was good to know. "So I can just leave?" I asked.

"Yes."

"And you think the Emperor's armada is going to accept that Felix never made it out of you?"

"I have already interfered too much," Holgotha said. "The rest is up to you, Commander. As your kind would say, 'Good luck with your future endeavors.'"

I grunted a good-bye. Then, I put on my spacesuit and helmet and headed for the exit wall.

***

The trek back to the patrol boat gave me time to think. How should I play this? I mean, in a sense, I had been to the holy mountain. That's how the Lokhars would see it. I'm not sure what Baba Gobo and his Starkiens would think.

According to Holgotha, Abaddon and enough Kargs in their warships had made it into our space-time continuum to give the Jelk a go for it. Yet Abaddon had appeared at least one thousand light-years away from Earth, on the other end of the Jelk Corporation.

Abaddon was winning the fight.

What could I make out of what the Forerunner machine had told me? It would appear that Abaddon did not have access to his billions of starships. That was something. I hated the idea that our sacrifice at the portal planet had been in vain. It would appear as if Abaddon had captured at least one Lokhar dreadnought in hyperspace, giving him the limited ability to cross from there to our universe. It seemed as if it had been a one-time occurrence. Otherwise, he could have brought *millions* of Karg vessels with him. In that case, Abaddon would have already beaten the Jelk and already been here.

The bulk of the Saurian fleets along the Jelk-Jade League frontier had left to help with the conflict. Even though Abaddon didn't appear to have millions of warships, he had better tech and used a superior strategy.

One thing was certain. It would be suicide for the two Lokhar fleets to bloody themselves in self-mutilation. I had to bring peace to the warring sides.

How could I do that?

The easiest way would be to lay down the law from on high. If I could make the Lokhars believe that I came with words from Holgotha, the tigers might set aside their differences and join forces in a grand crusade and against the right enemy.

Okay. I had my goal. Now, I needed a game plan to achieve it.

***

In the end, I went for broke.

Returning to the *Achilles*, I had Zoe patch me through to the chief Purple Tamika shuttle officer. With my head bowed as if with sorrow and respect, I spoke in a low monotone to her. It turned out she was another of the former Emperor's daughter-wives.

"The Emperor is dead," I said. "Yet, Holgotha wishes that we honor him as a Lokhar of noblest birth and highest honor. Speaking for the Sol Object, I decree three days of mourning for Felix Rex Logos."

The daughter-wife stood stiffly as she regarded me. "You think that I will mourn here in your star system?"

"No," I said. "Both fleets in the Alpha Centauri system must mourn. We must return at once and tell them the news."

"You wish to gloat?" she said.

Slowly, I raised my head to glare at her. "How dare you sully the honor of Emperor Felix Rex Logos? He was the greatest among us, the Grand Master of the Shi-Feng."

"Do not speak that name."

"Me?" I asked. "I am the victor. I saw the passing of the noble Felix Rex Logos. He spoke to me before he died. Do you wish to hear his final words or not?"

She watched me, and at last, she bowed her head. "Let us return to the fleets. You can tell the others your words. I will let them decide if you are genuine or not."

"Yes," I said. "Let us begin the days of mourning."

***

Many of those in the fleets mourned for three days while others cheered and celebrated.

Then, at my orders given in the name of Holgotha, the Forerunner machine of the First Ones, I demanded that all the highest officers of both fleets meet in our chosen battle cruiser.

Half of them came from Purple Tamika's armada. Half came from ours. The assembled sat in a large hall, facing a podium.

Admiral Saris of Purple Tamika waited along with Baron Visconti of Orange. Seer Sant came and so did the ancient Purple Tamika acolyte, Divine Griffin. Baba Gobo came with nine of his chief elders, which included Kaka Ro. Diana and

Murad Bey joined the throng. So did several of the late Emperor's daughter-wives. We packed the hall with dignitaries, admirals, generals and high priests.

Wearing my black uniform with silver trim and the .44 holstered at my side, I entered the hall and walked to the podium. Would hidden Shi-Feng assassins try to kill me? I expected it, ready to fast-draw and fire.

I faced the heavily Lokhar crowd, with Starkiens and humans sprinkled among them.

"I am Commander Creed," I said. "Many years ago, I went to the portal planet and returned inside Holgotha. Later, I traveled on Holgotha to raid Sanakaht. Because humanity needed warships, the Forerunner artifact agreed to my request. Several days ago now, the Emperor and I went alone into the machine. Today, I will tell you what happened."

The assembled crowd leaned forward in their chairs. I could see it in their eyes. They yearned to know. For some, it seemed as if this was a religious experience.

"First, I want to let you know that Abaddon lives."

Half the Lokhars moaned in dread. The other half looked stricken.

"He battles the Jelk in their core worlds, which lies on the other side of the corporation. Abaddon did not come through with his billions, but with enough starships to fight the Jelk in endless conflicts. Saurian border fleets departed our frontier long ago, leaving this part of the corporation defenseless. What happened next tells of our arrogance and stupidity. Freed from the pressure of Jelk-led assaults, we warred against one another. We fought for pride of place. Some in the league, like the Ilk, have ignored the old customs and laws, going their own way.

"No," I said. "Holgotha and the other Forerunner artifacts are not pleased. Why do you think Emperor Logos died in the Sol Object? Was it because of my superiority? I will tell you the truth. He died because in his arrogance he thought to bring brother against brother into war. Unknowingly, the Emperor fought Abaddon's battles for him."

"No!" a Lokhar shouted, standing to his feet. "You lie!"

I'd been waiting for that. Speed drawing, I aimed and fired a single round. The slug took him in the head, exploding his brains onto those sitting next to him.

Lokhars roared with outage.

"Shi-Feng," I said.

The rest of the Lokhars stood to their feet.

"Listen to me!" I shouted, with smoke trickling from the gun barrel. "Listen, you of Purple, Orange, Yellow, Green and Crimson Tamika. I just shot a Shi-Feng assassin. I knew they would attempt this. What you don't know is that Holgotha has told me to tell you to outlaw the ancient house of killers. Their days are over."

The old Purple Tamika acolyte pointed a trembling finger at me. "How did you know he was...?"

"Shi-Feng?" I asked.

"Do not say that name," Divine Griffin told me.

Of course, Holgotha hadn't said any such thing to me. I'd known because I'd seen the tiger begin the Shi-Feng blink. Since Sanakaht, I recognized the maneuver. I didn't tell the assembled crowd any of that, though.

"I know because I have been given knowledge," I said. "I saw into his heart and knew him as part of the outlawed assassin band."

The Lokhars stared at each other in wonder and disbelief. I could see the question in their eyes. Did the human speak the truth?

"Would you hear the rest of my words?" I asked. "If so, then sit down."

Diana and Murad Bey led the humans in sitting. The Starkiens followed their example. Finally, one by one, Lokhars began to sit.

"No!" a tiger howled. "He lies. We will never disband."

I shot him next, another Shi-Feng assassin. I suppose anything could have happened then. The meeting could have turned into pandemonium. Instead, I saw new expressions come over the tigers. They saw me in a different light. The Shi-Feng were supposed to be invincible. They always killed those they targeted. Yet, before everyone, I'd just slain two half-mythical assassins. In that moment, I think most of the tigers believed I was indeed the speaker for the Forerunner object.

Something troubled me then. The Shi-Feng attacked in triads. There should be another assassin lurking in the crowd. Yet...could Felix Rex Logos have lied to me? He said he was his own triad. These two assassins had been highly ranked Lokhars. I wondered if they completed the Emperor's triad.

Inspiration struck, but not about the Shi-Feng. It's weird how things work like that. In that moment, I knew how to cement the enemy Lokhar to me, how to win the diehards to my cause.

"Because of Holgotha's words," I said. "I am formally returning the articles of honor to Purple Tamika."

Many in the audience stirred, both enemy and friendly Lokhars. Clearly, my words shocked them.

"What do you demand as payment?" Admiral Saris called out.

Clutching both sides of the podium, I stared at her. "Not a thing," I said.

"Nothing?" Divine Griffin asked in bewilderment.

"That's right," I said.

Lokhars exchanged startled glances with each other.

"But..." Divine Griffin said. "This is not the way. Because you have the articles, you should extract grim oaths from us."

"That is the old way," I said. "That way died with the Emperor. I have returned with the new way. In order to defeat Abaddon, we must practice these methods." I paused for effect. Then, I leaned toward the crowd, lowering my voice. "Let me tell you a truth you might not know. You are Lokhars of honor. Instead of merely having your word, I want your hearts. You will fight the harder because of it."

"Meaning what?" Divine Griffin asked.

"Meaning that we must wage the greatest crusade of the age," I said. "Listen. The Emperor slew billions of humans when he ordered my world attacked and poisoned. Before he died, Felix Rex Logos repented of his heinous act. He asked me to ask you to atone for the deed."

"How can we atone?" the old acolyte asked.

"By beginning a holy crusade against the Saurian border star systems," I said. "First, everyone will help cleanse the Earth of poison. Then you must help me free the captured humans among the Jelk Corporation. They will come to Earth to live, incorporated among the free people. For centuries, the Jelk have stolen Earthers. Their children were born into slavery. Together we will free them and train them in the arts of war for the coming grand crusade."

"One against Abaddon and the Kargs?" Divine Griffin asked.

"You have spoken truth," I said. "We must all join together to defeat the evil one loose in the Orion Arm."

Those in the crowded hall thought about that. Finally, Admiral Saris stood to her feet.

There was something about her that compelled me to say: "Speak. Let us hear your words."

"Who will rule the Empire of the Lokhars? You, a...human?"

"No," I said. "Here's what Holgotha has to say on the matter. Purple Tamika has held the throne for many centuries. Now is the new era of Orange Tamika. They sent their best warriors to the portal planet and saved our space-time continuum. One particular Lokhar of great nobility returned from that grueling battle in hyperspace."

"Do you mean Doctor Sant?" Saris asked.

"Yes!" I shouted. "You have named the new Emperor of the Lokhars. Three cheers for the Emperor," I said, pumping a fist into the air. Noticing that that didn't get them excited enough, I drew the .44 and fired slugs into the ceiling.

As the smoke cleared from the barrel, one Lokhar after another stood to his or her feet. They began to roar and rave with approval.

In such a way Doctor Sant, Seer Sant, became the next tiger emperor, ending the civil war and bringing the Lokhars back together.

-35-

One year and twenty-one days after Seer Sant became Emperor Sant, the Patrol Boat *Achilles* led seven attack cruisers and three giant freighters through the Alpha Centauri AB system.

We were returning from an extended raid into the frontier region of the Jelk Corporation. The attack cruisers shepherded the freighters. They held the first human immigrants from formerly guarded Saurian worlds. Several million sons and daughters from kidnapped Earthers were coming home.

I stood on the patrol boat's bridge with Zoe Artemis, holding her hand.

"There's an incoming message for you, sir," the comm officer said.

"Put Baba Gobo on the main screen," I said.

A moment later, the ugly baboon peered at me. "Greetings, Commander Creed," the Starkien said.

I disengaged my hand from Zoe's and took several steps closer to the screen. "Greetings Baba Gobo," I said. "Have your people settled in?"

The Starkien frowned. "It is strange, Commander. We have wandered the star lanes for so long that none of us knows what it means to call a system home. The techs are finally dismantling our factory ships and bringing the machines onto selected asteroids. I already feel differently about Alpha Centauri."

"I'm glad to hear it," I said.

As per my secret bargain with Baba Gobo, I let the Starkiens settle star systems one jump from Holgotha. From a distance, they guarded the great artifact. It brought peace to their hearts, a serenity they had long been lacking. On behalf of all Starkiens, Baba Gobo had agreed to the Jade League's terms. No Starkien could enter a star system with a Forerunner artifact in residence. It would mean death to that Starkien. In return, the baboons became full-fledged members of the league. They also gained a new league title, the First Defenders.

From scavengers and pirate contractors, the Starkiens had gained honor, respect and recognition in the main league religion.

I'd pushed for that for several reasons. The greatest in my mind was that, because of the Starkiens, no one could just dash to Earth and strike fledgling humanity. They would have to wade through the First Defenders of Holgotha. The artifact still resided in the solar system. It meant the Starkiens guarded the various routes to Earth.

In time, the close Starkien presence might cause population problems. But that was something the future generations could worry about. For now, I was trying to insure humanity's survival and then our prosperity.

"How long until the Grand Fleet launches its main assault against the corporation?" Baba Gobo asked.

"Another year, at least," I said.

"The Starkiens will send warships."

"I'm counting on it," I said.

"Good voyaging, Commander," Baba Gobo said. "I have duties I must attend to."

"Of course," I said. "Good talking to you, old son."

The connection ended, and our small flotilla headed for the jump gate.

The Jelk still fought Abaddon, waging desperate war. Emperor Sant had sent scouts to the other end of corporation territory, to the core worlds. They were supposed to assess the situation. So far, none of the Jade League members had attempted to contact the Jelk. None of us trusted them. So, we had agreed to let the Jelk absorb Abaddon's hatred while we built up for the great contest.

That meant the Star Vikings raided Saurian-held worlds. We did so for several reasons. The most important was to gather humans for Old Earth. The second was to grab loot to pay for all the items our planet and people needed.

Some argued it weakened the Jelk against Abaddon. I said we had to strike while we could. Humanity had come perilously near extinction. Now, I wanted to pump us up and train the new people in the art of being free. That meant learning to run one's own life and learning how to defend what belonged to you.

The *Achilles* led the way through the jump gate. After shaking off the bad effects of jump, the comm officer turned to me.

"The jump gate guardians are demanding to speak with the captain," she said.

"Put the commodore on the screen," I said.

A moment later, I stared at Dmitri Rostov's Cossack features. My good friend had taken up guardian duties.

"Commander Creed," Dmitri said. "How did it go?"

"A few diehard Saurians refused to surrender," I said.

"They must be dead then," Dmitri said.

"That's right."

"Do you have time to board my flagship?" Dmitri asked. "Maybe we could play a game of pool before you head to Earth."

"Not today, I'm afraid. Maybe some other time."

"When?" Dmitri asked.

I grinned at him, shrugging.

He laughed and saluted. Then, his comm officer cut the connection.

The last leg of the journey to Earth proved uneventful. Together with Ceres, Holgotha happened to be on the other side of the Sun. That was fine with me. I knew now that the Forerunner artifact watched us. The other relics in the Orion Arm watched other races. I'd never forgotten Felix's question. "What is the true purpose of the Forerunner artifacts?"

These days, I believed that the old Emperor had come to distrust the ancient relics. He wanted to believe they helped us, but who really knew the answer. The artifacts said they awaited the Creator's reappearance. Was that just a saying? Maybe it meant until everything ended. Maybe they had their own nefarious game plan. I mean, why else had Holgotha gone to the portal planet? The artifact was the one who had first let Abaddon escape the collapsing universe.

The point was I didn't trust the giant machines. I didn't trust the First Ones, either.

What is the true purpose of the Forerunner artifacts?

If I could kill Abaddon and free Jennifer, and destroy Shah Claath while I was at it, I might make the goal of my life to know the purpose of the ancient machines. Today, and for a great many more tomorrows, I had a different task.

Soon enough, our flotilla began to brake. In the viewing port before me, I saw the beautiful blue-green planet of my birth.

"Sir," the comm officer said. "Council member Diana would like a word with you."

"I'd be delighted."

"She would like to speak to you privately."

"Nope," I said. "Put her up on the main screen."

The Amazon Queen appeared. She frowned at me. It seemed like a lifetime ago when I'd first met her on a Jelk freighter parked on Earth. She wore fancy clothes and looked better than ever. Alien tech allowed awesome facelifts.

"Commander Creed," Diana said. "I'm sorry to inform you that we aren't ready to receive the new immigrants yet."

I didn't want to hear that. "What's the problem?" I asked.

She licked her lips. "This is a delicate topic. If I could speak to you alone…"

"No, Diana. Tell it to me straight."

The scowl put lines in her forehead. "Creed, you never have understood politics. You like to point and snap your fingers, telling people to do this or do that. I have to persuade others, to cajole and prod."

"I understand politics just fine," I said.

"Power politics," she said.

Arguing with Diana made no sense. So, I waited for her to get to the point.

She pouted. She tried to outwait me, and finally she threw up her hands. "Why do you have to be so stubborn?"

"If he wasn't," Zoe said, "would any of us still be alive?"

Diana glanced at Zoe and then back at me. "Very well," she said. "It has to do with placement. Murad Bey demands the immigrants land in old Turkey. He hasn't ensured full sterilization of the ground yet. He also insists that at least half of the immigrants take his reeducation courses."

"The first group will land near Laramie, Wyoming," I said. "It's the cleanest part of the planet. Besides, that's where the new homes and industrial sites are waiting."

"I know all that," Diana said. "Murad Bey is claiming American chauvinism on your part. He could get ugly about this."

"Murad wants to start up the old problems?" I asked. "Is he serious?"

"Very serious, Creed," Diana said. "Everyone wants to make sure he gets his part of the pie. Murad Bey thinks we're colluding."

I closed my eyes and rubbed my forehead. The problems never ended. If it wasn't one thing, it was something else.

"I'll talk to him," I said. "Maybe if I promise to set the third group in his area of Earth that will help. He has to clean it up first. That will give us another six months before we have to worry about him."

"Talking to Murad would be a good idea," Diana said. "Remember, though, we want Murad Bey onboard with us. We want his heart in this."

"Got it," I said. "And Diana…"

"Yes?"

"Thanks for all your hard work. I don't know if I've told you how much I appreciate what you've done."

The Amazon Queen smiled. She knew how to look fantastic. "That's the right technique to use on Murad Bey. And thank you, Commander. It's good to hear some appreciation."

We ended the conversation shortly thereafter.

335

A half hour later, Luna Command called. Zoe spoke to them and gained clearance for our vessels.

At the same time, a lone ship rose from the cratered surface. The craft entered a docking bay in our patrol boat. The vessel's single occupant soon spoke to me alone in my quarters.

Looking grave, N7 sat in a chair.

"You have the secret report?" I asked.

"I do, Commander," N7 said.

As I said earlier, Sant had sent fast scouts to the Jelk core worlds. We wanted to know what was happening one thousand light years away. According to N7, one scout had returned with highly interesting news.

The android now told me the message, gained by capturing Saurians and convincing them to speak.

The Kargs had indeed come out of hyperspace. During our voyage to the portal planet, they had captured a Lokhar dreadnought as suspected. Somehow, the Jelk had learned of this. The corporation leaders didn't wait, but struck hard and fast once the Kargs appeared in our universe.

I suspect Shah Claath had doubled-crossed Abaddon. That would be just like the little Rumpelstiltskin. He would have told his brother Jelk the truth and they'd moved ruthlessly to destroy Abaddon's hyperspace-moving abilities.

In any case, the Jelk had lost most of their attacking battlejumpers during that first assault. They also managed to destroy the hyperspace craft, stranding the Kargs on this side. Afterward, Abaddon waged merciless war against the corporation. So far, the two sides decimated each other.

According to the secret report, it would be years before either side conquered the other. The Jelk knew their danger, and Abaddon understood he had to kill the red devils before he could consolidate.

Our task at present would be to let the Jelk and Kargs fight it out one thousand light-years away in the core worlds. As they did, we would build up. According to the report, it sounded like we still had time.

After shaking N7's hand, I returned to the bridge. From it, I led the way in the *Achilles*. Low Earth Orbit held hundreds of spaceships with half again as many defensive satellites. With the layers beginning in the other star systems, it would be almost impossible for an alien to do what the original Rhode Island-sized dreadnought had done those many years ago to Earth.

I had a nightmare, though. What if the Forerunner artifacts declared war against humanity? Sure, it might never happen. I didn't see any reason why it would. But if it did, how could we defend our planet against transfer technology? I'd raided Sanakaht. I knew the power of a transfer. I wanted to make Earth a fortress so no one could do that to us.

"Take us down," I told Zoe.

She instructed the pilot. He began entry procedures. Soon, the patrol boat left low orbit and entered the blue atmosphere.

I remembered the last time I'd touched down. Winds had howled, tossing the craft this way and that.

A lot had changed since Emperor Felix Rex Logos' passing. Nearly one hundred automated factories chugged on Earth, cleaning the planet. Twenty giant scrubbers cruised back and forth in the air, destroying toxins. The winds no longer howled. The purple, red and other crazy colors no longer made the sky look insane. The old blue had returned.

The patrol boat landed in Wyoming, five kilometers from the automated factory where the first Shi-Feng assassin had tried to kill me.

"I'm going to go outside," I said.

"Let me join you, Commander," Zoe said.

I shook my head. "I'm going alone. I...I need this."

Zoe stared into my eyes, nodding after a moment. Then she pecked me on the lips. I gave her a hug and headed for the hatch.

I had goosebumps on my arms as I entered the airlock. I wore a jacket but no vacc-suit, no breather or other protective devices. This would be my first time on the planet breathing the air since Antarctica so long ago.

The lock hissed, clanked and rotated. I opened the outer hatch and stepped onto Terra Firma.

337

I stood frozen, maybe a little frightened. Don't tell anyone I said that. I have an image to protect. Finally, I jumped out, landing on the dusty soil.

All the grass and trees, the bushes and funguses had died to the Lokhar bio-terminator. We had seeders putting Earth plants down. They would need time to root into the soil. Until then, this was a rock world waiting to begin.

How many cars had rusted away? How many old buildings were gone? The freeways crisscrossed in places, but there wasn't much else left from the pre-Alien Visitation Era.

Yeah, the automated factories chugged overtime. The humans in the freighters had debarked near the factories. They built new homes, planted and worked feverishly. They labored to ready our planet to receive millions upon millions of lost sons and daughters.

Humanity rebuilt its world, racing to catch up with all the other aliens. We'd come a long way since the day the Earth died. Now, it was the year the Earth was reborn. We had a fantastic challenge to motivate us. That should help to unite us quarreling humans for many, many years.

I walked away from the patrol boat, feeling the sunshine on my face. I yearned to walk past waving wheat fields and hear children laughing and dogs barking. That would come. We were rebuilding, and I led humanity in that.

In time, I would join the Grand Fleet. We had to slay whoever won the Jelk-Karg War. First, I wanted to enjoy my world. I wanted to swim in the waters and see the new sights.

"Creed!"

I turned around. Zoe Artemis ran after me. She waved, and her hair flowed in the wind.

Smiling, I waved back. A pang of guilt reminded me of Jennifer. Somehow, someday, I'd find and free her. What had Abaddon done to Jennifer?

Before I could think too much about my greatest failure, Zoe threw herself into my arms. We kissed. We hugged and laughed. Then, hand-in-hand, we walked on the Earth. I think we'd earned a few moments of peace. I planned to enjoy them while I could.

The End

28269484R00194

Made in the USA
San Bernardino, CA
23 December 2015